ALIX JAMES

THE
MEASURE
OF HONOR

THE MEASURE OF A MAN COLLECTION, BOOK THREE

A PRIDE AND PREJUDICE VARIATION

Blog and Website: https://alixjames.com/
Newsletter: https://subscribepage.io/alix-james
Book Bub: https://www.bookbub.com/authors/alix-james
Facebook: https://www.facebook.com/ShortSweetNovellas
Twitter: https://twitter.com/N_Clarkston
Amazon: https://www.amazon.com/stores/Alix-James/author/B07Z1BWFF3
Austen Variations: http://austenvariations.com/

Contents

For all you angst lovers... I am not responsible for your ruined hankies.

Chapter One

"HARRY, IS THAT YOU?" Darcy's voice echoed through Pemberley's halls, carrying a note of surprised delight. "What the devil are you doing back so soon? I did not expect you for two days yet."

Captain Harrison William Darcy stood in the doorway, a broad grin spreading across his sun-bronzed face. He looked every inch the dashing officer in his scarlet coat, his dark hair tousled by the wind. "The very same," he replied, his voice warm with laughter. "Have you forgot what your own brother looks like, Fitz?"

Darcy crossed the hall quickly, his usual reserve melting into a rare, affectionate smile. "It has been too long, brother," he said, pulling Harry into a tight embrace. For a moment, the weight of Pemberley, his responsibilities, his worries—all of it—fell away, and they were two boys again.

His brother slapped him on the shoulder with a bark of laughter. "Too long by half! I declare that I am going to enjoy my time off. No army drills, no orders—just a chance to sit by the fire with my favourite brother and eat Cook's food instead of rations."

Darcy took a step back, peering at his younger brother. It was strange— there was still the same warm light in those boyish eyes that had always been there, but beneath it, another expression there as well: a shadow, a strain that ran counter to the jovial words. "Is everything well?"

Harry's smile dropped momentarily, and then he brightened even more. "Well enough, Fitz," he said, squeezing Darcy's shoulder. "But come, let us not dwell on serious matters. I have some stories to share and am anxious to hear the latest from all of you in my absence. Shall we retire to the study? That journey's given me more than enough reason to drink."

Darcy nodded and ushered him down the hall to his library. The room was snug and cosy, full of the rich smell of leather-bound books and wood smoke. Darcy poured them each a glass of brandy, handing one to Harry before taking a seat by the fire.

Harry settled into the opposite chair, stretching his legs with a contented sigh. "Ah, it is good to be home," he said, sipping his drink. "I must say, Fitz, I have missed this—being here, with you, away from all the noise and chaos."

"And I have missed having you here, brother. Pemberley is far too quiet of late. But tell me, what news do you bring from the front? Back home two months already, and you could not write sooner to tell me I could have seen you in London? The first word I had of your return was three days ago when you wrote that you were coming here."

Harry made an abashed sort of frown. "I knew I would catch it from you for that. Sorry, Fitz. Things have been rather... unsettled. I wanted to come sooner, or at least write to you, but I thought I had better not tell you to come see me in London unless I could be sure I would still be there when you arrived."

Darcy took another sip from his glass. "Well, you look to be in one piece, thank Heaven. I confess, some of your letters have left me quite uneasy. Are things really so bad as all that?"

Harry shifted in his chair, a playful glint returning to his eyes as he leaned forward. "I came here to forget war for a time, Fitz. Tell me, how are things at Pemberley? Has Mrs Reynolds prepared any of her famous treacle tarts? I have been dreaming of them ever since I left France. And what of old Wilkins? Is he still puttering about, or has he finally decided to retire and enjoy his twilight years?"

Darcy chuckled, glad to see his brother's spirits lifting, even if only a little. "Mrs Reynolds is as formidable as ever, and yes, she has indeed made your favourite treacle tarts. I shall see to it that she brings some to you directly. As for Wilkins, he is as stubborn as ever. He insists he has no desire to retire and claims that Pemberley would fall apart without him. I fear we shall have to drag him away from his duties when the time comes."

Harry laughed. "Good old Wilkins. I cannot imagine this place without his griping about the new footmen or bending the stable boys' ears about conduct. And what of the neighbours? Are the Farnsworths still squabbling over that ridiculous border dispute? And the Carters—did they ever get those daughters of theirs married off, or are they still trotting them out like show ponies?

Darcy smiled wryly. "The Farnsworths are indeed still at odds with the Robinsons, though I suspect it is more for sport than any real grievance. As for the Carters, their eldest daughter finally married a minor baronet from Lincolnshire, but the younger ones remain, as you say, 'on parade.'" He paused, his gaze growing more serious. "And Uncle Matlock and Aunt Catherine are both well enough, though you know as well as I that 'well' is a relative term where our dear aunt is concerned."

Harry grinned. "Ah, Lady Catherine. Always a joy. And Lord Matlock? Still pressing you about those parliamentary ambitions?"

Darcy nodded. "As persistent as ever, though I have managed to avoid any firm commitments. For now, at least."

Harry's smile remained, but there was a flicker of something else behind his eyes—an unease, a tension that Darcy had seen earlier. He leaned forward, his voice softening. "But enough of my affairs, Harry. You have been deflecting long enough. What is really troubling you?"

For a moment, Harry's face froze, his smile becoming almost painfully tight. His eyes flickered with a brief flash of something—fear, perhaps, or reluctance—but it vanished just as quickly. He straightened in his chair, his expression brightening as if a new thought had occurred to him. "You always could read me too well, Fitz. You know, there *is* something," he began, his tone shifting. "Something rather... important."

Darcy waited, watching his brother closely.

A real smile crossed Harry's face. "I have met someone, Fitz. Someone quite remarkable."

Darcy raised an eyebrow, bemused by the abrupt change in conversation but intrigued nonetheless. "Ah, and here I was thinking you had some grave matter to share. So, you have found another pretty girl to occupy your thoughts, have you?"

Harry laughed, shaking his head. "This is different, I assure you. Her name is Elizabeth Bennet."

Darcy's eyebrow arched higher. "Elizabeth Bennet? Not a very distinguished name, is it?"

"The name may not be distinguished, but the lady herself certainly is."

Darcy sighed, leaning back in his chair. "And where, pray tell, did you meet this distinguished lady?"

Harry's smile widened. "I have been stationed in London for the past two months, you know. And while there, I frequently encountered an old school friend—Charles Bingley."

Darcy squinted, searching his memory. "Bingley? Is that not the son of the woollen miller?"

"Yes, yes, but he is also a gentleman of quality, Fitz. You must not be so quick to judge. Bingley is a good man, and he has been quite taken with a young lady from Hertfordshire who was staying in London with her aunt and uncle—a Miss Jane Bennet."

Darcy's frown deepened. "Another Miss Bennet... a sister, I suppose?"

Harry's grin grew even wider. "Elizabeth Bennet, yes. And before you ask, no, none of this may sound promising to you, but I assure you, she is quite remarkable. In fact, she is the very woman I have asked to marry me."

Darcy nearly choked on his brandy. He straightened in his chair, his eyes wide with disbelief. "You what? Harry, have you lost your senses? How do you mean to live? Does the lady have a sufficient dowry to support you both?"

Harry's expression sobered slightly. "No, she does not have much in the way of a dowry. But I just received my promotion, you recall, and we intend to live modestly. I believe we will be very happy, Fitz. I am certain of it."

Darcy's face remained sceptical, his brow furrowing. "And what makes you so certain of that, Harry? You have always been too quick to fall for a pretty face."

Harry leaned forward, his expression earnest. "Because she is not like the others, Fitz. She is intelligent and strong-willed, with a lively mind and a wit that matches my own. I believe you will like her—once you meet her."

Darcy sighed, setting his glass down on the table. "I suppose I shall have to meet her, then. But do not expect me to approve of this at once. You know our father always wanted better for you."

"I know, brother. But do promise to be on your best behaviour. I believe, once you see her for yourself, you will understand."

Darcy rolled his eyes, a reluctant smile tugging at his lips. "Very well, Harry. I shall reserve my judgment until I meet this 'remarkable' Elizabeth Bennet. I shall endeavour to be polite."

Harry laughed, raising his glass in a toast. "That is all I ask, Fitz. To Elizabeth Bennet and the hope that my dear brother might see what I see."

Darcy clinked his glass with Harry's, though his smile remained wary. "To Elizabeth Bennet," he echoed, his voice carrying a note of resigned amusement. "And to you, Harry. May you always find happiness—if not sense."

They both laughed, and for a moment, it felt as if nothing could shatter this happiness, as if the world was as it should be. But Darcy could not shake the vague sense of unease that had nested in his chest—this deep-down dread that was something not right. Harry was there, right in front of him, but the look in his eyes had changed. He was not the same man he was when he marched off to war.

T HE NEXT DAY PROVED a promising one for a hunt, with just the right sort of crispness in the air to invigorate the senses. But Darcy and Harry had intended something far more leisurely—a gentle ride through the estate to take in the green-covered hills and perhaps call on a few of Harry's old friends in the area. It felt like forever since they had been this relaxed with each other, and Darcy was determined to take advantage of his brother's sudden appearance. The sun was scaling the peaks, and the tree branches cast dappled shadows that danced around their feet while their horses stamped the ground to be off.

Harry leaned against the stable door, a contented smile on his face. "I must have said it a dozen times already, but it feels good to be home, Fitz," he said softly, his eyes scanning the familiar landscape. "There is something about this place... it calms the soul. I had forgot how much I missed it."

Darcy glanced at his brother, noting the lines of strain around his eyes, the way his shoulders seemed to bear an invisible weight. "I am glad you are here. You know Pemberley is not the same without you. And if I had known you were coming early, I would have had a better welcome prepared."

Harry chuckled. "I prefer the surprise, honestly. Gives me a chance to see you without your mask of responsibility." He hesitated, his smile faltering for a brief moment. "But there is something I need to ask of you, Fitz."

Darcy frowned. "What is it?"

Harry took a deep breath, his gaze fixed on the distant hills. "I want you to arrange a meeting with the family's solicitor," he said quietly.

Darcy's eyebrows knitted together in confusion. "The solicitor? For what purpose?"

Harry was silent for a moment, his expression thoughtful. Then, with a small, almost resigned smile, he turned to face Darcy. "I want to draft a settlement to offer Miss Elizabeth Bennet's father," he explained. "I want to ensure that she will be well cared for, should anything happen to me."

Darcy's face darkened with concern. "Why such morbid thoughts, Harry? You are on leave, not marching into battle. And you know how I feel about this impulsive engagement of yours. You have not even introduced me to the lady yet."

Harry shrugged, his smile growing softer, more introspective. "I just want to be prepared, Fitz. Life is unpredictable, and I want to know that Elizabeth will be safe, no matter what."

Darcy sighed, his hand rubbing his chin thoughtfully. "Very well. I will summon the solicitor. But you must promise me that you are not keeping anything from me. What is truly troubling you, Harry?"

Harry hesitated, his gaze dropping to the ground. For a fleeting moment, the mask slipped, and Darcy saw the shadow of something dark—something weighing heavily on his brother's heart. But then, just as quickly, Harry's smile returned, bright and carefree. "Nothing at all, Fitz," he replied with forced cheerfulness. "Come, let us not dwell on sombre thoughts. The day is too fine for that. Shall we ride?"

Darcy watched him for a moment longer, still sensing the unspoken burden his brother carried. But he nodded, deciding to let the matter rest for now. "Yes," he agreed. "Let us ride. I could use some fresh air myself."

They mounted their horses and set off at a gentle trot, the sun warm on their backs and the soft breeze carrying the scent of late summer blooms. For a while, they rode in companionable silence, the rhythmic ringing of hooves on the drive as the only sound. It was a moment of peace, a momentary escape from the concerns that plagued him.

But as they rode towards the stables, there was a shift in the air. The horses, usually calm and steady, seemed skittish, their ears flicking back and forth as if sensing something was amiss. The silence of the morning was shattered by dogs barking in the distance and a shrill whistle. Darcy looked in the direction of the noise and saw a gang of stable boys wrestling with two hounds that had somehow got loose.

"Looks like a successful hunt in the offing," Harry remarked with a grin. "What say you, Fitz? Shall we see if the old fox will put up quite the chase?"

Darcy smiled, though his eyes remained on the hounds. "Not today. What the devil is going on over there? Those boys should know better than to let them run this close to the stables. It is bound to cause trouble." His gaze shifted to the nearby grooms, who were distracted, watching the commotion with growing concern.

One of the younger stable hands was attempting to lead a high-spirited stallion across the yard—a new acquisition from the north, a horse Darcy had been meaning to examine more closely. The stallion was devlish fast, but known for his unpredictable nature, a beast with fire in his veins. Darcy frowned. The boy seemed to be struggling with the animal's bridle, his feet leaving the ground as the animal reared and tried to twist away.

"Easy there!" Darcy called out. "Bring him round—and leash those hounds!"

The stallion's ears twitched, he snorted, and for a moment, he seemed to settle. But then, a sudden snap—like a whip cracking in the air—broke the fragile calm. The sound was sharp and unexpected, shattering the quiet like a gunshot.

It happened in a heartbeat.

"Whoa, there!" Darcy shouted. The stallion squealed and tried to plunge away. The stable boy was struggling, his grip faltering as the stallion twisted, writhing in the air and striking out at his handler. Darcy cursed under his breath and spurred his own mount forward. The boy wouldn't be able to hold on much longer. He could see it—the stallion's agitation building, the bridle already slipping, half off one ear.

"I'll take him!" Darcy called as he closed the distance, urging his horse into a quicker trot. But even as he neared, the stallion plunged. He reared violently, yanking the reins from the boy's hands.

Darcy's heart lurched, his mind already calculating the danger. He reached out, stretching toward the bridle, but it slipped completely from the stallion's head, leaving the animal wild and free. The hounds were now barking in a frenzy, dragging their handlers towards the loose horse, and Darcy's own mount was trying to turn and escape. Darcy cursed again, leaning from his saddle, his fingers just grazing the stallion's crest before the bridle fell to the ground, useless.

The stallion twisted away from him, his eyes wide with a sort of animalistic mania. Darcy's breath caught as he saw the beast lunge directly toward Harry, who was mounted on one of Darcy's prized mares. The stallion, frenzied by his sudden freedom, charged at the mare, and Harry barely had time to react.

"Harry! Watch out!" Darcy shouted, his voice raw with panic as the stallion barreled forward.

Harry, caught off guard, turned in the saddle, his bright eyes wide with surprise. There was a split second where their gazes met—a fleeting moment where Darcy saw the realisation dawning in his brother's eyes, the flash of fear that was so out of place on Harry's usually confident face. The horse thundered closer, its hooves pounding the earth, throwing up clods of dirt in its wake.

It was too late. The stallion lunged at the mare, and she reared back in terror. Instinctively, Harry tried to pull the mare horse aside, out of the stallion's reach, but the movement was too sudden, too sharp. The mare, startled by the chaos and the scent of fear, reared up again, unbalanced by Harry's unexpected shift in weight. She tried to lash out at the stallion's unwelcome advances, but the ground was slick, and Harry was clawing for balance.

Darcy's heart pounded as he watched his brother struggle to regain control. "Harry, jump clear!" He spurred his horse forward, but what would he do even if he reached them?

The ground beneath them seemed to tilt, time slowing to a crawl. Harry's horse, unable to regain her footing, stumbled backwards. Harry fought to stay in the saddle, his hands gripping the reins tightly, but the force of the movement sent him flying. He was thrown from the horse, his body twisting in mid-air. Darcy reached out, as if he could somehow catch his brother, but he was too far away.

Time seemed to slow as Darcy watched helplessly, his outstretched hand still clutching the reins of a bridle that no longer mattered. He should have acted sooner—should have had the hounds sent away sooner, should have calmed the horse, should have tugged the bridle back over the horse's head.

But he had not.

Harry hit the ground with a sickening thud, his head striking a large stone hidden beneath the loose gravel. Darcy's breath caught in his throat. For a moment, everything was silent. The world seemed to hold its breath, waiting for something, anything, to break the stillness.

Then, chaos erupted. The stable hands rushed forward, shouting orders and trying to calm the remaining horses, who were now rearing and whinnying in panic.

Darcy's heart felt like it was going to explode, every breath a struggle as he urged his horse forward, leaping from the saddle before it had even fully stopped. He reached Harry in seconds, but it felt like an eternity. Harry's head was tilted at an odd angle, his breaths shallow.

"Harry!" Darcy's voice was raw with fear as he dropped to his knees beside his brother. Harry lay motionless, his face pale, a dark bruise already forming on his temple where his head had struck the stone. Blood trickled from a cut just above his brow, mingling with the dirt. His chest moved shallowly, each breath a laboured effort.

"Harry! Hold on, Harry... look at me." Darcy grabbed his brother's hand—it was limp. He should have seen the danger sooner. He should have noticed the skittishness of the horses, the distraction of the grooms, the stallion's unpredictable temperament. He should have called out sooner, done something, anything, to prevent this!

Harry wasn't moving. Wasn't opening his eyes. A cold dread settled in his stomach, his hands shaking as he gently cradled Harry's head. "Stay with me, Harry," he murmured, his voice trembling. "We will get you help. Just stay with me!"

Harry's eyes fluttered open, unfocused and filled with pain. "Fitz..." he whispered, his voice barely audible. His hand reached out, grasping weakly at Darcy's coat. "Do not..." Something rattled in his throat. "Eliza..."

But even as the words left his lips, his eyes began to lose focus again, his grip loosening. "Harry, no!" Darcy choked out, his voice breaking. "Harry, please, stay with me!"

His heart pounded with fear, every beat a desperate plea for Harry to hold on, for this nightmare to end. But even as the words left his lips, Harry's eyes began to lose focus, his grip on Darcy's coat loosening.

"Harry, no!" Darcy choked out, his voice rising with panic. He shook his brother gently, his hands moving to check his pulse, pressing against Harry's wrist as if willing the blood to keep flowing. His hands were shaking, his mind spinning as he leaned down, listening for any sign of breath, any faint rise in Harry's chest. There was a moment—a fleeting, unbearable moment—where he thought he felt something, a weak pulse, a shallow breath.

But nothing. Harry's chest remained still, the life slipping from him before Darcy's eyes.

"Harry, please, stay with me!" Darcy's voice cracked, breaking into a sob as he frantically checked again, his fingers searching for the pulse he knew wasn't there. He pressed his ear against his brother's chest, hoping—praying—for the faintest sound of a heartbeat. But the silence that greeted him was suffocating. His hands trembled violently as he tore open the buttons of Harry's coat, refusing to accept what was happening.

"No, no..." Darcy's words came out in a broken whisper as he lifted his brother slightly, shaking him as if the movement might jolt him back to life. "Breathe, Harry! Harry, no—" His hands shook as he fumbled to check his brother's pulse, pressing trembling fingers against Harry's neck.

"Help! Someone—!" Darcy's voice cracked, raw with desperation. The head coachman, who had been tending to the horses, sprinted toward them, his boots pounding across the yard as he reached Harry's side.

"Master Darcy! Move aside!" The coachman's voice cut through Darcy's panic as he rushed forward, dropping to his knees beside them. Darcy did not move at first—could not move, his hands still gripping his brother's lifeless body as if letting go would make it final. But the coachman's hands were firm as he gently pulled Darcy away, his face lined with urgency and terror.

Darcy scrambled back, his breath coming in gasps as he watched the coachman feel for a pulse at Harry's neck, checking his breathing with quick, practised motions. For a brief moment, Darcy clung to the hope that the coachman would find something he had missed—that Harry wasn't truly gone.

"Is he—?" Darcy's voice faltered, thick with desperation.

But the coachman's face turned ashen as he leaned back, his shoulders sagging with the awful truth. He looked up at Darcy, his eyes filled with sorrow, and shook his head. "He's gone, sir."

"No!" Darcy's denial tore from him, harsh and visceral. "No, he isn't! Check again—he cannot—" His voice broke into ragged sobs as he reached for Harry once more, his hands trembling as he clutched his brother's limp body. "He cannot be gone... he cannot!"

But Harry's stillness was unmistakable; the life that had once burned so brightly in him was now extinguished. A raw, guttural cry tore from Darcy's throat, the sound of a man who had just lost his world. He clutched his brother tighter, his voice echoing across the courtyard in a desperate wail.

It was as if the earth itself shifted beneath him, the solid ground vanishing into an abyss of grief. His breath came in sharp, shallow bursts, his chest heaving as the dark reality of what had happened hit him with the force of a tidal wave, knocking the breath from his lungs. His hands still gripped Harry's coat, the fabric damp with blood and dirt, as if holding on might somehow anchor him to this moment, might somehow undo the nightmare.

But no matter how tightly he held his brother, no matter how desperately he wanted to believe it wasn't real, Harry was gone—his bright, vibrant brother—snuffed out in an instant. There was no bringing him back.

The sudden shock of grief crushed him, a relentless, unbearable force that pinned him to the ground. The guilt wrapped around his heart like a vise, squeezing tighter with each passing second. "I should have stopped it—I should have done something!" Darcy's voice broke, his words barely coherent through the sobs that wracked his body. "It is my fault... all my fault..." His hands trembled as he held Harry close, his tears falling freely, unchecked. He should have been quicker, more vigilant, should have noticed the danger before it was too late. He should have saved his brother from this senseless, cruel accident.

But he had not, and now... now Harry was gone forever.

And it was all his fault.

Chapter Two

One Week Later

FITZWILLIAM DARCY STEPPED FROM the carriage onto the cobblestones of his London townhouse. The air was sharp with the late autumn chill, but it did little to stir him as he ascended the steps, his boots tapping against the stone with a quiet, steady rhythm. The streets of London, once so familiar, felt distant now, their hum muted by the suffocating presence of grief that clung to him like a shroud.

The door opened before he reached it, and Thompson, ever precise in his timing, stood ready with a deferential bow. Darcy glanced up only briefly, unwilling to meet the butler's gaze for more than a moment. The warmth of the townhouse beckoned, but it could not touch the cold that had settled inside him since that awful day.

"Welcome back to London, sir," Thompson said. "We did not know to expect you, but I shall call for refreshments at once. Your rooms are, of course, ready. Do you require anything, sir?"

Darcy stepped inside, the familiar scent of polished wood and soap wafting toward him. The fire burned in the hearth, but it felt like a hollow gesture, no comfort to be found in its warmth. The servants had gathered in the hall, faces expectant, as they always did upon his return. This time, however, their presence was unbearable. Every sympathetic glance, every gesture of respect, grated against the raw wound that had not yet begun to heal.

Without preamble, he turned to Thompson. "Have black drapes hung for the windows and place a hatchment over the door."

The butler inclined his head. "Yes, sir. At once." He hesitated for a moment, his brows knitting slightly before he spoke again, softer now. "May I ask, sir... for whom are we mourning?"

Darcy stared ahead, the question slicing through the quiet like a blade. His throat tightened. He had not spoken the words aloud in days, had scarcely allowed himself to think them. It had been easier, somehow, to carry on in silence, to push the truth to the corners of his mind where it might not overwhelm him.

"It was Harry," he said at last. "My brother."

The hall fell into a hush. Thompson's face, usually so composed, shattered with a grief he tried and failed to hide. Harry had been more than a master to the staff. The younger Darcy had always possessed a warmth, a vitality that reached even the most reserved among them. The suddenness of it, the cruel finality, struck them just as deeply.

Thompson opened his mouth, likely to offer some words of condolence, but Darcy cut him off before they could form. "No." His tone came out sharper than intended, and he sighed, softening. "Not now. No words."

He glanced at the gathered servants, their faces shadowed with sorrow and confusion. They all looked to him for direction, for guidance, as they always had, but the weight of their expectations crushed whatever strength remained. Harry had been loved here, in ways Darcy never had been. His brother's absence would linger in every corner of this house, a reminder of what had been lost.

"Do not place the knocker on the door," Darcy ordered. "I am not at home to anyone."

Thompson bowed again, and the others followed suit, their quiet obedience filling the space where words might have been. The fire crackled faintly behind them, but it offered no warmth, only a reminder of the quiet that would soon engulf the house.

Darcy turned from them, his steps purposeful but heavy as he made his way up the grand staircase. He needed the silence, the solitude. There would be no visitors, no platitudes, no more words. Not today. Not for some time.

H OOVES ECHOED ON THE narrow streets as Darcy's carriage wound its way
through the quieter parts of London. The weight of the black-edged envelopes
sent out earlier that morning still hung over him, heavier than the deepest grief. One had
gone to Lady Catherine, a duty he could not avoid. Her fury at being informed in such an
impersonal manner would likely arrive before any letter she could dispatch in response.
The other express had been addressed to Richard in Chatham... and Heaven only knew
what his cousin would have to say.

The Earl of Matlock, he had to face in person. The visit had been brief, filled with
formalities and hushed tones, the Earl's face darkened by the weight of sorrow. His uncle
had spoken little, nodding at each of Darcy's words, his eyes fixed somewhere beyond the
walls of the room. After a strained embrace, Darcy left. He would receive no further solace
there.

Harry's commanding officer had been next. Colonel Frederick Halton was a man of
stone-faced authority, yet even he could not entirely mask the sorrow that crossed his
features at the news. Darcy had delivered the message with military precision, keeping his
emotions locked beneath the surface, and then he had left, feeling no lighter for it. All the
formalities, the hushed exchanges, none of it made any difference to the truth. Harry was
gone.

Now, seated in the carriage alongside Harry's batman, a quiet, stoic fellow by the name
of Corporal Simmons, Darcy was bound for his brother's flat. The thought of entering
Harry's private world, of sorting through his belongings, was almost too much to bear.
But it had to be done. Every piece of his brother's life must be gathered, each object boxed
and taken to Darcy House for review. It was his duty now, the final act of care for the
brother he had never fully understood.

As they arrived at the building, Darcy's steps felt leaden as he approached the door,
the stark reality of the task ahead tightening around him. The batman followed in silence,
which was one of the few mercies allotted him this day. Harry had always spoken well of

the man, trusting him with more than just the care of his clothing and provisions. Now, the corporal remained solemn, his loyalty clear even in grief.

The door creaked open, revealing the stillness of the flat—untouched since Harry had last walked its halls. The faint scent of pipe tobacco lingered in the air, and a jacket, casually thrown over a chair, hung there as if its owner might return at any moment. Darcy paused, taking in the quiet that had settled over the room, a silence pressed against him with each passing moment.

"Let us begin," Darcy said quietly, more to himself than to Corporal Simmons.

The batman nodded and moved efficiently, collecting Harry's personal effects—clothing, boots, mementoes. Darcy, however, found himself drawn to the desk—Harry's desk—littered with papers, books, and scattered correspondence. He had always meant to sit down with Harry one day to understand the world his brother inhabited when he was away from Pemberley. But the chance for that conversation had long passed, and now only the cold facts of paper and ink remained.

He gathered the letters, keeping his hands steady despite the tremor of emotion that threatened to break through. He could not afford that now. Not here.

The hours passed in heavy silence, interrupted only by the occasional sound of a drawer being opened or a trunk being closed. Darcy's mind wandered to memories of Harry—his carefree smile, the way he had filled rooms with his laughter. There had always been something light about Harry, something that Darcy himself could never quite capture, no matter how hard he tried. Now, that light was extinguished, leaving behind only shadows.

Corporal Simmons worked quietly beside him, packing away the last of Harry's belongings with the same dutiful care he had shown to his master in life. There was respect in every motion, a silent acknowledgement of the man they both mourned. When all was packed, Simmons stood by the door, awaiting Darcy's final command.

"It will all go to Darcy House," Darcy said, his voice steady despite the ache that threatened to rise. "I will review it there."

"Of course, sir," the batman replied softly.

Darcy gave a nod of dismissal. Simmons would see the trunk to the carriage, thus discharging his final duty. For now, he needed a moment to himself. He let his gaze sweep the flat one last time before turning on his heel and stepping out into the cooler air of the hallway.

He had thought the task's bitterness would ease now that it was done, but it had not. The truth still tore at him, raw and unyielding. Harry was gone, and there was no sense of closure, no peace to be found in the empty rooms he had left behind.

As Darcy made his way back to the carriage, a new thought struck him with sudden clarity. *Bingley.* He had not yet spoken to Harry's closest friend, the man who had understood his brother's light-hearted nature better than any. The man who, more than anyone else, deserved to hear the news in person. Darcy could not bear the thought of writing Bingley a letter, of allowing the news to reach him in such a cold, impersonal manner.

No. This, too, must be done face-to-face.

With the decision made, Darcy instructed the driver to take him to Bingley's townhouse. His weariness lingered, crushing the very heart within his ribs, but there would be no respite until this, too, was done.

E LIZABETH BENNET'S FINGERS FALTERED on the keys of the pianoforte, the melody she had been attempting dissolving into a dissonant jumble of notes. She sighed in frustration and pressed the keys again, harder this time, but the chords still rang hollow. Music had never been her solace, not in the way it was for Mary, who played out her deepest thoughts with sombre grace. Elizabeth, by contrast, found herself only agitated by the exercise, the trembling in her hands betraying her inner turmoil.

Harry would return. Of course, he would. She *mustn't* doubt him. Yet the panicked thoughts clawed at her—unbidden, unwelcome.

She barely knew him. Their acquaintance, though filled with charm and laughter, had been brief, too brief to warrant the depth of feeling she had allowed herself to develop.

But he had promised.

After everything that had happened, Harry stepped up, and he promised. He had spoken of settlements, of engagements. He had done the honourable thing in the wake of the scandal. Surely, surely, he would not abandon her now! Her fingers trembled again, striking an off-key note that grated against her ears.

"Oh dear, I thought it was Mary who played out her dark feelings on the pianoforte," came her aunt's gentle, teasing voice from the doorway.

Elizabeth jerked her hands from the keys, feeling the faintest flush rise to her cheeks. "Aunt Gardiner," she said with a shaky breath, "I— I just needed to think. Reading was unsettling me today."

Her aunt crossed the room and stood beside the pianoforte. "Well then, perhaps a walk with Jane would do you more good. You know walking always cheers you."

Elizabeth gave a rueful smile and glanced out the window, where the streets of London stretched out beyond the glass. "At home, it does," she murmured. "But I have never been quite at ease walking about in London, and even less so now."

There was a pause. Her aunt's gaze lingered on her, and Elizabeth felt the weight of her unsaid thoughts hanging between them. "*Especially* now," Elizabeth added quietly.

Her aunt sat beside her, resting a hand on Elizabeth's arm. "Dearest, you are about to marry a man who will make his home here. If he is lucky, that is. If not, you might find yourself in Portugal or India or some far-flung outpost. Have you given thought to that?"

Elizabeth turned her eyes to the keys, her fingers hovering uncertainly above them. "I have," she said. "But the duty would not be so hard with Harry... I mean, Captain Darcy for company."

Her voice sounded steadier than she felt. It *was* true, was it not? She had fallen for his easy manner, for the way he had made her feel safe, even amidst the whispering crowd. His promises had held weight then, binding her future to his, despite the uncertain footing on which she stood. The rumours had already begun to swirl—quiet, cutting whispers about her reputation. A trollop... a tart, an easy conquest... If Harry did not return soon, if he failed to formalise their engagement, those whispers would only grow louder.

Aunt Gardiner gave her arm a gentle squeeze. "He will return for you, Elizabeth. I have no doubt of it. Captain Darcy is not the kind of man to leave a promise unfulfilled. He is an honourable man. Those whispers will be forgot in time, once you are safely wed. And then, my dear, you will be able to get on with your life—without these anxieties clouding your mind."

Elizabeth nodded, her smile growing a little steadier, though it still did not reach her eyes. "Of course," she agreed softly. "I can trust him to come back for me."

Her voice sounded almost convincing. She wanted to believe it—she truly did. Harry had spoken of duty and honour, had reassured her that all would be well once he spoke with his brother and finalised the arrangements. There was no reason to doubt him. He would return. He had to.

But her fingers trembled still as they hovered over the keys.

D ARCY KNOCKED FIRMLY ON the door of Bingley's townhouse, his mind dull and weary from the unrelenting business of the last few days. The butler opened the door swiftly, bowing crisply, and before Darcy could utter a word, Bingley himself appeared in the hallway, his face brightening at the sight of his unexpected visitor.

"Darcy!" Bingley's voice was full of unrestrained cheer. "Come in, come in! What brings you to London this season? Harry said you were firmly lodged at Pemberley. By Jove, had I known you were here, I should have called."

Darcy hesitated for a moment. It was never easy to deliver such news, but he had promised himself he would do this much for Harry. As much as he wanted to leave and bury the grief under the weight of duties and logistics, this visit was necessary.

"I am afraid this is not a social call, Bingley."

Bingley's face faltered, the smile wavering as he sensed the gravity in Darcy's tone. "What is it, man? Come in—sit down."

Darcy followed him into the drawing room but remained standing, staring down at his gloved hands. He did not wish to linger here, not in the warm comfort of a home that had no business housing such news.

"It is Harry," Darcy began, bracing himself.

"Harry?" Bingley repeated, his brow furrowing in confusion. "What of him? Has he returned with you from Pemberley? He was supposed to—"

"He is dead."

The words froze on the air, colder than the autumn chill Darcy had just left outside. For a moment, Bingley stood there, blinking at him, as if he had not heard correctly.

"I—what?"

"Harry is dead," Darcy repeated, his irritation rising despite himself. He had hated saying it once, and now twice felt like twisting the knife. "A horse accident... a week ago."

"No." Bingley shook his head, backing away, his eyes wide with disbelief. "No, that cannot be. Not Harry. We—we were supposed to..." His words cluttered to a halt, as if he had forgot how to speak. "We were meant to spend the autumn shooting—I was looking into leasing an estate, and he was going to join me there!"

Darcy looked away, pressing his lips together as Bingley's voice broke. He hated this—seeing others fall to pieces when he could not afford to do so himself. His own grief was buried deep, cold and tightly locked away. It had to be. His hands clenched at his sides as Bingley stumbled over to the window, his back to Darcy.

"We'd planned it all out," Bingley muttered, his voice barely above a whisper. "He... he was so looking forward to it. He told me he had not been out shooting in ages." Bingley's voice cracked, and his hand covered his face. He collapsed inward, his usual exuberance reduced to a fragile shell of the man Darcy knew.

Still standing, Darcy stared at the floor, wishing to leave—wishing to escape the room before he was forced to confront the feelings he had spent the last week avoiding. He shifted his weight, ready to excuse himself, when Bingley's voice broke the silence.

"We ought to drink to him," Bingley said abruptly, his words thick with emotion as he moved to the sideboard, fumbling with the decanters. "A man like Harry deserves that much, at least."

Darcy opened his mouth to decline, to tell Bingley that he had no wish to sit and toast his brother's memory—not yet, not in someone else's drawing room where he had not the leisure of shattering as he pleased. But something in Bingley's trembling hands, the sheer nakedness of his grief, made Darcy pause. Bingley needed this. And perhaps he needed it too, though he'd been refusing to admit it.

Without a word, he accepted the glass Bingley handed him.

"To Harry," Bingley said, his voice unsteady, tears spilling freely down his cheeks as he raised the glass. "To the best friend a man could have."

Darcy swallowed hard, his throat tight as he clinked his glass against Bingley's. He had not allowed himself to shed a single tear since that horrible day. There had been no time. No room. He drank, letting the burn of the liquor slide down his throat, and for a moment, the sharpness of it threatened to break through the stoic facade he had built around himself.

Bingley shoved his glass down, wiping his eyes with the back of his hand. He looked up at Darcy with a sudden expression of shock, as if something had only just occurred to him.

"Miss Elizabeth," he gasped, stepping forward, his face stricken. "Has—has she been told?"

Darcy blinked, caught off guard by the abrupt mention of the name. His brow furrowed. "Miss Elizabeth?"

"Yes, Elizabeth Bennet," Bingley stammered, his voice rising in urgency. "Does she know? Have you told her? Surely, Harry mentioned her. That was his whole purpose in going to Pemberley early."

Darcy shifted uncomfortably. "Harry mentioned her," he said carefully. "I know of the lady, yes."

Bingley stared at him with wide, pleading eyes. "Darcy, she must be told. She will be expecting Harry's return. You... you *do* know what she meant to him, don't you?"

Darcy exhaled slowly, setting his glass down with deliberate care. Oh, of course Harry had mentioned that proposal, but he had never written of the lady, never told Darcy how they met, never left any serious direction for her family. Darcy had assumed he would find something of her in the papers from Harry's flat—letters, something in his journal... if not, he was still prepared to assume that Harry's attentions were casual, the flirtation of a young officer enjoying his leave in town and speaking on a whim. Excitement, some desire to impress his older brother with such a large personal step.

But at Bingley's urgency, Darcy realised he might have underestimated the connection.

"I had hoped," Darcy began, "that you might speak to her. You are better acquainted with the lady. She would take the news better from a familiar face."

Bingley, his face streaked with tears, shook his head quickly, almost violently. "I—I cannot, Darcy. You do not understand. I... I am already in a delicate position with her family." He swallowed, wringing his hands. "But you... you are his brother. It should come from you."

Darcy frowned, his patience wearing thin. The last thing he wanted was to spend the day delivering more painful news, especially to a young woman he did not know. "I am not acquainted with Miss Bennet," he said, his voice clipped. "Nor have I the stomach to face a grief-stricken female today."

Bingley took a step closer, his expression imploring. "Darcy, please. You must understand—this is not just about grief. Her reputation... it's..."

Darcy raised an eyebrow, but Bingley's words faltered, his voice choking on his grief. Darcy remained silent, trying to piece together Bingley's disjointed ramblings. Surely, Bingley was referring to the usual consequences for a lady who had entered into an engagement. With Harry gone, Miss Bennet would face the unfortunate prospect of being considered unchaste—or, at the very least, unable to attach herself to another man until enough time had passed for mourning.

"It seems unfair," Darcy muttered, more to himself than to Bingley. "But time will heal the situation. She will move on once the appropriate period has passed."

Bingley, pacing the room in agitation, suddenly stopped and turned back to Darcy with renewed urgency. "No, it is more than that," he insisted. "You must go to her. Please, do not make me do this."

Darcy sighed heavily, pressing his fingers to his temple. Was not Bingley involved with the sister? Of course, he would not wish to make himself the bearer of bad tidings. But Darcy had come here to discharge his duty to Harry, not to become embroiled in Bingley's emotional entanglements. He did not wish to argue or press for details. It no longer mattered.

"Very well," he relented, though every muscle in his body resisted the idea. "I shall call on her tomorrow. But not today. I have not the strength for it."

Bingley opened his mouth to protest, but seeing the hard set of Darcy's jaw, he closed it again and nodded. "Thank you," he whispered, collapsing into the chair beside him, his face buried in his hands.

Darcy stood, his hand tightening briefly on the back of the chair as he steadied himself. He had to leave. The walls of the room felt too close, the air too thick with grief. He gave Bingley a short nod and turned toward the door.

"I shall see to it in the morning," Darcy said, his voice heavy as he stepped into the hallway. "Good day, Bingley."

Without waiting for a reply, he strode out of the house.

Chapter Three

"**I** RECEIVED ANOTHER LETTER from home this morning," Jane said quietly.

The soft scuffing of their boots on the walk was the only sound between them as Elizabeth and Jane wandered along the park's edge. The September breeze tugged at their pelisses, the crispness of the air warning of the colder months to come. It was one of the last fine days of the season, but the beauty of it was lost on Elizabeth. Walking through London's streets felt suffocating now, as if the very ground beneath her feet were ready to betray her with each step.

Elizabeth knew the contents of the letter before Jane spoke further. "Let me guess—Mama is beside herself again."

"She is worried, Lizzy. Terribly so." Jane's brow furrowed, her lips pressing into a thin line. "Her nerves have taken quite a turn. Papa says she barely leaves her room."

"When is Mama *not* beside herself?"

"Do not say that. You *know* this is different, and it is your doing. You cannot possibly make light of—" There was an edge to Jane's voice—a frustration that rarely surfaced in her otherwise serene nature. "She is right to be worried, Lizzy!"

The rebuke stung, but Elizabeth kept her expression neutral, her eyes fixed on the path ahead. "Worried about what? That I might be ruined? It seems a little late for that, Jane."

Jane sighed, her face pinched with so many unspoken thoughts. "You were not careful, Lizzy. You know how people talk in London. You—"

"I know!" Elizabeth cut in. She felt the weight of Jane's judgment as acutely as her own. "I know, Jane."

Jane seemed to hesitate for a moment, as if weighing whether to continue. When she did, her voice was sharp with frustration—a novelty for Jane. "I do not understand how it came to this. I would have almost expected it from Lydia, but not you! You... you let your feelings—"

"Run me to ruin," Elizabeth finished for her. There was no use pretending otherwise. She'd thought herself careful, thought Harry's affections were earnest enough to weather whatever scandal might follow. Now, she could hardly bear to look Jane in the eye. "I know."

Jane's lips tightened into a thin line, but she said nothing. Elizabeth could feel her disappointment, as cold and bitter as the autumn air around them. And she hated it. Hated that she'd put herself in this position, hated that her future rested on the shoulders of a man who had yet to fulfil his promise.

"He will come back for me," Elizabeth said, more to herself than to Jane. "He will make things right."

Jane was silent for a moment, her eyes on the horizon. "I hope so," she said at last. "But time is not your friend, Lizzy. What if the captain does not come—or what if he is delayed?"

The question hung between them, a heavy cloud of doubt that Elizabeth could not escape. Her chest tightened at the thought. What if Harry did not return? What if his promises, his easy smile, had all been lies in the end?

No, she could not let herself think that way. Harry had *said* he would come back. He had said he would make it right, and Aunt Gardiner insisted the Darcys were all known for being honourable.

"He will," Elizabeth muttered, as if saying the words aloud could make them true.

"Lizzy, you must be realistic. You have not had a single letter from him, and you ought to have by now. If Harry—if *Captain Darcy*—does not return... what will you do?"

Elizabeth clenched her jaw, fighting the sudden urge to lash out. "I shall not think about it," she said tightly. "Because I refuse to believe he will not."

The silence between them grew heavier, more strained. Jane had always been the calm, understanding one. But even now, Elizabeth could feel her sister's patience unraveling. Jane was trying—trying to be the kind, forgiving soul she always had been—but the worry of their situation was wearing on her, too.

And there was more than just Elizabeth's scandal to torment their imaginations.

"Will Mr Bingley call tomorrow?" Elizabeth asked, desperate to change the subject. "Uncle Gardiner has not been very... receptive to him lately."

Jane's shoulders sagged slightly, her face growing more troubled. "I do not know if he will be welcomed. Uncle Gardiner... he does not approve of Mr Bingley's—"

"Does not approve of him full stop?" Elizabeth raised an eyebrow, trying to inject some lightness into her voice, though her sarcasm fell flat. "Or disapproves of the company he keeps?"

Jane swallowed. "You know which one, Lizzy."

Elizabeth tipped her shoulders into a flippant shrug. "I am not surprised. Uncle Gardiner thinks all men from 'new money' are beneath us. A shame, really, when we are in desperate need of one."

Jane gave her a sharp look. "It is not that. You know Uncle Gardiner values honour above station or fortune. He is only protective of us."

"Too protective," Elizabeth muttered under her breath.

"And are you saying he is wrong to be so? After everything?"

Elizabeth crossed her arms inside her muff and growled. "It took Aunt Gardiner a full week to talk him into letting us out of the house. I hardly think we deserve to be gaoled like criminals. I say, what surer way is there to own all the horrible things people are saying about me than to refuse to show my face in public?"

Jane sighed again, though this time it was Elizabeth's words that had caused it. "Lizzy, I know you are angry—at all of this. But you must admit, we are in a delicate situation."

Elizabeth stopped walking, turning to face her sister. "No. *I* am in a delicate situation, Jane. Believe me, I am painfully aware of just how precarious my future is."

She saw Jane's eyes soften, guilt flickering across her face, but Elizabeth could not bring herself to apologise. Not for this. She had enough regret weighing on her heart without adding more to it.

They resumed their walk, though the ugly silence between them remained. Elizabeth had always relied on Jane's unfailing kindness, her ability to see the best in people, even when no one else could. But now, with the scandal hanging over them like a dark cloud, even Jane's resolve was beginning to crumble.

"And what of home?" Elizabeth asked, her voice quieter now. "What else does Papa say?"

Jane's expression grew pained. "He... he mentioned that Mr Collins is coming to look over Longbourn."

Elizabeth felt a sharp twist in her chest. "Of course he is," she said bitterly. "The vultures are already circling. And what does our cousin have to say about *me*, eh? Did Papa even have the stomach to put it down on paper?"

Jane winced at her tone, but said nothing.

Elizabeth bit her lip, forcing her voice to steady. "What will become of us, Jane? What if—" She stopped herself before the thought could take root.

"Stop, Lizzy. We cannot think that way."

Elizabeth twisted her mouth in a scowl and stared at the ground as they kept moving.

The park was growing busier now, more people out enjoying the last fine days of September. Elizabeth's eyes scanned the familiar faces, most of them belonging to the same social circles the Gardiners moved in. As they passed a group of ladies just ahead, Elizabeth stiffened, recognising Mrs Whitesmith and Miss Crandall, two women she had once exchanged polite pleasantries with at several gatherings.

But as they neared, the ladies' eyes flicked toward Elizabeth and Jane, lingering for a moment before turning away with cold indifference. Mrs Whitesmith raised her chin ever so slightly, her lips pursed, and the group swept past them without so much as a nod.

Elizabeth's blood ran cold. The cut direct.

For a moment, she stood frozen, fury rising in her chest, her breath quickening as the full force of the insult struck her. It was one thing to suspect her reputation was in tatters; it was another to see it confirmed in such a blatant, humiliating way. She could feel the heat in her cheeks, her hands clenching into fists as she turned, ready to march after them.

But Jane's hand was already on her arm, tugging her gently forward. "Do not," Jane whispered, her voice urgent. "Please, Lizzy. Let us go home."

Elizabeth's jaw tightened, but she allowed herself to be pulled along, her entire body trembling with anger. *How dare they?* How dare they look at her as though she were already fallen, already ruined?

Well... were they wrong? She *was* ruined. But that admission did little to soothe her pain and anger. Her feet dragged, and she had a very good mind to march on those ladies and make them speak to her face what they preferred to whisper behind their fans.

"*Please*," Jane said again, her hand tightening around Elizabeth's arm. "Please, let us go back to Uncle Gardiner's. Now."

Elizabeth closed her eyes for a moment, willing herself to calm. But the rage simmered just beneath the surface, threatening to spill over. She could feel the stares of the other passersby on her back, whispering, watching, waiting for her to fall.

"They will see," she muttered under her breath, her voice shaking. "They *will*."

Jane said nothing, but her grip on Elizabeth's arm did not loosen as they hurried away from the park, the fine day now marred by reality. Elizabeth could not help but wonder if this was all there was to her future—walking on the edge of ruin, dependent on the mercy of a man who may or may not return.

FITZWILLIAM DARCY LAY IN his bed, staring up at the dark ceiling. His eyes burned with exhaustion, but sleep would not come. Twice already, he had startled awake, gasping, drenched in a cold sweat, the terrible moment replaying again and again in his mind. The sickening thud, the way Harry's body had crumpled... each time, the nightmare tore through him, leaving him raw and heaving for breath.

He turned on his side, burying his face in the pillow, but it did no good. Sleep was a special kind of torment, an enemy he could not escape. And yet, as unbearable as his waking hours were, he could at least control his thoughts and direct them elsewhere. Awake, he could keep the grief at bay, if only for a little while.

Throwing back the covers, Darcy swung his legs over the side of the bed and sat up, running a hand through his damp hair. His chest felt tight, his skin stretched uncomfortably over muscles that twitched in an odd mixture of fatigue and restlessness. He could not lie here any longer, waiting for the next wave of nightmares to crash over him. He had to do something—anything—to stop the suffocating stillness.

The house was silent as he moved through the halls, his feet instinctively leading him to Harry's old room. They had brought the trunk from his flat here—where else could they take it? And though Darcy had meant to avoid the room entirely, now he felt a strange compulsion to see it. Perhaps, by confronting these relics of his brother, he could bring his mind to order—focus on the practicalities of Harry's belongings rather than the loss itself.

The door creaked softly as he pushed it open, the candle in his hand bathing the familiar room in a weak glow. And there it was—the trunk, sitting quietly at the foot of the bed as though it had been waiting for him.

He knelt beside it, his hands trembling slightly as he reached for the latch. For a moment, he hesitated. The thought of opening it, of seeing the things Harry had touched, had worn... it felt too intimate, too raw. But he forced his hand to move, lifting the lid slowly.

A wave of nostalgia hit him as the familiar scents of Harry's life rose up to meet him—the smell of leather, pipe tobacco, and the faint hint of the cologne Harry had always favoured. Darcy closed his eyes, letting the memories wash over him. He could see Harry as clearly as if he were standing before him, his broad grin, sun-browned face, and the mischievous spark that had never left his eyes.

Carefully, Darcy reached inside and lifted out the first item: an old brown coat, worn and weathered from use, one that Harry had often thrown on for informal walks or trips to town. Darcy ran his fingers over the fabric as though by touching it, he could somehow bring Harry back. For just a moment.

Next came a few shirts, neatly folded, though Darcy could tell they had been hastily packed by the batman. He lingered over a particular one, pulling it to his face, the scent of Harry's cologne still clinging to it. His breath hitched, but he forced himself to move on.

And then, buried beneath the shirts, his hand found something else—something softer. He tugged it free, his throat closing as he realised what it was: a handkerchief, embroidered with fine blue initials. Their mother's work, done just before she had passed. Harry had kept it with him ever since. Darcy had one just like it—a Christmas gift from her, and both brothers had treasured them, holding on to this last remnant of her care.

Darcy's eyes stung as he held the fabric in his hand. For a long moment, he simply stared at it, the memories of their childhood swirling in his mind. How often had he and Harry spoken of their mother, remembering her warmth, her gentle humour? And now, with Harry gone, that connection felt impossibly distant, lost to time.

His fingers lingered over a few more items, some trinkets Harry had kept—small souvenirs of places he had visited, letters from acquaintances—and then Darcy's hand brushed against something unfamiliar. He frowned as he pulled it out. It was a cravat, but not Harry's. The fabric was of lower quality, and there were still creases in it from a tight knot, carelessly left to rumple. That was not Harry's style. As he sifted through the items, more articles of clothing appeared—waistcoats and shirts, all of them unfamiliar. And then, Darcy recognised the battered whiskey flask.

A sneer curled at the edge of his mouth. *George Wickham.*

Of course. Harry had always been good friends with Wickham, despite Darcy's warnings. Father had condoned it, they were of the same age, and they had similar expectations in life—it made sense. They had been stationed together in Spain, spent endless hours together in London Wickham had wormed his way into Harry's life the way he always did—charming, manipulative, and entirely untrustworthy. These clothes must have been left behind after some stay at Harry's flat. Wickham was always turning up when he was least wanted.

Darcy shoved the cravat back into the trunk, anger rising in his chest. *Wickham.* The man had haunted their family for years, and even now, his presence lingered. Darcy had no intention of notifying Wickham personally of Harry's death. Let him find out through whispers in London, the way everyone else would. There was no part of Darcy that felt inclined to give Wickham the dignity of a personal notice.

With that thought, Darcy continued pulling things from the trunk—two of Harry's uniform coats, a few more cravats, and an old pair of boots. Each item felt like a piece of his brother being laid bare before him, and with each one, Darcy's control frayed a little more.

And then, at last, something inside him broke.

The sobs came, not in tears, but in ragged, anguished cries—sounds that tore from his throat, fierce and bitter. He clutched one of Harry's coats, his knuckles white as he pressed it to his chest. "No!" he choked out, his voice cracking with the force of it. "No, no, no..."

Harry was gone. The realisation crashed over him again and again, and no matter how tightly he held his brother's things, no matter how many times he screamed into the silent room, it would not change. Harry was dead. Nothing could bring him back.

For what felt like an eternity, Darcy knelt by the trunk, his face buried in Harry's coat as he raged—long, aching cries that shook his entire body with fury at himself. His chest heaved with the effort, but no relief came. Not even tears to soften the burn. Only more pain, more bitter denial.

Eventually, his body gave out, exhaustion taking hold. He pushed the remaining clothes back into the trunk, slamming the lid shut with shaking hands. He could not bear to look at any more of it. Not now. The memories, the pain, were too much.

But as much as he longed to collapse, to sleep and forget, Darcy knew there would be no respite. Not tonight. Perhaps not ever.

He stood, his legs unsteady, and left the room, his breath still ragged. He could not stay here, surrounded by Harry's personal things, drowning in the past. But neither could he attempt to sleep. There must be work to do—something practical, something that would give his mind a task.

The papers. Harry's papers had been brought down to the study, and sorting through them would be business. Something necessary. Something he could do to distract himself from the grief that had hollowed him out.

Darcy made his way down the hall to the study, his mind already shifting to the task at hand. The papers would require his full attention, and for now, that was what he needed most of all.

THE PAPERS SPREAD ACROSS Darcy's desk in an untidy sprawl, just as Harry had left them. Letters, maps, army orders—some crumpled and yellowed with age, others fresher, their ink still crisp on the page. He ran a hand through his hair, staring down at the mess. It was so typically Harry, to keep everything jumbled together, important or not, and Darcy had to force back the familiar flicker of irritation. Even now, with his brother gone, Harry's carelessness continued to haunt him.

A stack of letters sat in one corner, mostly correspondence with Harry's school friends. Darcy sifted through them absently. Here was a note from Tom Bertram, long-winded and full of good-natured banter. Another from some acquaintance in Bath, the paper already yellowing and forgot. None of it important. Darcy tossed them aside, his mind wandering.

He pulled out some outdated army orders, most of them several months old—why Harry had kept them, Darcy could not imagine. Outdated maps of the Spanish country-side, hastily sketched with faded notations, were crammed alongside scribbled lists and other half-formed thoughts that seemed entirely useless. Darcy almost laughed bitterly. Of course, Harry would keep a pile of rubbish mixed with crucial documents, as though one day all these scraps might suddenly become important.

But beneath the clutter, Darcy found other papers of more recent significance. His brother's last army orders, crisp and direct, made him pause for a moment. The reality of Harry's role—his life as an officer—felt distant now, as though it had belonged to someone else. Darcy shook his head and placed them aside.

Next, a letter from their uncle, Lord Matlock, its formal tone familiar and unre-markable. Darcy skimmed it quickly, more out of duty than interest. His gaze landed on another letter—this one from Richard, Harry and Darcy's cousin, who had been stationed in Chatham for the better part of the year. It was full of the usual bravado and casual news of military life that sounded like gibberish to Darcy. Richard's letter ended with an affectionate jibe at Harry for being "soft-hearted when it came to women." Darcy grimaced and set it aside.

His fingers lingered over the remaining papers when he noticed another letter, folded carelessly, its edges creased and worn, though the paper itself appeared relatively fresh. Unlike the others, this letter bore no coat of arms and no identifying marks beyond a broken wax seal. The seal was simple, without any stamp of identity—curious, given that Harry's correspondence usually came from those of good standing, their crests easily recognisable.

Darcy's brow furrowed as he picked it up. Something about the state of the letter—the heavy creases despite its newness, the irregular folding—ignited his curiosity. With a growing sense of unease, he unfolded it and began to read.

*C*APTAIN,

You will forgive the brevity and the lack of pleasantries, as neither are deserved. It has taken some time to find the words to put down in this letter, but now, with the situation grown desperate, I can no longer remain silent. You have wronged an innocent young woman, and in doing so, you have forever destroyed her prospects and left her in disgrace.

I write not for myself but for her, as it is not my honour at stake but hers. She believed your promises—believed that you were a man of your word, a man of honour. What a fool she was to trust you, to allow your sweet words to lead her down a path that has now left her with a ruined name and, worse, with child!

The child, at least, should have a name. You owe her that much. But what have you done, Captain? You have shunned her, acting as if you never saw her before. You have left her to bear the shame alone, abandoned her to face the consequences of your vile actions.

And now, you do not even dare to face the damage you have wrought. You are a coward, sir. A disgrace to your family name and to the uniform you wear. But I will not allow this to go unchallenged. You will make this right, or I will ensure the whole of society knows what you are.

I demand satisfaction. You will marry her and give the child a name, or I will see to it that your reputation is left in tatters. Do not think you will be able to threaten me in return, for I have no desire to protect myself, only her. I will not even sign my name, nor will I write hers, as you do not deserve the chance to save face. If you are the man you pretended to be, then you know precisely who I mean.

Do what is right. Marry her and restore what honour you have left.

D ARCY'S HAND TREMBLED AS he lowered the letter; the words burned into his mind. His breath came in sharp, uneven bursts, his heart hammering against his ribs. The desk beneath his palm felt cold and unforgiving, as though the ground itself had fallen away.

Harry? Harry had *ruined* a girl?

His mind scrambled, sifting through every memory of his brother, every conversation they had ever had about Harry's life in London. He had known Harry to be reckless at times—charming and careless with his affections, certainly—but this? The idea that his brother had left a young woman ruined, carrying his child, seemed impossible.

And yet, the letter. The fury, the pain, the demand for satisfaction... It all pointed to one undeniable truth.

Harry was gone, but the consequences of his actions remained. Darcy clenched the paper tightly, his knuckles white. *Bingley's words*, the man's insistence that Darcy must visit Miss Bennet himself, echoed in his mind.

Elizabeth Bennet.

Was it she? Could it be any other? Harry said he had pledged himself to the girl—this girl Darcy had never heard of, with no fortune and no family. Why else would he do such a thing? Was that a tacit admission of wrongdoing, and Darcy had failed to notice?

And Bingley... Bingley had all but begged Darcy to visit her, to break the news of Harry's death in person. At the time, Darcy had dismissed it as an overabundance of sentiment, but now... Now, the pieces were beginning to fit together.

The sickening realisation washed over him. This Elizabeth Bennet girl was ruined. A chit of no means. carrying a fatherless child. And it was Harry's fault.

Darcy's hand slammed against the desk, the letter crumpling in his grip. His brother had left a girl pregnant, abandoned her to shame and ruin. And now, it fell to him to fix it.

There was only one thing Darcy could do.

Chapter Four

D ARCY PACED THE LENGTH of his study, his boots scuffing the polished floor as he tried, yet again, to find a reason not to go. The direction to the Gardiner household sat neatly on the desk, written in Bingley's hastily scribbled hand, taunting him. Every instinct screamed at him to ignore it, to turn back, to let the matter dissolve into the shadows from which it had emerged. What if the girl was a fortune hunter? What if the accusations were false?

He paused, gripping the back of a chair tightly as his stomach churned. What if she was innocent—deceived into bestowing affections she ought not to have been asked for? What if everything in that wretched letter was true? His brother had seduced her, left her with child, and now—now it fell to him to salvage what little remained of their family's honour.

Darcy groaned, the burden of his duty settling like iron in his chest. If this was true, he had no choice. He *had* to marry her. The thought was enough to turn his stomach over again. He could feel the bile rising, threatening to overcome him, and without thinking, he hurried from the study, barely making it to his chambers before he was violently ill.

His whole body shook as he leaned over the basin, panting heavily, trying to steady himself. He closed his eyes and forced himself to think of Harry. His brother, full of life and laughter, now gone... and it was Darcy's fault.

His brother, who had left a woman ruined, carrying his child—a child Harry had meant to claim, if Darcy's own incompetence had not robbed him of that chance. Darcy clenched his fists, anger mingling with the grief and guilt that never quite left him. It was his *duty* to make this right. His father would have expected no less of him.

But still, the nausea persisted. What if this girl—this Miss Elizabeth Bennet—was nothing more than a cunning schemer? What if she had led Harry on, seeing in him an easy target, a way to ensnare a man of fortune? The thought twisted Darcy's gut further. He could not—*would not*—sacrifice his future for a fraud! No matter what the letter said, and no matter how guilty he felt.

Yet... Darcy's stomach roiled again, and he only barely dodged the necessity of another trip to the basin. How could he even think of his own needs and wants now? He had lost that right! If this girl were truly carrying Harry's child—a *Darcy*—he would have to marry her. There was no other option. His family's honour demanded it, and so did his devotion to Harry's memory.

Straightening, Darcy splashed cold water on his face and steadied himself in the mirror. He was pale, gaunt from sleepless nights, but his resolve had solidified. His mind was made up. He would confront Miss Bennet. He would see the truth in her face when he told her of Harry's death. If she was genuine in her grief, he would know. If she were truly... as the letter said... he would be able to see it.

And if not... well, he had every intention of offering her a generous settlement and leaving her to whatever fate awaited a woman who had ruined herself for a lie.

He dressed quickly, the stiff cravat and fine coat feeling like a kind of armour, though it could do little to protect him from the fiery darts he had already aimed at himself. His manservant hovered nearby, watching with concern, but Darcy waved him off with a terse nod. There was no time for hesitation now.

"Have the carriage brought round," he muttered.

The carriage ride was a blur of nerves and nausea. The horses' hooves clattered along the cobblestones, and each jolt sent another wave of biliousness through him. The closer they came to Gracechurch Street, the more Darcy's mind snarled with panic. What kind of woman was this Elizabeth Bennet? Why had Harry entangled himself with the niece of a tradesman? Oh, Bingley had insisted their father was a gentleman, but still—Harry had known better! He *needed* a wife of some fortune, someone to match his status, not the daughter of a country squire. It was irresponsible, reckless!

And yet, despite his irritation, despite the gnawing dread, Darcy felt the heavy pull of duty. The thought of the girl's grief, the child she might be carrying—it all sat like a stone in his stomach. If Harry had indeed wronged her, then Darcy had no choice. He would do what was necessary, as always.

As the carriage drew to a halt in front of the Gardiners' modest townhouse, Darcy swallowed hard, his palms already damp with sweat. He shot his cuffs, trying to shake the trembling from his hands.

"Wait for me," he instructed the driver, his voice tight. He would not be long. This meeting could end quickly if the woman proved to be a fraud.

Darcy strode to the front door, his lip curling as he looked over the house. The Gardiners were tradespeople, after all—wealthy, perhaps, but still beneath the Darcys in rank. Even a younger son could have done better than to tie himself here. *Harry, what did you do?*

He knocked firmly, steeling himself. The door was opened by a manservant who looked at Darcy with mild surprise, his expression quickly shifting to a professional mask.

"I am here to speak with Mr Gardiner," Darcy said, his tone clipped, formal.

The manservant's brows flickered upward slightly, but he nodded. "Mr Gardiner is not in, sir. He is not expected to return until later this evening."

Darcy hesitated, frustration bubbling to the surface. For a moment, he considered turning away, postponing the inevitable. But no. He had steeled himself for this meeting. Been ill over it. Barely forced himself into the carriage. It *had* to happen today.

"Then I would speak with Miss Elizabeth Bennet," he said, his voice firmer than he felt.

"Your name, sir?"

He swallowed. "Darcy."

The manservant's face altered ever so slightly—curiosity, perhaps? A hint of disdain? But the man bowed, gesturing for Darcy to follow him inside.

"Please wait here, sir," the manservant said as he opened the door to the hall. Darcy's pulse quickened as he heard murmured voices from the drawing room just beyond.

"Excuse me, ladies," the manservant's voice filtered back. "There is a Mr Darcy calling for Miss Elizabeth."

Darcy's breath felt like it was going to burst his chest. He could feel sweat gathering at his collar as his palms grew clammy.

There was an immediate outcry from within the room, voices rising in surprise and—joy? Darcy stiffened. Surely, this woman was desperate. Already, she had pinned her hopes on him. It was enough to make his stomach turn once more.

"He is here?" one voice exclaimed, full of breathless relief. "Oh, thank Heaven!"

"Show him in!" another voice added, trembling with emotion.

Darcy swallowed hard, tugging at his cuffs once more, and forced himself to step forward, his legs leaden. His hands felt slick as he wiped them against his coat and entered the drawing room.

The first thing he saw was three faces turned toward him—two young women and an older lady. The woman in the middle was striking—blonde, with a graceful composure about her that immediately put Darcy at some ease. He fervently hoped this was Elizabeth Bennet. A woman like her would be manageable. Decent. He could see her pale expression, her hands folded neatly in her lap, the perfect picture of restraint.

But then his eyes shifted to the other young woman—*her*.

The brunette stood, her body almost vibrating with tension, her eyes bright with feeling. Her dark hair framed a face alive with some internal storm, her whole being quivering as if the mere sight of him had sent a shock through her.

Darcy's stomach sank, the blood rushing in his ears. *Please, let it not be her.*

But it was.

She took a step forward, her confusion apparent as she tilted her head, the colour rising in her cheeks, her nostrils flaring with the weight of emotions just barely contained. Her lips parted, trembling slightly, and when she spoke, her voice was tight, uncertain, as if she was barely holding herself together.

"Harry?" she whispered. Her eyes searched his face, widening with dread. "Where is Harry?"

T HE AIR IN THE drawing room was suffocating. Elizabeth sat with her hands clenched in her lap, her knuckles white beneath the thin fabric of her gown. Jane sat beside her, her face composed, though the tension in her every movement was impossible to ignore. Aunt Gardiner, seated across from them, stared silently at the window, her hands folded in her lap, but it was clear she was not looking at anything. The silence between them had a presence of its own, pushing in on all sides.

It was another day gone. Another day without a word from Harry.

Elizabeth could feel her whole body trembling, though she did her best to hide it. Her leg jiggled beneath her skirts, the only outward sign of her unravelling nerves. She had been pacing the room earlier, but Jane had insisted she sit down—probably to stop the relentless movement. It had not helped. If anything, being still made the anxiety worse.

Where *was* Harry? Had something happened? He had promised—promised to speak with his brother, to finalise everything. But now there was nothing. No word. No sign of him. And with every passing day, the silence became more unbearable. The stares they received when they went out, the whispers when they passed others in the street—it was enough to drive anyone mad.

The soft sound of Jane's voice finally broke the oppressive quiet. "Perhaps... perhaps we ought to return to Longbourn," she said gently, though her eyes never left the carpet. "We would not face such—such censure there."

Mrs Gardiner did not speak, but her expression spoke volumes. The lines around her mouth tightened, her lips pressing together, though she said nothing. It was a look Elizabeth had grown used to—one of helpless frustration. Her aunt was caught between sympathy for her and the reality of their situation, and no amount of reassurance from Elizabeth would change that.

Elizabeth scoffed, shifting in her seat. "Do you truly think Longbourn will offer any sanctuary? I am under no illusions, Jane. The good people of Meryton are likely just as scornful as the fine people of London. Did not Kitty write to us complaining of the lack of invitations?"

Jane looked up, startled by Elizabeth's sharp tone. "But... perhaps they will come to understand—once... once everything is settled. Papa could put something in the paper. After all, you *do* have a proposal—"

Elizabeth laughed, a short, harsh sound devoid of any real mirth. "A proposal? A proposal is only worth as much as the man who makes it—and right now, that man is nowhere to be found." She shook her head, a bitter smile tugging at her lips. "Even if we were to announce it, Jane, do you really think the people of Meryton would care? Besides, it is not for Papa to announce. That duty lies with Captain Darcy, not him."

Her voice cracked slightly as she said it. Captain Darcy. The man who had changed... changed *everything*, the man who was supposed to have settled all by now. Where *was* he?

Before Jane could respond, there was a knock at the door. Elizabeth froze, her heart leaping into her throat.

"Miss Elizabeth," the manservant said, stepping just inside the room. "There is a Mr Darcy calling."

For a moment, the world seemed to stop. The breath she had been holding for what felt like days released in a rush, and Elizabeth leapt to her feet, her heart pounding with relief.

"He's here," she gasped, her voice barely above a whisper. "Harry—he's come back!"

Jane and Mrs Gardiner exchanged a glance. "He is here?" Jane cried. "Oh, thank Heaven!"

"Show him in!" Aunt Gardiner told the manservant.

Elizabeth's whole body surged with hope, with the overwhelming joy that Harry had returned at last. All of her worry, all of her fear, melted away as she turned to the door, expecting to see the familiar face of the man who had promised to make everything right.

But when the manservant stepped aside, it was not Harry who entered the room.

Elizabeth faltered, her breath catching in her throat. For the briefest of moments, her mind played tricks on her—*surely, this was Harry?* The man standing before her had a similar build, a powerful familial resemblance, but no—this man was older, his face more square, his bearing more severe. Handsomer, perhaps, but his eyes—his eyes were not Harry's laughing green-blue. They were dark, intense, and searching.

Elizabeth's heart sank into her stomach. The relief she had felt just seconds before vanished, replaced by a sharp sense of confusion.

"Harry?" she said, her voice wavering with uncertainty. She shook her head, frowning as she took a step forward. "Where is Harry?"

Elizabeth's pulse pounded in her ears, her whole body suddenly rigid with confusion and a flicker of apprehension as the tall, dark-haired man glanced uncomfortably toward Jane and her aunt. His presence seemed to fill the room in a way that made it difficult for her to breathe. He bowed stiffly in her direction, his movements measured and formal.

"Miss Bennet," he began, his voice deep and subdued. "I am Fitzwilliam Darcy."

Her heart sank. *The brother. The one whose approval Harry sought.* Her throat tightened, her hands clenched into fists at her sides. Was he here to forbid their marriage? Was he here to inform her that Harry had failed to secure his blessing? A sudden surge of defiance welled up within her. She would not cower before him, no matter how imposing or exacting he might be.

"Mr Darcy," she said, her voice firm, her chin rising slightly as she met his gaze with civility. "Where is Captain Darcy? Has he returned to London?"

For a moment, Fitzwilliam Darcy seemed to falter. His eyes, dark and intense, flickered with something that made Elizabeth's heart twist. He shifted uncomfortably, looking almost—no, it couldn't be—broken.

He opened his mouth to speak but hesitated as if the words would not come. Finally, his voice, when it emerged, was uneven, stilted, as if forcing itself out. "Harry... is... is dead."

The words crashed over her like a tidal wave, deafening her to everything but that single, terrible truth. *Dead?* Her vision blurred, the room tilting dangerously as the ground beneath her seemed to disappear. "No..." she whispered, her breath coming in ragged gasps. She shook her head in denial, her heart beating so hard it hurt. "No... no..."

Mr Darcy stood before her, his face ashen, his eyes locked on the floor as though he could not bear to look at her. Elizabeth could see it now—the truth written plainly in his expression. It was real.

Harry was gone.

"No!" she cried out, louder this time, her whole body trembling uncontrollably. It felt as if something inside her had been torn open, an unbearable agony tearing through her chest. Jane and Mrs Gardiner rushed to her side, their hands reaching for her, trying to hold her up, trying to comfort her with soft words she could not even hear. Their murmurs blended into the background, meaningless in the face of the storm raging within her.

She tore away from them, stumbling forward as sobs wracked her frame. Her mind barely registered her actions as she lunged toward Mr Darcy, her fists pounding against his broad chest, her voice rising in desperate, broken gasps.

"Take it back!" she sobbed, her fists striking him again and again, her words coming out in a torrent of anguish. "Tell me it isn't true! Tell me it's a lie!"

Mr Darcy did not speak. He stood motionless, enduring the force of her grief, his face drawn tight with pain. At last, his hands reached up, gentle but firm, and closed over her wrists, stilling her frantic movements. His grip was strong—too much like Harry's, the resemblance too painful to bear.

"If I could..." Mr Darcy's voice broke, and he swallowed hard, his eyes filled with an ache that mirrored her own. "If I could take it back, Miss Bennet, I would."

Her legs gave way beneath her, and she crumpled to the floor, her sobs overpowering her completely. The world around her seemed to fall away, leaving her in an abyss of grief and disbelief. Harry, her Harry, was gone. The man who had both stolen her future and promised her another, the one she had pinned all her hopes on, was gone forever.

She barely felt the hands of Jane and Mrs Gardiner trying to pull her up from the floor, their voices soft but panicked as they murmured reassurances that fell on deaf ears. They could not comfort her. No one could. Her life was over.

"Elizabeth, come now," Jane whispered, her voice quavering as she tried to coax her sister back to her feet. "You must not—"

Aunt Gardiner spoke over her, her tone far more urgent as she glanced toward Mr Darcy. "I should send for my husband. He is at the warehouse, but I will have him return at once. Mr Darcy, will you wait? We shall—"

Elizabeth heard the words only dimly as she struggled to stand, pushing away from her aunt and sister. Her knees were shaking beneath her, but fury began to rise, burning through the haze of her grief. She locked eyes with Mr Darcy, her voice ragged with the sharp edge of desperation.

"How did it happen?" she demanded, her voice trembling with anger.

Mr Darcy had turned away, his gaze fixed on the window, the muscles in his back tensed as if he were bracing himself for the onslaught of her grief. He did not speak, but the silence was its own cruel answer.

Elizabeth's voice shook with frustration as she shouted at his back. "*How* did it happen?"

Mr Darcy turned, his face pale and lined with pain. His gaze flicked toward Mrs Gardiner and Jane, and he spoke, his words slow, carefully measured. "May I... may I request the honour of speaking to Miss Elizabeth alone?" His voice wavered, the weight of his grief evident in every syllable. "If she is willing."

"Absolutely not!" Mrs Gardiner was quick to protest, stepping forward with a fierce shake of her head. "Elizabeth is in no state to—"

Elizabeth cut her off, her voice sharp and unyielding. "I have nothing to fear from Mr Darcy, Aunt. And what reputation is there left to care about?" She turned back to him, her eyes burning with determination. "I want the truth. Let him stay."

Mrs Gardiner looked torn, her mouth opening as though to argue, but Elizabeth's resolve held firm, and at last, her aunt sighed, glancing at Jane. "Very well," she said reluctantly. "Jane, come with me."

Jane looked desperately between her sister and Mr Darcy, but with a final pleading glance at Elizabeth, she allowed herself to be led out of the room. The door clicked shut behind them, leaving Elizabeth alone with Mr Darcy in the thick silence that followed.

Elizabeth stood where she was, her hands trembling at her sides, her eyes never leaving Darcy's pale face. She had no tears left—only a fierce, aching need to know.

"What happened?"

D ARCY COULD NOT BRING himself to look at her. The sound of Elizabeth Bennet choking back sobs, fighting for composure, was unbearable. Whether her tears came from the heartbreak of losing Harry or from the desperate realisation of her circumstances, Darcy could not know. But the devastation was unmistakable. She was utterly destroyed by the news—whatever her feelings for his brother had been.

Darcy paced to the window, his fingers tugging at his cravat as though he were suffocating. He was too warm, too cold—his body unsteady beneath the crushing guilt. How was he to face her? How was he to tell her how it happened? That it was his fault? She had demanded the truth, and he could not deny her, though each word felt like a stone lodged in his throat.

She spoke again, her voice tight and ragged. "What happened?"

Darcy clenched his jaw, staring out at the empty street beyond the window, the autumn light too sharp against the glass. He drew in a breath, but it was shallow, trembling. He had relived the moment so many times already, each time tearing at his mind as if it were happening all over again. How could he put this into words for her?

Slowly, haltingly, he turned back to her. She was watching him, her eyes red and swollen, the torment etched in every line of her face. She deserved the truth, no matter how it broke her further.

"It was... it was an accident," he began. "We were at Pemberley, preparing for a ride. It was supposed to be nothing more than a leisurely morning." He stopped, his mouth dry, but forced himself to continue. "There was a new horse. Barking dogs, one of the stable hands... a boy, inexperienced... was struggling with it. The stallion was nervous, high-strung—lunging for Harry's mare."

He saw her flinch, but he had to keep going. He owed her that much. "I tried to calm the horse, but—" Darcy's voice caught, his throat tightening. He swallowed hard. "The horse bolted. It charged straight toward him. I shouted to Harry, I—I tried to warn him, to reach him. But it was too late."

Elizabeth Bennet's hands clutched the arm of the chair, her knuckles white, her breath coming in shallow, ragged gasps.

Darcy's voice faltered, and he looked down, staring at his boots, his fists clenching at his sides. "He... he tried to move aside, but his horse was startled. It reared. He lost his balance and was thrown."

The silence between them grew heavier, more suffocating. Darcy could barely hear his own thoughts over the sound of Elizabeth Bennet's broken breathing. He closed his eyes for a moment, gathering the strength to continue.

"Harry... hit the ground," Darcy said, his voice strained. "His head struck a stone. I— I ran to him, but..." He looked up at her then, forcing himself to meet her gaze, though the anguish in her eyes was nearly unbearable. "There was nothing I could do. He was—he was gone."

She shook her head, her body trembling violently. She was mouthing the word *no*, over and over, as if she could reject the truth he had just given her, as if she could will it away. Darcy's heart twisted painfully in his chest as he watched her. *Oh*, he knew that look. Too well did he know it, for it had stared back at him in his own mirror. And nothing he could say would offer her any comfort.

"I tried..." His voice cracked, and he had to pause, struggling to regain control. "I tried to save him, but... it was over in an instant."

Elizabeth's sobs tore through the silence once more, and Darcy felt as though he were drowning in her grief, in the terrible reality he had delivered to her. His brother was gone, and now so was any hope of peace for the woman sitting before him.

There was nothing left to say.

Darcy stood for a long moment in the oppressive silence, his thoughts tangled in a whirlwind of grief, guilt, and something he could not quite name. Shame lowered his gaze, but curiosity lifted it again.

She was not... unpleasant to look at. Not at all. Harry had always favoured brunettes, and though Darcy had never openly admitted it—even to himself—he had found the same appeal in women with dark curls, women with a certain fire in their eyes.

But Darcy had always held himself to different standards, ones that dictated he would marry for station and fortune, not for some fleeting attraction. Looks were irrelevant to him, especially now. This had nothing to do with beauty or desire. It was about necessity. Harry had left this woman in an impossible position, and Darcy, in turn, felt the crushing weight of responsibility for his brother's mistakes. He would make it right because Harry no longer could.

With a heavy breath, Darcy finally turned to her. "Miss Bennet," he began, his voice even but detached, "you are... distressed."

Her eyes, red and swollen, widened in incredulity. *"Distressed?"* she echoed, her voice sharp with disbelief. "You must be the coldest, most unfeeling man alive, to put it so lightly! Of course, I am distressed!" She took a breath that trembled on the edge of fury. "I am broken by the death of the man I meant to marry!"

Darcy flinched inwardly but held his composure. She was right, of course. But he could not allow himself to be moved by her emotion. He was here to face the consequences of Harry's actions, not to unravel himself in the face of her grief. "You were rather... attached to him, then," he said, his voice softer now, hesitant.

She closed her eyes, her hands trembling as she tried to gather herself. "Yes," she said, her voice faltering, her words nearly lost in the sobs she tried so desperately to hold back. "Yes, I was terribly fond of him... but..."

Her hesitation, the way her voice caught, sent a cold dread through Darcy's veins. He took a step closer, his gaze narrowing as he tried to read the emotions flickering across her face. "There is more, is there not?"

Her expression shifted, her face paling as though she had been struck. She broke away from him, turning toward the fireplace, her shoulders shaking as she paced away. Darcy watched, holding his breath as if it could help him hear hers better as she stood by the mantel, staring down at the hearth with her back to him. Her frame trembled from head to foot, and he could see the effort it took for her to hold herself together, to remain standing.

Then, in a small voice, she spoke. "You know?"

The words sent a deep, sinking feeling through him. Darcy closed his eyes briefly, his heart crashing in on itself. So, it *was* true. The letter—the horrible accusations—were not some madman's rant. His stomach churned with the knowledge that his worst fears had been confirmed. She had been left ruined, and Harry—his brother—was responsible.

"I do."

She turned to face him then, her eyes still brimming with tears, but there was something else in her expression now—a spark of strength that he hadn't expected. Despite the tremor in her body, she squared her shoulders, lifting her chin as though she could still summon some remnant of pride. "So, what now?"

Darcy's throat nearly closed up as he looked at her. It was all more than he could stomach—Harry's death, this woman's ruined future, his own overwhelming guilt. He closed his eyes for a moment, as if he could find some escape, some answer that would make this easier. But there was none. There was only one course left to him.

He turned away from her, his gaze falling to the floor. "I think," he began slowly, the words heavy in his throat, "that we need to speak with your uncle, Mr Gardiner."

Chapter Five

Elizabeth squeezed her fingers tightly against each other with all the strength in her hands. If she must sit and wait, she would find some way of burning off the anxiety that tingled in her limbs. Her aunt and Jane sat close beside her, their concerned glances flitting toward her as though they were waiting for her to shatter into a thousand pieces.

Outside, in her uncle's study, Mr Darcy and Mr Gardiner were discussing—no, *arguing*—over her future. She did not need to hear the words to know what was happening. Her fate was being decided by two men, without her, and whatever came of it would be delivered to her like a final, cold judgment.

"Lizzy," her aunt murmured, trying to soothe her, "at least Mr Darcy came. That is something, is it not? He must wish to offer aid in some form."

Elizabeth said nothing, her eyes fixed on the flickering flame of the hearth. She knew better. *Aid?* What could Mr Darcy offer that would save her now? Even if he were generous enough to give her a settlement—a lifetime's worth of security—it would not be enough to save her reputation. In fact, it would make things worse. People would whisper about her being a rich man's paid woman, living off the shame of Captain Darcy's indiscretion. No, money could not mend the ruin she had brought upon herself.

Her sisters were ruined, too—*every* Bennet daughter stained by the disgrace. There would be no invitations, no respectable proposals. And even though Elizabeth might scrape by on Mr Darcy's generosity, her future would never be honourable again. It was over. Her chance for marriage, for any semblance of normalcy, had been buried with Captain Darcy.

She covered her face with her hands, trying to hold back the sobs that threatened to escape. *Harry!* She had been looking forward to a life with him, a life she had convinced herself she could be happy in. No, he was not a man of fortune, but what did *she* have? A country girl with nothing more than an ageing father with an entailed estate and hardly any dowry to offer? They had been well-suited, or so she had thought. They got on well, and he had been there when she needed him. But now... he was gone, and with him, any hope of salvaging her life.

Jane leaned closer, placing a hand on Elizabeth's arm. "Lizzy, do not despair. We will think of something. There is always hope."

Elizabeth sniffed sharply and brushed Jane's hand away. "Hope?" she muttered, her voice edged with bitter humour. "For what, Jane? That a respectable man will suddenly appear and overlook the fact that I have ruined our family name? No. I've no illusions about what I have done." She laughed, though there was no mirth in it. "If I were truly clever, I would find a way to disappear quietly. Perhaps I'll take up residence in a small, forgotten cottage in the middle of nowhere. Live on my own means, far from the eyes of those eager to gossip."

"Lizzy, do not speak like that—"

"Oh, but why not, Jane?" Elizabeth retorted, forcing herself to smile through the tears that pricked at her eyes. "Let us not pretend. I brought this upon myself. There is no use in sugar-coating it. I have made my bed, and I shall lie in it. Though, in truth, I suspect it will be a rather lumpy bed, without so much as a decent pillow to rest my head on."

Her aunt shifted in her chair. "Elizabeth, you must not speak so. We will find a way to make things right—"

But Elizabeth shook her head. "Make things right? Aunt, I appreciate your optimism, but we both know there is no 'right' to be found. What's done is done. I shall face whatever ruin may come with as much dignity as I can scrape together."

She managed to smile again, though it was a hollow thing, and quickly wiped her eyes before the tears could fall. She would not cry. There was no room for tears. If she could not have honour, at least she would have her pride.

Even as she began mentally crafting her escape plan—imagining a solitary life far from society's prying eyes—the drawing-room door opened. The manservant stepped in, his face as impassive as ever, but Elizabeth felt her stomach twist at the sight of him.

"Miss Elizabeth," he said. "Mr Gardiner wishes to speak with you in his study."

For a moment, Elizabeth's breath staggered, her heart in her throat. Her fate was waiting for her beyond that door. She barely registered her own words of agreement, her feet moving of their own accord as she stood and allowed herself to be led from the drawing room.

Each step felt like a step toward the gallows, her pulse quickening as the hallway stretched before her. She could feel Jane's eyes on her back, could hear her aunt's murmured reassurances, but none of it penetrated the fog of dread that had settled in her chest.

Before she knew it, she was sitting in her uncle's study, her hands folded tightly in her lap as she faced her uncle across the heavy desk. The room smelled of leather and ink, the fire casting long shadows along the bookshelves. But it was not her uncle who held her attention—it was the tall figure standing near the window, his back turned to the room.

Mr Fitzwilliam Darcy.

Not the Darcy she knew. Not the man she trusted, but a taller, more formal shadow of him.

His hands were locked behind his back, his posture rigid, as if he were holding himself together by sheer force of will. Whatever had passed between him and her uncle, it did not seem like a discussion in which she had much say. Her heart hammered, her throat dry as she swallowed hard.

Elizabeth's voice was hoarse when she finally spoke. "Am I to be enlightened now?"

D ARCY STOOD BY THE window, his gaze fixed on the street below, though he saw none of it. His fingers twitched at his sides, every muscle tense as he fought the urge to turn and face Miss Bennet. He had no desire to look at her, not now—not while the reality of what was being arranged hovered like a weight he could not shrug off. But he could hear her behind him, could feel the oppressive silence filling the room as Mr Gardiner prepared to speak.

This was how it had to be. The arrangements had been made, the proposal delivered, and, despite the doubts roiling within him, Darcy felt a grim satisfaction in having done what was necessary. Mr Gardiner, for his part, had proven surprisingly reasonable. Darcy had expected more resistance, more outrage, from the man who had written that damning letter to his brother.

But there had been none. Darcy had not even been required to produce that letter for reference, nor even to speak of it directly. They understood one another well enough. Gardiner had listened to his proposition with calm deliberation, and the relief that passed through the man's expression had been excruciatingly clear, despite the civility with which he masked it.

The Gardiners, it seemed, had been at a loss as to what to do with Miss Elizabeth. The affection the man bore for his niece was evident, but so, too, was his frustration. Darcy had recognised that same quiet exasperation in the aunt and sister he had met earlier. Miss Elizabeth's actions had been reckless, had dragged her whole family into the mire of disgrace, and yet... Gardiner had agreed to Darcy's terms without hesitation. A quiet marriage. As soon as possible. Darcy would even secure a special license so that the whole affair could be conducted within the privacy of the Gardiner home. No public spectacle, no fanfare, and—most importantly—no witnesses beyond the immediate household.

Gardiner had, with some hesitation, asked about bringing her family from Longbourn to witness the marriage, but Darcy had declined. The family, surely, would prefer to distance themselves from this scandal, and it would be better for all if the matter were patched up quickly and discreetly from afar.

And besides, he was in mourning. As would she be now.

Darcy had assured Gardiner that he would settle a generous amount on Miss Elizabeth, that she would have enough to ensure a future of relative comfort—respectable enough, if she played her role. The rest would depend on her. This marriage, this arrangement, was about necessity. There was no room for sentiment, no room for the romantic gestures she might have once dreamed of with his brother.

As Mr Gardiner spoke, relaying the details of the arrangement to the lady, Darcy kept his back to the room, staring at the empty street outside as though it might somehow offer solace. Occasionally, he dared to glance over his shoulder at Miss Bennet. Her face was pale, her hands folded tightly in her lap, but he could see the rising colour in her cheeks as Gardiner continued to speak. She was angry—rightfully so—but she was holding herself together for the moment. He had expected this much from her, though her silence unnerved him more than her anger.

What was she thinking? Was she cursing him for robbing her of the man she had meant to marry? Did she even know it was his fault? The heat of her gaze on his back felt like a physical thing, and despite his attempts to remain impassive, Darcy could not ignore the scathing reproach that built with every passing second.

When Gardiner finished, the silence that followed was deafening. Miss Bennet did not speak, but Darcy could feel her eyes burning into him, daring him to turn and face her. For a long moment, he could not force himself to move. There was something whenever he looked into her red-rimmed eyes, something that pierced through his carefully constructed walls, striking him with an emotion he could not quite name.

Finally, he turned, his throat working as he swallowed. There was a strange, unaccountable urge in him to apologise to her, to offer some small word of regret for the way things had turned out. But the words stuck in his throat. He could not give her that. And he certainly could not offer her the ridiculous, romantic gesture of kneeling before her as though this were a love match.

Instead, he forced the words past his lips. "Will you accept my terms?"

Elizabeth Bennet's face tightened, her jaw working as she fought to steady herself. He could see the tremor in her shoulders, the way her hands clenched in her lap as though she were holding herself together by sheer force of will. She swallowed hard, her whole body shivering with the effort to control her emotions.

"Yes," she said, at last, the word clipped, devoid of any joy. It was a word of resignation, one that felt like a death knell in Darcy's ears.

The room seemed to close in around him. That single word—small and sharp—had sealed not just her fate, but his own. He had set this course in motion, and now he would live with it, no matter how it felt like his own doom.

"Very well." Darcy bowed to her, then to Mr Gardiner, his throat constricting. "I will send my man of business with the settlement offer. The rest of the details will be arranged." He straightened, his voice cool and formal. "We will be married by the end of the week. After the ceremony, I intend for us to leave for Derbyshire without delay."

He glanced once more at Miss Bennet. Her jaw was set, her cheekbones sharpened by anger, the fire in her eyes still burning, though she remained silent.

She nodded once, not trusting herself to speak.

Darcy bowed again, a stiff, perfunctory gesture, and without another word, he turned on his heel and left the room.

Four Days Later

T HE MORNING LIGHT FILTERED through the thin curtains, casting pale shadows across the small room. Elizabeth sat at her dressing table, staring at her reflection. Her hands trembled as she tried to pin up the last of her hair, but it was no use—her fingers were clumsy today, shaking with a mixture of nerves and something that felt a great deal like terror. Reluctance. Her heart was heavy with the knowledge that this day—her wedding day—felt more like a sentencing than the beginning of a new life.

What a cheerless occasion! If only there were something to look forward to, something to soften the blow of leaving everything and everyone she knew behind. At least now, Jane could have a future. Perhaps Mr Bingley might return, and perhaps her uncle would let the gentleman see her. The possibility was small comfort, but comfort all the same.

She turned her gaze to her reflection again. *What sort of man was Fitzwilliam Darcy?* The question lingered in her mind like a dull ache. Harry had told her very little about his brother, though she supposed she had never asked. There was never time for such things. She had been so focused on her own plans with Harry, so caught up in the notion that her future was secure, that she had never thought to learn more about the man to whom she would now be bound—the substitute husband.

In truth, she had known little about Harry either, but at least she had known him personally. His body language, his clear, open expressions—she could read him easily. His face was pleasing, his manner comfortable, and she had felt safe with him, as if everything would work itself out in time.

Fitzwilliam Darcy, however, was another matter entirely. Harry had spoken of his brother as a man of duty, a man who could be relied upon, someone whom Harry clearly admired. But to Elizabeth, the portrait he had painted was of a severe man, rigid and cold. Someone who would do what was required of him, but without finding any joy in it. A dutiful husband, yes, but one whose sense of obligation left no room for warmth or affection. A cold, impersonal marriage awaited her.

Her hands trembled more violently as she fumbled with a hairpin, and she let out a soft sigh of frustration, dropping it onto the table. At that moment, there was a gentle knock at the door. Aunt Gardiner stepped in quietly, saying nothing as she crossed the room. She came to stand behind Elizabeth, resting her hands on her niece's shoulders. Their eyes met in the mirror, and Mrs Gardiner offered a small, tight smile.

Elizabeth sniffed, her fingers idly plucking at the borrowed gown she wore, smoothing the soft fabric as if it might distract her from the day ahead. "The lace is lovely," she murmured. "Thank you for lending it to me. It is much finer than anything I brought from Longbourn." She hesitated, the corner of her mouth lifting in a faint attempt at humour. "Except for my ballgown. But a girl can hardly get married in a ballgown. Only think what my future husband would think of that!"

Mrs Gardiner's smile wavered, and she sighed. "We should have taken the time to alter it," she said, her hands gently squeezing Elizabeth's shoulders. "It is a bit too large for you."

Elizabeth shook her head, forcing a small, bitter laugh. "I will only be wearing it for a few minutes," she replied, her eyes fixed on her lap. "I'll be changing into my travel attire soon enough. Besides, I doubt my husband will care one way or another." She swallowed. "He probably already thinks me more indecent than I am."

Mrs Gardiner's expression tightened, her lips thinning as she fell silent. Her hands stilled on Elizabeth's shoulders, her touch now more of a quiet comfort than anything else. The silence between them grew, and Elizabeth stared at her own reflection until her gaze blurred and she almost forgot that was herself in the mirror.

After a long pause, she focused to meet her aunt's eyes in the mirror once more. "Is Pemberley truly as beautiful as you have always said?" Her voice was tentative—all she wanted was some scrap of hope to cling to.

Mrs Gardiner smiled again, this time a little more earnestly. "Yes. Pemberley is everything I have described and more. If nothing else, Lizzy, you will have beautiful grounds to walk on. Better than London. It is a fine estate."

Elizabeth nodded, her fingers still toying with the lace of her gown. *Beautiful grounds.* That did sound... not awful. But would she walk them alone? Fitzwilliam Darcy certainly did not seem like the kind of man to join her. She could not imagine him strolling through gardens or engaging in quiet conversation. Certainly, he would not stoop to daydream or jest with his wife. He would do his duty; that much was clear, but she doubted he would ever be more than a stranger to her.

There was another knock at the door, this time softer. Jane slipped into the room, her face filled with gentle concern. She smiled at Elizabeth's reflection in the mirror, then came to her side, taking her hands in her own. Elizabeth turned on the stool to face her sister fully.

"Mr Darcy has arrived. And the clergyman is with him."

Elizabeth felt her blood run cold. Her heart gave a sickening lurch, and she paled, her grip tightening on Jane's hands.

Jane squeezed her fingers. "Lizzy... it is not too late." Her voice trembled ever so slightly. "If you wish to call it off—if you truly cannot bear it—you do not have to go through with this."

For a moment, Elizabeth could not speak. Her mouth felt dry, her head light, as if the room were spinning. But then she drew in a deep breath, steeling herself against the flood of emotions threatening to overwhelm her. She gave Jane's hands a final squeeze and squared her shoulders, rising to her feet.

"Yes, Jane," she said softly, her voice firm despite the tightness in her throat. "It *is* too late."

She stepped away from the dressing table, her movements slow and deliberate, every step taking her closer to the fate she could not avoid.

Chapter Six

D ARCY STOOD AT THE front of the room, his eyes fixed on the doorway, waiting for the woman who was soon to become his wife. It had been four long, uncomfortable days since his last encounter with her, and now, as the ceremony approached, he wondered how this moment would play out. Would she falter? Would she face him with anger or resignation? Or would she crumble, overwhelmed by the prospect of a marriage neither of them wanted?

But when Elizabeth Bennet entered the room, he was struck by the way she held her head high, her shoulders squared with quiet dignity. She walked toward him with measured steps, and though her face was devoid of any smile, her gaze met his unflinchingly. That alone made an impression on him. She did not shrink from him, nor did she show any outward signs of fear or shame, as he might have expected from a woman in her position.

There was no warmth between them, but he could not judge her for that. He had no smile for her, either.

He bowed slightly as she came to stand beside him and offered her his hand, palm down. It was a formal gesture, one made more from duty than any sense of gallantry. She stiffened, he noticed, a slight flicker of hesitation crossing her face. Then, with a subtle arch of her brow, she placed her hand lightly on the back of his.

It was the briefest of touches, barely there, but it was enough. Together, they walked toward the clergyman. Darcy was aware of every movement, the swish of fabric, the soft tap of her shoes against the floor. As they approached the man who was to solemnise their union, his eyes caught on the gown she wore. It was too loose, the fabric bunching slightly at her waist and dragging a little on the floor.

So, she had already grown too much to wear clothing that fit her properly.

The sight of her in that ill-fitted gown only cemented in his mind the gravity of what he was doing, and why. He was marrying her for necessity, to preserve what honour could be salvaged. As they stood before the clergyman, his mind wandered for a moment, wondering just how far along she was. A month? Perhaps more? Harry had returned from the Continent in mid July, so it was long enough to be certain of some things. He supposed that time would reveal the answer soon enough. For now, this was simply another step in fulfilling his duty.

The clergyman began the ceremony, his voice low and solemn as he read the words of the marriage service. Darcy kept his gaze forward, trying not to let his attention drift toward the stony faces of her family, who watched the proceedings with expressions ranging from discomfort to sadness. But it was Elizabeth who drew his notice again, despite himself.

Her face was not cold like the others. It was alive with feeling, each emotion—grief, resignation, perhaps even anger—flitting across her features. She did not mask it, and it made her impossible to ignore. Darcy found himself watching her from the corner of his eye, fascinated by the way her expressions changed with each vow spoken. He had to force himself to look away, to remind himself that this was duty, nothing more. It was not the time to be captivated by the movements of a woman's face.

They repeated their vows, their voices steady and formal, though her words were coloured with something that his own were not—emotion. When it came time for the clergyman to bless their union, Darcy listened with both relief and dread. It was done. The union was legally sealed.

They turned together, the formality of the moment still hanging in the air between them. There was no kiss, no gesture of affection, not even a perfunctory brush on the cheek. That would have been far too intimate for the circumstances. Instead, Elizabeth faced her family, her expression unreadable once more.

Her aunt and sister approached her first, their embraces awkward and brief, the kind given when there is nothing left to say. Then Mr Gardiner came forward, offering his hand to Darcy with some hesitation. The handshake was quick; no words were exchanged, just a shared acknowledgement that this was the best solution they had.

Darcy's attention returned to Elizabeth, watching as she gathered the oversized skirt of her gown with practised grace. Her face was set, determined, but her eyes were shadowed with something he could not quite place. She looked at him, their gazes meeting briefly before she spoke.

"I will go upstairs to change for our travels."

Her voice was steady, though he detected a faint tremor beneath it. She turned without waiting for his response, walking toward the door with that same quiet dignity she had shown since the moment she entered the room.

Darcy watched her go. *Mrs Darcy.*

It was done.

I T HAD BEEN ONLY half an hour since the wedding ceremony, and now Elizabeth was already standing in the hall of her husband's townhouse. She had not been given a tour, nor offered much of an introduction to her new life. No, they had stopped only long enough for Mr Darcy to change out of his wedding attire and have another carriage brought round from the mews for the long journey to Pemberley.

She had been introduced to the housekeeper, Mrs Hodges, who had greeted her with polite deference, offering whatever refreshment she might require. The housekeeper's eyes had been kind, though Elizabeth could not miss the black armband worn in quiet mourning. The sight of it stirred something in her chest—they were grieving for Harry, too.

But the reminder did little to soothe the knot of anxiety in her stomach. She had only just changed from her wedding gown into her travelling attire, and the thought of sitting down to eat or drink anything seemed impossible. "I require nothing, thank you. I am ready for our travels," Elizabeth said, her voice tight. She offered a sparse smile to Mrs Hodges, who looked at her with sympathy but said nothing more.

"Would you like to sit by the fire, ma'am? You may be comfortable here until Mr Darcy is ready. It will not be long."

Elizabeth hesitated but then nodded, allowing herself to be shown to a seat in the drawing room. The fire crackled softly in the grate, a quiet, warm sound that soothed her, though it did little to ease the scattered pounding of her pulse. Her gaze drifted around the room. A pianoforte sat in one corner, polished and elegant, its keys gleaming in the firelight. Who played that? Did Mr Darcy?

Harry used to. He said his mother had taught him, and she had seen him exhibit one evening at a party, with Mr Bingley laughing over his shoulder and turning the pages for him like he would for a lady. For a brief moment, she pictured Harry sitting there, in that drawing room with her, his fingers deftly moving over the keys as he played. He had been so skilled, better than she could ever hope to be. It seemed a lifetime ago now.

Her attention shifted to the few books placed neatly on a side table—decorous and untouched, from what she could tell. She wondered if her new husband had placed them there out of a fondness for reading or simply to give the room a more refined air. Did he even read at all? There were so many things she did not know about him. So many things she had never thought to ask when she had envisioned marrying his brother.

Well, she would have time to discover the answers. More time than she had ever bargained for.

The moments passed slowly, the quiet of the room oppressive as she waited. She stared into the fire, trying to calm the wild thoughts swirling in her mind. Only fifteen minutes later, her husband returned, dressed now in his travel attire. He greeted her with a brief nod, informing her that the carriages were ready. Without another word, they left the townhouse, their departure marked only by the faint sound of the door closing behind them.

Two carriages set off—one carrying them, and another behind with their trunks and two servants she had yet to meet. The cobblestones beneath the carriage wheels clattered rhythmically, the noise filling the silence between them. Elizabeth swallowed, her gaze fixed out the window, watching the dark streets of London slip by. It was easier to focus on that than to meet his steady gaze.

But she felt him looking at her, the weight of his attention almost searing her flesh, until finally, he broke the silence. "Are you well, Mrs Darcy?" His voice was measured, polite, as though they were merely strangers exchanging pleasantries.

Elizabeth nodded, not trusting herself to say much. "Yes," she answered softly, her hands twisting together in her lap. What else was there to say?

The silence returned, thick and heavy, as the carriage rolled over the uneven cobblestones. Elizabeth continued to stare out the window, watching the city fade into the distance, but her thoughts were far from the road. Her new husband said nothing more for several long moments, and she wondered if he had already given up on conversation. Perhaps that was for the best.

Then, without a word, he reached into a leather bag at his side and pulled out a book. He opened it with quiet deliberation and began to read, the rustle of the pages the only sound breaking the silence between them.

Elizabeth kept her eyes on the window, her heart sinking further. This was how it would be, then—duty, formality, and silence.

They did not speak again until the first change of horses.

T HE CARRIAGE ROCKED GENTLY as it pulled into the courtyard of the coaching inn, the sound of the horses' hooves dulled by the deep gravel beneath the wheels. Elizabeth leaned forward slightly, peering out the window, her gaze sweeping over the inn. It was a quaint, well-kept place, and as the carriage came to a halt, she noticed the staff bustling about in preparation for their arrival. Clearly, Mr Darcy had sent word ahead.

When the door swung open, and Darcy stepped out first, offering his hand to her, she hesitated only a moment before taking it. His grip was firm, but as detached as it had been all day. He gave no indication of emotion, no sign of any lingering warmth or even duty-bound affection. She allowed him to help her from the carriage, and together they approached the inn.

The innkeeper greeted them at once, bowing low before Darcy, his face bright with the kind of welcome reserved for a long-standing patron. Elizabeth stood silently, watching the man as he spoke to her new husband with the familiarity of one who knew him well.

It struck her that Darcy's influence must extend far beyond his estate in Derbyshire, and though she had expected it, seeing it in practice unsettled her.

But then something shifted. The innkeeper's eyes fell on the black armband Darcy wore, and in that instant, the man's demeanour changed. His welcome became even more deferential, his tone hushed with a respect that bordered on reverence. It was clear that the sight of the mourning band had altered everything for the man, but he did not dare ask who Mr Darcy mourned. It was as though the very presence of that black cloth forbade any inquiry.

Elizabeth followed silently as the innkeeper led them up a narrow staircase. When he opened the door to the upper floor, she discovered with some surprise that Mr Darcy had reserved the entire level for them. A small, well-appointed dining table stood in the main bedroom, already set with a meal for two. The maids lit the fires in the adjoining rooms, moving quickly, their heads bowed as they worked.

When the last of the servants had finished their tasks, Darcy turned toward the doorway, his hand raised in dismissal. "That will be all, thank you," he said curtly. The maids curtsied quickly and hurried from the room.

Elizabeth stood uncertainly by the table, watching the flames flicker in the hearth, her hands clasped before her. She felt... lost, in a way. Everything about the evening had been conducted with such cold precision. There had been no conversation, no acknowledgement of their circumstances beyond the necessities. Mr Darcy had spoken to her only in passing, his attention focused elsewhere, as if the very thought of addressing her directly required some great effort.

Or he felt soiled by the association.

As he turned to leave the room, presumably to take one of the other chambers for himself, Elizabeth was overcome by a sudden burst of frustration. She stepped after him, her voice catching before she called out, "Mr Darcy?"

He paused, half-turning toward her, his face unreadable.

She swallowed, her heart beating faster. "Are you... are you not going to join me? To eat, I mean."

For a brief moment, his expression froze, as if her question had caught him completely off guard. There was a flicker of something in his eyes—surprise, perhaps—but it vanished almost as quickly as it appeared.

"I am not hungry," he said, his voice stiff. "Please, enjoy it yourself." There was a finality to his tone, one that discouraged any further inquiry.

Elizabeth stood there, the silence between them growing heavy. "I see," she murmured after a moment, though in truth, she did not see. She could not understand him, could not begin to fathom what was going through his mind. He had arranged for these sumptuous accommodations, a lavish dinner suitable for a wedding night, and yet he had no intention of sharing even a loaf of bread with her?

With a nod that seemed more of a dismissal than anything else, Darcy turned and entered the other room, leaving her standing in the dim light of the hallway, staring after him in confusion.

Why? The question ate at her, and she could not shake the sinking feeling in her chest. Why would he reserve such extravagant accommodations if he had no intention of observing their wedding night? Was it not customary for a couple to share such a moment, to sit together, to acknowledge their new life as man and wife?

And as for the things that usually came *after* the meal... why, had he no interest in *that*, either? Not that she was personally eager to sample Fitzwilliam Darcy's conjugal talents, but....

Nothing?

Her mind tumbled like water over a rocky stream, trying to make sense of it, but no answer came. The only explanation that rose to the surface, bitter and undeniable, was that he must despise her. He could not even bear to eat with her, much less fulfil any other expectations of their marriage. Had she misunderstood everything about this arrangement?

Heart sinking, Elizabeth returned to the table, though the sight of the food now turned her stomach. She poked at the plate before her, but she had no appetite, no desire for the fine meal laid out so carefully. Her thoughts were too tangled, too weighed down by the events of the day.

What had she done?

D ARCY LAY IN THE darkness, his body restless and his mind a hopeless snarl of thoughts. The bed beneath him felt impossibly large, and no matter how many times he shifted, he could find no comfort. He was too hot and then too cold, sweat prickling at his skin one moment, then shivers creeping up his spine the next. His thoughts whirled in endless circles, never settling, never letting him rest.

And his stomach. His cursed stomach growled and twisted, reminding him that he had not eaten all day. He had been too knotted up with anxiety, with guilt, to even think about food. But now... now the hunger gnawed at him, a sharp, insistent pain that he could not ignore. He should have eaten something. Perhaps he should have joined her for the meal, but the idea of sitting across from Elizabeth, newly his wife, was unbearable.

She would have assumed things, he thought bitterly, his fists clenching at the sheets. She would have expected him to act the part of the husband, to consummate this marriage. As if the consummation had not already happened! No, he had no intention of touching her, not now, perhaps not ever. If she delivered a son, that would be enough. Harry's child would be Darcy's heir, and that would be the end of it.

Or at least, it *should* be the end of it. But Darcy could not shake the nagging thoughts that lingered. Tomorrow, perhaps, he should ask her more details about her condition, about how far along she was...

No. No, that would be too much, too soon. He could not face that conversation yet. He *knew* enough. That would suffice for now. As soon as they reached Pemberley, he would summon a midwife, someone discreet. That would settle the matter.

He tossed and turned again, his mind racing in circles. It was impossible. He would never sleep, not like this. His stomach gave a loud growl, and he pressed a hand to his abdomen, feeling lightheaded from the lack of food. He considered going down to the innkeeper, asking for something to eat, but the thought of doing so was too humiliating. The innkeeper would know. Everyone would know. The grand meal Darcy had arranged for the wedding night, enough to feed six men, had been left untouched by the man who paid for it.

It would only prove what everyone would soon suspect: that Fitzwilliam Darcy's marriage was a sham.

No. He could not do that. But... there *was* food waiting in the next room, more than enough. And she was likely asleep by now. Perhaps if he were careful—quiet—he could slip into the room, take something from the table, and leave without disturbing her.

The thought seemed ridiculous, but his hunger felt as if it would swallow him whole, forcing his hand. Slowly, Darcy slid out of bed, the cold air hitting his skin as he pulled on his banyan. He moved silently down the hall, pausing outside her door. It might be locked. He would not be surprised if it were, but when he tested the latch, it gave way easily.

His hand stilled on the door handle as the implications of that hit him. *She had left the door unlocked.* Purposefully. In case her husband came to exert his marital rights in the night. Darcy's throat tightened, and he pushed the thought away before it could take root.

He opened the door carefully, slipping inside. The room was dark, lit only by a faint sliver of moonlight streaming in through the window. He strained his ears, listening for any sound. Her breathing was soft, steady—a deep rhythm that told him she was asleep.

Thank Heaven.

He eased toward the table, his footsteps as light as he could manage. The food was still there, untouched. Darcy's brow furrowed as he took in the sight of it. She had not eaten, either? That was not good. Not good for the child. His jaw set with concern. She could not neglect herself like this. Today could be excused—he understood the shock, the grief—but it could not continue.

He was just reaching for a loaf of bread when a sudden whimper broke the silence. Darcy froze, every muscle in his body tensing. He turned his head, his breath catching in his throat as he saw her shift beneath the blankets, the fabric rustling softly as she tossed.

For one terrifying moment, he thought she was going to wake and find him there, standing like a fool in the middle of the room. Or worse, that she would assume somet hing... other than what he intended. He held his breath, waiting.

But after a few moments, she stilled again, her breathing evening out once more. Darcy exhaled, his heart still hammering in his chest. The room was quiet again, but his nerves were on edge, every sense heightened.

He should leave. He had what he came for—there was no reason to stay.

And yet...

In the faint moonlight, he could just make out the shape of her lying in the bed, her hair loose from its pins, scattered across the pillow like dark silk. Darcy could not help it. He crept closer, until he was standing over her bed, peering down at her.

Her features were soft, her expression calm—so different from the tense, hardened face he had grown accustomed to over the past days. In sleep, there was no trace of the turmoil, no sign of the pain or grief that usually marked her.

She was... Darcy gulped. She was *beautiful*.

The thought struck him like a blow, and he tried to shake it off. But as he stood there, looking down at her, something tugged at his core. He understood now... at least a little... what Harry had seen in her. Darcy had witnessed her intelligence, the way her eyes flashed when she spoke, the fire in her spirit. But there was something more to her, something deeper that he had not seen before.

Perhaps one day... The thought slipped through his mind before he could stop it. Perhaps one day, he might see her like this again, in happier times. When she was not in shock or grief-stricken by the loss of his brother.

Without thinking, his hand twitched, as though to reach for one of the loose curls resting on her cheek. He could almost feel the softness of it beneath his fingers.

That was when he knew he had to leave. *Now.* Before he lost whatever self-control he had left.

Chapter Seven

ELIZABETH WOKE EARLY, HER head throbbing with the dull ache that often followed a restless night. She had probably ground her teeth all night, and now her jaw was stiff and sore as a result. Sighing, she lay still for a moment, staring at the thin slice of morning light filtering through the curtains. The events of the previous day weighed heavily on her mind, and the reality of her new life began to settle more firmly in her chest.

There was no point in staying in bed. With reluctance, she rose and began to dress herself, her movements slow and methodical. The room was cold, and she shivered slightly as she fumbled with her stays. She was almost finished when a knock came on the door.

Elizabeth hesitated, her fingers stilling on the laces of her gown. Was this her husband, come to... she knew not what, but who else could it be? She squinted. "Come?"

The door creaked open, and a young maid entered, looking mildly surprised to see Elizabeth already up and dressed.

"Oh! Beg pardon, ma'am," the girl stammered, taking a step back. "I didn't realise—"

Elizabeth blinked in surprise. "It's quite all right," she said, pulling her gown more tightly around herself. "I did not expect anyone this early."

The maid dipped a quick curtsy and introduced herself. "I'm Susan, madam. I rode with you and Mr Darcy from London. I'm to be your lady's maid, that is... if you approve, Mrs Darcy."

Elizabeth raised an eyebrow. "Approve? Why on earth would I not approve?"

Susan fidgeted with the hem of her apron, her face flushing a little. "Mr Darcy... he was not sure what your preferences would be, so he secured the closest maid at hand before we left. But I'm not a proper lady's maid, you see. I don't have the training..." Her words trailed off nervously.

Elizabeth took a deep breath, not quite sure what to make of this new development. *Of course*. Mr Darcy, as ever, thinking of every detail, even in the midst of such... complicated circumstances. "I am sure I shall be quite pleased," she replied, trying to offer a reassuring smile. "Thank you, Susan. I only wonder that I did not know of you sooner."

"Oh. Yes, well, the master said I shouldn't trouble you, and yesterday the horses were changed so fast whenever we stopped... and last night, I meant to follow you up to your room, but the master was with you, so I thought it best if I did not... did I do wrong, ma'am? I should have come later, shouldn't I?"

Elizabeth shook her head. "Think nothing of it, Susan. I am pleased to know you now."

The maid brightened a little, though her nervousness didn't fully leave her. "I meant to help you dress this morning, ma'am, but I see I've come too late."

Elizabeth nodded, smoothing her skirts absentmindedly. "It is quite all right. I have managed."

Susan took a step toward the table near the fireplace. "Shall I have some breakfast sent up for you, madam?"

Elizabeth shook her head, glancing toward the table. "I expect there is still some bread and cheese left from last night. That will suffice." But as her eyes landed on the table, she paused, her brow furrowing. The bread was gone. And most of the cheese tray, as well.

Her eyes narrowed. Now, who had taken it? Did she possibly stuff herself on that whole loaf of bread and forget about it?

"Is something wrong, ma'am?" Susan asked, her voice hesitant as she followed Elizabeth's gaze.

Elizabeth snapped back to attention, quickly clearing her throat. "No, it is nothing," she said, though she was not at all convinced that was the case. She took a breath and forced herself to focus. "I am ready to depart. Do you know when the carriage will be prepared?"

Susan blinked in mild confusion. "I... I don't, ma'am. But I can certainly find out."

Elizabeth shook her head. "No, naturally, I will speak to Mr Darcy myself." She gave a quick, somewhat self-deprecating smile, realising how detached she must seem from her own journey.

Susan smiled. "If you have no further need of me, Mrs Darcy, I will see to the preparations."

"Very well," Elizabeth said as Susan curtsied and left the room.

When the door closed, Elizabeth's gaze returned to the table with its missing food, and she wandered over to inspect it more closely. Had someone entered the room last night? Her husband? He was supposed to be the only one on this floor. Surely, if he had come in, she would have woken... or he would have awakened her. The thought sent a strange, uneasy shiver down her spine. But then again, she had slept fitfully—perhaps she had been more deeply asleep than she realised.

Still, the thought of Mr Darcy entering her room, so silently, so discreetly, unsettled her in ways she could not fully explain. What had he been doing in here? And why had he left without a word? Without... anything but a loaf of bread?

D ARCY STOOD BESIDE THE carriage, his hands clasped behind his back, his eyes fixed on the inn. It had been... ungallant, he supposed, not to wait for his wife upstairs to escort her down, but he could not face her in the close intimacy of her room. He would rather not think too much on that particular arrangement, anyway. It was better, cleaner, to meet her here—on neutral ground—before they departed.

He pulled out his pocket watch, glancing at the time, and turned to his coachman. "Are we ready to depart?"

"Aye, sir," the coachman replied, giving a quick nod as he tightened the straps on the horses. "All's prepared."

Darcy nodded, satisfied, though he still felt a twinge of anxiety as he glanced back at the inn. Where was Elizabeth? He was told she was dressed ages ago. Susan, Elizabeth's maid, had already climbed into the second carriage, and after a brief hesitation, he strode over to her.

"Susan," he said, his tone brisk but not unkind. "Where is Mrs Darcy? Is she not ready to depart?"

The maid's eyes widened, and she fidgeted nervously. "She... she is, sir. She was down early. Said she wished for a moment to herself." She pointed beyond him, behind the carriages.

Darcy narrowed his eyes, looking in the direction Susan pointed. A small stand of aspen trees stood beside the inn, casting long shadows over the grass. There, on a rock overlooking a stream, sat Elizabeth. Her back was to him, her figure poised and still, though there was something almost dreamlike in the tilt of her head, as if her thoughts had taken her far away from reality.

Her shoulders were straight, her back composed, but her fingers fidgeted in her lap, and as Darcy drew closer, he realised she was humming softly to herself. She had not heard him approach.

"Good morning, Mrs Darcy," he said, his voice cutting through the stillness.

Elizabeth jumped, her hum dying on her lips as she turned sharply to face him. "Mr Darcy," she breathed, recovering quickly. "I did not hear you."

"I apologise for startling you." He hesitated for a moment, unsure of what else to say. "Are you well?"

She stood, brushing her hands lightly over her skirts before meeting his gaze. "Yes, quite well. And yourself?" There was a slight tilt to her head as she asked the question, her tone polite but with an edge of curiosity.

Darcy blinked. He had not expected her to ask after him. It was only common courtesy, of course, but there seemed to be something beneath her words today that unsettled him—something he did not care to examine too closely. He nodded, a little too jerkily. "I am well enough."

Elizabeth regarded him for a moment longer, then thinned her lips into what could pass for a smile. The gesture was stiff, but it softened something in him. He found himself extending his hand toward her, an offer he had not entirely intended. "May I escort you to the carriage?"

Her brow arched in a peculiar, playful way that was entirely unbefitting a woman supposedly in mourning for her lost love. Despite himself, Darcy felt a flicker of warmth in his chest. He had seen that look before, fleeting as it was, and there was something about it—something in the spark of her eyes—that stirred something almost... fond.

Foolish, he told himself. *Very foolish.*

Still, he clasped her hand as she accepted his offer, and they walked toward the carriage together in silence. The air between them was thick, full of unspoken thoughts and words neither seemed ready to utter. When they reached the door, Darcy helped her inside, his hand firm around hers, but his touch remained distant, careful not to linger. She settled herself onto the seat first, smoothing her skirts, and he followed, ducking slightly to avoid hitting his head on the low frame.

As soon as he sat down, the narrow confines of the carriage seemed terrifyingly stifling. It had not seemed so... so *close* yesterday, but today, he felt as if they must be trading breaths in the small space. Though he tried to position himself as far from her as possible, their knees brushed almost immediately. Darcy froze for a moment, feeling the warmth of her leg against his, and before he could think, he jerked his knee away, straightening his posture awkwardly.

"I—my apologies," he muttered, feeling the heat rise in his cheeks as his body stiffened in embarrassment. He had not been this unsteady, this unsettled, in years.

Elizabeth's gaze flicked up to meet his. "No need," she said quietly, her voice controlled, though the hint of a smile tugged at the corner of her lips. "It is rather... cramped."

Cramped. *Yes*, Darcy thought, desperately grasping for that simple explanation as he nodded. "Quite."

He shifted again, trying to give her more space, but the carriage offered none. Their knees collided once more, and this time, he noticed her fingers tighten just slightly in her lap, though she made no further comment. Instead, she glanced at him from beneath her lashes, her expression unreadable, but he could feel her watching him.

"Please, be comfortable," she said after a long moment, her tone not entirely unkind. "I am not made of glass."

Darcy blinked, caught off guard by her directness. Her words should have put him at ease, but instead, they stirred something else entirely. There was a confidence in her manner, a quiet but undeniable strength that reminded him of... *Harry*. He swallowed hard and nodded, though he still hesitated before allowing himself to settle back into the seat.

"Very well," he said, his voice a little too formal. "Thank you, Mrs Darcy."

Her brow arched again at the formality, and a ghost of a smile passed across her lips before she turned her gaze back to the window, leaving Darcy sitting there, his heart pounding far too fast for such a simple exchange.

For a few moments, neither of them spoke. The carriage lurched into motion, the horses' hooves ringing against the cobblestones. Darcy glanced at her from the corner of his eye. Elizabeth was watching him—staring, really—with a gaze so intent it made him shift uncomfortably in his seat. There was something impertinent in the way she looked at him, as though her eyes were full of unasked questions, probing deeper than he wanted them to.

His eyes fell on the bag of books he kept in the carriage, and an idea came to him—an impulse, really, but it felt like the right one. Without thinking too much on it, Darcy reached for the bag, pulling out one of the volumes. There, that would keep his mind occupied! He drew it out, but paused.

And instead of opening it for himself, he held it out toward her.

Elizabeth blinked in surprise, her eyes widening slightly as she looked at the book in his hand. After a moment, she took it from him, a small smile curling at the corners of her mouth. A real smile, not the stiff, forced one she had shown him before.

The sight of it did something to him, something he could not explain. He swallowed and quickly tugged out another book, opening it as if it were the most pressing matter in the world.

It was easier than trying to understand what she was thinking.

As the carriage continued its journey, Darcy found his gaze wandering to her occasionally, though he quickly returned to his reading each time. He did not want to admit it, even to himself, but the questions in her eyes—questions he could not answer—were beginning to unsettle him.

He could still feel the warmth of her knee against his.

FOR FOUR DAYS, ELIZABETH had ridden in silence, watching the countryside roll by as they journeyed toward her new home—toward Pemberley. In the beginning, she had been stiff with uncertainty, her body still and her mind preoccupied with the strange new existence she found herself in. But, little by little, she had grown somewhat more comfortable.

Her husband had been nothing if not polite. He did not speak often, and when he did, it was usually brief—a question about her comfort or the arrangements for their next stop. Yet, she had begun to notice a certain... attentiveness in his behaviour. After the first day, when she had mentioned being chilled, the next morning found the carriage equipped with extra bricks to keep her warm. And then there was his constant, quiet attention to her meals—ensuring that she ate, even though he never seemed to partake with much enthusiasm himself.

Odd. Very odd indeed. He had not touched her, had barely spoken to her, yet he took care of her as if she were a fragile object in his charge. It left her feeling uneasy, as though there were invisible boundaries drawn between them that neither dared cross.

He was kind, and in some ways, even considerate. Yet there was a distance between them that she could not penetrate, an icy reserve in his manner that left her wondering. Did he truly dislike her? Or was this how all gentlemen behaved when thrust into an arrangement such as theirs?

She glanced across the carriage now, her eyes falling on the book in his hands. He had been reading for much of the journey, a quiet and focused figure in the opposite seat. From time to time, she would catch him frowning slightly at the page, his brow furrowing in concentration, and she had found herself longing to ask him about it. Not that she dared.

But she recognised the title—*The History of the Decline and Fall of the Roman Empire* by Edward Gibbon. Papa had that same book. She had read it once, not long ago, though she imagined that most men of his standing would think it beyond a woman's comprehension. Still, she wondered what he thought of it. Did he agree with Gibbon's assessments? What opinions might he hold on the fall of civilisations? Elizabeth longed for an intellectual conversation, even if it were with a man as guarded as Darcy, but she had said nothing. He gave no indication that he wished to discuss anything at all with her.

What would Pemberley be like? she wondered instead, her thoughts drifting. She was the mistress of an estate she had never seen, married to a man who had spoken perhaps four dozen words to her in total. It was an odd reality to reconcile. What would his household be like? How many servants would she oversee? Would they all regard her with suspicion or contempt, knowing too much of her sudden entrance into their world?

And she... she must surely be a disgrace to all of it. She had imagined many things when contemplating her future, but never this—a marriage of necessity, bound to a man who seemed to tolerate her at best, and to whom she was a burden at worst.

Her eyes returned to his book, still tempted to say something, to offer a comment about Gibbon's work. Perhaps she could ask what he thought of the empire's inevitable fall, or mention that she had read the same text. But as she opened her mouth, her courage faltered. What if he dismissed her thoughts? What if he did not wish to share any of his opinions with her?

Before she could decide, she noticed a subtle shift in Darcy's posture. He straightened slightly in his seat, closing the book and tucking it away in the leather bag beside him. His gaze turned toward the window, and a change came over him, as though some invisible signal had alerted him to their surroundings.

Elizabeth blinked and followed his gaze, realising what had caught his attention. They must be close now.

She turned her head toward the window as well, her heart beginning to race just a little. In a matter of moments, she would see Pemberley for the first time. Her new home. Her new life.

What kind of mistress would she be? What kind of wife?

Her hands fidgeted in her lap, smoothing the fabric of her gown as she gathered her courage. This was it—her new role, her new duties. Whether she liked it or not, her future was now inexorably tied to Fitzwilliam Darcy and Pemberley.

T HE CARRIAGE RUMBLED TO a halt at last, and Darcy felt the tension in his body tighten further as he glanced at Elizabeth. She, too, was looking out of the window, her eyes widening slightly as the imposing structure of Pemberley came into view. Her lips pressed together, and Darcy could not help but wonder what she was thinking. The estate was massive, sprawling out in front of them in all its grandeur. It was home to him, but to her... she must feel as though she had stepped into another world entirely. And he had to confess, after four days of marriage, he still... had no idea what her home had been like.

Darcy stepped out of the carriage, his face impassive as he scanned the front of Pemberley. Everything was prepared for their arrival, as he had instructed. The staff, dressed in mourning black, stood in a neat row at the entrance, waiting to greet their new mistress. But despite the orderliness of the scene, Darcy's stomach twisted with discomfort.

He was used to the servants knowing his business. It was the way of things, and it had never bothered him before. But now—now it was different. He could feel their eyes on him, their curiosity thinly veiled behind the professionalism they wore like armour. They were too intelligent not to have noticed the absurdity of his sudden marriage. It had been only days since Harry's death, and here he was, returning with a bride. A bride who would be brought to childbed in rather short order.

No, they were not stupid. They must have guessed some scandal lay behind it all, and the idea of it made Darcy's face burn.

Elizabeth stepped down from the carriage, and Darcy offered his arm. She hesitated, her eyes flickering toward the waiting staff. She must have sensed their scrutiny as well. But then, to his surprise, she squared her shoulders and took his arm. Her grip was steady, her chin lifted just slightly as they walked together toward the house.

At the top of the stairs, Mrs Reynolds, the housekeeper, stepped forward, her face solemn but respectful. Darcy's eyes swept over the black mourning band on her sleeve, and the lump in his throat closed up.

"Welcome to Pemberley, Mrs Darcy," Mrs Reynolds said, her voice steady, though there was a trace of something else beneath the formality. Curiosity, perhaps. Maybe even pity.

Elizabeth inclined her head. "Thank you, Mrs Reynolds. It is an honour to meet you."

Darcy watched the exchange closely. How would his new bride manage the introductions? Elizabeth had never met the housekeeper, knew nothing of Pemberley or the people who had served his family for years. She must feel completely out of her depth. But despite that, she was calm, composed—more composed than he had expected. Thank Heaven for small mercies. If he had to be bound to a stranger, at least she had some concept of decorum.

"I hope you find everything to your liking, ma'am," Mrs Reynolds continued, her gaze flickering briefly to Darcy before returning to Elizabeth. "If there is anything you require, please do not hesitate to ask."

Elizabeth smiled, a tight but genuine gesture. "Thank you, Mrs Reynolds. I am certain all will be well."

Darcy's eyes lingered on her as she spoke, noting the faint tremor in her hands, the way her fingers fidgeted ever so slightly with the fabric of her gown. She was holding herself together, barely, but she was doing it. He could see it in the way she stood, poised but taut, as if she were fighting against her own nerves.

The other servants curtsied and bowed as they were introduced, their eyes averted but sharp. Darcy could almost hear the thoughts running through their minds. *Why had the master married so suddenly? Why had he brought this woman to Pemberley when the house was still draped in mourning?* His skin prickled with humiliation.

He had always been a private man, but for the first time, he felt exposed. Vulnerable. He could sense the whispers that would follow them into the halls of Pemberley, the quiet conversations held behind closed doors. He had always trusted his staff to remain discreet, but this... this was different. He could not escape the truth, and neither could they.

"Mrs Darcy," he said, his voice tight. "You must be fatigued. I can have a maid show you to your rooms."

Elizabeth nodded, though he could see the exhaustion in her eyes, the strain in the set of her shoulders. She looked as if she might collapse at any moment, and he doubted she had taken a full breath since they stepped out of the carriage. But as she followed the maid towards the stairs, her gaze was pulled toward the open doorway of the drawing room. Her eyes wandered, taking in the grand entrance hall as they passed, the soaring ceilings, and then she turned her head to the side, catching sight of the open door to the ballroom.

Her feet seemed to move of their own accord—still following the maid, to be sure, but her steps carried her nearer to the doorway as they passed. Darcy followed silently behind her, observing with growing curiosity. He gave a signal to the maid, asking her to wait on her mistress. After all, there was no harm in letting the new Mrs Darcy admire the house as she pleased.

She stepped towards the drawing room, her hand resting lightly on the doorframe, her eyes sweeping over the elegant furnishings, the delicate china, and the artwork that adorned the walls.

For a moment, she seemed lost in thought, her fingers brushing the wood of the door as she absorbed the space. Then, without a word, she moved on, her attention drawn next to the ballroom just beyond. Darcy kept pace with her, his gaze narrowing as he watched her. Her steps had slowed, and her posture had shifted slightly,

As they neared the ballroom, Darcy saw her body sway ever so slightly. Alarm shot through him. Her hand gripped the edge of the doorframe, and she paused, her face flushing scarlet. Darcy moved behind her, close enough to see the way her neck seemed to go limp. She paused, her hand gripping the edge of the doorway as she gazed into the ballroom, her expression distant.

"Mrs Darcy?" he asked, his voice sharper than intended.

She did not answer. And then he saw it—the moment her body gave way, her knees buckling, her face paling now as she swayed again, this time more violently.

Before anyone could react, Darcy was at her side. "Elizabeth!" The name left his lips before he had even registered the alarm surging through him. He caught her just as she began to fall, his arms going around her as she slumped against him.

"Mrs Darcy!" Mrs Reynolds hurried forward, her face lined with concern. "Fetch water, quickly!" she called to one of the maids, who dashed off at once.

The maids sprang into action, but Darcy could only focus on the woman in his arms, her body limp against him. For a brief, terrifying moment, he thought she had fainted entirely. What the devil had happened? He had not known she was unwell—how had he missed it? And what was he supposed to do now?

Before he could gather his thoughts, she stirred slightly, a soft, pained sound escaping her lips. Then she rolled in his arms and, to his horror, she was sick.

The maids gasped, but Darcy tightened his grip, holding her steady as she heaved again. His arms trembled, his mind blank with shock. He had no time to react, no time to process what was happening. All he could think to do was hold her, to keep her from collapsing completely.

Mrs Reynolds was already issuing orders, directing the maids with practised efficiency. "Help carry her upstairs, sir. Please, sir."

Darcy, still at a loss, nodded dumbly. He lifted Elizabeth into his arms, her body rather... firmer in his arms than he expected, and turned toward the stairs. The maids rushed ahead, but Darcy barely noticed them.

All he could focus on was the woman in his arms—and the sinking feeling that he had failed her... failed Harry... Heaven knew who else. Without knowing even how, or what he could have done differently, somehow he was sure of that—that he had failed in every possible way.

Chapter Eight

"NO, NO, I AM not... that will not be necessary, Mrs Reynolds, thank you. I—"

But Mrs Reynolds only smiled and spread another coverlet over her feet. "No trouble at all, ma'am. Would you like another pillow?"

Elizabeth was already propped against four pillows, surrounded by a level of comfort she neither asked for nor needed. The fire crackled gently in the hearth, and the maids bustled about, bringing trays of warm milk, ginger tea, and stoking the fire yet again.

She had politely refused the biscuits earlier, and now the thought of the salty chicken soup they were offering made her stomach turn. She was not ill—just embarrassed. Why did they insist on treating her as though she were on the verge of collapse? It was like heaping burning coals of humiliation on her head.

Mrs Reynolds had been doting over her all afternoon, with the kind of quiet insistence that was difficult to refuse. Each time Elizabeth had tried to tell her she was perfectly well, the housekeeper's response was the same: "The master has ordered that you have your every need attended, Mrs Darcy. It is my pleasure to see to it."

The master had ordered it. That was all Elizabeth needed to know—this was not about her preferences or comfort. It was about Mr Darcy's expectations. And he was making his desires known—she was to be a pet of sorts, a doll to be set on a shelf... or a disgrace to be kept hidden in her rooms. She was not sure which yet.

Mrs Reynolds would not budge, no matter how many times Elizabeth insisted that she needed no special treatment. No one seemed to believe her that it was not illness or physical frailty that had twisted her stomach and wrung out her sentiments earlier, but the emotional exhaustion of being thrust into a role she had never asked for, married to a man who barely seemed to acknowledge her existence. That, and she had simply run out of air until her vision swam black.

But she was not about to say that.

Her palms were itching. The muscles of her legs crawling with nerves, and she was far too warm. How many perfectly good daylight hours had she been stuck in bed, receiving all this pampering? And now, it was dark, and she had yet to see or speak with the man who had brought her here. The one who had bounced in the carriage with her for days and then bore her upstairs in his arms.

By the time the second glass of warm milk arrived, Elizabeth had lost her patience entirely. This was absurd. She was no child to be soothed into sleep with warm milk, nor an invalid needing constant attention. She needed space, perhaps a little air, not mollycoddling.

"No, truly," Elizabeth said again as one of the maids set the tray down by her bedside. "I assure you, I am perfectly well. There is no need for all this." But even as she spoke, she could see the maids were not about to listen to her. They were only following orders, after all.

They fussed with the fire again, laid out her nightclothes, and smiled as though they had fulfilled some crucial duty. Elizabeth's gaze drifted toward the adjoining door—the one that led to Darcy's room. She had avoided looking at it all day, but now, with the maids finally gone, it loomed large in her thoughts.

He was right there. Not far away at all, separated only by a door. What was he doing? Was he sitting in silence, brooding as she imagined he might? Did he feel as adrift as she did? Or was he content to keep his distance, to avoid the awkwardness of their new reality?

What lay beyond that door? A doting husband, the man who had so tenderly carried her upstairs even over her protests? Oh, how humiliated she had felt! Even more so when he had hastened from her presence... disgusted by her.

Well, why wouldn't he be? She had probably soiled his coat. Elizabeth scowled and blew out a sigh that feathered the hair around her face. What a *perfect* way to make an impression on the household.

But that was enough pitying herself. She rose from the bed, the need to move spurring her into action. She could not lie here any longer, passive and waiting for something—anything—to make sense. Her feet carried her to the door before she had fully considered what she was doing.

Her fingers curled, poised just above the handle, the smooth wood cool beneath her knuckles. What would he say if she knocked? Would he welcome her, or would she be met with cold indifference? The uncertainty churned in her stomach, but she had never been one to shy away from difficult moments. She could not go on like this, cut off from him entirely, not knowing where they stood.

After a moment's hesitation, she knocked.

The sound felt too loud in the silence that had blanketed the room. She waited, pulse quickening, her breath held as she listened for movement on the other side.

The door creaked open, and Elizabeth's breath caught in her throat. There stood Mr Darcy, not in his usual immaculate attire, but in a nightshirt. His collar was loose, baring his throat and a small glimpse of his chest. The sight was utterly unexpected, and she stepped back, her mouth suddenly dry.

She had never seen a man like this; not with such dishevelled intimacy, and her eyes lingered longer than they should have on the curve of his exposed neck. The dark hair curling at the top of his nightshirt. His chest rose and fell in an uneven rhythm, and she realised he was breathing more quickly, though his face betrayed none of the same discomposure.

When she finally dragged her eyes back to his face, his expression was carefully neutral, distant even. "Mrs Darcy," he began, his voice low, "are you unwell?"

She drew her shoulders back. "Do I look unwell?"

"You were... somewhat discomposed earlier."

"Yes, how kind of you to point that out. I..." She cleared her throat. "I must thank you for helping me. The, ah... strains of travel, and the house... I fear I was overwhelmed."

Mr Darcy thinned his lips. "Quite understandable. I trust the servants have attended you properly."

"Oh, yes. It seems that is all anyone cares about—making sure I am 'well.' I have been so pampered and coddled that I fear if such treatment continues, I shall not remember how to walk or even eat for myself."

His brow furrowed ever so slightly, but he responded with a calm, almost clinical tone. "You are frustrated by being cared for?"

Elizabeth offered a strained smile. "No. I am only asking to have some say in that 'care'. Please, I know you told Mrs Reynolds to look after me, but I could hardly move under all the blankets and the steamed milk and roaring fire and three different kinds of tea—it is a bit much."

"It is their duty to look after the mistress of the house. Just as it is my duty to ensure they fulfil their roles."

She could not help it—the absurdity of his detachment, the way he spoke as though everything was a mere transaction, grated on her nerves. She huffed and rolled her eyes, more in frustration than anything else.

At once, his posture stiffened, his jaw tightening as a sudden sharpness entered his voice. "Do you find this amusing, madam? Do you think any of this is a joke?"

Elizabeth felt her heart skip at the sudden shift in tone. "No," she replied, her voice quieter now, though the frustration still simmered beneath the surface. She folded her arms across her chest, half in defiance, half in defence against the strange emotions swirling around her.

"Then you take matters with far too much levity, madam. I ask you, when *is* it appropriate for a husband to merely neglect the fact that his wife became physically ill?"

She clenched her teeth, but then exhaled, trying to force a bit of reason into her tones. "No, of course. You are perfectly right, sir, and I *do* appreciate your consideration. I wonder, Mr Darcy, do you mean to observe all your husbandly duties with such devotion?" The words slipped out before she had fully formed them in her mind, and for a moment, she feared she had gone too far.

He stiffened, and she saw the muscles in his throat move as he swallowed. His Adam's apple bobbed up and down, and though his face remained carefully controlled, she detected something—a flicker of discomfort, or perhaps something else entirely. His lips parted, and he made a small noise in his throat as though to speak, but then he hesitated.

"I prefer," he said slowly, drawing back just slightly, "a certain... decorum, madam. I am still in mourning, after all. As are you, I thought."

The words hit her with an unexpected force, and Elizabeth's cheeks flushed with embarrassment. She had not meant to suggest... Had he thought she was trying to seduce him? Heat spread down her neck.

"That was not my intent!" she stammered, feeling foolish and exposed. "I... I merely wished for you to speak with me. Perhaps take tea or... oh, bother! I did not mean... whatever it is that is so odious to you, but—" She stopped, biting her lip, unsure how to continue. How could she explain her growing frustration, her sense of isolation in this marriage, without making herself seem foolish or desperate?

Darcy's face gave away nothing, but there was no mistaking the way he pulled back, distancing himself, both physically and emotionally. His gaze shifted, avoiding hers as if the very act of meeting her eyes would soil him, or shatter whatever careful control he was holding on to.

Elizabeth's stomach twisted. What had she expected? A warm exchange, a moment of understanding between them? She had sought only a small reprieve from the loneliness that had engulfed her since their hurried marriage. Yet, all she had managed was to widen the chasm between them.

She swallowed against the bitter taste of regret. He would not look at her, and each second of silence was like a door closing, shutting her further out. She had misstepped, that much was clear. What had begun as a tentative attempt to understand her husband had turned into something far more awkward, far more distant.

W HAT THE DEVIL *WAS* that?

Darcy had retreated to the high-backed chair by the fire as if it were a refuge, his breath coming in short pants as his pulse still hammered in his ears. Had she... *truly* said that? He needed a drink. Not for the alcoholic haze it promised, but for something to do with his hands, something real and tangible on his tongue to remind him what reality was. Shakily, he poured out the decanter.

He brushed a hand absently over his forehead, the brandy swirling in his glass as he tried, and failed, to steady his thoughts. The amber liquid warmed his throat, but instead of calming him, it set his nerves alight. He stared into the flames in the hearth, watching them flicker and dance, but all he could think of was Elizabeth—her words, her tone, the challenge in her eyes.

How could she say something like that? He took another sip, hoping the drink might dull the sharp edge of his thoughts, but it only sharpened them. Proposing... what exactly had she been proposing? "Husbandly duties." What else *could* she have meant?

Did she truly believe he would... What did she *think* of him? His mind reeled.

Had she no respect for the memory of his brother? Regardless of the... er... nature of their relationship, had she no remorse for Harry, who was barely cold in his grave? The very thought sent a wave of nausea through him, one that no amount of brandy could settle.

He had married her out of duty, out of responsibility. Surely, she must understand that. This was no arrangement made for his pleasure, or even his needs. She owned all the benefits here, and she had acted as if he still owed her something. Did she not care for Harry at all? Or was he, himself, merely a transaction to her now, a way to secure a future when her original plan had crumbled? The idea twisted in his gut, a mixture of regret and something far darker.

He clenched the glass, staring at the golden liquid sloshing within as his hand shook. He had already begun to writhe under the weight of his decision, the regret settling deeper with each passing hour.

The devil of it was that when he was with her, his mind almost forgot. She would fix those eyes on him, and he could not entirely say he was his own master. Was that how she had bewitched Harry? He had married a seductress! A seductress who put on all the airs of innocent gentility, convincingly enough that when she was before him, he swallowed it all like the veriest gull.

This was supposed to be simple. He was not supposed to be bouncing between bewilderment and shock at every turn.

But it was done—there was no turning back. The deed had been sealed the moment he said those vows. He was bound to her now, in a way that felt suffocating, in a way that made him question whether he would survive it at all.

Elizabeth... she was not what he had imagined. Her spirit, her independence—it had seemed almost admirable when he had first heard Harry speak of her. But now, having seen one or two glimpses of her stubborn defiance, it felt more like a trial. Why? Should she not welcome his care? Did she not realise how vulnerable she was? As if anyone needed to be told! As if the proofs were not ample enough.

For mercy's sake, she had *vomited* in front of the household, nearly collapsed at his feet, and yet here she was, insisting she did not need anyone's help. His lips pressed into a thin line, the brandy no longer tasting sweet but bitter as it sat heavy in his mouth. He wanted to rage at her obstinance, her pride, but the anger quickly gave way to confusion. What did she expect? Did she truly believe she could bear this all alone?

The fire cracked, the only sound in the room save for the soft ticking of the mantel clock. Darcy tried to focus on the flames, to let their warmth soothe the tension in his body, but then he heard it—the faintest sound coming from the adjoining room.

Elizabeth.

His body stiffened instantly, his grip tightening on the glass as he strained to listen. It was just the sound of her moving, shifting in bed perhaps, but it ignited something in him. The brandy coursing through his veins now burned hotter, setting fire to his already frayed nerves.

She was going to test him at every turn, he thought, staring hard into the fire.

Every. Single. Turn.

He could feel it already. Perhaps she had given him little enough trouble on the journey, but the look in her eye—that openly curious one, the one that seemed to second-guess his decisions—it had only grown each day. He would have no peace, no respite from this constant push and pull between them. She questioned him, she challenged him, and worse—she made him question himself.

Darcy brought the glass to his lips again, but it did nothing to calm the storm within him. His mind whirled with a hundred thoughts, each one more unsettling than the last. How would he survive this marriage—this strange, awkward union with a woman who seemed determined to have her own way, regardless of what was right, decent, and proper? With every moment that passed, it felt more like a trap he had willingly walked into.

D ARCY TOSSED IN THE darkness, his sheets twisted and damp with sweat, but sleep would not come. The silence of the house was oppressive, the faint crackling of the fire doing little to soothe him. He shifted beneath the blankets, but it wasn't discomfort from the bed that kept him awake. Something else stirred him—the faintest noise from the adjoining room.

He stilled, listening.

Elizabeth.

She was still awake, too. He could hear her pacing again, the soft creak of floorboards under her steps. Then, after a moment of stillness, a different sound reached his ears—a muffled, broken sound.

She was weeping.

Darcy sat up straighter, feeling an ache rise in his chest as the sound of Elizabeth's quiet sobs filtered through the door. Each stifled breath, each ragged sigh seemed to strike him like a blow, a reminder of the number of ways he had failed to make the world right again. She was grieving, and though she tried to muffle her sobs, it was as if her sorrow was seeping through the very walls.

Well, perhaps... perhaps there was something genuine in her, after all.

Any other respectable husband would rise, go to his wife. The urge to comfort her, to offer some small solace, tugged at him. But as his feet hovered above the floor, he stopped. What would he do? How could he be of any help at all? He imagined stepping into her room, the awkward creak of the door as he entered uninvited, his presence looming in the faint candlelight. She would look up at him, her face streaked with tears, her eyes red from holding back sobs.

And then what? He swallowed hard. What would he say? The sight of her grief, so raw and exposed, would be more than he could bear. Would she want him to hold her? Heavens above, he could not do it. The intimacy of it, the vulnerability—he was not prepared for that. He was not prepared to confront her pain or his own.

The idea of being the one to comfort her, to hold her while she cried, was unimaginable. He had no right. Her tears belonged to his brother; her grief was not his to share, and yet he felt the sting of it as if it were his own.

He closed his eyes, clenching his fists as though willing himself to act, but he remained frozen, paralysed by his inability to offer what she needed. The sheer intimacy of her pain, the thought of crossing that fragile boundary between them—it was more than he could manage. She would turn those tear-filled eyes on him, and he would be helpless. He could not offer her what she truly wanted. He could not be Harry.

And perhaps that was what frightened him the most.

The moments dragged on, his mind a whirlwind of doubt and self-recrimination. What could he possibly say? "I'm sorry"? For what? For binding her to a life she had not chosen? For trying to replace a brother who could never be replaced?

Darcy's hand hovered over the spine of the book on the table, one he'd turned to so many times before in search of solace. But tonight, the thought of reading—of trying to escape into the pages—felt empty, meaningless. Words would not drown out the sound of Elizabeth's muffled sobs. The words on the page were a feeble defence against the storm raging inside him.

Frustration surged within him, a heat rising in his chest that he could not quell. He pulled back from the book as though it had burned him, his fingers curling into fists. This was not grief he could face with quiet contemplation. He pushed away from the bed with an abruptness that startled even him, his pulse pounding in his ears as he fled the room.

He needed out—needed space, something physical to release the wrath inside. His footsteps echoed through the darkened halls as he made his way to the billiards room, the sharp crack of his heels against the marble floor the only sound in the sleeping house. The strain in his jaw was almost enough to fracture his teeth, and he could feel his anger building, pressing against his ribs like a vise.

The door to the billiards room loomed before him, and he shoved it open with more force than necessary. The quiet of the room, the stillness of the balls lying perfectly arranged on the table, mocked him. He grabbed the cue stick and lined up the first shot, not caring about form or precision. He simply wanted to hit something, anything, to release the fury that clawed at his insides.

With a sharp snap, the balls scattered across the table. The satisfying crack of impact sent a brief jolt through him, but it was not enough. He lined up the next shot and struck harder, watching as the balls flew in all directions. Still, it was not enough.

As he played, the memories flooded him, unbidden and relentless. He could almost see Harry standing beside him, the two of them laughing as they used to on nights like this. Harry, always quick to jest, always a step ahead in their friendly games. They'd spent hours in this room together, knocking the balls across the table, sharing drinks and conversation. There had been no distance between them then, no weight of guilt hanging between them like a spectre.

But now... now there was nothing but silence, and that silence was suffocating.

Darcy struck another ball, harder this time, his hand shaking as the memories overwhelmed him. Harry's smile, his laughter, his reckless energy—they played before Darcy's mind like scenes from a life he couldn't bear to look at anymore. The glaring ache of it all—his brother's absence, the emptiness left behind—was too much. He wasn't strong enough to carry it.

The next shot missed entirely, the ball spinning away uselessly. His hands trembled as he tried to line up another, but the cue slipped, and his control faltered. The frustration boiled over, the calm mask he'd forced on himself shattering under the pressure. With a sudden, raw burst of rage, Darcy slammed the cue stick down on the edge of the table.

The sharp crack echoed in the empty room, and the cue snapped in half, splintering in his hands. For a moment, he stood frozen, staring at the broken pieces of wood, the room suddenly eerily still. Then the dam burst.

A guttural scream tore from his throat, filling the silence with his anguish. It was as if everything he had been holding in since Harry's death—the guilt, the rage, the helplessness—erupted in that single, terrible sound. His hands clenched around the broken cue, his knuckles white as he threw the pieces across the room, sending them clattering against the wall.

He collapsed against the table, his chest heaving, his breath coming in ragged gasps. His arms trembled as they supported him, and his vision blurred with the force of his emotions. The rage was still there, bubbling beneath the surface, but now it was mingled with something even darker: guilt.

He had failed. He had failed to save Harry, and now he was failing everyone else, too. Elizabeth, Pemberley, even himself. Every time he closed his eyes, he could see that terrible moment in the stable yard—the moment Harry's horse reared, the moment his brother was thrown to the ground, the way his head struck the stone. And every time, Darcy saw himself standing there, powerless, helpless, too late to stop it.

He squeezed his eyes shut, his hands gripping the edge of the table so tightly that his knuckles ached. His body shook with the force of his rage. He could have saved him. He *should* have saved him. And now, no matter what he did, nothing would make it right.

Chapter Nine

Elizabeth awoke to the quiet crackling of the fire, the room warm and bathed in the soft glow of morning light. Her gaze shifted to the bedside table, where a tray laden with offerings had already been laid out for her. Warm broth, tea with cream, ginger tea, milk, and even a glass of lemon water—enough to satisfy an entire household, it seemed. She sighed and shook her head, half-amused, half-exasperated by the unnecessary fuss.

"Do they think I am the Queen of England?" she murmured to herself, swinging her legs out of bed.

She reached for the dressing gown draped neatly at the foot of the bed and slipped it on, the soft fabric offering a small comfort against the chill of the morning air. Her stomach rumbled, reminding her that, fuss or no fuss, she was, indeed, hungry. She sat down at the small table near the window and began to eat, her thoughts wandering to the excessive attention that had become a constant part of her new life at Pemberley.

Well, it was better than poor treatment, though she couldn't help but feel a touch of exasperation. Her protests to the servants—and to Mr Darcy himself—seemed to have gone entirely unheeded. A new day, but the same overabundance of care. The same hovering concern for her well-being, as if she were made of the finest porcelain, in danger of shattering at the slightest breeze.

After a while, the soft knock at her door announced Susan's entrance. The maid stepped inside, her expression calm but slightly uncertain, as if still unsure of her place in Mrs Darcy's service. "Good morning, Mrs Darcy," she said. "Would you like help getting back into bed? Or perhaps some more tea?"

Elizabeth sighed but smiled through it. "Susan, truly, I am quite well. I do not need to be confined to bed all day, nor do I require any more tea at the moment. I would, however, like to be dressed and perhaps have a tour of the house."

Susan blinked, a moment of hesitation passing over her face. "A tour, ma'am?"

"Yes, a tour," Elizabeth said firmly, but with a touch of humour to soften the demand. "Surely the mistress of the house ought to know her own home, ought she not?"

Susan looked doubtful but nodded. "Of course, Mrs Darcy. If that is what you wish."

The maid hurried to fetch Elizabeth's clothes, and Elizabeth patiently allowed her to assist in dressing, though her thoughts kept returning to how unnecessarily elaborate the morning routine had become. But when it came time for her hair, it quickly became clear that Susan was far from proficient. Her attempts to style Elizabeth's hair were clumsy at best, the pins slipping from her fingers or jabbing painfully into Elizabeth's scalp.

After the third—or was it the fourth?—time Susan's fingers fumbled with the plaits, Elizabeth sighed, her patience thinning. "Here, let me," she said, gently taking the hairbrush from Susan's hand.

The maid's face flushed with embarrassment. "I'm sorry, ma'am, I—I know I'm not a proper lady's maid. The master said—"

"Nonsense," Elizabeth interrupted with a smile, expertly pulling her hair back and twisting it into a simple, elegant knot at the nape of her neck. "You've been perfectly helpful. Besides, I'm no great connoisseur of fashionable styles myself. And given we are in mourning, there's little need for frills and fuss, don't you think?"

Susan's shoulders relaxed slightly, though the blush remained. "I'll try to improve, Mrs Darcy. I promise."

"You'll manage splendidly, Susan. There's no need for perfection. And look, let me show you a little trick with these pins. My hair is rather thick, so if you angle them just so..." Elizabeth demonstrated as she worked, guiding Susan through the motions. "There. It holds, see?"

Susan nodded, watching carefully. "Thank you, ma'am."

"Now," Elizabeth said with a bright smile, "I think I am quite ready for that tour."

Susan led Elizabeth down the winding halls of Pemberley, her footsteps almost inaudible on the thick carpets. As they approached Mrs Reynolds, who was directing a few maids in the main hall, the housekeeper turned to greet her new mistress, her brow slightly furrowed as if surprised to see Elizabeth up and about so early.

"Mrs Darcy," Mrs Reynolds said, her voice warm but cautious, "I trust you are feeling better today?"

Elizabeth offered her a small smile, trying to dispel any concern. "Yes, thank you, Mrs Reynolds. I was quite fatigued yesterday—overwhelmed, really. But I am well now and eager to familiarise myself with my new home. It is all a bit daunting, you see, and I should like to make it feel less... unfamiliar."

Mrs Reynolds studied Elizabeth for a moment, perhaps assessing whether her new-found energy was truly genuine. Then, with a nod of approval, she relented. "Of course, ma'am. It would be my pleasure to show you Pemberley."

They began with the mistress's morning room. It was a bright, cheerful space with tall windows that overlooked the gardens, the autumn sun spilling over the deep greens and golds of the estate. The walls were covered in delicate floral wallpaper, and a dainty writing desk sat by one of the windows, facing out to the rolling hills. A soft chaise lounge, upholstered in pale blue, rested beneath a large portrait of Lady Anne Darcy, her serene expression watching over the room. So, *that* was where Harry had got his smile.

"This is where you may take breakfast or spend your mornings, Mrs Darcy," Mrs Reynolds explained. "It was the former Mrs Darcy's favourite room, especially in spring when the gardens are in bloom."

Elizabeth nodded, her fingers lightly trailing over the back of the chaise. It was a beautiful space, but still, she felt like an intruder. "It is lovely," she said quietly, her gaze drifting to the portrait. "Perhaps, in time, I shall come to love it as she did."

Mrs Reynolds smiled politely and led her through the main rooms of the house. They passed through the formal dining room, with its long mahogany table that gleamed beneath the light of the crystal chandelier. The chairs, upholstered in rich velvet, were arranged with meticulous precision, and Elizabeth imagined grand dinners hosted here, the table filled with guests she had yet to meet.

Next, they entered the portrait gallery, where the likenesses of Darcys long past stared down from their ornate frames. Elizabeth glanced up at each one as they passed—some stern, some thoughtful, all proud. She lingered briefly before the portrait of Darcy's father, a man whose presence still seemed to fill Pemberley, even in death. His eyes were strikingly like his eldest son's—intense, watchful. She moved on quickly.

The arboretum was next, its glass walls a marvel of light and greenery. Even now, as the season began to turn, the plants inside thrived, their deep greens contrasting with the golden hues of the trees beyond the glass. A faint scent of herbs and jasmine filled the air, and Elizabeth could imagine escaping here during the colder months when the estate would be covered in snow.

"Mr Darcy takes particular pride in the arboretum," Mrs Reynolds said. "He tends to visit it often, especially when he requires solitude."

Elizabeth nodded. The space indeed felt like an escape, a small refuge in the vastness of Pemberley. She filed that detail away, supposing it might become a place she sought out herself.

They passed through several more "public" rooms, each grander than the last. The drawing room, with its polished floors and fine furnishings, caught Elizabeth's attention when her eyes landed on the grand piano in the corner. She moved toward it, her steps slowing as she recalled a conversation with Harry. He had described this very room to her once, his voice filled with fondness. Their father had bought the piano for their mother, not long before her death, he had said. It was meant to bring her some happiness in her final days, but she scarcely lived long enough to play it.

Elizabeth's fingers drifted absently over the keys, barely grazing them as she hummed a familiar tune, the one she and Jane used to play together. She smiled faintly at the memory, though it quickly turned bittersweet. She missed Jane more than she could express—her confidante, her sister. The distance between them felt like another chasm to cross.

"Would there be pen and paper somewhere I could use to write a letter to my family?" she asked Mrs Reynolds, her voice soft as she stepped away from the piano.

"Of course, ma'am," the housekeeper replied, gesturing to a writing desk neatly tucked into the corner of the room. "There is paper and ink here, as well as in the library and the morning room. If you prefer, we can arrange for a desk in your chambers, should you wish for more privacy."

"The library?" Elizabeth perked up, interest flickering in her eyes. "I have not yet seen it."

"It's not far, Mrs Darcy. Would you like to visit it now?"

"Yes, please," Elizabeth replied, eager to escape the quiet melancholy the drawing room had stirred in her.

They made their way down another hallway, passing by a closed door that Mrs Reynolds said led to Darcy's study. A footman stood outside, awaiting orders, and Elizabeth felt a strange pull as they passed. Mr Darcy must be inside, working diligently, no doubt. She walked on, but found herself glancing back occasionally, wondering what occupied him behind that door.

They entered the library, and Elizabeth stopped short, her breath catching at the sight of it. It was magnificent. The room was lined with tall shelves, all crammed with books of every kind. A grand, dark oak desk sat near the centre of the room, and a fire crackled warmly in the hearth. Large windows let in ample light, illuminating the richness of the leather-bound volumes and the warm, inviting atmosphere of the space.

"This is the library," Mrs Reynolds said softly, as if sensing that Elizabeth needed a moment to take it all in. "It was remodeled by the late Mr Darcy, and the master spends much of his time here when he is not attending to business matters."

Elizabeth nodded, her eyes scanning the titles on the shelves. There was something comforting about the room, something personal, even though she had never stepped foot in it before. Here, perhaps, she could find some solace. A private place, away from the eyes of the servants, and perhaps, even away from her husband. For now.

She ran her fingers over the spines of the books as she moved toward the desk. "I think," she said quietly, "I shall enjoy spending time here."

D ARCY SAT BEHIND THE large mahogany desk in his study, papers spread before him, the heavy scent of wax and ink thick in the air. The fire crackled quietly in the grate, doing little to chase away the sombre chill that had settled over the room. He had been at this for over an hour—attempting, and largely failing, to work through the business of his brother's affairs. Each document, each letter, seemed to sting him anew with Harry's absence, a constant reminder of the loss that had gutted him.

His focus strayed easily this morning, his thoughts wandering before he could make sense of the words in front of him. Every now and again, he would pick up a letter, glance at it, and then set it down again, none of which could hold his attention. His eyes moved to the clock on the mantel. Time slipped away, and he had accomplished next to nothing.

Then, a thought struck him—Elizabeth. He had not looked in on her since the previous evening, since that difficult exchange at her door. He had left her in the capable hands of the household, but still... it seemed his duty to inquire after her.

Rubbing his temple, Darcy leaned back in his chair and called for the footman standing by the door. "Go ask after Mrs Darcy," he instructed, his voice terse with exhaustion. "Find out how she is this morning."

The footman bowed and departed swiftly, leaving Darcy alone with his thoughts again. He stared at the papers on his desk, his mind wandering once more to Elizabeth. It was not... too intimate, his asking after her. Nothing that ought to make him uncomfortable. Surely, seeing to her welfare was one way of caring for Harry, of doing right by his memory.

Several minutes later, the footman returned. "Mrs Darcy is having her breakfast, sir."

Darcy nodded, satisfied in some measure. "Very good," he murmured, dismissing the servant with a slight wave of his hand. At least she was being looked after. It allowed him a small measure of peace, a fleeting sense that he was fulfilling his duty to Harry.

With that settled, he turned his attention back to the grim task before him, his eyes scanning the next set of letters. Some were dull matters—correspondence with Harry's superior officers, general documents of army life. A few were personal notes from comrades. And then, Darcy found it—a letter informing Harry of his promotion to Captain for meritorious service in battle.

A faint, almost involuntary smile tugged at the corner of Darcy's mouth. He could picture Harry receiving the letter with that irrepressible grin of his, the one that had always made him seem so much younger. His father would have been dismayed, no doubt. George Darcy had never wanted his youngest son leading battle charges, placing himself in danger, exposed to bullets and sabres. But Harry—brave, reckless Harry—had risen through the ranks with distinction.

He had been a hero. A flicker of pride mingled with the sorrow. No one could deny it. A hero of the nation. And yet, for all his valour and bravery, for all the battles fought and victories won, Harry had perished not on the battlefield, but here—at Pemberley. The place where he should have been safest. A horse slipping in the stable yard. A tragic, senseless end.

Darcy's fingers traced the edge of the paper, the memory of that day fresh and brutal. The irony of it twisted like a knife in his chest. An experienced cavalryman who had survived the horrors of war, only to be felled by a skittish horse on familiar ground!

But even that, that preposterous twist of fate, did nothing to erase the brave man Harry was. The man Darcy admired like no other. How George Wickham must have festered over Harry's promotion! Wickham, who had been given the same Lieutenant's commission as Harry, only through their father's misguided generosity.

Their father once insisted that Harry take orders and enter the church. It had been destined for him, that living at Kympton. But Harry—always stubborn, always independent—had refused, choosing instead the more dangerous path. Wickham had been only too eager to step in, to claim the living for himself, and Darcy had fought him at every turn. Wickham had no business leading a flock! Entering a position of trust, where monies for the poor would pass through his hands, where innocent maidens might be tempted to confide in him?

And so, Darcy had fought—for months, arguing with his father over the notion of promising this living to Wickham, since Harry did not want it. Eventually, his father had been swayed, and Wickham, deprived of an easy life as a country parson, had joined Harry on the Continent instead. It was a bitter twist of fate. Darcy had thought it unwise at the time—those two, too close for his liking—but there had been no separating them.

At least Harry had risen above Wickham. He had proved himself, time and again, while Wickham had remained the same twisted, wretched man he had always been.

Darcy let out a long breath, carefully placing the letter back onto the desk. He had been staring at it for far too long. His eyes were blurring, his mind weary from the weight of it all. The morning had nearly slipped away, and he had made little progress.

A fleeting thought crossed his mind: Would Mrs Darcy be leaving her room today? He hoped, in some strange way, that she would remain upstairs. It would be easier if he saw as little of her as possible, at least for now. He could barely keep his thoughts straight, let alone navigate the complexity of their new life together.

His hand reached for another of Harry's documents when a knock came at the door. A footman entered, his posture rigid.

"Colonel Fitzwilliam has arrived, sir."

Darcy's hand stilled over the papers, his mouth setting into a grim line. He should have expected this—Richard would come, of course—but it still took him by surprise. He stood, jerking the front of his waistcoat into place. "Show him in."

As the footman departed, Darcy braced himself. At least it was Richard and not the earl or Lady Catherine. There were certain... conversations he had yet to explore with anyone, and he had not yet decided how to go about them. The door opened, and Colonel

Fitzwilliam strode in, his sharp eyes already taking in the sight of his cousin behind the desk.

Darcy straightened, his emotions a carefully controlled mask as he faced his cousin. "Richard."

They had always shared a comfortable camaraderie, though their bond was often steadied by the presence of Harry, the younger brother who had tied them both together more closely than they were to each other. Now, with Harry gone, Darcy felt the strangeness of it—the gap that neither he nor Richard could fill alone.

Richard stood there, quiet for once, his mouth pressed into a thin line. Without a word, he crossed the room and embraced Darcy. It caught him off guard. He stiffened, unused to such an overt display of emotion. For a moment, he was unsure how to react, his hands hovering awkwardly before he finally returned the gesture with a hesitant pat on Richard's back.

They stepped back, Darcy clearing his throat, unsure of what to say. He moved toward the sideboard where the decanter of brandy waited, grateful for something to do with his hands. "A drink?" he offered, his voice steadier than he felt.

Richard heaved a sigh. "I'd say I need one, and it seems rather improper to refuse when you look so grim."

Darcy poured two glasses, handing one to his cousin before taking a deep drink from his own. The liquor burned on its way down, but he welcomed the sting, if only to focus on something other than the crushing sense of loss between them.

Richard watched him, his expression more serious now. He sipped his drink and set the glass down, his brow furrowing. "How did it happen, Darcy?"

Darcy sighed heavily and looked down. "It was the horses. Harry was riding one of my mares... a stallion spooked at some dogs, got loose in the stable yard and charged the mare. She reared, and Harry couldn't control her in time. He was thrown." Darcy swallowed, the words bitter on his tongue. "He hit his head. There was nothing anyone could do."

Silence settled over them as Richard processed the information. Darcy glanced at him briefly, unsure what to expect from his cousin.

After a moment, Richard let out a broken laugh. He ran a hand through his hair, shaking his head. "It's shocking. Stupid, even. That something so... simple could have killed him." His voice wavered at the end, but he quickly swallowed back the emotion, trying to maintain some semblance of control.

Darcy nodded, unable to trust his own voice. It *was* stupid, absurd in its simplicity—a fall, a horse, a stone on the ground. He sat across from Richard, the two of them sharing a silence that felt deeper than words, a commiseration that neither knew how to put into language. They sat like that for a time, the quiet only broken by the occasional clink of glass against wood as they set their drinks down.

Eventually, Richard sniffed, wiping a hand over his face, and turned to Darcy. "What about the arrangements?"

Darcy frowned, unsure what he meant. "The arrangements?"

"For Harry. I got an emergency leave to come help with... well, his affairs. I thought you might welcome the help in dealing with the army," Richard explained, his voice gentle but probing, as if waiting for Darcy to lean on him, to admit that the burden was too heavy to bear alone.

But Darcy shook his head and waved the offer aside. "It has already been dealt with. The army—everything has been managed."

Richard leaned back in his chair, swirling the brandy in his glass. "And the family... they'll have their thoughts. You know Lady Catherine always meant to have one of the Darcy brothers marry Anne. Your father warned her off of you, but Harry... well, he needed a wealthy bride, I suppose. Lady Catherine may now be looking to you for satisfaction. And my father's probably already considering the disposition of Harry's inheritance from your mother. He was supposed to—"

"Richard," Darcy interrupted, his voice strained.

Richard looked up, startled by the sudden gravity in Darcy's tone. Darcy's hand gripped the back of his chair as he stood, then he began pacing, his thoughts tangled. He tried to force the words out, but they lodged in his throat, thick and unwieldy. *How could he explain this?*

"There is... something else," Darcy managed, his voice rough. "Something they do not know yet."

Richard's expression sharpened, his eyes narrowing as he focused on Darcy with a growing concern. He raised the glass to his lips, taking a slow sip. "What is it?"

Darcy stopped pacing and stood before the fireplace, his back turned to his cousin. He stared into the flames, watching as the flickering light cast shadows over the room. "Harry left someone behind."

Richard's brow creased. "A woman?"

Darcy didn't answer immediately. He could hear Richard's mind turning, the assumptions forming in his cousin's voice as he continued, his tone becoming more incredulous. "Surely not... not some mistress, I hope. You don't mean there's a woman claiming that Harry left her with child, do you? And demanding a fortune from you, no doubt."

Darcy stiffened, his throat constricting as he tried to swallow down the ache that had been building for days. He couldn't speak, couldn't bring himself to confirm or deny Richard's words. Instead, he resumed his pacing, feeling the walls of the room closing in on him.

Richard sat up straighter in his chair, his glass still in hand. "It *is* something like that, isn't it?" he said, his voice dropping as though he dreaded the answer. "Darcy, for Heaven's sake, what have you done?"

Darcy stopped abruptly, turning to face his cousin. His voice came out hoarse, low. "She was no mistress, Richard. She's a gentleman's daughter."

The words hung in the air between them, laden with significance. Richard's face paled, his brow furrowing as the full weight of what Darcy was saying began to sink in. He set his glass down slowly, the movement deliberate as if he needed a moment to absorb the implications.

"Oh, good Lord," Richard muttered, running a hand down his face. "What is this, Darcy?"

Darcy's lips tightened. His chest felt heavy, his breath uneven as he struggled to continue. "Elizabeth Bennet. She is... was... Harry's intended."

Richard stared at him, disbelief flickering in his eyes. "Harry's intended?" he repeated slowly, as though he needed to hear the words again to make sense of them. His voice was low, measured, but Darcy could see the storm gathering behind his cousin's expression, the confusion, the anger, and perhaps even pity.

Darcy nodded once. "Yes. He had every intention of doing the honourable thing and marrying her, but... but he died before he could formalise the engagement. There was no time for settlements, no official announcement."

Richard exhaled sharply and looked away, shaking his head as if trying to clear it. "A gentleman's daughter..." He sighed, rubbing the back of his neck. "And you've been left to deal with this mess? Surely—surely that's all there is, Darcy? You're not suggesting..."

Darcy swallowed hard, his chest tightening. He looked down, unable to meet Richard's eyes for a moment, and forced himself to say the rest. "I married her."

Chapter Ten

Pemberley, Derbyshire
Tuesday, September 23

M Y DEAREST JANE,

   I hardly know where to begin, but I suppose it is best to start with the facts before I wander into more pleasant fictions. You will be relieved to hear that I have arrived at Pemberley without any great disasters—though I fear you will laugh when I tell you that I am being treated as though I am made of the most delicate porcelain. Truly, you would think I had never walked in my life, given how eager everyone is to fetch and carry for me! I am half-expecting a footman to stand beside me while I breathe, in case I should take too deep a sigh.

   Still, I must confess that Pemberley is every bit as grand as I had imagined, perhaps even more so. The house sits like a crown upon the landscape, with rolling hills, forests, and a lake that gleams in the distance. The library, where I now sit, is so vast that I believe it could house all the books in Hertfordshire and still have space left for a dance. And yet, for all its beauty, I confess the silence of the place weighs on me, though you know how I dislike admitting such things.

   But now to the more serious matter. You have likely guessed by now that I am struggling to reconcile myself to Harry's death. I have tried, dearest Jane, to keep my spirits high, but the truth of it is this: I miss him. I miss the life we might have had together, the ease of his company, the sense that, with him, I might have found a kind of happiness I scarcely dared to imagine. But now, well... now that future is gone. I am a different Mrs Darcy now, and the name fits about as comfortably as a borrowed pair of gloves.

I do not mean to alarm you, Jane. Please, do not let my words trouble you overmuch. I am well, I assure you. The servants—there are more than I could ever hope to remember—are all fussing over me, making sure I have tea with milk, tea without milk, tea with mint, and tea with some lemon in case I should feel a faint need for refreshment. I have not gone without a meal, a warm fire, or a comforting word since I arrived. If anything, I am rather overwhelmed by their kindness.

As for Mr Darcy... well, he is exactly as you might expect. He is every inch the reserved, proper gentleman Harry described, with just as many thoughts locked behind that stoic brow of his as he has books in his library. He is polite and considerate, yet it feels as though there is always some great distance between us, as though he cannot quite bring himself to look at me too long. I believe he is grieving, too, though you know men show such things differently. He is not unkind—far from it—but he is not... Harry. I suppose that is the real difficulty.

Pemberley itself is beautiful beyond words, as I said, but it feels strange to be mistress of so fine a house when I still feel like nothing more than Elizabeth Bennet of Longbourn. Can you picture me here, Jane? Strolling these halls as though I belonged to them? No, I cannot either.

But do not worry about me. I have taken up residence in the library for now—imagine, me with so many books!—and I promise to write often. If nothing else, I shall have no shortage of time to write you very lengthy letters. Please, give my love to dear Mama and Papa and tell them that, despite everything, I am well enough and that I have found a quiet comfort here, in my own way.

Yours ever,

Elizabeth

E LIZABETH SAT BACK IN the chair, staring at the words she had written, the pen hovering just above the paper. She had done what she always did, hadn't she? Made light of the things that twisted her heart, put a mask of good cheer over the cracks in her composure. The truth was far more complicated, more tangled in grief and confusion than she would ever admit to her family.

She let out a quiet sigh and glanced up at the rows of bookshelves towering over her. It was impossible to escape the grandeur of Pemberley, no matter how many jokes she tried to make about the endless tea or the over-attentive servants. The house seemed to breathe with its own ancient weight, and she—Elizabeth Bennet of modest means and spirited nature—felt out of place in its shadow.

Setting the pen down, she folded the letter and sealed it, her fingers moving absently. At least writing to Jane had provided some solace, even if she had glossed over the more painful truths. If she focused hard enough, she could almost convince herself all would be well. After all, she was Mrs Darcy now, and that title should mean something. Shouldn't it?

Her thoughts drifted again to Harry—his laughing eyes, the warmth of his voice, the way he had promised her a future that was now lost forever. And now, here she was, bound to a man who barely looked at her, a man who grieved as she did, but in a way she could not touch.

Elizabeth stood, the letter in hand, and moved toward the window. The view outside was beautiful, indeed, but it felt distant, almost like a painting that she couldn't quite step into. She pressed the letter to her chest, the only comfort she had at that moment being the knowledge that her family, at least, was far from this strange new world she found herself in. They were safe. Her sisters might now marry. Her marriage had ensured that hope, at least.

T HE ROOM SEEMED TO freeze. Richard's mouth opened, but for a few moments, no words came. He stared at Darcy, stunned. "You... married her?" His voice was almost a whisper, as if he couldn't quite believe it. "*You?*"

Darcy nodded, his expression grim. "Yes. I've married her."

Richard leaned back in his chair, his eyes widening as the enormity of the revelation settled over him. He ran a hand through his hair again, his usual composure faltering in the face of such unexpected news. "But why? For the sake of propriety? Surely... there were other ways to manage this. You didn't have to..." His words trailed off as his gaze sharpened, understanding dawning in his features. "You think... you think she's carrying Harry's child, don't you?"

Darcy's jaw clenched. He turned away, pacing the room again, his hands flexing into fists as he struggled with his thoughts. "I don't think," he began, his voice low, "I know."

Richard let out a long breath, his shoulders sagging as he leaned forward, resting his elbows on his knees. He seemed to be searching for something to say, but no words came immediately. Finally, after a long silence, he asked, "And does she know? Does she know what you suspect? Has she told you..." Richard coughed, gesturing vaguely with his hand.

Darcy stopped pacing, his back still turned to his cousin. His voice was strained when he answered. "She is not stupid, Richard. Of course, she knows. We married in haste because of the scandal. Perhaps we have not discussed anything in explicit detail because there are some things I do not wish to speak of or hear about. The honourable thing has been done. That is enough."

Richard sat up straighter, his tone hardening. "Darcy, you can't just marry a woman under those circumstances without knowing specifics. Were there any others for her? Are you sure Harry was the man? And how far along—"

"I will speak to her on the matter," Darcy cut in sharply, spinning to face Richard again. "But what would it accomplish now, in the middle of this? What would it change? I did what I had to do—what Harry would have done if he'd lived." His voice softened at the end, his resolve crumbling slightly under the weight of everything unsaid. "I had to protect her. And him."

Richard was silent for a moment, his sharp gaze watching Darcy closely, measuring his words. Finally, he let out a slow breath, the tension easing just a little. "And you think this is what Harry would have wanted? For you to marry her?"

Darcy's mouth tightened. He didn't have an answer to that. It was the one question that had plagued him since the day of the wedding. What would Harry have wanted?

What would he have done? He had no way of knowing for certain. All he knew was that he had to do something, had to preserve his brother's honour, even if it meant sacrificing his own.

"I don't know what Harry would have wanted," Darcy admitted, his voice rough. "He named her—said what he meant to do, but I've no idea what... Either way, it is done now."

Richard ran a hand over his face, visibly exhausted by the revelation. "Good Lord, Darcy." He leaned back in the chair again, his eyes scanning the room as if looking for an escape from the enormity of the situation. "You said the family does not know?"

Darcy shook his head. "Not yet."

"And Lady Catherine?" Richard asked, his voice heavy with irony. "I'm sure she'll be overjoyed to hear you've married without consulting her."

Darcy gave a wry smile, though it held little humour. "She'll find out soon enough." He paused, his expression hardening. "But it does not matter. This is my decision. No one else's."

Richard sighed again, rubbing the back of his neck. "So, what now? What do you intend to do?"

Darcy's gaze drifted to the window, the distant hills of Pemberley just visible through the glass. He was not sure what the future held, what lay ahead for him and Elizabeth, but there was no turning back now. He had made his choice.

"She is my wife," he said quietly. "I will see to her... and to Harry's child. We will make the best of it."

Richard shook his head, though the edge of his earlier frustration had softened. "I hope you're right, Darcy. I truly do."

E LIZABETH FELT AS THOUGH the very walls of Pemberley were closing in on her. Every corner, every room, was carefully tended, polished to gleaming perfection, but for her, it only added to the suffocation. There was hardly a moment to herself, with servants at every turn anticipating her smallest needs—needs she hadn't even realised she had. The first time she had attempted to pick up a fire poker in her morning room, a maid had appeared as if summoned by magic, taking the poker from her hand with a swift, deferential bow. It left Elizabeth feeling like an ornament, something fragile and delicate, to be protected from every small exertion.

Her chest tightened again as she stood near the hearth. She needed air, space—something beyond the thick air of Pemberley's endless rooms. She stepped toward the bell-pull, and a few moments later, Susan appeared in the doorway.

"My pelisse, if you please," Elizabeth requested, keeping her voice calm, though her pulse was already quickening with the urge to escape. "I should like to go out walking."

Susan hesitated, her face colouring slightly. "I'm afraid, madam, your pelisse is still on the laundress's line. It... was soiled yesterday when you—"

Elizabeth closed her eyes briefly, suppressing the irritation that rose at the mention of her illness. She had not forgot, and she had no desire to be reminded of it. "Then fetch me something else," she said with a sigh.

The maid bobbed her head and rushed to the trunk where Elizabeth's things were hastily stored, emerging with a heavier cape than she would have chosen for the mild autumn air. Still, it was something, and Elizabeth was not inclined to quibble. She pulled the cape around her shoulders, fastening it with a sharp tug.

"Shall I fetch a parasol, ma'am?" Susan asked, her voice full of dutiful eagerness. "Perhaps a footman to show you about the grounds?"

Elizabeth turned to the girl, shaking her head. "No, thank you, Susan. I should like to walk alone." The words came out with a bit more edge than she intended, but she couldn't help it. She wanted—*needed*—to be left to her own devices for once.

Susan's eyes widened slightly, but she made no protest. Instead, she dipped another curtsy. "Very well, ma'am."

Elizabeth nodded, taking a breath as she stepped past her maid and out into the hall. The air in the corridor felt a touch cooler, cleaner, though not nearly enough to settle the unease simmering within her.

Once outside, she found herself on the lawn, circling the house in long, deliberate strides. She paused here and there, scanning the grounds, trying to decide where to go. Pemberley stretched out in every direction, offering more paths and gardens than she could possibly explore in one afternoon, but none of it felt... hers. Not yet.

The lawns, though perfectly manicured, were not what she needed. Elizabeth's eyes drifted past them, toward the wilder stretches of garden that lay further from the house. With sudden resolve, she made her way down a path that led into the gardens. The riot of end-of-season flowers and autumn foliage closed in around her, their vibrant colours almost too bold, too alive for her unsettled heart. She continued walking, her steps purposeful as the path wound through the gardens and out toward the lake in the distance.

The lake. She could see it glimmering faintly through the trees, its surface smooth and clear as glass, mirroring the changing sky above. A small breeze stirred the water, and Elizabeth paused at the edge, staring out at the reflection of the towering trees lining the shore.

Harry must have walked here, along this very path, stopping by this very lake. She could almost see him—his bright smile, his easy laughter. Perhaps he had brought Bingley here, or even some other friends from his regiment. She tried to picture Harry strolling these grounds, but the image faded almost as soon as it had come.

No, the one who most belonged here was not Harry. It was *him*.

Fitzwilliam Darcy. Her husband. The master of all this.

As much as she tried to push it away, his presence crept into her thoughts—his tall, silent form, his intense, unreadable eyes. She imagined him walking here, his long strides cutting through the serenity of the landscape. This place suited him, did it not? Its stateliness, its quiet grandeur.

Elizabeth felt a shiver that had nothing to do with the cool air. She pulled the cape tighter around her shoulders and turned away from the water. She would keep walking. Perhaps if she kept moving, she might finally begin to feel as though she belonged here. Or, at the very least, she might find a way to make peace with the strange, unsettling new life.

"**D**ARCY, I SIMPLY DO not understand. You could have done this different-ly—you *should* have done this differently. You could have paid her off, settled the matter quietly, from a distance. You didn't have to—"

Darcy took a slow sip of his brandy, letting the warmth slide down his throat as he listened to his cousin's rant. It was nothing he had not already considered himself, and yet Richard's words stirred something raw in him. He could have paid a settlement, yes. He could have spared himself this marriage and moved on, free to wed some other woman of fortune and high standing. But none of that would have salvaged the one thing that mattered—Harry's honour.

His silence was a shield, one Richard couldn't easily penetrate. He kept his eyes on the fire, the amber light flickering over the rim of his glass, refusing to give Richard the satisfaction of an agreement, though, in the depths of his heart, Darcy knew his cousin was right. He *could* have done all those things, but none of them would have been enough.

Richard, impatient with Darcy's quietude, began to pace again, his boots tapping sharply against the floor as he circled the room. He stopped in front of Darcy, his eyes blazing with frustration. "It is not too late, you know."

Darcy looked up from his glass, a quizzical frown tugging at his brow. He scoffed lightly. "Not too late? And how, exactly, is it not too late?"

Richard shifted his weight from one foot to the other, glancing aside before meeting Darcy's gaze again, a faint discomfort in his eyes. "I know you too well, Darcy. You have not... fulfilled *all* the legal requirements, have you?"

Darcy's face went ashen, and his hand froze around the glass. The implication of Richard's words hung heavily in the air, and it took him a moment to find his voice. "You mean to say... the marriage...?" He set his brandy aside, his pulse quickening. "It is no one's business whether I have consummated my marriage or not. No one could challenge the legality of it. There were witnesses. The ceremony was done properly, as it should be."

Richard sighed, running a hand through his hair. "Yes, I comprehend that. You know as well as I do that even if my father or Lady Catherine wished to contest it, they couldn't. But *you* could. If you avowed—"

Darcy cut him off, his tone sharp, defensive. "I gave my word, Richard. I will keep it."

Richard hissed in exasperation, pacing away toward the window, muttering under his breath. He stood for a moment with his back to Darcy, shaking his head as though trying to argue still. But then, suddenly, he froze. His gaze locked on something outside, and his posture stiffened.

Darcy, still standing beside the fire, noticed the way Richard had gone completely still. He frowned, setting down his glass and walking to stand beside his cousin. "What is it?"

Richard gestured wordlessly to the window.

Outside, in the soft autumn light, Elizabeth was walking toward the garden. She wore a billowing cape that fluttered around her as she moved, the heavy fabric catching the breeze. The cape—while practical in the cool air—did her figure no favours, and yet, something in the sight of her made Darcy's throat tighten. She looked small, dwarfed by the grandeur of the estate, her steps uncertain as she explored the grounds. There was an air of quiet resolve about her, though. As if she, too, was trying to find her place here, to claim some small piece of this vast, unfamiliar world.

Darcy forced himself to look away, clearing his throat. "I suppose she is... familiarising herself with Pemberley," he said, the words clipped and cold. "It is her home now, after all."

Richard glanced at Darcy with a bemused expression, but said nothing.

For a moment, the room was filled with an uncomfortable silence. Darcy swallowed hard, his eyes drifting back to the window despite himself. He couldn't deny the odd ache in his chest, the way his thoughts tangled when he saw her out there, walking the grounds he loved. But he forced it away, unwilling to linger on whatever that feeling was. This was duty. Nothing more.

Finally, he straightened his shoulders, breaking the silence. "You might as well meet Mrs Darcy now. Come. I will introduce you."

Without waiting for Richard's response, Darcy turned and strode toward the door, determined to maintain control of the situation, and perhaps even of his own unruly emotions.

Chapter Eleven

E LIZABETH SAT ON A stone bench overlooking the lake, pulling her cape a little tighter around her shoulders as her eyes lost themselves in the rippling reflections. Her thoughts swayed between sadness and solace when she heard the unmistakable sound of footsteps along the path behind her. Startled, she turned, expecting a servant, but instead saw Mr Darcy approaching with another man—a stranger.

Darcy's expression was formal, as ever, and his bow stiff. "Mrs Darcy," he said, his voice level. "May I introduce my cousin, Colonel Fitzwilliam."

Elizabeth blinked and then brightened slightly at the name. "Colonel Fitzwilliam?" she repeated, standing to greet him. "Captain Darcy spoke highly of you."

The colonel, a man of average build with a thoughtful, dignified bearing, offered a polite bow in return. His countenance was softened by the black armband he wore, a silent reminder of their shared grief. "And I am equally pleased to make your acquaintance, Mrs Darcy," he said, though his eyes flicked briefly to Darcy. Elizabeth noticed the exchange between the cousins—a glance passed as if Darcy had offered an unspoken caution, and she wondered at it.

Colonel Fitzwilliam seemed to acknowledge Darcy's restraint, but he returned his attention to her, greeting her with a warmth that relieved some of the knots in her stomach. "I am sorry we meet under such circumstances, but I am glad to finally be introduced to the lady who... well, who has joined our family."

"Thank you, Colonel," she replied quietly. "I am honoured."

An awkward pause hung in the air, the colonel shifting slightly. Darcy remained nearby, silent and watchful. The swelling grey cloud that often accompanied his presence seemed to linger, and Elizabeth began to feel the familiar anxiety stirring in her chest. Colonel Fitzwilliam seemed to notice, though, and he was quick to change the tone of the conversation.

"Tell me, Mrs Darcy, where does your family hail from?" he asked, leaning casually against the stone that had been her seat, as if inviting her to ease into the conversation. "I understand you are not from Derbyshire?"

"No," she replied. "My family lives in Hertfordshire, at a modest estate called Longbourn. We are... provincial by comparison to Pemberley, I fear."

The colonel appeared delighted by her response, casting another glance at Darcy, who stood with his arms crossed, his face inscrutable. "Provincial?" he echoed, his voice light with amusement. "I find that hard to believe. I've always thought the charm of smaller estates lies in their simplicity and warmth. Tell me, do you miss it?"

Elizabeth hesitated, feeling the full weight of that question. "Very much so," she admitted, though she was careful not to allow too much emotion to creep into her voice. "But I suppose anyone would miss the familiarity of home, when thrust into such... grand surroundings."

"Grand surroundings, indeed," the colonel said, glancing around them. "Pemberley does have a way of making everything else seem... less." He leaned in conspiratorially. "But I gather you are adjusting well, from what I can see?"

Elizabeth could not help but smile, even as her eyes flicked toward Darcy. "Am I? You must be quite observant, Colonel, for I feel as though I am still finding my way around both the house and... other matters."

"Ah, well," Colonel Fitzwilliam replied with a grin, "the mark of a good officer is to observe without being noticed."

Elizabeth let out a quiet laugh, one of the first genuine ones since her arrival. It was a relief to speak with someone who didn't seem to carry the same oppressive gravity that her husband brought into every room. Colonel Fitzwilliam, despite his military bearing, was light-hearted and easygoing. He was more like Harry in spirit, and that thought warmed her.

"You were stationed in Chatham, as I recall. Is that so, Colonel?" she asked.

The colonel straightened in some surprise. "Why, yes, I was. Intended to remain there all winter, and quite sorry for myself over it. Harry was the lucky one, stationed in London since May, after his stay on the Continent, the blighter."

She smiled faintly. "I believe he arrived in July, Colonel. And if one accounts for the summer heat, perhaps he did not have the better assignment. I daresay Chatham at least catches a breath of the sea breeze now and again."

"Indeed, it does. There it is—I cannot even complain because you have found me out. What of you, Mrs Darcy? I let my own tales run on without pausing to listen to yours. Tell me, are you fond of walking? I imagine the grounds of Pemberley are quite different from those you've explored before."

Elizabeth breathed a little, glad for the change of subject. "I am, though I have not had much chance to explore the grounds yet. What little I have seen is beautiful, but I imagine it will take time to truly know this place."

Darcy shifted from one foot to the other, drawing her eye to him. There was something rather odd in his gaze just now—she would almost call it protective or disapproving or... well, she could not quite read it.

Colonel Fitzwilliam gave a knowing nod. "Yes, Pemberley does have a way of revealing itself in layers. Every time I come here, I find something new—though I expect you will know it better than I in no time."

Elizabeth smiled, warming to the colonel's easy manner. He had a way of drawing her out, encouraging her to speak with a familiarity that felt natural rather than forced. "I hope so," she replied softly. "It is certainly a place worthy of admiration."

A brief silence followed, heavy with unspoken grief. Then Colonel Fitzwilliam shifted the conversation again, his tone lighter. "I understand you were lately in London. Do you prefer it to the countryside?" He leaned against the low wall near her bench. "Or is the quiet appeal of the country more to your taste?"

Elizabeth let out a soft laugh. "The quiet does have its appeal, especially when compared to the bustle of London. There, it is easy to feel one is constantly being watched or judged." She paused, her smile faint. Oh, she had felt *very* judged in London. "The countryside offers privacy, a kind of sanctuary."

"Privacy is indeed a rare commodity in the city," the colonel agreed with a nod. "I must confess, I prefer the freedom of a long ride in open fields myself."

"Captain Darcy once mentioned you rode well. He said you were the only man in uniform who could keep up with him."

Colonel Fitzwilliam chuckled. "Ah, Harry had a tendency to embellish, but I thank you for the compliment on his behalf. He, however, was the better rider by far. He made it seem effortless." His expression softened with a touch of sadness as he added, "There was a lightness about Harry, wasn't there? He had a way of making even the most difficult situations bearable."

"Yes," Elizabeth murmured, her throat tightening at the memory of Harry's ready laughter, the way he had seemed to put everyone at ease. "He did."

"So," the colonel continued, shifting to stand more comfortably beside her, "did Harry ever regale you with tales of my many misadventures in the army? He had a particular talent for making me the subject of his stories—whether true or exaggerated."

Elizabeth raised a brow. "Oh, he may have mentioned a certain incident involving a horse that nearly threw you into a stream—though he insisted he was blameless in the matter."

"Ah!" Colonel Fitzwilliam threw his head back with a laugh. "Blameless, was he? Typical! Let me assure you, Captain Harold Darcy had a knack for trouble. He decided it was a fine time to start a race while I had only just mounted my horse. And I nearly ended up in that stream, though I suspect that was his intent all along!"

"I can imagine him doing just that," she said, shaking her head fondly. "He had quite the mischievous side, didn't he? Though I imagine you gave as good as you got."

"On occasion," the colonel admitted with a grin. "Though, more often than not, Harry managed to outmanoeuvre me. There wasn't a dull moment when Harry was around. He could charm anyone, from the lowliest private to the general himself. But there, I suppose that is enough talk of... of horses and whatnot." The colonel swallowed.

Elizabeth glanced over at Darcy, who remained silent but was watching them intently. The colonel followed her gaze, stiffening as if realising he may have overstepped.

Darcy cleared his throat and stepped forward, his expression tightening. "I believe it is time to return to the house," he said, his voice a little too firm to be entirely polite.

Elizabeth blinked, her enjoyment of the conversation abruptly cut short. He left little room for argument in his stiff posture. There was nothing to be done but to nod in acquiescence.

"Of course," she said, her voice more subdued than before. She turned back to Colonel Fitzwilliam, her smile faltering. "It was a pleasure speaking with you, Colonel."

"And with you, Mrs Darcy," he replied, though his smile seemed tempered.

Darcy extended his hand to escort her, and though she took it, there was a slight chill between them now. She could feel the warmth of the conversation dissipating as they walked back toward the house, the noose of her new life tightening around her neck once more.

"Y OU WERE FLIRTING WITH Mrs Darcy!" Darcy accused, his voice low but unmistakably sharp. "I warned you to be polite, but I never imagined you would be... whatever that was. I tell you, it was indecent! Harry gone barely a fortnight, and you *flirting* with..." He broke off with a hiss and a growl.

The drawing room was quiet, save for the faint crackle of the fire. The late afternoon sun streamed through the windows, casting long shadows across the room, but the warmth of the setting did little to ease the underlying friction between them. Darcy sat upright in his chair, his back rigid, trying to keep control over the frustration simmering inside him. He had been calmer since Elizabeth had left to retire upstairs, but now, with Richard sitting across from him, that calm was slipping away.

Richard raised an eyebrow, pausing mid-sip to lower his glass and stare. "Flirting, was it? Well, I would never claim to be anything less than charming," he replied with a smirk, though the humour quickly faded as he saw Darcy was in no mood for it. "But really, you think I was trying to woo your wife? Even you cannot be so blind."

"And what, precisely, do you mean by that?"

Richard sighed, setting his cup down with deliberate care. "I was testing her," he said, leaning forward as if to emphasise the point.

Darcy's eyes narrowed further. "Testing her? In what way?"

"I wanted to see if she was genuine," he said. "Or just another pretender. You know the type—a fortune-hunter or an adventuress, someone who finds a wealthy family to attach herself to and takes advantage of the situation."

Darcy crossed his arms, almost afraid of what was coming next. "And?"

Richard lifted his teacup again, taking a slow, deliberate sip before answering. "She's authentic."

Darcy's brow furrowed in surprise, though he tried to maintain his composure. Somehow, he had expected to hear the opposite. "What makes you so certain of that?"

"Because that story she told about the horse was true," Richard replied, setting his cup down again. "She also knew I had been stationed in Chatham, and she corrected me when I gave the wrong date for Harry's return from Spain. Unless you've been sharing personal details about Harry and me with her, which I doubt, those are things Harry must have told her himself."

Darcy felt a flicker of something—relief, perhaps?—but he did not allow it to show. He kept his arms crossed, his expression neutral. "Go on."

Richard leaned forward once more, his voice lowering slightly. "And there's something else. The way she spoke about getting to know the estate... there was humility in it. She wasn't pretending to know more than she did, wasn't putting on airs, and isn't trying to elevate herself. She's no adventuress, Darcy. But she is hiding from something."

Darcy's frown deepened. "What makes you think that?"

"It was in her face when I mentioned London. Whatever happened there—she's happy to be away from it. Happy to be here, at Pemberley, where no one can reach her. She's keeping a low profile for a reason."

Darcy grunted, leaning back in his chair. "That is no surprise," he muttered. "We both know why she would be happy to escape that sort of gossip."

"Indeed," Richard agreed, his tone more serious now. He glanced down at his cup before continuing, "But what are you going to do now? You are married, and quite stubbornly so. You've got a problem on your hands, one that's going to become very obvious to the world soon enough. The earl is not going to be pleased, to say nothing of the rest of society."

Darcy's skin crawled at the mention of the looming consequences. The Earl of Matlock, not to mention Lady Catherine and others, would certainly have opinions once word spread. But it was Richard's next question that sent a jolt through him.

"Do you expect to find any measure of happiness in this marriage, Darcy?" Richard asked quietly, his voice cutting through the room like a blade. "To make all this suffering and trouble worth it?"

Darcy swallowed hard, his pulse suddenly loud in his ears. His hand gripped the teacup tighter than necessary, and for a moment, he could not speak. Happiness? That was not even a possibility in his mind.

"No," he said, his voice flat and final.

Richard studied him for a moment, his expression unreadable. "Are you sure about that?" he asked carefully. "The lady seemed rather forthright and intelligent. Sensible of her circumstances but willing enough to smile. She wasn't a punishment to speak to or to look at. Just because she isn't an heiress—"

Darcy cut him off, the words coming out more sharply than he intended. "She is carrying Harry's child, Richard. That is all that matters."

The room fell silent, the finality of Darcy's words hanging in the air like a lead weight. Richard said nothing for a long moment, his eyes darkening with understanding. Darcy set his cup aside, no longer able to stomach the tea.

"I will give her what Harry could not," Darcy continued, his voice low, almost bitter. "That is my duty. And that... is the end of it."

E LIZABETH STOOD BEFORE HER wardrobe, staring blankly at the few gowns she had brought from Longbourn. Her fingers drifted to the satin hem of one—a gown with a torn bodice that had been damaged... on another occasion. She sighed.

Well, there were still two hours before she had to dress for dinner. Perhaps she could mend it, but really, what was the point? What did it matter what she wore when her husband scarcely looked at her and seemed content to keep her hidden away, shut in her room?

No, that was unfair. He had told her they would be having dinner with the colonel. Had given her the option of whether she wished to join them—they would honour the dictates of her feelings on the matter. Perhaps she might be too fatigued, he had suggested.

Too fatigued for a dinner in her own home? She could endure that, surely! The colonel, at least, was good company, and with him there, Darcy would be forced to speak. That would be better than sitting alone in her room again, staring at the walls, the suffocating silence around her. Her world had shrunk to that small, stifling space—her isolation at Pemberley pressing in on her more each day.

Elizabeth rifled through the remaining gowns. She had little that suited a formal dinner—nothing like the gowns of silk and satin worn by fashionable ladies of London.

Her husband had mentioned sending for a modiste soon, but even the prospect of new clothes did not excite her vanity. What she craved was some sense of belonging, perhaps some gowns that made her feel part of this new role she had been thrust into, rather than the intruder she feared she was.

Her hand fell on that evening gown—once the best one she owned, now a sad ruin of stitches and muslin. If she sat down with her needle now, perhaps the damage could be repaired, hidden...

A knock interrupted her thoughts. Startled, Elizabeth turned toward the door. "Come in."

The door opened to reveal Mrs Reynolds, and behind her, a stately older woman whom Elizabeth did not recognise.

"Mrs Darcy," Mrs Reynolds began with a curtsy, "this is Mrs Watson." She gave no further explanation, merely glanced between the two women before excusing herself.

Elizabeth stared after Mrs Reynolds for a moment, baffled by the sudden introduction. She looked back at the woman, who had stepped inside and was now watching her with a small smile.

"Mrs Watson," Elizabeth repeated, carefully masking her confusion. "I... forgive me, but I did not know I would be expecting... a guest."

"No trouble, madam," Mrs Watson said, folding her hands in front of her. "Mr Darcy sent for me. I am here to assist you." Her smile remained, serene and polite, but Elizabeth noticed a curious note of familiarity in her voice.

"To assist me?" Elizabeth echoed, still unsure of the woman's purpose. Perhaps she was a trained lady's maid? "I see. And to what do I owe this... attention?"

"Mr Darcy asked that I attend to your well-being, madam," Mrs Watson replied, taking a seat across from her as if she had done this many times before. "He expressed some concern for your health."

Elizabeth blinked in surprise. Of course. More of his excessive attentions. "My health?" she repeated, frowning slightly. "I assure you, I am quite well."

Mrs Watson's smile softened, but she remained where she sat, composed and patient. "That is good to hear, madam. Though I was informed that you had been feeling unwell yesterday—perhaps a bout of fatigue or... other symptoms?"

Elizabeth's frown deepened. "I believe I can safely say I was only overwhelmed," she said slowly. "The journey was rather long, and I had not eaten since daybreak, but I assure you, there is nothing amiss."

THE MEASURE OF HONOR

Mrs Watson nodded, her gaze still fixed kindly on Elizabeth. "Overwhelmed, perhaps, by your condition?"

"My... condition?" What condition could the woman possibly be referring...?

Oh.

The blood drained from her face as realisation suddenly dawned on her. "Wait... you are not under the impression that I am—"

Mrs Watson blinked in surprise, her smile faltering. "Mr Darcy did mention... well, that is to say, it is not so unusual for a young bride..."

The rest of the woman's words faded into the background as Elizabeth's head spun. Her stomach clenched, her heart pounding in her ears. Darcy believed she was *pregnant?* That explained the constant coddling, the hovering servants, the endless attention to her every need.

That explained why he had married her. He believed she was with child.

Harry's child.

"Oh," she whispered, taking a shaky step back from the woman. "Oh, no!"

Mrs Watson rose, alarmed by Elizabeth's sudden reaction. "Madam, please—"

Elizabeth held up a hand, shaking her head as she turned toward the door. "No, please, Mrs Watson. Forgive me. I must... I must speak with Mr Darcy."

Without another word, she hurried out of the room.

Chapter Twelve

ARCY SAT RIGIDLY IN the library, attempting to focus on the book before him,
though its words blurred under the wheel of his thoughts. Across from him,
Colonel Fitzwilliam reclined in his chair, absorbed in his own reading—or so it appeared.

Yet Darcy could not shake the sensation of his cousin's quiet judgement, simmering
just beneath the surface. The words Richard had spoken earlier still seared his mind,
stinging more than they should. His cheeks burned each time Richard turned a page,
even though the colonel never lifted his gaze from the text. Still, Darcy felt his cousin's
unspoken rebuke, his unwelcome opinions, like an iron pressing against his skin.

He shifted uncomfortably in his chair, trying to bury himself in his book. But then,
the muffled sound of hurried footsteps interrupted the stillness. Darcy glanced up, his
senses sharpening as he heard voices outside the door. Elizabeth's voice—frantic, edged
with something he could not quite place—sent a jolt of apprehension through him.

"Is Mr Darcy inside?" Elizabeth's voice rang through the hallway, urgent and breathless.

The footman outside the door replied, "Yes, Mrs Darcy, the master is in the library."

An instant later, the door opened, and Elizabeth appeared in the doorway. Her eyes
were wide, her face pale, her entire posture trembling.

A nameless dread seized Darcy's heart, and he rose to his feet at once, striding towards
her. "Elizabeth! Are you unwell?"

She shook her head, but her gaze darted past him, landing briefly on the colonel seated
behind. "I need to speak with you," she said in a low voice, her expression still stricken.
"Alone. It is urgent."

Darcy glanced over his shoulder, catching Richard's raised brow, but without a word, he turned back to her and nodded. "Of course," he said quietly, stepping aside and gesturing toward the door. "Come with me."

He led her out into the hall, the pit in his stomach deepening as they made their way to his study. What could have overset her so?

Elizabeth's hands trembled in his as they walked into his study. Darcy closed the door behind them and led her to the centre of the room, but she seemed unable to find the words right away. Her breath hitched in her throat as she fought to calm herself.

Darcy stepped closer, eyes searching hers. "What has happened?"

Elizabeth gulped some air. "A—a woman came to my room just now. A Mrs Watson—did you know of this?"

Darcy stared at her, his mind struggling to keep pace with her words. Watson? *Oh*... yes. Mrs Watson. That made perfect sense—he had sent for Mrs Watson himself, arranging for a tactful, capable woman to take stock of... well, Mrs Darcy's health. It was only right that he should have sent for someone.

But why was Elizabeth looking at him like this, pale and wide-eyed, trembling on the spot?

"Yes," he nodded slowly. "I sent for her. I was assured she was competent and discreet. Why are you alarmed? Did she harm you?"

Elizabeth shook her head, her breath coming in short, quick gasps. Her eyes darted to the door, then back to him. "No, she did not harm me. But..." She swallowed, her voice thick with emotion, as if she could barely get the words out. "I fear you are under a serious misapprehension."

Darcy frowned. "What misapprehension?"

Elizabeth's hands twisted before her, her face paling even further. "I... I am not with child. I have never been."

The air in the room shifted, as if all the breath had been sucked out. For a moment, Darcy could do nothing but stare at her, frozen in place as her words slowly sank in.

Not with child?

But... that made no sense! Of course, she was! Why else would he have had to marry her? He blinked, his throat tightening, and the room seemed to tilt.

"You are not... pregnant?" His voice came out in a strangled laugh, as if he could not even believe the words when he spoke them aloud.

Elizabeth shook her head, her eyes filled with a burnished glaze that threatened tears. "No. Why did you think I was?"

His mind reeled, grasping for explanations that slipped further from reach with every passing second. His heart pounded in his chest, fury and disbelief warring within him. *Not pregnant?*

"I thought you were because your very manner confirmed my suspicions! The day we met, you asked me if I knew of your... reproach."

"And you said you did! I thought you knew the truth, the facts of what happened! You did not say anything about me being with child."

Darcy hissed, stalking a short circle and then rounding on her again. "I did not think I *had* to! You vomited all over the floor yesterday! The ill-fitting clothing, your sickness—how are those not dead giveaways?"

She paled, her mouth slackening as she looked at him like he had grown an arm sprouting out of his forehead. "Coincidences! A borrowed gown and a bit of travel sickness, exacerbated by sheer terror of the size of this house! And you took these as proofs that I was *pregnant*?"

"What about the scandal?" he demanded, pacing away from her again, unable to face the truth unravelling before him. "Why did Bingley insist? Why did Gardiner practically beg me to marry you?" His thoughts raced, flashes of that chaotic moment returning—the letter, the rumours, Gardiner's desperation.

Elizabeth tried to speak, her voice breaking as she stumbled over her words. "There was an... an incident. Harry... that is, Captain Darcy, he—"

Darcy cut her off, his frustration boiling over. "The letter! The letter from Gardiner, accusing Harry... telling him about how he had wronged you... what, then? What about that?"

She blinked, confusion clouding her expression. "What letter?"

His anger surged, and he strode to his desk, yanking open the drawer where he had stashed the wretched thing. He pulled it out and practically threw it into her hands. "This letter! The one I found among Harry's papers. Read it!"

Elizabeth fumbled with the paper, her hands shaking as she unfolded it. He watched her face as she read, her lips moving silently over the damning words. He saw the colour drain from her cheeks, the way her shoulders sagged as the weight of the letter's contents hit her.

"Harry... betrayed me?" she whispered, the words barely audible, her voice cracking with disbelief. "He... who *is* this girl?"

Darcy snatched the letter back, fury coursing through him. "Is this not about you? Is this not your uncle's hand? Is this not why Gardiner was so eager to marry you off? Why everyone was so bloody insistent that you needed protection?"

Elizabeth shook her head frantically. "No, no! It is not my uncle's hand, I swear. Nor my father's. I would know if it were—I had no cause for anyone to make such accusations. Do you think they made this up to... I don't know what! But this is not... not about me."

Darcy's vision blurred, the room spinning around him as his world collapsed in on itself. "Bingley," he hissed, his voice trembling with rage. "That fool! His stupidity has done this. He swore there was some great secret, some private catastrophe that warranted my personal attention. What the devil was it? Did Harry step on the lace of your ball gown? Spill his wine on your fichu?"

"Mr Darcy, please! Mr Bingley was right when he said... well, I suppose I do not know *what* he said to you, but matters truly were quite desperate!"

"Aye, desperate, indeed. You had no dowry. No other prospects, and the one you had got your hooks into inconvenienced you by dying before he could be leg shackled. What bothersome timing!"

Elizabeth straightened, her eyes suddenly blazing with a fire he had never witnessed. "I am no fortune hunter. Take it back!"

"Why should I? It is the truth, is it not?"

Her features flushed. "Do you think I *wanted* to find myself here? Stuck with a man who hardly speaks to me? Given no opportunity to refuse because of the misdeeds of others?"

He barked a caustic laugh. "Refuse! There is a good joke. You would refuse me? My wealth? The comforts of being Mistress of Pemberley? Tell me something I could believe."

Her mouth twisted into a dark scowl. "You cannot conceive it, can you? Do you think I *planned* to entrap you? That I would not a thousand times rather run back to Longbourn this instant, back to the comforts of my family and far away from your condescension?"

He slammed his fist on the desk, the sound echoing in the room. He couldn't stop himself, couldn't hold back the torrent of emotion that poured out of him. "You are a fine one to talk. You think *you* have been inconvenienced? What about me? I was swindled! Fooled into sacrificing my honour on a broken altar! Now, I am bound to a woman I never intended to marry over a child that never existed!"

The words spilt from him, sharp and bitter, and he couldn't stop himself from thinking of the humiliation, the endless shame. Egad, what was he to tell Richard now? What about the rest of the world? This could not be undone!

His chest heaved with fury, the betrayal cutting deeper than anything he had imagined. He had done this to himself, bound himself to a lie, to a woman who—

No. He couldn't think of her now.

"What am I to do now?" he shouted, the anger erupting from him like a storm. "In Heaven's name, what am I to *do?*" His voice broke, and for a moment, the room fell silent, save for the sound of Elizabeth's outraged sob.

"How dare you, sir," she whispered. "You think only of your own misfortune? You blame *me* for this?"

"Indeed, madam. Who else is there?"

Elizabeth drew herself up once more, but her composure was shattered. More sobs quaked in her chest, and the cords of her neck flickered under her skin as she choked on what remained of her courage.

And then she gushed into a gasping torrent of rage and grief—a wordless fit of humiliation and despair that broke freely over her face.

He couldn't bear to hear it. The tears, the apologies she owed him but was surely too proud to render. He could not stomach any of it. They only made it worse, reminding him of how deeply entangled he had become. He turned away from her, his hand gripping the back of a chair, his knuckles white with the force of it.

"Just... leave me," he said, his voice hoarse.

He heard her stifled sob as she hurried from the room, the door closing softly behind her, leaving Darcy alone with the bitter taste of betrayal and his own unbearable regret.

ELIZABETH BARELY REMEMBERED HOW she had managed to slip out of the house. Her heart pounded, her chest constricting as she fled down the steps, past the hedgerows, and toward the garden maze. She had no idea how to pass through it, had never had a chance to explore it. She only knew that she had to escape the suffocating walls of Pemberley, the biting lash of her husband's words still ringing in her ears.

It felt as if the world was closing in around her, each step carrying her further into a labyrinth of emotions she had no strength to navigate. The autumn breeze whipped against her face as she stumbled through the gravel paths, her eyes stinging with unshed tears. How *dare* he? How could he hurl such accusations at her as if she were a schemer, a fortune hunter, and not a victim of circumstances?

Reaching the entrance of the garden maze, she hesitated, then plunged into its quiet, hoping the high hedges would shield her from the eyes of the household staff. She needed to be alone. She needed to scream, to shout, to demand answers from a world that had suddenly betrayed her in the worst possible way.

The sharp edges of the maze walls blurred as she pushed deeper inside, past the clipped hedges and neatly ordered paths. Oh, how she hated them all! Hated their unfamiliarity, hated their perfection. Hated the man who had brought her to live among them.

Yes, that was the word she was searching for. She *hated* Fitzwilliam Darcy.

But that was still his ring on her finger. His name she had legally taken, in desperation for some sort of way out of the chaos her life had suddenly become. All because she had tried to help someone.

Harry. Oh, Harry! How could he put her in this position?

But it was worse than the scandal that had ruined her life, wasn't it? There was more... *oh*, so much more. Stopping suddenly, she pressed her hands over her face and let out a sharp breath.

"How *could* he?" The words screamed from her lungs before she could stop them. Harry had promised her—no, *shown* her—that he was honourable, dependable. Yet, here she was, left reeling with the knowledge that he had wronged someone else, that he had carried a secret she had never suspected. She dropped her hands, staring blankly at the hedge in front of her.

Her breath hitched, the searing disbelief mingling with the anger still pulsing through her veins. He had seemed so genuine, so noble, but that letter—that vile, cruel letter—had revealed a truth she could scarcely comprehend. Another woman? A child? How could the man she'd thought so honourable have hidden something so terrible from her?

Was *no* one to be trusted?

She stopped at a bend in the path, her breath coming in ragged bursts, her hands trembling as she reached out to steady herself against the cool stone of a nearby bench. The tears she had fought so hard to keep at bay now spilt over, hot and furious, racing down her cheeks.

How had it all come to this?

Darcy had married her out of pity—no, worse—out of obligation to some false idea, bound by a sense of honour to a mistake he had never intended to make. And now... now she was trapped in a marriage with a man who despised her, all because of Harry's lies and Darcy's pride.

And such abominable pride! What did he think she had done? Rejoiced at the news of Harry's death so she could deceive and entrap the wealthier brother? How could anyone even dream up such an accusation? But Fitzwilliam Darcy seemed ready to believe it of her. He had said as much, had he not?

She sank onto the bench, burying her face in her hands as sobs wracked her body. It was not only Darcy's cruel words that cut so deeply. No, it was the sting of Harry's betrayal, the realisation that even the man she had been willing to trust, to marry, had deceived her. If Harry was capable of such duplicity, who was left in this world to trust?

Her sobs quieted, though the ache in her chest refused to subside. She raised her tear-streaked face to the sky, her eyes narrowing against the fading light. It all felt so hopeless. What was she supposed to do now? Stay locked away in this miserable arrangement, waiting for a future she could not shape or understand?

DARCY WAS STILL TREMBLING with fury as Elizabeth fled the room, the soft click of the door closing barely reaching his ears. For a moment, he stood rooted in place, his hands still gripping the edge of his desk as if it were the only thing anchoring him to reality.

Not pregnant?

The words echoed in his mind, colliding violently with every assumption, every justi-fication that had driven him to this unwanted marriage. How had it all gone so wrong? His fists clenched, the raw indignation flaring in his chest like a flame that refused to be snuffed out. She had deceived him—*they* had deceived him!

Without another thought, Darcy pushed himself from the desk and stormed toward the door. He needed to be out, to breathe, to get away from the suffocating weight of the truth that had just shattered his world. His thoughts were a hopeless jumble, clouded by a contempt that grew with every passing second.

Elizabeth Bennet was not Harry's beloved. No longer could he think of her as the woman who, in his imagination, had at least had some claim on his brother's heart. No, she was merely a woman Harry had felt *obliged* to pledge himself to for some nebulous reason, just as Darcy had done. But Harry had failed to keep his promise, leaving Darcy to shoulder this wretched burden alone.

She had trapped him, bound him to her under false pretences, and now he was stuck. The thought sickened him.

Reaching for the door, Darcy flung it open, striding purposefully toward the stables where the wide-open air might give him a shred of clarity. But then, in the distance, he saw her.

Elizabeth.

She was running, her figure disappearing toward the gardens, her skirts gathered in her fists as she fled. There was something wild in her movements, something desperate, but Darcy could not bring himself to care. If she wanted to escape, then so be it. She could run, cry, scream—none of it would change the fact that she had made a fool of him. That she had tricked him into believing he was saving her from ruin when, in truth, there had been nothing to save.

His breath came short and fast, the rage still simmering under the surface, but he turned sharply on his heel. He could not bear to follow her, to confront her again in this state. No, what he needed was something to expel the fury that was building in him, something to crush beneath his hand. The stables would not suffice. He needed to vent this rage in a place where no one could see, where no one could hear the depth of his humiliation.

The billiards room. He stalked down the corridors, his long strides eating up the distance as his chest heaved with every step.

Once inside the familiar room, the dark wood panels and gleaming green felt barely registered in his mind. His eyes locked on the cue sticks arranged neatly on the wall, and without thinking, he snatched one from its holder. The smooth wood was cool against his hand, grounding him for a brief moment, but it was not enough. The storm inside him still raged, and he needed *something* to release it. His gaze flicked toward the table, the memories of Harry and him playing together rushing back, unbidden, unwelcome.

He twisted the stick in his hands as the rage bubbled forth in a wrathful howl. "Harry, you *idiot!* How could you *leave* me with this?"

Darcy's grip tightened on the cue, his knuckles going white as he fought the urge to snap it over the edge of the table. He had done it once before, and the desire to repeat the motion surged within him. But this time, something held him back. It would have been too easy to break the cue, to smash it into splinters and pretend it was enough to release the fury inside him.

But he could not do it.

His hand trembled as he raised the cue stick, and then, with a guttural cry, he brought it down hard on the table, stopping just short of breaking it. His whole body shook, the muscles in his arm straining as he held the stick above the felt, frozen in a moment of indecision.

He wanted to destroy something, anything, but for some reason, he could not bring himself to act on the impulse. His restraint mocked him, a bitter reminder that even in his darkest moments, he could not let go. The fury roiled within him, trapped with no outlet, until finally, in a fit of impotent rage, he hurled the cue stick across the room.

"Damn it, Harry!" Darcy shouted, the sound of his voice reverberating off the walls, filling the empty space around him. His chest heaved, and for a moment, the only sound was the harsh rhythm of his own breathing.

A moment later, the door to the room swung open, and Richard hurried inside, his expression a mixture of alarm and confusion. "Darcy! What the devil has happened?"

Darcy stood rigid, still trembling with anger, his hands clenched into fists at his sides. He couldn't answer at first, couldn't find the words to articulate the depth of the betrayal he felt.

"Darcy?" Richard pressed, stepping closer. "Talk to me, man! What is it?"

Darcy's jaw worked, the words struggling to emerge as he turned away, pacing to the far end of the room. His mind was a whirlwind of rage and confusion, too chaotic to form into coherent sentences. But Richard wouldn't leave. He stood there, waiting, his presence a reminder that Darcy could not run from this.

"*She lied!*" Darcy finally managed to choke out, his voice low and venomous.

Richard frowned, his brow furrowing in confusion. "Who lied? Elizabeth?"

Darcy turned on him, his face contorted with fury. "She was *never* with child. The whole reason—the *entire reason* I married her was based on a lie! There was no child. There was *never* a child!"

Richard's eyes widened in shock. "What? You're saying... that none of it was true?"

Darcy let out a bitter laugh, the sound harsh and hollow. "She confessed it to me just now. Said she had no idea why I thought she was pregnant." He ran a hand through his hair, pacing the length of the room once more. "I thought I was saving her, Richard! I thought I was doing what Harry couldn't. And now... I'm shackled to a woman I never intended to wed, all for a lie."

Richard stared at him, thunderstruck, as if he didn't know how to respond to the sheer force of Darcy's anger. "Darcy, I—"

Darcy cut him off, his voice cracking with frustration. "I've never been so *humiliated* in my life! I—" He stopped, his chest heaving as he struggled to contain the raw emotion spilling out of him. His hands shook at his sides, and he turned away, unable to face his cousin's pity.

For a moment, there was only silence between them, the weight of Darcy's confession hanging in the air.

Darcy stalked the room, his thoughts a chaotic whirl that he couldn't seem to control. What was he supposed to do now? He had tied himself to Elizabeth Bennet, believing all the while that he was saving her from disgrace, preserving his brother's honour. And now... now it was all a lie.

"What are you going to do?"

Darcy whirled around, teeth clenched. "What *can* I do, Richard? I'm married. Bound to a woman based on a deception. And for what?" His voice shook with the force of his anger. "I've made a promise—no, a solemn oath! You ask what I'll do? I'll keep it, damn it."

Richard stood still, assessing him. "There is still the option of an annulment."

Darcy let out a derisive laugh, stalking toward the far wall as if the suggestion itself were an insult. "An annulment?" he snarled, raking his hands through his hair and tugging hard as if to wrench some sense of order from the chaos in his mind. "You think that would solve it? Break my vow as if it meant nothing?"

Richard crossed his arms, leaning against the billiards table. "The vow was made under false pretences, Darcy. You didn't know the truth."

Darcy froze, his back to Richard, staring at the dark panelling on the wall as if it could somehow hold the answers he sought. His body was still trembling with rage, but beneath it all was a deep, gnawing confusion. He couldn't see a way out of this.

Richard continued, his tone calm but firm. "You could release her, settle her somewhere else, far from Derbyshire. Give her the chance to start anew without your name binding her. It wouldn't be breaking anything if the promises were made based on lies."

How convenient he made it sound! Darcy let out a slow, tortured breath. *An annulment*. It would be the easiest path, would it not? He could wash his hands of the whole wretched affair. Give her some settlement, send her away, and forget this ever happened.

But even as the idea began to settle in his mind, something recoiled in him. The very thought of breaking a vow, even one made in ignorance, was unbearable. His father had raised him to honour his word, no matter the circumstances. How could he turn back now when he had sworn to protect her? To give her the life his brother could not?

He clenched his fists at his sides, his head hanging low. "I cannot... I *will* not..." His voice faltered, but he forced himself to continue. "I cannot annul the marriage, Richard. She is my wife now. For better or worse."

Richard exhaled slowly, clearly trying to gauge his cousin's resolve. "Are you sure, Darcy? No one would blame you for wanting to undo this. Even the law would be on your side."

"I don't care about the law!" Darcy snapped, his anger flaring again as he turned to face Richard. "I gave my word. Whether or not it was based on a lie, I will not be the man who casts his integrity aside as if it were nothing."

Richard studied him for a long moment, his expression unreadable. Then, without another word, he pushed himself off the billiards table and nodded slowly. "If that's your decision, I'll respect it." He turned toward the door but hesitated before stepping out. "But, Darcy... this isn't something you can carry alone. If you need—"

"I don't need anything," Darcy interrupted, his voice cold, final. "Just... leave me be for now."

Richard nodded, though his expression held a hint of reluctance. Then, without another word, he stepped out of the room, leaving Darcy alone with the crushing agony of his thoughts.

Chapter Thirteen

ELIZABETH'S BREATH TREMBLED AS she sat on the cold ground, knees tucked beneath her chin. Her cheeks were raw, her eyes swollen from the torrent of weeping she had unleashed—grief and fury, all tangled in knots so tight she could scarcely unravel them. The whole world had twisted around her, suffocating her beneath the weight of betrayal. Not only Darcy's cruel words but the realisation of Harry's duplicity ravaged her mind, leaving her hollow.

How could Harry have *done* that to some girl? And then laughed and charmed *her* just as if he were the finest gentleman ever to kiss a lady's hand?

She exhaled slowly, wiping her damp cheeks with the back of her hand, and at last, something tugged her from her despair—the biting chill of the evening air. She glanced up. The world had darkened without her noticing. It must be growing late, and the maze, with its towering hedges, now loomed around her like a shadowy cage. For a moment, panic flared. She could no longer see any sign of the house lights. Just the rising moon, casting its pale glow over the maze.

A huff of a laugh escaped her, bitter and faint. "Well done, Elizabeth," she muttered under her breath, her voice trembling as she rubbed her arms, trying to stave off the cold. "Lost and stranded in the middle of a garden maze. Brilliant idea."

Her thin gown was no match for the evening air, and without her pelisse or cloak, the chill was starting to seep into her bones. She had dashed out here in a blind rage, seeking refuge from the pain coursing through her, and now it seemed she was paying for that impulsiveness. It was as if the world itself was mocking her foolishness.

For a moment, she stayed there, eyes closed, trying to summon the energy to stand. There was no one to blame but herself, was there? She was entirely alone, no one to come searching for her—no one who would care, truly. She had brought this on herself, after all.

But she was not about to freeze to death out of sheer stubbornness. Huffing again, she pushed herself up to her feet, though the world swayed slightly with exhaustion and emotion. She had to get back, find the house somehow, even if she dreaded every step back towards it. The maze was vast and unfamiliar—she hadn't even explored it yet, had hardly walked Pemberley's grounds at all, and now she had the distinct feeling she had taken more than a few wrong turns.

She glanced up at the moon, casting its pale light across the garden. There were no stars visible beyond the clouds, but at least the fixed position of the moon gave her some sense of where north might be. But she had no idea where the house lay in relation to that. Would she even find her way back?

Why bother?

The thought crept in before she could stop it. The sharpness of it sent a dull ache through her chest. What was the point in struggling back to a house that could never be a home? Where she was unwelcome—reviled, even. The chill in her heart ran deeper than the night's cold.

Her husband didn't want her. She was bound to him, yes, but only because of some mistaken sense of duty. And her family? They had all but cast her out, their letters distant, concerned only with the potential for further disgrace. Who did she have now? Where could she find refuge?

Elizabeth's legs began to tremble, not from the cold but from the weight of all that she had lost. She hadn't even realised she had stopped moving until she was huddled against the base of one of the hedge walls, her arms wrapped tightly around her knees.

The path forward—back to the house, to her marriage, to her family—felt utterly bleak. She rested her head on her knees and let her eyes flutter closed. And curse it all, those blasted hedges were dense enough to block her view of the house, but not enough to keep out the evening wind. A change of weather, no doubt—an icy breeze was dipping through the branches and biting at her skin as it picked up.

What was the use? Who would care if she never found her way out?

"Just let me be lost," she whispered. She curled up tighter against the base of the hedge, hoping its thick branches would at least shield her from some of the wind—enough to find some rest.

It was so tempting to give in to the darkness around her, to let it consume her. After all, wasn't it easier than continuing to fight a battle she had already lost?

*H*OW COULD *I HAVE been so stupid?*

The question circled endlessly through Darcy's mind, refusing to be silenced. His thoughts ran like a vicious current, too powerful to escape. He had been so certain, so sure he understood every facet of the situation. Yet, here he was, undone by his own misjudgment.

Had his grief for Harry clouded his reason? Had it driven him to act too hastily? The unsettling truth was staring him in the face—he had rushed ahead, abandoning the careful judgment that had always been his safeguard.

He brooded in the dim light, the shadows of the room stretching long and cold around him. His glass of brandy sat untouched beside him. He couldn't bring himself to drink it. The taste of his own failure was enough.

But all the signs were there! Bingley sent him on that wild goose chase, pleading with him to address that... chit... in person. Mr Gardiner had fairly puddled to the floor in relief when Darcy had tendered his offer. Now, what *other* cause could there be?

But Elizabeth herself had provided the strongest clues. Her desperate grief when he told her about Harry—how much of that had been genuine sorrow for his brother and how much sheer panic that her golden goose was gone? But that did not even matter. It should have, but it did not. What mattered was the material fact he had supposed.

She hardly ate on the journey. She had an odd, greenish cast to her skin. The loosely fitted clothing he kept seeing her in—granted, her travel gown seemed to fit well enough, but Darcy had known women in their sixth month who could conceal it all beneath the bulky folds of a heavy travelling cloak.

But the sickness when she had reached Pemberley... That, he could not so easily explain away.

Travel fatigue, she had said. The disturbance of all that motion and unravelling equilibrium. Gad's teeth, but *who* simply toppled over and vomited *after* they had already got out of the carriage? No one but a pregnant woman.

Or someone caught in a lie, perhaps. Was that it?

But no... Darcy had been wracking his memory all evening. Had she *ever* explicitly said... even implied...? He curled his fist by his hand, biting into his knuckles as if the pain could help him recall.

"You know?"

That was all she had said in reference to her situation. No leading statements, no overt hints. Just an acknowledgement that there was *something* shocking to be covered up. If it was not a pregnancy, what was it?

Whatever it was, he had not found it out. And that left him with one inescapable conclusion: no one was at fault for his own misery but him. Much as he longed to place the blame squarely on Elizabeth, on Bingley, on Mr Gardiner and even Harry, it was his own rashness, his failure to gather all the facts before diving into this ill-fated marriage, that had landed him here.

Why had he been so eager to believe that fantasy? Because it gave him some means of action? Since he could not save Harry, he had to try to save *something*, even if that thing were merely a figment of imagination and coincidence? What a fool he was!

His thoughts were interrupted by a knock at the door. Darcy clenched his jaw, unwilling to entertain any company, least of all Richard. He ignored the knock, hoping his cousin would take the hint and leave him in peace.

But the knock came again, more insistent this time. Darcy remained silent, his anger simmering beneath the surface.

The door creaked open, and Richard's voice broke the stillness. "Darcy?"

Darcy did not answer, his eyes fixed on the window, his back to the door. The soft shuffle of boots across the floor told him that Richard was not planning to leave.

Richard came fully into the room, first pacing toward the bed and then coming back around until he stood before Darcy's chair in the darkness. "There you are. What the devil are you doing?"

Without looking up, Darcy muttered, "Trying to drink the cellar dry. And I need no assistance."

Richard snorted. "Well, that will have to wait," he said, tossing Darcy's coat toward him.

The coat landed in Darcy's lap, but he made no move to put it on. "Why?" he asked tersely, feeling little inclination to entertain whatever Richard wanted.

"Because Mrs Darcy is not in the house."

Darcy's head snapped up, the words jolting him to his feet. "What do you mean, she is not in the house?"

Richard's expression darkened as he glanced towards the window. "The housekeeper cannot find her. Her maid has no idea where she has gone. She has been missing for some time now, and it's starting to look like rain."

Darcy shot up from his chair, his limbs suddenly tingling with urgency. Elizabeth, out there, alone? The grounds were vast, and she had no real understanding of them. She could be lost, hurt—anything could have happened to her. His anger dropped to a dull simmer, tamped down by a surge of worry so intense it left him breathless.

He grabbed his coat from the floor and yanked it on, moving toward the door without a second thought. Richard followed, his own coat already on. They reached the hall, but just as Darcy was about to plunge down the stairs, he paused.

"Wait," he said, abruptly turning back toward his room.

"What are you doing? We need to go!"

Darcy ignored him, striding quickly back into his room. He crossed to the wardrobe and pulled out a second heavy cloak. Elizabeth would be cold when he found her. The autumn chill was well upon them for the season, and she had run out without any proper protection from the elements.

With the cloak in hand, Darcy returned to the hall, his expression grim. "Let's go."

D ARCY TOOK LONG, MEASURED strides across the front lawn, his heart thrumming in a rhythm of controlled urgency. The wind had picked up, the air heavy with the scent of rain, and though he kept his face composed, his thoughts tumbled in relentless pursuit of where she might have gone.

Richard had already sprinted toward the lake, a quick exchange between them deciding their separate paths. Darcy had hesitated for a moment, feeling the pull to follow. Water seemed to calm Elizabeth—or at least occupy her thoughts. She had admired the lake earlier that day, as well as the stream outside the coaching inn on their first day of travel. It was entirely possible she might have gone there. What if she had slipped in the mud, lost her footing, and fallen in?

But no, if she had been at the lake, surely someone would have seen her. The grounds were not deserted—even now, the footmen were spreading out in search of the mistress. He had questioned them all, and apart from an undergardener saying he had seen Mrs Darcy on the lawn earlier, no one could provide any clues.

Which meant she had hidden herself. How very fitting—her deception found out, her lie exp....

Darcy sighed as he gripped a tighter fist, his eyes scanning the bobbing lanterns around the grounds. Whatever else might be said of her, he could not for certain say that she had lied.

In fact, it could be said that she came to him with the truth as soon as she had discovered his misapprehension. She *had* looked somewhat overwrought when she asked to speak with him. Or was she simply a good actress who only came to confess because the midwife would have exposed the truth? And because Elizabeth Bennet, now Mrs Darcy, had already got what she wanted?

His knuckles ached and he forced himself to shake out his hand, draining some measure of his wrath away with it. None of that mattered now. He would not leave the worst woman in the world out by herself in the night to face a storm alone.

Suppose she had got into a drayage cart and run away to Lambton? No, that made no sense. Why would she leave her conquest behind so easily?

Darcy tried to recall the exact look on her face, her manner when they spoke those heated words. She had been... he squinted up at the clouding sky. *What* had she been?

Furious. Quaking in rage and humiliation, almost as violently as he was. And she claimed she wanted nothing to do with him or with Pemberley... said she even would have refused him, if she'd had that choice.

Could he believe any of that? Darcy cast another look around the darkened grounds—the open areas, the pleasure gardens, the folly on a distant hill—all places ladies fancied for a few moments of quiet. But if he were right about her feelings the moment she fled the house, she would have sought none of those. They were too exposed. After their last encounter, she would have sought the very opposite.

She had been too raw, too frantic.

It was a test, he supposed—a test of his ability to interpret her feelings, assuming he was operating with facts at this point. Others were searching the places that made sense, where a normal lady might have wandered. Only a fool would stumble into something close and dark with nightfall approaching.

A fool, or someone so desperate for privacy that they cared nothing for their own safety.

He turned toward the maze, its tall hedges looming ahead, shadowed under the dull, thickening sky. A place to hide. It made sense. If she had felt anything like the riot of wrath and confusion that raged within him, the maze would offer solitude, a place where no one could see her—where she could storm her feelings out in peace.

The entrance yawned before him as he stepped inside, the slightly taller grass here swishing softly against his boots. The branches reached high overhead, cutting off much of the fading light, leaving only the faintest outline of a path stretching ahead. Darcy pressed on, his mind circling like the twisting corridors around him.

How far had she gone? How long had she been out here?

He moved quickly through the narrow walkways, taking each turn with purpose, only to be met by more endless hedge walls. His breath grew more laboured as he forged ahead, sweeping his eyes over every nook, every corner, his heart thumping harder with each wrong turn.

He had searched the maze many times as a boy. He remembered the frustration, the helplessness of feeling trapped within its tall boundaries. How had he forgot just how vast this place was? But this was no child's game—this was different. If she were lost in here, alone in the growing darkness, what state might he find her in?

That was when the rain began. It started as a faint drizzle, soft and barely noticeable, as Darcy moved deeper into the maze. He hardly registered it at first, so focused was he on the search. But as he pressed on, the drizzle thickened, the air growing colder, heavier, the dampness seeping into his skin.

Another wrong turn. Egad, this was *his* home. His maze! He knew it like the back of his hand, but in the darkness, the path looped back on itself, leading him in circles. If even he could become lost so quickly, what hope would she have? If she were truly out here. His pulse quickened, anger flaring at the thought of her wandering aimlessly, at his own inability to make sense of this labyrinth.

"Elizabeth!" His voice carried down the twisting paths, swallowed by the dense walls of the hedge. There was no answer.

He stopped, leaning against the hedge for a moment, the rough branches scratching his palm. His mind throbbed with every worst possibility. Had he overlooked a turn somewhere? Was she elsewhere, at the lake, or even inside the house now, safe and warm while he bumbled in circles like a fool?

He started forward again, his foot catching awkwardly on a root, his balance slipping so that he very nearly dropped his lantern.

"Blast!" He barely kept himself from falling, his hands catching the hedge, breathing hard as the irritation simmered into something hotter.

He cursed under his breath and pressed on, turning left this time, trying to recall the maze's layout. He was losing time, losing even the moonlight behind gathering clouds—losing patience. Perhaps this was madness. Perhaps—

What if she had fallen somewhere? What if, blinded by tears or rage, she had slipped into one of the many ditches along the path? Or worse—what if she *had* found her way to the lake with the mud so treacherous? No one would see her in the dark. Perhaps not ever again.

The rain pelted his face, soaking through his shirt and dripping from his hair, but he didn't care. Elizabeth was out here, somewhere, and he could not leave her. His breath was heavy, a mix of exhaustion and anxiety, and just as he considered turning back—perhaps he had gone the wrong way after all—his foot collided with something soft.

Elizabeth.

He lifted the lantern to shine on her. Her small, curled form was huddled against the base of the hedge, barely visible in the deepening shadows.

Darcy simply stared, the sight of her stealing his breath. She was drenched, her dark hair matted and tangled from the rain, her face pale and drawn. Her knees were pulled tightly to her chest, her arms wrapped around them in a feeble attempt to shield herself from the cold.

Darcy dropped to his knees beside her, his heart hammering in his chest. "Elizabeth!"

She did not stir. Rainwater trickled down her face, her lips pale and trembling.

His hand closed over her shoulder, shaking her gently. "Elizabeth, wake up!"

A low groan escaped her, and her eyes fluttered open, though her gaze was unfocused, distant.

"Mr... D-Darcy?" Her voice was faint, nearly swallowed by the relentless downpour.

Relief washed over him, though it was quickly overshadowed by fear. She was far too cold—her skin icy beneath his fingers, her body trembling uncontrollably. He shrugged off the extra cloak he had brought and draped it over her, enveloping her in the heavy, soaked fabric.

"You're freezing," he muttered, his brow furrowing as he tucked the cloak more tightly around her. "You should never have come out here."

"I... g-got l-los-st..."

"What were you thinking, wandering into the maze alone just before dark? No lantern, no cloak? What a stupid thing to do!"

She lifted her head fractionally, her eyes glittering in the weak light of his lantern even as her teeth chattered uncontrollably. "W-want-ted t-to g-g-get aw-way ffr-from-m *y-you*."

Darcy stiffened, his mouth frozen. He tried to make some reply, but there was... nothing.

And no time to examine it now. He shook his head.

"We need to get you back inside." Without waiting for a response, Darcy bent down and scooped her into his arms, lifting her easily. Her body trembled violently, and her legs were likely so numb from the cold that he doubted they could support her weight. She certainly would have no powers to coordinate her limbs.

The rain continued to fall in sheets, soaking them both through, but Darcy paid it no mind. He held her close, shielding her as best he could, and moved through the maze as quickly as the uneven paths allowed, the cold biting into his skin with every step.

The path twisted and turned, and he cursed the complexity of the maze under his breath. Elizabeth had got her arms around his neck, and though he was grateful that she was in some part, at least, helping him by holding tight, he was nearly afraid she was going to choke him. But every muscle in her body was rigid with cold—she probably could not have slackened her grip on him even if she tried.

Finally, after what felt like an eternity, the maze gave way to the open lawn, and Darcy spotted the faint glow of lights from the house in the distance. Thank Heaven! He had finally remembered which turns to take. He clutched her closer, her body still shuddering in his arms, and carried her inside.

Chapter Fourteen

ELIZABETH SAT TREMBLING BY the fire, her skin still pale from the cold that had seeped into her bones. Mrs Reynolds bustled about, directing Susan and another maid to bring more blankets and stoke the fire higher. The housekeeper was attentive, even gentle, as she tucked a thick woollen blanket around Elizabeth's shoulders while Susan rubbed her hands with a warm towel.

For all her shivering, Elizabeth's mind was sharper than ever. Her thoughts were crisp and numerous, though none made sense. Why were they treating her with such care? She was no one of consequence—certainly not someone deserving of this level of attention. And yet, Mrs Reynolds behaved as if it were the most natural thing in the world to tend to her, as though Elizabeth truly were the proper mistress of Pemberley. There was no hint of disdain, no reproach.

This was the same kindness she had experienced the previous day—when they all thought she was with child. Was that still what they believed? Did they not know? Surely, the rumours had reached the servants by now. Darcy's shouts of outrage had to have been loud enough for the entire household to hear. Perhaps, like Mr Darcy, they had assumed the worst—that she had deliberately taken advantage of him.

And yet, despite all of that, here they were. Kind, patient, and unfailingly attentive, as if she had not just made a fool of herself by getting lost in the maze like some careless child. As if she had not been dragged to Pemberley by a man who wed her under false pretences.

What would they think of her when they learned the truth? The truth that had already shattered her own sense of self-worth. Would they feel deceived? Would they think her an imposter, imposing on the family, clinging to an honour she did not deserve? Would anyone even give her a chance to tell what the truth was?

Elizabeth bit her lip, glancing warily at Mrs Reynolds, half expecting some sign of disapproval to reveal itself. But the housekeeper merely smiled gently as she handed her a cup of hot tea, urging her to drink.

"Thank you," Elizabeth managed to murmur, her teeth still chattering slightly as she took the cup with both hands. The warmth of it against her palms was a small comfort, but it did little to quiet her confused thoughts.

Why were they still so kind? She hadn't meant to deceive anyone, of course. The misapprehension had come from Mr Darcy, and yet surely they would feel slighted, misled. It seemed only natural. But no—their kindness never faltered. The maids brought more blankets, more tea, more coals for the fire—not as if she were some foolish interloper, but as if she belonged in this place.

She sank deeper into the chair. Perhaps she could permit herself... just this little indulgence, letting herself take comfort in their care, for she truly needed it now. Her teeth slowly ceased their chattering, though the tremors in her hands took longer to still. She was finally beginning to feel the warmth spread through her body again, the deep cold of the night beginning to leave her, though the confusion in her heart lingered like a shadow.

But there was another question that troubled her most of all: why had Mr Darcy come for her personally?

She could still see him—his face set in grim determination as he carried her through the maze, his arms strong around her, his coat sodden, and his body shivering from the cold. Why had he come out in the rain, risking his own health, for a woman he clearly despised? He had every reason to hate her. His words had made that painfully clear, had they not?

So why had he searched for her? He could have had his servants do it. Why had he carried her in himself, soaked and shivering, clutching her to his chest to impart what little warmth his body could provide? Why order her every comfort, lingering in the hall, dripping wet himself, until he saw her fire built up to his satisfaction?

"Are you feeling warmer, Mrs Darcy?" Susan asked, helping Elizabeth into her bed as Mrs Reynolds finished preparing the room.

Elizabeth nodded, though her thoughts were elsewhere. She allowed herself to collapse into the pillows, her body exhausted, though her mind still whirled with the strange contradictions of her situation. The warmth of the blankets was comforting, but it only served to remind her how entirely dependent she was on the goodwill of these people—people who, for all she knew, might soon turn against her when the truth was fully understood.

"Thank you, Susan," Elizabeth murmured, watching the fire flicker in the hearth, trying to make sense of it all.

Just then, there was a soft knock on the door. Elizabeth looked up in mild surprise, sitting up a little in the bed. Mrs Reynolds opened the door to reveal another maid, who curtsied politely and stepped inside.

"Mr Darcy sent me, ma'am," the maid said.

Elizabeth blinked, her heart giving a strange little flutter. "What does Mr Darcy want?"

The maid smiled faintly. "The master wished to know if you were well, ma'am. He was concerned."

Elizabeth's lips parted in surprise, and she stared at the maid, at a loss for words. Mr Darcy was still concerned? That he should ask after her well-being at all was bewildering. The same man who had practically accused her of trickery and deception was now sending messages to inquire about her health?

"I see," Elizabeth said softly, nodding more out of reflex than understanding. She was too drained to ask further questions, too perplexed to know what to make of it. "Tell him I am well, and... and tell him thank you."

The maid bobbed a curtsy. "The master will be pleased to hear it, ma'am."

Elizabeth watched the door close, her mind tumbling through a dozen thoughts. She was too tired to untangle any of them, too exhausted to make sense of the strange contradictions that now coloured her every interaction with Mr Darcy.

She lay back against the pillows, pulling the blankets tighter around her, her body finally relaxing after the cold ordeal of the evening. But her mind would not rest. No matter how she tried to calm herself, one question refused to be silenced: Why would he care?

It made no sense. None of it made sense.

But as the exhaustion overtook her, Elizabeth's thoughts slowly dulled, the questions slipping into the haze of sleep. She was too tired, too drained to seek answers tonight.

ELIZABETH'S BODY SLOWLY WARMED the next morning, a gentle, comfortable stirring to awareness. Despite the storm of emotions that had carried her to sleep, she felt surprisingly refreshed. Her eyes fluttered open, and she stared at the canopy above her bed, blinking in confusion. What time was it? The room was bright, the sun streaming in through the curtains some maid must have opened earlier. Had she truly slept through that? She sat up and squinted at the small clock on the mantle across the room. Ten o'clock!

In Hertfordshire, at Longbourn, she would have been up, dressed, and perhaps even out for a walk by now. She did not know the established routine here, at Pemberley, but everything seemed slower, more languid. Perhaps the Darcys were too well-to-do to keep country hours.

She sat up, glancing toward the bellpull by her bed. Was she meant to summon her maid? Surely, in a grand estate like this, the mistress did not dress herself. But after last night's ridiculousness, Elizabeth could hardly bring herself to ask anything more of the servants. She had already been such a bother. How could she impose further?

No, she would dress herself. The act of relying on someone to button her gown—an entirely unnecessary indulgence—felt too much like an acknowledgement that she belonged here. And she did not. Not truly.

Elizabeth slipped from bed and dressed herself in the quiet of her room, her fingers still stiff as she fastened each button with care. Once dressed, she paced the floor for a while, trying to decide what to do.

She had to speak with Mr Darcy again, distasteful as the duty was. Perhaps there was a way out of this entire mess for both of them. He had made his disappointment and anger plain enough—he felt she had deceived him, tricked him into marriage. Surely, he would be as eager to be rid of her as she was to leave.

It hadn't even been a real marriage yet. Not in every sense. The thought sent a flush of both embarrassment and determination through her. Yes, an annulment was the only solution. Surely, he would agree.

The only question was where to find him.

Elizabeth was unfamiliar with Mr Darcy's habits. She wandered downstairs, aimlessly passing by several maids and footmen who offered deferential nods and greetings as she passed. Too uncomfortable to ask any of them for help, her pride stiffened her spine. She would not appear desperate.

The most sensible place to look for him would be the breakfast room, so she made her way in that direction. When she entered, however, she found not Mr Darcy but Colonel Fitzwilliam. He sat at the table, casually picking at his plate with a steaming cup of coffee beside him, the morning post spread out on the table.

Elizabeth curtsied, intending to turn away and resume her search, but the colonel looked up and called after her. "Mrs Darcy!"

She paused, then reluctantly turned back toward him. "Good morning, Colonel."

The colonel smiled warmly and gestured toward the table. "Looking for Darcy?"

She hesitated, but there was little point in pretending otherwise. "Yes, I am."

Fitzwilliam nodded and gestured toward a window. "He went out riding early this morning and has not yet returned. Do join me—unless, of course, you would rather keep up the search?"

Elizabeth felt the flush rise to her cheeks, and she offered a small, reluctant smile. "Thank you, Colonel. I suppose I might sit for a moment."

She took a seat at the table, folding her hands in her lap. Colonel Fitzwilliam set the paper aside and offered her a kind smile. "How are you feeling after your ordeal last night?"

She drew an unsteady breath, surreptitiously wiping her palms on the fabric of her gown under the table. "Stupid."

Fitzwilliam chuckled and leaned back in his chair. "I can imagine your pride must have taken a bit of a bruise."

"Pride?" she asked, raising a brow. "What makes you think I have any?"

The colonel grinned, then took a sip of his coffee. "Just a guess, Mrs Darcy." He folded the paper and set it aside entirely, giving her his full attention. "Have you met all the maids yet?"

Elizabeth blinked, taken aback. "I am not..." She trailed off, then cleared her throat. "I mean, it is not a title I ought to hold."

Fitzwilliam scoffed lightly. "Merely the shock of it all. You will get on well enough once you've adjusted."

Elizabeth shook her head, unable to conceal her disbelief. "Do you honestly believe I ought to consider staying here as Mrs Darcy? Surely, you know your cousin married me believing I was with Harry's child. And that... that was not true."

The colonel shrugged as if the matter were not as serious as she thought. "I have heard of marriages that began for far less auspicious reasons. Why should that trouble you?"

Elizabeth's eyes widened. "Because the entire thing was a lie... or rather, a misunderstanding. How can there be any truth or honesty in that?"

He gave her a knowing look. "Which was it then—a lie, or a misunderstanding?"

Elizabeth shifted in her chair, the hairs on the back of her neck prickling. "A misunderstanding, on my part."

The colonel nodded. "And surely, on Darcy's part as well. Darcy has never lied in his life. I am not even sure he knows how."

She leaned forward slightly, shaking her head in frustration. "That does not matter. We both misunderstood one another."

Fitzwilliam regarded her curiously, his gaze thoughtful. "Your honour must mean a great deal to you, Mrs Darcy. Even to the point that you would injure yourself to uphold it."

Elizabeth blinked, surprised by the insight. After a pause, she nodded. "Yes. It does."

The colonel grunted softly, then leaned back in his chair again. "In that, you and Darcy are well matched."

She stiffened. "There is nothing well matched about us."

The colonel merely smiled, twirling his empty coffee cup in his hands for a moment. Then, he looked up. "May I ask you something?"

Elizabeth hesitated, but eventually nodded. "You may."

The colonel's tone shifted slightly, taking on a more serious note. "Were you truly in such dire straits after Harry's death? I shall not ask after the specifics, but did he owe you the... ah... the fulfilment of a promise?"

Elizabeth swallowed, the sting of Harry's betrayal still fresh in her heart. She wetted her lips and slowly nodded. "Yes. But I understand I am not the only one."

The colonel stood and crossed to refill his coffee cup. "That reply will do for the present." He glanced at her plate. "Now, try some of Cook's smoked ham. It is excellent."

D ARCY SWUNG HIMSELF OFF his horse, the reins slipping from his gloved hand
as he passed the animal to the waiting groom. His breath came in ragged bursts,
his chest heaving. He had galloped for miles, and though his horse was now done in,
Darcy himself had been inclined to gallop several more before returning to the house.
The moisture in the air, the chill of the day should have cooled him, but his body was
drenched with sweat, his pulse still hammering in his ears.

"Walk him around, cool him down," he ordered the stable hand, his voice gruffer
than he intended. The young man nodded silently and led the horse away, leaving Darcy
standing alone for a moment in the dim, misty morning.

He dragged a hand through his damp hair, frustrated that the exertion had not given
him the clarity he sought. His muscles ached from the ride, his hands stiff from gripping
the reins too tightly, yet none of it had lessened the confusion in his mind.

How had everything spiralled so wildly out of control? He had set out with every
intention of fulfilling his duty, of righting the wrongs his brother had left behind, only
to find himself entangled in a marriage he never wanted. And worse, in a marriage based
on a misunderstanding that could have been avoided had he simply exercised his usual
restraint, asked the right questions, and investigated more carefully before acting.

Indignant outrage warred with a bitter disappointment in himself, both emotions
fighting for dominance as they had since the moment Elizabeth had confessed the truth.

Yet... why had she said it? And why had she fled the house after her confession? Why
would a woman who had supposedly tricked him into marriage, who had every reason to
want his protection, now claim she wanted nothing to do with him?

He had turned it over and over in his mind all night. That one declaration, uttered with
such biting conviction, had haunted him long after he had returned to his bedchamber.
Elizabeth had been vulnerable, freezing in the rain, her teeth chattering from the cold,
and yet she had found the strength to tell him that she wished to be well rid of him.

Women of lesser character would indulge in such histrionics merely to invoke pity, to garner sympathy after an argument, but Elizabeth's words had not rung with such false tones. She had meant them.

Why? What could she possibly stand to gain by pushing him away? He could not understand it, and the not knowing stung him worse than any sense of betrayal. It did not fit the narrative he had constructed in his mind—the one where she had schemed, had manipulated him into this marriage. Yet, if she had truly schemed, why now would she act as if she wanted no part in it?

Darcy shook his head, pushing the thoughts aside for the moment. He wasn't ready to solve that mystery just yet. His limbs ached, and his head felt muddled.

As he reached the house, he handed off his hat, coat, and gloves to the waiting footman. "Where is Colonel Fitzwilliam?" he asked, though he had little inclination to see anyone. His voice sounded too harsh, even to his own ears, and he swallowed to steady it.

The butler bowed slightly. "The colonel is in the library, sir. With Mrs Darcy."

Darcy clenched his jaw, his teeth grinding against one another as the words landed. He had hoped to find Richard alone. The prospect of speaking to his cousin had been a welcome one—someone who could help untangle the mess in his mind—but now that option was clouded by the presence of Elizabeth.

Of course, she would be with him. Richard had probably sought her out to soothe troubled waters. He always had possessed a way of making people feel at ease, of engaging in conversation without judgment. Richard probably thought he was helping or something stupid like that.

"Very good," Darcy muttered, dismissing the butler with a curt nod. He could not face her yet.

He strode up the stairs, his feet heavy against the wooden steps as he made his way to his room. The prospect of shedding his damp clothing and dressing in something dry and comfortable was the only thing he could cling to for a shred of relief. If nothing else, he would regain some semblance of dignity before deciding what to do next.

Chapter Fifteen

D ARCY DESCENDED THE STAIRS, his footsteps echoing in the stillness of the hall. Questions still ate at him, but he was determined to shake them off, if only for a few hours. Once at the bottom, he turned toward his study, bypassing the morning room where he had no appetite to sit for breakfast. Work would be his solace. Letters, correspondence—anything that required his attention and drew him away from the rat's nest of emotions he had been trying so desperately to untangle.

Once inside the study, he closed the door behind him and moved to his desk. The familiar scent of ink and paper greeted him, and he breathed in deeply, finding comfort in the structured order of his workspace. The correspondence awaited him in a neat stack, and he pulled out the first letter, breaking the wax seal with his usual precision.

Lord Matlock's handwriting stared up at him—a formal inquiry about the state of Harry's affairs, no doubt. Darcy read the lines with measured focus, responding in his mind as he went along. His uncle was predictable in his inquiries, and the letter held no surprises. With a sigh, he set it aside and moved to the next, a report from his steward about a tenant dispute. Another straightforward matter. He scribbled a few notes in the margin, prepared to send instructions later.

And then, his eyes fell on the familiar handwriting of his aunt, Lady Catherine. Of course, it had only been a matter of time before she had something to say about Harry's death. Darcy picked up the letter, turning it over in his hands. He was tempted to leave it unopened. Lady Catherine's words would hardly be of comfort—they rarely were—and he was in no mood to be lectured on what *ought* to be done for the sake of the family's future.

But the next letter in his stack caught his eye. The agent handling the disposition of Harry's London flat. Darcy frowned, feeling the ever-present acid burn in his stomach. The agent had written to update him on the sale of the flat, no doubt. And the matter of Harry's lingering affairs was always a difficult subject.

With a resigned sigh, Darcy returned to Lady Catherine's letter. Better to hear from her than to dive into the mess of Harry's things just yet. He cracked the seal and scanned the contents quickly.

As expected, her words were far from heartfelt. Lady Catherine was more concerned with Anne's prospects now that Harry was gone than with offering any true condolences. Darcy scoffed as he read her presumptuous demands. She insisted, as he feared she would, that it was now his *duty* to step into Harry's place and marry Anne, ensuring the continuation of the family line.

Darcy shook his head, unable to contain his exasperation. Anne? He could never marry Anne. Not before, and certainly not now. Neither he nor Harry had ever had any desire to marry her before, and the idea of Darcy wedding his sickly, petulant cousin to birth the next heir of Pemberley was utterly preposterous.

If only Lady Catherine knew the truth—that he had already married a woman in Harry's place, albeit for reasons that were far from ideal. And truth be told, he would rather marry Elizabeth all over again—with all her defiance, her sharp words, and the misunderstandings that plagued their union—than marry Anne. At least Elizabeth had spirit and spoke for herself—rather too much, as it happened. He could not imagine living with a woman like Anne, who was silent, meek, and obedient to the point of paralysis. A doormat.

And at least Elizabeth had appeared to truly mourn for Harry. He doubted Anne could even work up a single tear. If she thought of his brother at all, it was probably with disdain for dying instead of obliging her.

Darcy shuddered at the thought. No, he would never have that.

Lady Catherine's letter was set aside to be dealt with later, when he had more energy for the inevitable confrontation that would follow. Instead, he picked up the agent's letter, bracing himself for the details of Harry's London flat.

But as he read, the letter slipped from his fingers, landing on the desk with a soft thud.

London

14 September

M Y DEAR MR DARCY,

  I write to inform you of an alarming discovery regarding your late brother's London flat. When I arrived to inspect the property for a potential buyer, I was greeted by an unsettling scene. The flat had been ransacked, with locks broken, furniture overturned, and drawers pulled out from their places. The rooms were left in utter disarray as if someone had been searching for something of value.

  Fortunately, all papers, money, and personal effects had already been safely removed under your instructions, but it is evident that the intruder was not aware of this. I can only surmise that the culprit hoped to find something remaining that would be of use to them.

  In light of this situation, I seek your guidance on how you would like me to proceed. Would you prefer that I inform the local authorities? I can also make inquiries with the neighbouring tenants and the building staff, though I fear this may not yield any leads. Nevertheless, I await your instructions.

  Yours sincerely,

Woodrow Barker

Agent for Darcy Estates

D ARCY'S PULSE QUICKENED, FURY rising within him like a storm. Who would *do* such a thing? Someone must have known that Harry was dead, or at the very least, absent from London for some time. It had to be someone who had been watching, waiting—someone close to Harry, or someone who had been keeping an eye on the Darcy family.

The idea of it festered, a deep, seething rage building as he rose from his desk, unable to sit still any longer. He paced the study, his hands clenched into fists at his sides. How could anyone so disrespect the dead? Who would stoop so low as to rob Harry's flat, to violate what little remained of his brother's life?

He prowled back and forth, his mind racing with possibilities. Perhaps the Earl had made Harry's death more public than Darcy had intended. Or perhaps someone had discovered the Darcy house in mourning, knowing that no one would return to London for some time.

But what were they after? There was nothing of value left. Nothing that could be taken—unless, of course, Harry had hidden something that Darcy missed. Money, military papers, letters, and personal articles, Darcy had already secured. But what if he *had* missed something? What if the person who broke in had been searching for more than just money?

Unable to contain his anger any longer, Darcy stormed down the hallway toward the library, where he knew Richard would be. His fury radiated off him in waves as he threw open the door, his voice sharp with urgency.

"Richard! I need to speak with you at once!"

Richard looked up casually from where he sat by the fire, a bemused smile playing at his lips. "Ah, the lion has emerged from his lair," he drawled, one brow arching.

Darcy's gaze swept across the room, and he froze for a moment as his eyes landed on Elizabeth, standing by a bookshelf. She was composed, her posture erect, meeting his gaze without flinching. She did not look away or shrink under the heat of his anger. In fact, she appeared...challenging. Impassive.

His anger faltered slightly, a ripple of something else passing through him as he swallowed and inclined his head curtly, acknowledging her without offering a proper greeting. It was far from polite, but it was the best he could manage at the moment.

Elizabeth arched a brow in response, her chin lifting slightly, as though daring him to say more.

Darcy quickly turned his attention back to his cousin. "Richard, if you can spare a moment...?"

Richard rose reluctantly, offering Elizabeth a short bow. "Of course," he said smoothly, though there was a glint of curiosity in his eyes. "Beg your pardon, Mrs Darcy."

Darcy barely waited for Richard to follow before leading the way out of the room, his mind still consumed with the questions that plagued him. Someone had ransacked Harry's flat. Someone wanted something from Harry even after his death. And Darcy was going to find out who.

D ARCY LED RICHARD SWIFTLY into his study, his pulse still thrumming with a potent mix of anger and disbelief. He shut the door firmly behind them and crossed the room in long, impatient strides. Richard leaned against the back of a chair, arms crossed, watching Darcy pace.

"I just received word from my agent in London," Darcy began, his voice low, barely controlled. "The one managing the disposition of Harry's affairs. Someone broke into his flat."

Richard straightened, his casual demeanour falling away. "What? Are you certain?"

"Locks broken, furniture tossed about, drawers rifled through. The place was ransacked." Darcy's voice grew more clipped as the rage simmered under his skin. "I had already been there, when I was in London, so I know there was nothing left—no papers, no personal effects, no valuables. But someone was looking for something, all the same."

Richard let out a slow breath, clearly shaken. "That's... appalling. To disrespect the dead in such a way—what sort of monster does that?"

Darcy's jaw clenched, and he turned back to his desk, gripping the edge until his knuckles turned white. "Someone who knew Harry was dead. Someone who wanted something from him—something specific."

"Any idea who it could be?" Richard asked, brow furrowed, clearly trying to process the shocking news.

Darcy turned back to his cousin, his eyes sharp. "Do you know of any associates of Harry's in the army or in London? Someone with reason to believe there was something in that flat worth taking?"

"Do you mean besides George Wickham?"

Darcy clenched his jaw. "Anyone."

Richard shook his head slowly, his brow lined with thought. "Harry and I barely crossed paths these last few years. We were stationed in different places, and even in army circles, there were assignments we couldn't discuss. Too many secrets to keep. You know that."

Darcy raked a hand through his hair, his frustration mounting. He looked back at the note on his desk, the words swimming before him. "What about Charles Bingley? Did Harry ever introduce you to him?"

Richard's eyes narrowed as he considered the question. "Bingley? A couple of years ago, perhaps. But I haven't seen him since. Surely, you don't think Bingley could have had anything to do with this?"

Darcy shook his head, though the doubt lingered. "No, not directly. But Bingley might know something. He was close enough to Harry—enough to know that something was wrong."

Richard sighed heavily, rubbing his temples. "For Heaven's sake, Darcy. Why don't you just ask Mrs Darcy what she knows? She was closer to Harry at the end than either of us. She has secrets of her own, I daresay."

Darcy's lips tightened. "I have been meaning to. But yesterday... and then last evening... there simply has not been an opportunity."

Richard raised an eyebrow, clearly unimpressed with that excuse. "Now seems like just such an opportune moment, wouldn't you say? The lady is quite at her leisure."

Darcy swallowed. He tapped his fingers on the desk, considering his next move. His study, with its heavy air of authority, was hardly the place for such a conversation. It would intimidate her—no, that was not right. She was not easily intimidated, but it would put her on the defensive. He needed her to feel comfortable, free to speak openly.

"You are right," Darcy finally said. "I will speak to her now."

D ARCY PAUSED OUTSIDE THE library door, his hand resting on the latch. He had intended to stride in with confidence, but now, standing here, uncertain of how to approach her, he hesitated. How was he to greet her after everything that had passed between them? What could he possibly say to set her at ease while still getting the answers he needed?

She was not a stupid woman. He had no idea what her character truly was, but this much, he could say for certain. She was intelligent, and she had enough self-awareness to deal with him frankly. Perhaps he would start there.

He pushed the door open, stepping in quietly so as not to startle her. The soft crackle of the fire greeted him first, filling the room with a warmth that might do something to soften the chilly reception he expected. His eyes fell on Elizabeth, curled up in an oversized chair by the fire, deeply absorbed in a book.

Her hair, just at her temples, had slipped loose from its pins, letting the shorter wisps trickle in unruly waves around her ears, the flickering light catching in the strands. One foot was tucked beneath her in the chair, the other dangling lazily over the side, her body relaxed, as if for the first time in weeks, she had found a brief moment of peace.

Darcy's breath caught in his throat. There was something painfully intimate about the scene—something that stirred within him a vision of domesticity he had not allowed himself to entertain. It was the kind of scene he had imagined once, long ago, for his future—a wife by the fire, reading quietly, content in their shared company.

The sight of Elizabeth like this, so at ease, brought an unexpected pang to his chest. *Why*, after a lifetime of meeting and rejecting candidates who were infinitely more appropriate prospects, did it have to be *this* woman who made that feeling swell in him?

He hated to disturb her, but there was no avoiding the conversation. Clearing his throat, he took a step closer. Elizabeth stirred but did not startle. Her eyes, dark with contemplation, snapped up to him immediately, her attention fully on him now. She shifted in her chair, straightening herself but still holding the book loosely in her lap.

Darcy hesitated for a moment, then gestured to the chair opposite her. "Would you mind if I joined you for a moment?"

Elizabeth blinked, her expression cool and unreadable. "It is your house, Mr Darcy."

He gave a small nod of acknowledgement, somewhat chastened by her reminder, and sat down in the chair she had indicated. As he settled into it, his eyes remained on her, watching her more closely than he had before. Despite the fire, her pallor was still noticeable, and there were faint shadows under her eyes, the telltale signs of strain and exhaustion.

A sharp spear of guilt twisted within him. Had he put those marks there? Had his misjudgment and harsh words taken their toll on her more deeply than he had realised?

"I... I trust you are feeling better today?"

Elizabeth sighed, brushing a loose strand of hair behind her ear as she gave him a wary look. "Why is everyone so concerned about my health?" she asked, her tone edged with weariness. "I assure you, Mr Darcy, I am very well."

Darcy's eyes sharpened as he leaned forward slightly, meeting her gaze more directly. "There were reasons for such concern. Some perhaps unfounded, but not all of them."

Her expression softened for a moment, then she waved a hand dismissively. "There are none now. As I said, I am quite well."

He nodded, though the answer did little to settle his nerves. Clearing his throat, he began to speak again, but before he could get the words out, she cut him off.

"What has happened?"

Darcy looked up sharply. "What makes you ask that?"

Elizabeth arched a brow, her gaze steady. "You did not call the colonel out of the room so urgently to invite him to tea, I imagine. Something has happened."

A small, reluctant smile tugged at the corner of Darcy's mouth, though he quickly suppressed it. He could not help but feel a glimmer of appreciation for her directness, her sharp reasoning. "Yes," he admitted. "Something did happen. But before I explain that, I need to understand your real history with Harry. How did you meet my brother?"

Elizabeth's expression tightened for a moment, her hands stilling on the book in her lap. She took a breath before answering, her voice quieter now. "We were introduced through Mr Bingley. My uncle and Mr Bingley had business contacts in common, and they crossed paths at a few parties. Mr Bingley demonstrated an immediate interest in Jane, and about a month after they began courting, Mr Bingley introduced me to Captain Darcy."

Darcy tilted his head, his eyes narrowing slightly. "Did my brother declare his interest in you right away?"

Elizabeth shook her head, a faint, rueful smile on her lips. "No. In fact, one of the first things he said to me was a rather delicately phrased announcement that he was not free to marry where he chose. He even said he envied Mr Bingley that liberty."

Darcy sat back in his chair, surprised by the revelation. "He told you that?"

"He did," she said, her voice tinged with sadness. "He was quite clear, though not unkind. I think he wanted to put me on my guard—to ensure that no matter how much we enjoyed each other's company, he would not form an attachment he could not satisfy."

"You were in company often?"

"Yes." She nodded. "We passed several evenings keeping one another entertained. We had something of an agreement, he and I—he would keep close to me and I to him because we understood each other's intentions. He did not have to fear that I would form expectations of him, and I was quite confident that he would advise me which 'gentlemen' in the room to avoid. We talked a great deal—came to know one another rather well over cards and piano performances, and even danced a few times. But there was nothing more than that."

Darcy's gaze grew more intent as he studied her. "What changed, then?"

Elizabeth's throat worked, and she glanced down, fumbling with the pages of the book in her lap. "That is a long story, Mr Darcy."

He crossed his legs, leaning back in his chair with an air of quiet determination. "I have all afternoon to hear it," he replied, his voice firm but not unkind.

Elizabeth stilled, her eyes flickering up to meet his, and for a moment, she was silent, as she considered how to begin.

Chapter Sixteen

London
One Month Earlier

"Miss Bennet, you'll have me thoroughly out of breath if we keep this pace!" Elizabeth's partner teased, spinning her through the final turn of the dance.

Elizabeth laughed, her breath coming quick as she curtsied. "Then I have done my job well," she replied. "Be sure to save something for your next partner, sir." Her heart still fluttered with the exhilaration of the reel, the music lingering in the air as couples began to leave the floor.

The gentleman laughed and bowed with a flourish. "I daresay you have ruined me for the evening, Miss Bennet. A pity you haven't a dance left this evening, or I should have asked for a second."

"A pity, indeed." Elizabeth curtsied in reply to the compliment. Her partner led her to the edge of the dance floor and moved off. She glanced eagerly around the crowded room because Captain Darcy had spoken for her next dance. She couldn't help but smile. His easy charm had always made their conversations light and enjoyable, and besides, his tall, athletic figure made him a highly diverting partner. She had been looking forward to her dance with him all evening.

But just then, she caught sight of him slipping out toward the portico, his steps seeming hurried and unnatural. How very odd! Captain Harold Darcy was always prompt to claim her hand, and he never left a lady waiting. Perhaps he forgot? Strange, but surely there was a reasonable explanation.

Elizabeth made her way through the clusters of dancers pairing off for the next set, the sound of laughter and clinking glasses fading behind her. Curious—and with a sense of expectation fluttering in her chest—she made her way toward the garden doors, weaving through the throng of guests who lingered near the edges of the ballroom.

The cool evening air greeted her as she stepped out onto the terrace, the muffled strains of music fading behind her. The contrast was refreshing, the crispness of the night calming after the warm bustle of the ballroom. Lanterns lit the portico, casting soft pools of light across the stone walkway while the faint scent of autumn leaves mingled with the last bloom of summer roses.

Elizabeth strolled along the length of the portico, her heart light with the pleasant anticipation of a quiet moment with her favourite gentleman. They were friends, she and he—friends who understood one another well enough to know they could never be more, and that had opened the door to an artless, open sort of camaraderie that she had grown to depend on through these long evenings among strangers. The night was peaceful, and the stars glittered faintly overhead, making the scene all the more inviting.

As she approached, the sound of voices broke through the serenity. She slowed her steps, her brow furrowing as shouts of anger reached her ears. A low, harsh murmur carried on the breeze, the words indistinct but unmistakably tense.

"Blast you, if you so much as breathe a word of this, your career is over, Darcy!"

Elizabeth hesitated, peering through the shadows toward the covered portico where the voices seemed to be coming from. The light of a nearby lantern flickered, and the glow of glass doors nearby illuminated two figures standing close together. Her breath caught—one of the men was unmistakably Captain Darcy in his dress uniform. The other was also in uniform, but she did not recognise him yet.

What was happening? Elizabeth moved a little closer, her curiosity mingling with concern as she tried to make sense of the situation. The other man—a lieutenant, by his insignia—was entirely unfamiliar to her. The lieutenant snarled, shoving Harry back a step before lunging again. His fist sailed through the air, narrowly missing Harry's face as he ducked.

Harry, his own expression fierce, landed a solid punch to the man's jaw. "I don't care about my career!" he snapped, his voice thick with frustration. "What I care about is you doing the right thing. You can't walk away from this, and you know it!"

The lieutenant spat, his lip split from the blow. "You're a self-righteous prig, just like your brother. Always spouting honour and duty like it's some bloody holy grail."

Harry pushed him again, slamming him against the stone railing, teeth gritted. "This isn't about me. It's about the men you've betrayed. And not just the men, curse you!"

"You don't understand the half of it," the lieutenant growled, struggling under Harry's grip. "But if you keep your mouth shut, you won't have to. You think your family name and your brother's wealth can save you? I'll have you court-martialed, Darcy. They'll see you hanged for treason before I let you ruin an entire regiment."

"You're already ruined. I saw everything. I have records, proof, and I'm sick of hiding behind my promotion to keep quiet." Harry's voice dropped dangerously low, his face inches from the lieutenant's. "I swear it."

The lieutenant sneered, managing to shove Harry off just enough to regain some ground. "Let's see how much you care about your honour when it's your neck on the line. You say anything, Darcy, and you're finished."

Elizabeth moved closer, the words each sounding like a drum beat in her ears. *Treason? Betrayal?* Her heart raced, panic clawing at her as she tried to make sense of what was unfolding before her eyes.

Should she call for help? No, that would only expose Harry, and clearly, he had come out here specifically to avoid that. Should she turn back? Yes, yes, that seemed... But what about the captain?

Her spine stiffened, a trickle of courage finding its way into her limbs. Surely, the protection of her sex would be sufficient to break up this unpleasantness. No officer would be so ungallant as to discommode a lady at a party, no matter how heated his conversation might be. Captain Darcy might even be spared the ignominy of a duel if she were tactful enough.

She cleared her throat. "Excuse me, sir, but I believe you have waylaid my dance partner for the next set. If you would be so kind as to return him to me undamaged, I should be terribly obliged."

The lieutenant's gaze shifted, catching sight of Elizabeth's figure hovering near the edge of the portico. His eyes narrowed, and an icy grin spread across his face. "Well, well, what have we here? A little bird caught spying, is it?"

Harry's head whipped around, his eyes widening in horror as he saw her. "Elizabeth—"

Without warning, the lieutenant lunged toward her, his hand snatching at her hair, yanking her toward him. Elizabeth gasped, the sudden pain wrenching through her scalp as she was pulled into the fray.

"Let her go!" Harry's voice cracked with fury as he stepped forward, his hands raised in a placating gesture. "Release her. This doesn't have to go any further!"

But the lieutenant only grinned, his grip on Elizabeth tightening. "Oh, I think it does, Darcy. A promise for a promise."

Elizabeth's mind reeled as her hands twisted behind her head, trying to at least lock the lieutenant's grip close to her scalp so he couldn't rip her hair from its roots. *Promise* what? What was this man holding over Harry?

Harry's expression shifted, the anger giving way to something far more unsettling—panic. He glanced around as though seeking an escape. "We can settle this between us. With honour. There is no need to involve an innocent lady!"

The lieutenant laughed, pulling Elizabeth closer to peer into her face. "She does not look so innocent to me. I assume she has some attachment to you since she has exposed herself coming out here to look for you."

Elizabeth tried to make a lunge away, feinting to the right with her upper body even as her heeled shoe drove into the toe of his boot. "Let me go!"

The lieutenant winced, but his grip did not weaken. Instead, he whipped out a blade and pressed it to her throat. "Have some manners, Miss," he tsked.

Elizabeth snapped her head back, trying to twist away, even as Harry lunged forward in alarm. "Elizabeth!" he shouted. "Leave her be!"

The lieutenant started slowly dragging Elizabeth backwards. "Savage little chit, isn't she? You always did like the saucy ones. Very well, you shall have her, but I need some assurance, Darcy—a worthy diversion to make sure you don't speak of this. We wouldn't want the higher-ups getting word that you were having 'doubts.' Not while certain notables happen to be just inside. I say, it's going to be difficult to explain your dishevelled state once you return to the ballroom."

Elizabeth's heart hammered in her ears. *What* was he talking about? Her pulse raced until she was lightheaded, her breath coming in short, panicked bursts. She couldn't allow Harry to be ruined—or worse. Whatever this was, it sounded worse. The music from the ballroom was still playing, voices and laughter drifting through the glass door just behind

Harry's back. More open doors surrounded them on all sides. Any moment, someone could walk out.

"Let her go back!" Harry snarled, yanking the lieutenant's arm. But the man's grip remained locked in Elizabeth's hair, the knife at her throat, and the way he was twisting her about between them kept the captain at bay.

"Try again. What say you, my pet?" the lieutenant crooned into her face. "How shall you explain what you saw? Do you have any strokes of genius to offer our rather dull-witted Captain Darcy?"

"I... I could..." Elizabeth's voice trembled, and pain-filled tears were stinging her eyes, but she forced herself to speak. "I c-could say I w-was out here. W-with Captain Darcy."

A stream of fresh tears coursed down her cheeks as the lieutenant gave her scalp another vicious yank. "You'll have to be more specific."

She gulped. "A-alone. In a... l-liaison."

Both men stared at her, their eyes locking on her with different expressions. The lieutenant looked quite satisfied, but Harry's face paled with shock. "Elizabeth, no! You'll be ruined."

He was right. Her hair was now a snarled mess, her face streaked. Moreover, Harry's lips were swollen, his brow sweating, and both of them had rumpled clothing. No one could look at them and believe they had been innocently taking the air. She wouldn't have to *say* anything. All the worst things would be assumed.

But what other option had she? There was a knife at her throat—a knife that could well fly into the captain's chest next.

The lieutenant's smile widened. "Oh, how perfect," he sneered, his grip tightening. "A tradesman's daughter, aren't you? I'm sure Fitzwilliam will love that."

Before she could make sense of his words, the lieutenant yanked her brutally forward, ripping at the neckline of her gown with his fist and then making a quick slice downwards through chemise, stays... everything until it bit lightly into her skin. The fabric tore with a sharp, sickening sound, and Elizabeth's world spun.

Her chest was exposed—all of it—to the cool night air, and her skin burned with shame. Elizabeth was too shocked, too humiliated to even scream. Her breasts were bare, her modesty completely stripped away in an instant. She tried to cover herself, her arms trembling as she attempted to cross them over her chest, but the lieutenant spun her like a rag doll, throwing her directly into Harry's arms.

"Do enjoy your evening, Captain," the lieutenant hissed. He shoved them both into the glass doors of the ballroom, the noise of the party just beyond.

Elizabeth stumbled, her body colliding with Harry's as he caught her in his arms. The earth tilted, the cold glass of the ballroom doors pressing against her back. Inside, she could hear the music, the chatter... and the voices growing closer. No one could have missed hearing the crash of their bodies colliding with that glass door.

Elizabeth barely registered the lieutenant's escape as he vaulted over the railing and disappeared into the night. All she knew was the cold weight of Harry's red coat suddenly around her shoulders, the way his hands—usually so sure and steady—trembled as he pulled the fabric around her, trying to shield her from the world. She was still shaking, still panting in horror, her mind struggling to make sense of what had just happened.

"Brave Elizabeth! Are you hurt?"

"I—" she stammered. "I'm sorry, I shouldn't have— I didn't mean to—"

"Shh." Harry's voice was soft, soothing, as he smoothed her hair back from her face, his eyes filled with a sorrow that Elizabeth could not understand. "You probably saved my life tonight. Do not apologise."

She could barely comprehend his words. Saved his life? How? She was the one ruined, her gown torn open, her body bared for all to see.

Harry cupped her cheeks in his hands, his breath warm against her skin as he leaned in and pressed a gentle kiss to her forehead. "I will make this right," he promised. "I'll not see you suffer for—"

And that was when the door behind them opened.

Elizabeth's uncle stood in the doorway, his eyes widening in shock as the entire ballroom seemed to fall silent. All around them, guests stared—at Elizabeth's torn gown, at the way she stood pressed against Harry, his coat around her bare shoulders. The scandal, the ruin, the destruction of her reputation was complete.

Elizabeth didn't hear the gasps or the whispers that followed. The only covering she had was the thin veil of Harry's promise as he stood before the stunned crowd, shielding her from their judgment.

But even with that—whatever he proposed to do—nothing could ever make this right.

Darcy's stomach was queasy after Elizabeth's confession. He sat quietly for a moment, staring at her across the room as the firelight flickered against the walls. The idea of his brother, who had always carried himself with honour, being drawn into something so dark, sat ill with him. Harry had always been something of a golden child, kissed by good fortune, never touched by scandal or corruption, even when the army called him away.

And yet, Elizabeth's account rang with truth—apart from a chillingly accurate description of her attacker, there was no falsehood in her eyes, no trace of manipulation. Only pain.

"Were you injured?" he asked in a tight voice.

Elizabeth's eyes wavered and fell. "The... ah... when he cut my gown..." She lifted a shoulder. "It is not quite healed. Nearly—it was not deep, but it was long, and a tender place to..." She cleared her throat and kept her eyes on the floor, her cheeks scalding red.

"Wickham," Darcy growled. "That lieutenant... I know who he was."

Elizabeth looked up, her brow furrowing slightly. "Who?"

"George Wickham," he said, the name bitter on his tongue. "A man who grew up alongside us. My father treated him like a son. Harry viewed him very much like a brother—the only time I ever knew him to misjudge anyone. Sentiment, I suppose. But Wickham... he never cared for honour or loyalty. His resentment toward Harry and me festered for years, and he has always sought what was not his."

Elizabeth frowned. "Why would he threaten Harry? What could he gain from it?"

"Your guess is as good as mine. They were always 'friendly' as far as I knew. Too friendly for my taste." Darcy let out a slow breath, his fingers tapping lightly on the arm of his chair as he considered the question. "Wickham is the sort of man who seizes every opportunity, no matter how vile. He must have seen Harry as a threat—someone who might expose him, though Heaven only knows what for."

Her lips parted slightly, and she looked down again, her fingers tracing the spine of the book in her lap. "After that night, I asked Harry who the man was, what they had been arguing about. But he would never tell me. He said it did not matter."

Darcy's gaze narrowed, his mind piecing together the puzzle with increasing clarity. "Harry was protecting you. Wickham had already used you as leverage once, and would not hesitate to come after you again. Harry knew it. He kept you in the dark because it was safer for you not to know."

Elizabeth's hands tightened around the book. "I see that now," she said, her voice soft. "But I should not have been involved at all. I should have returned to the ball at once, but I thought I was helping. Instead, I put myself at the centre of it. I made it worse."

Darcy leaned forward, resting his arms on his knees as he studied her closely. "You were not to blame. You made a decision in the moment, as anyone would. And you did not know what was truly at stake. How could you have?"

Elizabeth's head bowed slightly. "I am no child of fourteen! I heard what the lieutenant said. I should have realised that it was not just a quarrel between gentlemen over some female but something far more dangerous."

Darcy's jaw tightened. "You could not have known the depths to which Wickham would stoop. He has always found ways to destroy what others hold dear. And you were—" he stopped himself, the words catching in his throat.

Whatever she claimed about the supposedly platonic relationship she shared with Harry, Darcy would have been very shocked, indeed, if Harry did not feel *something* beyond friendship for her. A fond affection, at the very least, but Darcy suspected Harry's feelings had tended somewhat deeper than that. Had not Harry even claimed that much to him the day he died? Elizabeth was exactly the sort of woman Harry had always fancied, and Wickham was not blind.

Elizabeth looked up at him, a shadow passing over her face. "What?"

Darcy shook his head, leaning back in his chair. "It does not matter now. What matters is that Harry acted with honour. Even to the last conversation he and I had—he spoke of protecting you."

A heavy silence settled between them. Elizabeth diverted herself by thumbing the edge of a page, and Darcy stared absently at her fingers as she did so, his mind twisting on one pertinent question. What the devil had finally ruptured between Harry and Wickham? Whatever it was, it seemed that the girl formerly known as Elizabeth Bennet had been caught in something far beyond her control.

And, so, she *did* need him. Just as sorely as she would have if there *had* been a child.

Elizabeth broke the silence. "I still do not understand why Harry never explained. I asked him... I begged him to tell me what had instigated that, but he refused. It was as if he feared I might expose something, even unintentionally."

Darcy met her eyes, the firelight reflecting in their depths. "Harry must have had his reasons. He likely believed that the less you knew, the safer you would be."

Elizabeth gave a small nod, though she still seemed lost in her thoughts. Her voice was quiet when she spoke again. "And now, it is all too late."

Darcy felt a pang of sympathy, though he kept his expression guarded. "Harry did what he could. But I will not let Wickham's actions go unanswered."

Elizabeth's gaze snapped up, her eyes widening. "What will you do?"

He swallowed and shifted in his chair. "I wish I knew. I would like to assure you that I will find out what Harry discovered, what Wickham was hiding. I would like to say that I shall ensure that justice is done. But I... I've no idea where to begin."

For a moment, Elizabeth looked as though she might say something else, but she remained silent. Darcy studied her carefully. She had been through much more than he had realised, and her obvious honesty now made him... respect her. Yes, that was the word. His anger toward her had not fully dissipated—more because of the tangled web of his own feelings than any actual wrongdoing on her part. He could no longer deny that she had been trying, at least, to act with integrity.

Still, he hesitated. The conversation had softened, but it had not erased the distance between them. She was still holding herself aloof, and he was not yet ready to let down his guard entirely.

Elizabeth's voice broke the silence again, softer this time. "What about that letter?"

He stirred, his attention refocusing on her face. "To which are you referring? The one I received today or the one I showed you yesterday?"

She pursed her lips in thought. "What did you receive today?"

"Someone—and it seems painfully obvious who—broke into Harry's flat. Tossed the furniture, broke things. I cannot think what there might have been left to find, but he was looking for something."

Elizabeth's eyes widened. She caught her breath and looked quickly back to her lap.

Darcy's curiosity spiked. "What do you know?"

She shook her head. "Nothing. But you recall—I told you, I think—Harry did say he had proofs of... something."

"Then I suppose I begin searching through his effects once more." He ran a hand through his hair. "Though Lord knows what there is left to find."

"And what of the *other* letter? There is a... a need to answer there, as well."

Darcy set his teeth. "What do you want me to do? Shall I find that woman and marry *her*, too?"

Her features blanched, but this time, she did not drop her eyes. A sort of fire sparked in them, and she sat somewhat taller. "If you chose to, you could. But that would not be my business."

He snorted. "How so? The last I checked, I was bound in the eyes of the law and God to someone else."

"Not... in all ways," she reminded him.

Darcy's gaze met hers, and for a moment, he considered. What *were* they to do now? Should he carry her upstairs this very moment, seal the uneasy pact they had made with a union of the flesh? As... appealing as that notion suddenly sounded, he could not, just yet.

"What do you wish?" he asked her instead. "I will not bind you unwillingly, but you would have no alternatives at all if we..." He swallowed.

She drew a long breath, her shoulders lifting as her gaze studied him. "I do not know. I... I wish for a miracle, I suppose."

He grunted as his legs uncrossed. "I am no miracle, madam. But I am a man of my word, and I gave mine to you." He pushed out of the chair and began to leave the room, but before he passed her, he stopped.

Elizabeth was looking up at him now, her expression unreadable. Darcy could feel the tension still lingering between them, though something had shifted. It was not trust—certainly not—but there was a flicker of understanding, of shared purpose, however tenuous.

"And I gave mine to you," she whispered.

Darcy looked away, his thoughts still tangled with anger, regret, and confusion. "I will ensure this is resolved."

Chapter Seventeen

Longbourn
26 September

MY DEAREST LIZZY,

I hope this letter finds you well, or at the very least, in better spirits than when we last parted. I have so much to tell you, though I scarcely know where to begin. I have returned to Longbourn at last. Aunt and Uncle Gardiner thought it best, given the unfortunate stir your... situation has caused. They have been so kind, never once uttering a word of reproach, though I know the scandal has cast a shadow over some of Uncle's business dealings. They would never confess it openly, of course. When I suggested that perhaps I should return home, they merely agreed with me, as if it had been their own idea all along. My only sorrow in leaving was, of course, knowing I should never again see Mr Bingley.

But, dear Lizzy, you cannot imagine what I have to tell you next! It seems that fortune has not abandoned me entirely. Only this morning, word arrived that Netherfield Park has been let—to none other than Mr Bingley himself! I could hardly believe it at first. It seems he has chosen to take that country house he talked about, after all, and he chose Hertfordshire to settle in. Oh, Lizzy, I scarcely dare to hope, but what else could this mean? I have said nothing of this to Mama, for you know how she would fly into a fit of matchmaking the moment she heard, but I did confide in Papa. He was as he always is—that is to say, he gave no assurances, but I believe he understands my feelings well enough to call on Mr Bingley as soon as he is settled. I do not presume too much, but I am hopeful that Mr Bingley wishes to renew his courtship, despite everything that has transpired. Perhaps not all is lost, after all.

Enough of my own news, though I wished to share some cheer with you. How are you, Lizzy? I have been loath to inquire too directly, not wishing to upset you further, but you must know how I worry for you. I do hope you have found some measure of peace at Pemberley, though I know how difficult things must have been. Do you feel settled there? I pray that Mr Darcy is treating you well and that you feel safe, at least, even if all else is uncertain. I know the past weeks have been a trial beyond anything either of us could have imagined.

Sadly, it seems no one in London has believed the truth of what happened that night. They all persist in believing that Captain Darcy was the cause of your ruin. I am mortified to report that there are even some who claim he... ravished you out there, and that you were saved from further disgrace only by a hasty marriage to conceal what they suppose must come next. Some, knowing the wealth of the brother, even claim you planned such an incident for personal gain.

It is the most dreadful falsehood, but no one will be swayed from it. I am heartsick that such rumours continue, but perhaps there is a small mercy in this: the scandal has not followed us here to Hertfordshire. Not, at least, in all its particulars. Instead, Mama is almost insufferable in her triumph. It seems she cares little for what the world says about you, so long as she can boast of having a daughter married to a man of ten thousand a year. There are even those (not friends of mine, I assure you) who whisper that you must have been very clever to secure such a husband by... whatever means necessary. I blush to write it, but you know how people can be.

Still, the scandal has done nothing to dampen the spirits of Kitty and Lydia. They remain as wild and heedless as ever, and I fear that nothing short of a miracle will bring them to any sense of propriety.

Papa sends his love and promises to write "when he has a spare moment," though you know as well as I do that is merely a euphemism for "when he can bear the thought of losing you well enough to put it down on paper." Do not read anything personal into his oversight—scandal or no, he speaks of you fondly, Lizzy, and I hope you know how much you are missed here. Please, write soon, and tell me how you fare. I long to hear from you and know what is truly in your heart.

With all my love,

Jane

E LIZABETH LAID JANE'S LETTER gently on the desk, her fingertips lingering on the edges as she stared down at the familiar handwriting. A fortnight had passed since her arrival at Pemberley, and despite the chaos of her entrance into this strange new world, she could not deny the beauty that surrounded her. Aunt Gardiner had been right—Pemberley was more than an estate. It was a world unto itself, a place so vast and magnificent that Elizabeth felt at once a sense of awe and, strangely, a creeping loneliness.

She stood from the desk and moved toward the window, gazing out across the grounds. The autumn light stretched across the vast lawns, casting the house and the surrounding gardens in a soft, golden glow. She had begun to learn her way around the estate, taking long walks along the paths winding through the woodlands and toward the sparkling lake. She marvelled at the natural beauty, but it was the quiet that often lingered with her after these strolls. It was a quiet that both soothed and unsettled her, reminding her at every turn how little she truly belonged here.

Elizabeth could not deny that she had already come to know more of the household staff, at least. Mrs Reynolds had been patient and kind, introducing her to the daily responsibilities that would now fall under her care. Just yesterday, the housekeeper had shown her the journals kept by the late Mrs Darcy—Fitzwilliam and Harry's mother—detailing her role as mistress of Pemberley. The records of her routines, her wisdom in managing both the estate and the people who depended upon her left Elizabeth feeling both grateful and wholly inadequate. It was a world so foreign to her that, even with guidance, she feared she could never live up to such an example.

Yet, the greatest mystery of all to her remained her husband.

Fitzwilliam Darcy had been nothing if not kind since their conversation about the scandal that had ruined her reputation. He could have shunned her, like everyone else. But he had responded... rather like his brother. He had listened, he had respected, and he had not pressed her further. In fact, if anything, he seemed to be warming to her by slow, cautious degrees, his demeanour gradually softening. But even as he showed kindness, even as he grew more familiar with her presence, he remained distant. Polite, but never more than that.

There had been no further talk of an annulment—not even a hint, in fact. And though Elizabeth had expected at some point he might again broach the subject, despite his prior assurance to the contrary, he had done nothing of the kind. Instead, he had ordered a modiste to Pemberley to create new garments for her, each one suitable for her role as mistress of a house in mourning. He had taken steps to ensure she was properly dressed, properly positioned, and properly cared for.

That very morning, as she had been preparing for the day, he had approached her with the household accounts—a thick ledger in which the domestic finances were recorded. He had handed it to her almost casually, explaining that Mrs Reynolds had handled it until now, but it would be Elizabeth's responsibility going forward. There had been no ceremony to the act, no hint of reluctance, but it was clear in his gesture that he intended her to step into this role, to stretch and grow into the position of his wife.

For that, she could not complain. He was respectful, thoughtful, and generous. He was everything one could want from a husband in terms of duty and care. But he never spoke to her beyond the necessities. She felt as though she were living beside him rather than with him, and though she had nothing to reproach him for, she could not help but feel the yawning gulf between them.

She sighed softly, returning to her desk and picking up her pen. Jane deserved a letter, especially after such warm, encouraging words. But what could she say without alarming her sister? Without revealing how hollow and isolated she felt, despite the beauty of her surroundings?

Elizabeth dipped her pen in ink, the words coming slowly at first.

My dearest Jane,

I hope this letter finds you well, wrapped in all the comforts of Longbourn, though I daresay even the familiarity of home cannot entirely ease the strain of your sudden departure from London. I am deeply sorry that Aunt and Uncle Gardiner's position was compromised on my account. They are far too kind to admit it openly, but I know their burden has been heavier than any of us could wish. And I can only imagine your regret in leaving Mr Bingley behind—such a gentleman in every sense, and the only man I ever fancied who might be worthy of my dearest sister.

But what delightful news to learn that Netherfield has been let to none other than that same gentleman! My dear Jane, this is no small coincidence. I confess it brings quite a smile to my face. I can hardly suppose a man of his means would settle so near without some particular aim. How modest you are in your hopes, but I cannot help feeling certain that you are on the verge of great happiness. Though I do hope, for all our sakes, that Mama does not get wind of this just yet. You may, perhaps, enjoy a short time of privacy... at least until everyone sees you in the gentleman's company, then all hope of discretion will be long gone.

As for myself, I must report that I am remarkably well for a woman who has landed in so grand a place quite by accident. Pemberley is truly everything Aunt Gardiner claimed it to be—dare I say, even more? The lake, the gardens, the sweeping woodland paths—Jane, you could live here a lifetime and still not see every inch of its beauty. How anyone could ever tire of it, I cannot imagine!

The housekeeper, Mrs Reynolds, has been most kind in introducing me to the responsibilities of the mistress. (I daresay she is determined that I shall succeed in the role whether I like it or not.) Just yesterday, she placed in my hands the journals of the late Mrs Darcy—no light reading, I assure you! I admit, the task feels rather like stepping into a stranger's shoes, but I am told that with time, one grows accustomed to it.

Now, I must address the matter you are surely most curious about: Mr Fitzwilliam Darcy. He remains something of an enigma to me. He has been kind, unfailingly so, but Jane, he is more reserved than I ever imagined. I cannot pretend to understand him—though I do wonder if that, too, might come with time. He treats me with every courtesy, and you may rest assured that I am perfectly safe here.

Mr Darcy is grieving, that much is certain. I would not expect anyone to recover from such a loss so quickly. One great comfort to him, I believe, is Colonel Fitzwilliam's company. Perhaps you may recall that Captain Darcy spoke fondly of his distinguished cousin, and I daresay none of his praise of that gentleman's fine qualities was overstated. He has, I believe, brought some measure of relief to a mournful household. However, I understand he is to leave us to return to his regiment on the morrow, and I can but hope for better days ahead, even as my rather stoic husband and I must learn to get on without the colonel's leavening presence.

Please give my love to Mama and Papa, and to our dear sisters. I am greatly relieved that the entirety of the scandal has not followed you back to Hertfordshire with all its vicious tales, and I trust Mama will continue to shine the best possible light on the affair, however little circumstances deserve it.

As ever, I send you all my love and shall eagerly await your next letter—especially if it contains news of a certain gentleman's intentions.

Yours always,

Elizabeth

With a soft sigh, Elizabeth folded the letter, sealing it carefully. Time would tell if the hopes she had woven into her words would ever be more than that.

"NOTHING. NO SIGN OF anything unusual in the letters, maps, stray bits of rubbish or even personal mementos I brought back from Harry's flat."

Richard growled and crossed his knees. "You said some of Wickham's things were in that mix. Anything of interest?"

Darcy kept pacing. "Not unless you count a battered flask that smelled as if it had been used to store soiled stockings. A cravat that was hardly worth the laundress's bill, and a shirt or two that would serve better as boot rags."

"I assume you checked all the pockets of all the garments?"

"What do you think? I've written to my friends at the club," Darcy said, pausing mid-stride, his hand resting on the back of a nearby chair. "Some of them knew Harry in his last months in London—when he first returned from the Continent—but no one seems to have answers. Yet."

Richard stared at his glass. "What does Bingley say?"

"Bingley corroborated Elizabeth's version of events," Darcy began, his voice tightening slightly.

"Were you expecting otherwise?"

Darcy sighed. "No. No, I already believed her. But he did embellish some details that she had left out. How the scandal spread after she was found with Harry on that portico. Elizabeth was shunned, as you would expect. According to Bingley, even the

Gardiners—despite their loyalty to her—became deeply cautious about whom they associated with, for fear of further damaging their reputation. His business saw some... setbacks."

Richard raised an eyebrow but remained silent, his gaze fixed on Darcy as he continued.

"Bingley tried to defend her, of course. He called on her and Miss Bennet at the Gardiners' house, hoping to provide some support, but even Mr Gardiner refused to receive him. He feared Bingley's association with Harry would only worsen the situation."

Richard's expression darkened slightly. "So the blame fell squarely on Harry."

Darcy nodded gravely. "Yes. And it did not help that Harry came to the Gardiners' house the very morning after the scandal broke to offer for her. They would have excoriated him if he had *not* done so, but naturally, it gave the appearance of a guilty conscience. In truth, Bingley said it was an impossible situation. Society was determined to think the worst of her—and of him."

Richard shook his head, his face grim. "And now you, Darcy. You understand that, do you not? You have assumed whatever disgrace was heaped on them."

Darcy swallowed. "It is not as if I stand to lose anything but my pride. My investments are secure, and I have no other siblings to marry off. Give it time. Another scandal will rise in this one's place."

Richard emitted an almost soundless chuckle. "It's always like that, isn't it? But this one will not be forgot quite so easily as you seem to believe. The truth is often irrelevant once the whispers start. But did Bingley know anything about Wickham? Would he even recognise him if he saw him?"

Darcy shook his head. "He knew Wickham in school, of course, but said he never saw him at all in the last five years. Claimed he did not even know Wickham was in London until after that evening, when Harry told him what happened. I find that odd because Wickham and Harry used to be thick as thieves. How did Bingley not associate with Wickham as well as Harry last summer?"

Richard grunted. "Whatever happened between them must have begun when they were in Spain together."

"Agreed."

"I have made some inquiries of my own. There is a young sergeant of my acquaintance who, I believe, was at Badajoz with Harry. Perhaps he can shed some light on matters."

Darcy grunted. "A sergeant? He would have to have been close to Harry or Wickham for his observations to be of any use to us. I am not pinning my hopes on that connection, but it is something."

"Something, yes. Had Bingley nothing else to say?"

"Only that Harry was adamant about the marriage. He told Bingley directly that he intended to go through with it, that he was determined to protect Elizabeth from his mistakes. Bingley... he seemed to think Harry felt responsible for more than just the scandal."

Richard's eyes narrowed. "You mean because of Wickham?"

Darcy nodded slowly. "Yes. But no one seems to know why Harry was at odds with Wickham. Bingley only remembers Harry becoming more agitated whenever the subject of Wickham arose, as if Harry was holding something back. And now we may never know what it was."

Richard leaned back in his chair and took a measured sip of his drink, watching Darcy's relentless pacing with a mild, almost exasperated expression. "And yet, here you are, determined to chase this phantom of guilt. You know Harry would never have laid this burden upon you, Darcy."

Darcy's lips pressed into a thin line. "I cannot let it go so easily. Whatever Harry was involved in—whatever led to that confrontation with Wickham—I owe it to him to set it right. I owe him at least that much."

Richard sighed and set his glass down on the side table. "You owe him your grief, yes. But Harry is gone, cousin. You cannot rewrite the past by unravelling his secrets."

Darcy's hand tightened on the chair back as he stared at the floor, frustration rippling through him. He had always prided himself on his ability to handle things—his family, his estates, his responsibilities. Yet now, he felt powerless, constantly one step behind the truth. Harry had always been reckless, but what had driven him to risk everything? Why had Wickham been involved? None of it made sense.

Darcy resumed his pacing, only stopping again when he approached the window. His gaze drifted outside, across the lawn, where he saw Elizabeth walking alone.

For the first time all day, some of the burdens twisting his gut into knots seemed to ease, if only slightly. There she was, striding across the grounds with that same quiet confidence he had begun to associate with her alone. Her long strides, the purposeful way she carried herself—it struck him that she had grown to be a part of Pemberley's vast expanse, comfortable enough to walk it as if it were her own.

A book was tucked under her arm, and a warm cloak hung about her shoulders as if she intended to be out for some time. Her path led towards the lake, though the sky had begun to darken with the threat of rain. Darcy's gaze lingered on her figure. Somehow, seeing her billowing cape, the springy way she moved, as if daring the elements to challenge her, chipped away at the tension that had gripped him all day.

He couldn't quite understand it. Where once he had regarded her presence with mistrust—perhaps even resentment—he now found a strange sense of reassurance in her unflinching honesty. Elizabeth had been in his home for a fortnight, and during that time, her candour had stripped away the artifice he was so accustomed to in others. There was something almost comforting in the way she moved across the grounds as if she belonged nowhere and everywhere all at once. She faced the world as she faced him—with a straightforwardness that, rather than feeling confrontational, now struck him as deeply genuine.

For reasons he could not yet name, her presence calmed the storm of his thoughts. She was not the enemy he had once believed her to be. No, she was something far more disarming—someone he could... almost trust.

"Interesting sight, is it not?"

The voice startled him, and Darcy turned to see Richard standing silently beside him, his gaze also fixed on Elizabeth's retreating form.

Darcy tore his eyes away, giving Richard a quick glance before looking back at Elizabeth. "What did you say?"

Richard smiled wryly. "You know, it would be no dishonour to Harry's memory if you allowed yourself to fall in love with her."

Darcy blinked, stunned by the remark. "What? What are you talking about?"

"You heard me the first time," Richard said, his tone casual, as if discussing the weather. "It is only an observation."

Darcy scoffed, shaking his head in disbelief. "Love? Since when has love ever been a requirement for marriage? I meant to honour her, to offer her protection. That is what Harry wanted. That is enough."

Richard arched a brow. "Perhaps for some people, yes. But not for you, and you know it."

Darcy's mouth tightened, and he crossed his arms defensively. "Elizabeth and I are nothing alike. I do not even know what sort of things she enjoys or what sort of family she comes from."

"Well, you could always ask her."

Darcy said nothing, though his eyes found Elizabeth again as she continued walking toward the lake. It was true... he *could* ask her. Thus far, he had supposed that bringing up anything of her past must necessarily also bring pain. But that could not possibly be true, because he had heard her laughter ringing in the halls of his home. And Harry had spoken of her as a ready wit, an engaging personality. A woman with such an effortless, artless laugh had to have some root for that sort of pleasure. Something in her upbringing or background that gave joy rather than grief.

Richard gave a soft, knowing hum, his voice lowering. "I have seen you watch her, you know."

Darcy's brow furrowed, his gaze snapping back to his cousin. "Why should that be remarkable? She is my wife. I watch over her, as is my duty. She has been thrust into circumstances no one could have prepared for."

"That is not what I mean. You watch her, Darcy, and I see something else in your eyes. You breathe differently when you look at her. Slower, more relaxed. I daresay even your pulse is calmer. There is no need to deny it."

Darcy stared at Richard, words caught in his throat, as his cousin's casual observation struck a deep, unsettling chord. He had not realised it himself, but now that it had been said aloud, it felt... true. How many times over this past fortnight had he found himself watching Elizabeth without meaning to? How often had the sight of her calmed the tempest in his chest?

"I—" Darcy began, but he stopped, shaking his head as he turned back toward the window. "There is nothing more to discuss."

"Very well," Richard said, stepping away with a small shrug. "If you have no further need of me, I will see to my packing. Early morning tomorrow, after all."

Darcy did not respond, his eyes fixed once again on Elizabeth's distant form as Richard quietly left the room. Alone now, Darcy continued to stare after her, a swirl of emotions stirring within him that he could not quite name or understand.

Chapter Eighteen

THE SOFT CLINKING OF silverware on china echoed faintly through the cavernous dining room, filling the space where conversation ought to have thrived. Darcy sat at one end of the long, gleaming table, his gaze wandering over the ornate wallpaper, the heavy curtains—anything but the figure seated opposite him. Elizabeth, at the other end, sipped her soup—her posture as impeccable as ever, but her face almost devoid of expression. The footman stood by, watching over the formalities, though his presence only deepened the feeling of awkwardness that clung to the air between them.

Darcy cleared his throat softly, his eyes flickering to Elizabeth, who remained focused on her meal. "The weather today was... agreeable," he ventured, though even he heard how strained it sounded.

"Indeed," Elizabeth replied with a small nod. "Clear skies, though a bit colder than expected for this time of year. The colonel should experience an uneventful journey."

"Quite so." He glanced down at his plate, cutting into his food more forcefully than intended. Silence fell again, more oppressive than the last. Darcy stole a glance in Elizabeth's direction, hoping for some sign, some expression that might help him understand her better. But her face, though serene, gave nothing away. She was a puzzle he could not quite solve, and the distance between them—both physical and otherwise—felt insurmountable.

Darcy cleared his throat again, this time more purposefully, and cast about for another subject. "The cook has outdone herself with the pheasant," he remarked, though the compliment felt hollow even to his own ears.

Elizabeth paused, setting her fork down with deliberate care. "Yes," she agreed, though her tone was just as neutral. "The seasoning is... complex."

He nodded, unsure of how to prolong the conversation. His eyes darted across the expanse of the table, the polished silverware gleaming in the candlelight. The formality of it all only served to make the space between them more daunting.

"I trust your new gowns have all arrived?"

"Yes, thank you," Elizabeth replied, her eyes meeting his briefly before she returned her focus to her plate. "Susan is attempting to hem one that arrived too long, but I fear she is so nervous sewing the satin that she is like to puncture herself."

He stiffened slightly, guilt tugging at him for not having procured a proper maid for her. "Mrs Reynolds is... efficient," he said, searching for the right words. "I shall ask her if she can refer someone more capable to assist you."

Elizabeth gave him a polite smile. "I am in jest, sir. I think Susan has managed well enough so far, and I rather like her."

Another stretch of silence followed, punctuated only by the faint clink of cutlery. Darcy felt as though the sheer size of their unspoken words was crowding the room, and he struggled to break through it.

There was... something else that had entered his mind this afternoon. A duty... if one wished to call it that. One that, with Richard out of his house, he might turn his mind to a little more decisively. But matters between them had not yet warmed sufficiently for *that*, and he had no idea how to stoke the embers of an unkindled fire.

"You seemed to enjoy walking by the lake this afternoon," he offered, feeling slightly foolish the moment the words left his mouth.

Elizabeth's lips quirked slightly, as if amused by his attempt. "Yes," she said, setting her spoon down with a small sigh. "It offers a sense of calm, I suppose."

His gaze flickered over her, lingering on the softness of her features, the ease with which she spoke of something so simple. For the first time all evening, there seemed to be a flicker of connection between them. But it vanished as quickly as it had come, leaving Darcy floundering once more.

They continued in this manner—brief exchanges that never quite took root, leaving both of them glancing uncomfortably at each other between phrases. Finally, Elizabeth looked up, catching him watching her. She folded her hands in her lap, raising an eyebrow.

"Mr Darcy, perhaps you can solve a mystery for me?"

His brow furrowed. "What mystery is that, Mrs Darcy?"

Elizabeth reached for her wine glass and tilted her head before drinking of it. "I cannot, for the life of me, recall what colour your eyes are. As you are seated so far away, I find myself at a distinct disadvantage. Perhaps I ought to acquire a pair of spectacles, like some poor, feeble old man, so I will not have to rely on my rather poorly-informed memory."

Darcy's lips twitched despite himself. She had caught him off guard, and for the first time all evening, he felt the coolness of the distance between them lessen just a little. "You are welcome to come closer and discover for yourself."

Her smile widened, and without hesitation, Elizabeth rose from her chair. Darcy, feeling something stir in him, jerked to his feet as well, his movements so hasty that he knocked his knee on the underside of the table. But he would not let such a thing hinder him now. He gestured to the footman, who had stepped forward to assist the mistress, but Darcy reached her first. "I shall manage."

With a steady hand, Darcy lifted her plate and wine glass from their places and carried them to the chair beside his own. He set them down with care, then pulled out the chair for her, his hand lingering briefly on the backrest as she sat.

As she sat beside him, she leaned forward as if scrutinising him closely. "Ah," she said with mock seriousness, "I quite had it in my head that your eyes were blue, but I see now they are, in fact, brown. So dark a brown they are nearly purple. How silly of me to forget."

A small, genuine smile tugged at Darcy's mouth as he shook his head. "It was Harry who had blue eyes."

Elizabeth's expression softened slightly, and she tilted her head, correcting him gently. "No. His eyes were green. Shafts of blue, you are correct, but shot through with golden spikes, which, I fancy, he must have inherited from your mother, if that portrait of her in the drawing room is a good likeness."

Darcy paused, thinning his lips as he glanced downward, a momentary shadow crossing his face. "Yes," he murmured, "you are right. They were green—just like hers."

Darcy watched her as they resumed their meal, the silence between them after their brief exchange about Harry's eyes both comforting and unsettling. She was too sharp an observer to have "forgot" his eye colour, but it was a cleverer ruse than anything he had come up with.

Elizabeth had opened the door to something—a kind of levity, a natural ease in their conversation, and yet, he found himself unable to step fully through it. He glanced at her, seated beside him now, her fingers lightly tracing the rim of her wine glass, as if waiting for him to say something more.

But what? His tongue was as good as stuck to the roof of his mouth. Richard's words from the previous day echoed somewhere in the back of his thoughts, a lingering reminder that he had duties, responsibilities to fulfil in this marriage beyond mere civility. He needed an heir—Pemberley needed an heir, and she was the woman to whom he had given his name. The very idea of it, of Elizabeth as the mother of his children, sent an unfamiliar warmth crawling through his veins. He could still scarcely separate her in his mind from Harry, and yet, at some point, he would have to make her his own.

How could he voice such thoughts? He was unsure whether he could even begin that conversation without tripping over himself.

"Mrs Darcy," he began haltingly, "I thought perhaps tomorrow, we might attend religious services at the village church."

She turned her head slightly, her expression neutral, though a flicker of interest crossed her face. "Yes," she said, nodding. "I had wondered when that might come to pass. It has been some time since my arrival."

He nodded, grateful that she had not resisted the idea. The truth was, they could not continue hiding away forever, as if the walls of Pemberley would shield them indefinitely from the world's gaze. It was time they presented themselves as the master and mistress of the estate, mourning period or not. He cleared his throat again. "It will be good, I think... for the household, and the neighbourhood, to see us... together."

Elizabeth gave a small smile, pausing as she lifted her fork to her lips. "Indeed," she said lightly, "I suppose it is time for me to be paraded out like a new portrait in the gallery." Her tone was teasing, but there was a deeper understanding there, too. Surely, she knew as well as he did what would be expected of them as the new Mr and Mrs Darcy.

Darcy managed a faint smile, but his heart pounded harder in his chest. This was all more difficult than he had anticipated. Did other arranged marriages stutter and falter so in early days? Egad, no wonder so many men took mistresses. Not that he would ever... it was not the way his father had carried on, and he meant to do no differently. But there was probably some simplicity in the transactional nature of...

Egad, but his wife was beautiful. That expression in her eyes—eyes so rich and glorious that no painter could ever set them down properly. And it was silly, but he never could keep his gaze off the brown silk of her hair when it pulled loose from its pins, as it was trying to do now. Like the rest of her, it was almost feral, and... well, it made his upper lip sweat and his toes ache, and everything in between... warm. His eyes followed the curve of her wrist as she ate and fell naturally to the sweep of her décolletage and the soft curve of her body beneath.

Could he ask her? His hand shook on the spoon.

He could almost hear his father's voice in his head. *"It is not for the husband to ask as if begging favours not owed. A wife has a duty to fulfil. Her husband must not treat her unkindly, but there is little room for sentiment in the matter."*

Darcy's stomach churned, and suddenly, the syllabub turned bitter in his mouth. Hang it all, it was more... complicated than that! Even if Elizabeth had never been... *that*... with Harry, there were too many feelings, too much unknown between them for him to... No, he could not form such expectations—at least not here, in the dining room, with the footman watching. But he would have to at some point, and the sooner, the better.

His mind flitted between thoughts, between his desire to know more about her, his sense of duty, and the sudden awareness that perhaps... perhaps with enough wine, enough small talk... tonight might be the night he needed to confront the full reality of their marriage.

Elizabeth, still slowly picking away at the last of her dessert, glanced at him from the corner of her eye as if sensing his restlessness. She said nothing, but her presence alone seemed to stir something deeper in him. It would be... no punishment for him to...

Darcy gestured to the footman for a refill of his wine glass. Perhaps that would even out his nerves.

Elizabeth was watching him now—watching as he drained half the glass in one go and set it down with nerveless fingers. She gave him a strange look, then directed her attention back to her dessert.

"I suppose you must have had a letter from Mr Bingley recently?" she asked.

That brought some air back into his lungs. Yes, words. Plain, simple words. He could manage that. He cleared his throat. "I had another letter yesterday. He said he is preparing to move to the country."

Her brows arched as she sipped her wine. "I understand that as well. It seems that your friend has leased an estate barely three miles from Longbourn."

Longbourn...? oh! Yes. The estate in Hertfordshire where her family lived. He had been meaning to ask her about that. Three sisters? Four?

"I was not aware of such a happy coincidence," he replied in the evenest tone he could manage.

"You think it a coincidence, sir?" She smiled slightly. "Jane does not, though her modesty leads her to dissemble somewhat. I hope their reunion is somewhat happier than their parting was."

He swallowed and stared at his plate. "Indeed."

"Sir, if I may be so frank, you seem somewhat out of sorts this evening."

Darcy looked back up at her. "Do I?"

"I would assume the colonel's absence has something to do with your more sombre mood? Or is it some measure of dissatisfaction with the present company?"

He stiffened. "Not at all, I assure you. In fact, I was hoping to... to come to know you better, now that there are... fewer distractions. Er... what did you say all your sisters' names were?"

Elizabeth set down her spoon and turned to face him a little more. "Jane, you have already met. She is my elder sister. Then Mary is nineteen, Kitty is seventeen, and Lydia is fifteen." She leaned a little closer. "And I am no longer nineteen, but not yet one and twenty, in case you wished to know."

Darcy smiled. "Twenty-seven," he said, gesturing to himself.

She nodded. "A very sensible age. Why, I should think you would have outgrown every silly thing by that age. I wonder if I shall ever attain it, myself."

"There is a difference between sensible and glum," he said lowly. "And, for my part, what you term 'silliness' might, in fact, be the perfect weapon against sorrow."

Elizabeth paused, studying him. For an instant, her face reflected something rather profound, but then she brushed it off and brightened her expression. "Yes, that it may. But you have not seen true silliness until you have met my younger sisters. Perhaps you will change your tune on that notion. I daresay it is to your good fortune that you never had to bear the rather constant embarrassment of what three younger sisters can wreak on a young lady's social endeavours."

He nodded, and his throat tightened slightly. "I had a sister once. She... and my mother... it was a difficult pregnancy from the start, and neither of them survived the birth."

Elizabeth straightened and pierced him with a more curious look. "I did not know that. I am sorry, sir. Your father must have taken it very hard."

"He did. Refused to even give the child a name for a proper burial, so Harry and I had to come up with something to tell the clergyman."

"And?"

Darcy lifted his shoulder. "Father's name was George, and Mother's name was Anne, so we called her Georgiana. A rather cumbersome name, but we were only eight and twelve at the time."

A pang of sympathy crossed Elizabeth's features. "It sounds as if you chose very well, indeed." She toyed with her spoon, turning it over uselessly in her fingers. "Are there... or were there... any other Darcys I should know about?"

He shook his head, and was proud of the even, controlled timbre of his voice as he said, "I am the last of the line."

Her eyes lifted to his, touching them for a moment, before she nodded faintly and resumed her dessert. The reddish tint to the edge of her ears—that could *not* be his imagination. She had understood more than simple words in his statement.

Yes, perhaps it was time to consider... *more.* His palms ached with nervous perspiration as the thought recurred to him. She was his wife, the one he had pledged himself to. It only made sense. And the pleasures of such a union would surely not be all physical. If he could forget, for a few moments, how she had come into his life, and put aside, at least for one evening, all memories of what he had lost when he gained her, perhaps that would be something of a beginning. Something to build on. Surely, he found her appealing to his mind as well as his senses.

The way she moved and spoke—so breezy and confident. Honest and artless, even when she was in jest. There was nothing timid or coy about her. In that, she complemented him well. She could be warm when he was reticent, blunt when he had no patience for artifice, and apart from Richard... or Harry... she was the only person who spoke to him without flattery or deference.

They finished their dessert in near silence, Darcy's heart now hammering with a mounting urgency. He pushed his plate aside, glancing at Elizabeth as she sipped from her wine glass. *Now or never.*

"Would you allow me to escort you upstairs, Mrs Darcy?" His voice was steady, though inside, it felt like a thousand hornets were trying to break out of his skin.

Elizabeth blinked, setting her glass down as the colour rose in her cheeks. *Oh, yes...* she was not insensible to the turn of his thoughts. Darcy gulped as a shot of nervous pain speared his chest. *He could do this, he could do this...*

"Of course," she said, offering him a small smile as she stood from the table.

Darcy rose as well, his movements almost automatic as he stepped forward to offer his arm. She took it, and together, they made their way towards the staircase. His pulse quickened with every step, his mind racing ahead to what he might say when they reached her room.

Should he kiss her when he left her at her door? Say he would ask the pleasure of knocking in half an hour? Better yet, he could offer to assist her himself... Would that feel too abrupt, too presumptive?

But his thoughts veered dangerously close to other possibilities, and the more he considered it, the more his body seemed to stir with warmth, a yearning he could barely control. Yes, he would, by Heaven. If not now, then when?

But as they began to climb the stairs, Elizabeth's pace faltered, and she sucked in a sharp gasp.

Darcy immediately looked down, concern flooding his voice. "Are you well?"

Elizabeth's face was flushed, her hand pressed against her abdomen. She looked up at him, clearly embarrassed by something. "It is nothing," she said quickly, but the forced smile did not fool him.

"The pheasant?" he guessed. "Something in the seasoning? Or perhaps too much cheese?"

She shook her head, a bashful smile warming her features with a little more sincerity. "No, nothing like that."

Darcy frowned, his brows drawing together. "Are you sure?" he asked again, his worry deepening. "You are tense and beginning to double over. Are you in pain?"

Elizabeth sighed, biting her lip. "I... I believe I need my maid," she said haltingly.

"Your maid?" Darcy echoed, still confused. "Shall I fetch her?"

She hesitated, then, with a glance around, she motioned for him to lean closer. "Please, Mr Darcy, it is rather delicate... My, um, my... I find myself suddenly out of sorts, and... well, I do not wish to... move."

Darcy stared at her, utterly perplexed. "Out of sorts?" he repeated. What in the world was she—

Elizabeth sighed again, her face now fully flushed. "Mr Darcy, it is quite obvious you have not been a husband long," she said softly, almost wryly. "I mean my courses, sir. And I am rather unprepared... and wearing a new silk gown, and... well, I should very much like to return to my room."

His mind suddenly caught up with the situation, and Darcy's face heated in embarrassment. "Oh," he managed, feeling utterly out of his depth. "I... I see." He swallowed. "Is there anything I can... do?"

Elizabeth winced, her posture stiffening as her hand instinctively returned to her middle. "I think I must move gingerly, but I am not sure how I can—" she began, but Darcy was already moving.

Without waiting for more of an answer, he scooped her up into his arms, carefully cradling her as he moved toward her room. Elizabeth's body stiffened at first, but after a moment, she relaxed, though her cheeks still blazed with embarrassment.

"It is a gallant gesture, but it might not help," she murmured, but Darcy was already focused on the steps. Her proximity was both a comfort and a new kind of distraction. The firmness of her frame in his arms, the way her body fit so naturally against his—it stirred something in him, something primal and instinctual. But he forced those thoughts away, reminding himself that this was neither the time nor the place for such considerations.

Finally, he reached her room, where her maid immediately sprang up to help the mistress. Darcy gently set Elizabeth down at the door, ensuring she was steady on her feet before stepping back.

"Thank you," Elizabeth said, her voice soft, though her gaze avoided his.

Darcy nodded, and retreated swiftly to his own room. He had managed to dodge the inevitable tonight, but there was no denying it—his feelings were changing, and sooner or later, he would have to face them.

Chapter Nineteen

"**D**O YOU ATTEND SERVICES here every week, sir?" Elizabeth asked as they approached the chapel, her breath visible in the crisp morning air.

Darcy gave a slight nod, his expression unreadable. "When I am in residence, yes."

The churchyard was quiet, the soft murmur of the congregation gathering inside only just audible. Elizabeth glanced at the stone chapel ahead of them. It was small, humble compared to the grandeur of Pemberley, but somehow fitting for the peaceful village setting. As they reached the entrance, she could feel eyes upon them—villagers and tenants alike, all eager to catch sight of the new Mrs Darcy.

Darcy stepped forward, holding his arm out to her, and she entered the chapel. Inside, it was modest but well-kept. It rather reminded her of home, actually. The pews were polished to a shine, and the windows allowed in shafts of pale morning light. Elizabeth's gaze roamed over the congregation, expecting whispers or side glances, but to her surprise, none came. The people smiled at her warmly, nodding their heads in greeting, and she found herself easing just a little.

"Good morning, Mr Darcy," a man said, bowing slightly as Darcy led her to their seat.

"Good morning, Mr Fletcher," Darcy replied, his voice steady, though a small smile tugged at the corner of his mouth. "I trust your family is well?"

"Quite well, sir. Thank you."

They took their seats near the front, and Elizabeth watched as more parishioners entered. There was no sense of judgment, no hushed murmurs about her sudden arrival at Pemberley. She had braced herself for it, but instead found only curiosity and welcome.

Mr Smythe, the parson, stepped up to the pulpit. His manner was gentle, but there was an authority in the way he addressed the congregation. "Brothers and sisters, I have prepared some thoughts this week on the nature of kindness—true kindness, which comes not from obligation, but from the heart."

Elizabeth blinked in surprise. This was not the staid, formulaic sermon she had expected. His words felt personal, as if each sentence was crafted with care, and she could see that the congregation was listening—truly listening. Even Darcy, usually so composed, seemed to be paying closer attention to the sermon than to anything else she had ever witnessed.

Elizabeth leaned slightly closer to her husband. "Was it you or your father who appointed Mr Smythe to this living?" she whispered.

Darcy glanced at her briefly, before turning back to the pulpit. "It was my father's decision, but he consulted me on the matter. I have never had cause to regret it."

Elizabeth nodded thoughtfully. The sincerity of Mr Smythe's words seemed to reach every corner of the chapel, and she found herself drawn in, despite herself. For once, the sermon did not feel like a lecture, but rather a conversation—one that stirred reflection rather than mere obedience.

As the service concluded, Darcy rose and led her to the exit. Outside, the villagers gathered to greet them. One by one, they filed past, offering kind words and deferential greetings.

"Mr Darcy, how good it is to see you back in the village," an elderly woman said with a welcoming smile. "We have missed you."

"Thank you, Mrs Hardwick," Darcy replied. "I trust your granddaughter is well?"

"Yes, sir, very well. And she asked me to send her regards to you."

Elizabeth stood quietly by Darcy's side, listening as he spoke to each person by name, inquiring about their homes, their families, and their health. He knew them all—down to the smallest detail—and the way they responded showed a deep respect and appreciation for him.

"Good day, Mr Darcy, Mrs Darcy," Mr Smythe greeted them as they neared the church door. His wife, a slight woman with a kind face, curtsied beside him. "It is an honour to have you both with us."

Elizabeth curtsied in return. "Your sermon was most thoughtful, Mr Smythe. I found it refreshing."

The parson's face brightened. "Thank you, Mrs Darcy. It is always my aim to offer something of use, rather than mere words. I am glad it spoke to you."

As they exchanged pleasantries, Elizabeth noticed Darcy's attention drift. His gaze slid away from Mr Smythe, moving toward the churchyard in the distance. She followed his line of sight, her eyes settling on a large monument just beyond the chapel grounds. The name "Darcy" was engraved in bold letters across the stone. Iron fencing encircled the family plot, with carefully tended grass within—except for a rectangle of bare earth, where the grass had not yet regrown.

A shiver ran through her. *Harry.* The wound of his loss, though muted in recent days, seemed to stir again as she looked at the fresh grave.

Darcy's arm stiffened under her hand, his posture rigid, though his face betrayed nothing of his emotions. He inclined his head toward Mr Smythe, murmuring a polite farewell. Then, without another word, he gently guided Elizabeth away from the church, his hand firm on hers as they walked toward the waiting carriage.

Elizabeth wanted to ask, to say something that might offer him comfort, but the set of his jaw told her that this was not the moment. The grief was there, just beneath the surface, but he was not ready to share it—not yet.

As they climbed into the carriage, Darcy remained silent, his eyes fixed ahead as the driver clicked the horses into motion. The village and church slipped away behind them, but the image of that grave lingered in Elizabeth's mind. It was not just the loss of a brother—it was the loss of everything Darcy had once known, the last link to the family he had cherished. And she, an outsider, had stepped into that void, unsure if she could ever fill the space left behind.

E LIZABETH SAT AT THE polished desk in the mistress's morning room, her pen hovering above the paper as she glanced over the household expenditures for the week. Sunlight streamed through the tall windows, casting a soft glow on the elegant furnishings. She had been at this task for some time, pausing every few moments to rub her temples. The numbers were familiar now, but managing an estate like Pemberley was a new responsibility for her. She had called for Mrs Reynolds to help clarify certain details, and the housekeeper was due to arrive shortly.

The door creaked open, and Mrs Reynolds entered with her usual quiet efficiency. Elizabeth greeted her with a nod and motioned for her to take a seat.

"Thank you for coming, Mrs Reynolds," Elizabeth began, gesturing to the ledgers spread out before her. "I've been reviewing the accounts, and I have a few questions. First, I see certain sums set aside here for gifts to the tenants. Could you clarify how those gifts are usually distributed?"

Mrs Reynolds folded her hands in her lap. "Yes, ma'am. Traditionally, we send out small gifts each quarter—usually produce from Pemberley's own stores, along with items from the store in the village. It is something the tenants look forward to."

Elizabeth frowned slightly, tapping the edge of her pen against the paper. "And what of the harvest party? I've noticed a budget set aside for that, as well, yet I do not believe it was held this year."

Mrs Reynolds hesitated for a moment before answering. "That is correct, ma'am. The harvest festival is a longstanding tradition here at Pemberley. But given the household is in mourning this year, we did not think it appropriate to hold such festivities."

Elizabeth nodded. "No, it would not have been," she agreed softly, but her brow furrowed in thought. "However, I cannot help but feel that something should have been done. The tenants likely anticipated some kindness, even if not the party itself."

Mrs Reynolds looked down at her hands. "No, madam. Nothing has been done in place of the usual celebration."

"Well, we must set that right." Elizabeth sat back in her chair, considering for a moment. "Perhaps, instead of a party, we might assemble somewhat larger gift baskets for each tenant this quarter," she said slowly, as the idea formed. "Something generous—from Pemberley's winter provisions, along with dress goods and useful supplies from the village, and do not stint. It could see each family through the winter more comfortably."

A beaming smile spread across Mrs Reynolds' face. "That is a wonderful idea, ma'am. I can certainly arrange it."

Elizabeth smiled in return, handing back the accounts. "Then let us do that, please. And I hope, when the time becomes more appropriate, that you will be so good as to introduce me to the families."

Mrs Reynolds curtsied. "It will be my pleasure, Mrs Darcy. I shall set about it at once."

Elizabeth nodded and returned her focus to her writing, satisfied with the decision. But just as Mrs Reynolds was about to leave the room, she stopped and turned back, as if something had slipped her mind.

Elizabeth lowered her pen, raising an eyebrow. "Yes, Mrs Reynolds?"

The housekeeper hesitated. "There is another matter, ma'am. In the course of things, I had scheduled a thorough cleaning of Captain Darcy's private chambers." She paused, watching Elizabeth carefully. "The dust must be attended to, the linens freshened, but I thought it best to inquire if the master would wish the room to remain undisturbed, or if he has any other instructions."

Elizabeth let out a slow breath. This was delicate territory, and she felt unsure how to navigate it. "And what were Mr Darcy's previous instructions regarding the room?"

Mrs Reynolds' face softened with a hint of sorrow. "There were none, madam. Only the master's grief kept us from entering the room. He... he has not spoken of it since Captain Darcy's passing. But it has been a month, and I thought it right to bring it to your attention."

Elizabeth nodded thoughtfully, her fingers drumming lightly on the desk. She understood the housekeeper's concern, but she also knew how sensitive her husband was on this subject. "You are right. The room should be cleaned," she said slowly. "But I think it best if we delay by a day or so. I will speak to Mr Darcy and prepare him for the task."

Mrs Reynolds curtsied once more, clearly relieved. "As you wish, madam. I shall await your instructions."

Elizabeth watched her leave, then set down her pen and sighed. This conversation with her husband would be anything but easy.

THE SOFT SCRATCHING OF ink on paper was the only sound this morning in Darcy's quiet study. His mind was absorbed in the day's work—letters from his steward regarding Pemberley's tenants, matters of trade, and a reply still waiting to be written to a friend in London. But just as his focus sharpened, a firm knock came at the door.

His brow furrowed. He had given instructions not to be disturbed.

"Enter," Darcy called, setting the quill down and leaning back in his chair.

The door creaked open, and a footman stepped into the room, bowing slightly. "Mr Darcy, your uncle, the Earl of Matlock, has arrived and wishes to see you."

Darcy straightened in his chair, surprise flickering across his features. "My uncle?" He had received a letter from the earl only yesterday, and there had been no mention of an impending visit. For him to appear so suddenly... Something must be amiss. "Very well. Show him in at once."

The footman bowed again and disappeared through the doorway. Darcy rose from his desk to receive him but was at a loss as to what manner he should affect. Why had his uncle come unannounced? There had been no surprises in their correspondence. Darcy had informed him of everything—everything pertinent, at least. His marriage, the affairs at Pemberley, even his inquiries about Harry. No, this was unexpected, and Darcy found his pulse quickening as he moved toward the hearth to greet him.

The Earl of Matlock entered the room seconds later, his presence as commanding as ever, though today there was a weariness to his countenance that Darcy did not miss. His uncle's usually brisk step was slower, his face shadowed with something akin to strain.

"Uncle," Darcy greeted him with a nod, coming forward. "This is an unexpected visit. I trust all is well?"

The Earl gave a brief nod, his eyes scanning the room, though they were clouded with something Darcy could not quite place. "Nephew," he said. "You will forgive my distraction. I arrived at Matlock only yesterday—I left London in some haste. Matters... have arisen that I felt could not wait."

Darcy's unease deepened. "I see," he said slowly. "Please, have a seat."

His uncle hesitated, glancing toward the leather armchair near the hearth, as though torn between his urgency to speak and the polite formality of sitting. After a moment, he relented and took the offered seat.

Darcy offered his uncle a drink, gesturing toward the decanter on the side table, but the Earl shook his head with a brusque wave of his hand. "No, no, I need my wits about me, Nephew. This is not a conversation for muddled minds."

Darcy raised an eyebrow but said nothing, taking a seat opposite his uncle and settling himself. He waited, observing the way his uncle's usually composed features twitched with agitation, his fingers tapping a restless beat on the arm of the chair. It was clear the earl was trying to find his words, but Darcy knew better than to press him. Whatever it was, it would come out soon enough.

Finally, the earl let out a heavy breath, his eyes flashing with frustration. "You cannot begin to imagine the scandal that is bursting out everywhere in London."

Darcy sighed, shifting slightly in his seat. "I am certainly aware of it, Uncle. I assure you, there is nothing you can say that would surprise me."

The Earl grunted in a mixture of disbelief and irritation. "Oh, I have no pity for you, Nephew, if that is what you are expecting—for whatever personal reproach you have brought upon yourself by marrying Harry's chit." He spat the word as if it left a bad taste in his mouth. "I still cannot credit your foolishness there, but that is not what I am referring to."

Darcy's eyes narrowed. His voice was low, firm, as he interrupted, "You speak of *Mrs Darcy*, Uncle, and you will remember that the lady is under my protection. You will speak of her with respect."

The Earl's expression darkened further, but he rolled his eyes with a muttered, "Undeserving of the Darcy name, if you ask me." He waved a dismissive hand. "Do you even know the sort of family you've bound yourself to, Nephew? The scandal they've been embroiled in?"

Darcy's gaze didn't waver. "I know of them. But when I discovered the oath my brother was unable to keep, I could do nothing less than ensure it was fulfilled."

"She was not even carrying his bastard! An artful ruse, though not an original one. How the devil did she hoodwink *you*, Darcy? I always thought you had more sense than that."

Darcy jerked to his feet and gestured towards the hall. "There is the door, Uncle, if you should feel inclined to use it. What is done is done, and I am satisfied with the outcome."

"'Satisfied,' you say? A few rolls in the sheets will clear the stars from your eyes—I should have thought they would have done, already. You are fortunate that you find *me* at your door today, and not Lady Catherine."

Darcy did not move, but crossed his arms. "Lady Catherine would have the same answer from me. You can have nothing more to say on the subject that I will hear with equanimity. Now, state your business or have a drink to Harry's name. I care not, but you will cease insulting Mrs Darcy."

For a moment, they stared at each other in tense silence. The earl subsided, though the sourness on his face remained. Clearly, he was far from pleased with Darcy's choice, but the topic had been deflected for the time being.

"Very well," the earl muttered, though his voice still carried a faint edge of displeasure. "But I am not here to speak of the woman." He fixed Darcy with a sharp look, his lips thinning. "I am talking about Harry."

Darcy studied him, feeling a cold knot forming in his stomach. He turned away without a word, crossing the room to the decanter, after all. Whatever this was, it sounded like a conversation that required more than just words. Darcy poured a generous portion into two glasses, his hand steady, though his heart was beginning to race. He returned to his seat, offering one of the glasses to his uncle.

The Earl hesitated for a moment, then accepted it with a curt nod.

Darcy sat back down, the glass in his hand warming between his fingers. "I am aware that Harry had found himself in some sort of strife before his death," he said carefully. "But I have not been able to uncover the full nature of it."

The Earl let out a bitter, humorless laugh. "Strife? Is that what you're calling it? It would be very well if you never had to hear the truth of it, but that is no longer possible."

Darcy's jaw tightened. He took a measured sip of his drink before setting the glass down on the small table beside him, his voice cool and steady. "Then it seems we have much to discuss."

The Earl stared into his glass for a long moment before he spoke again. "The day before I left London, I was speaking with Colonel Halton—he served with Harry in Spain."

"I am familiar with Halton. It was he to whom I gave the news of Harry's death."

"A good man, well-connected. He had some... knowledge of what had happened in Spain."

Darcy's heart stuttered, and he leaned forward in his chair, his brows knitting together. "And what did he say?" His voice was low, quiet—too quiet, perhaps—but the tension in his words betrayed his growing unease. He set his glass down, his hands resting on his knees, ready for whatever bombshell his uncle was about to drop.

The earl thinned his lips, as if tasting something sour, and his eyes narrowed. Darcy had never seen his uncle this way—uncertain, even hesitant.

"It's not something I want to believe, and God knows it's not something I ever wanted to hear confirmed," the Earl muttered. "But Halton... he knew Harry well. And what he told me lines up with whispers I'd already been hearing in certain circles."

Darcy straightened, his body tense as he braced himself. "Out with it, Uncle."

The Earl scowled, his jaw tightening as if the words themselves caused him pain. "Captain Darcy—Harry—is said to have committed treason."

Chapter Twenty

"N o!" Darcy exclaimed, his voice rising in disbelief. "This must be some mistake! Harry was loyal—honest! He would never betray his country. He could not even betray a dog!" His fists clenched on the arms of his chair as he glared at his uncle. "What is the nature of this absurd claim?"

The Earl of Matlock sighed. "There was an incident during the siege at Badajoz. Harry—you recall, he was then a lieutenant—and his men were in the thick of it, taking heavy fire on the wall."

Darcy's breath strangled. His mind filled with the image of his younger brother, Harry, in the hellish chaos of battle. "Badajoz..." he murmured, his voice faltering as he struggled to imagine the violence and bloodshed his brother had witnessed. His chest tightened painfully. "Go on."

The earl hesitated. "It was bloody—though they claimed it a victory. But even in London, we heard of the tremendous casualties, so one can only imagine how hideous..."

Darcy could only nod. His throat felt dry, unable to swallow. He could picture it now: Harry standing against the storm of gunfire, defiant in the face of death. But there was more, and Darcy dreaded hearing it.

"During that battle," the Earl continued, "there is a claim—one made by an undersergeant, mind you—that Harry gave the order for his men to stop firing. To retreat. To give way and let the enemy surge over the wall they were defending."

Darcy's brow furrowed deeply, the shock giving way to anger. "What?" he barked, standing abruptly. "Why would he do that? He would never!"

"I do not know the reasons, but that is the accusation. Harry is said to have ordered a retreat at the most crucial moment of the battle."

Darcy's mind whirled as he paced the room. "Harry was made captain after that battle," he said through gritted teeth. "For his valour! How can they now accuse him of treason?"

The earl shook his head. "It was political wrangling, from what I can gather. The undersergeant made his accusation, but Harry, with his connections, his name, managed to... redirect the narrative. He undermined the evidence, retelling the tale in a way that cast him as the hero."

Darcy stopped in his tracks, his breath coming fast and shallow. "You expect me to believe that Harry—my brother—would threaten others to save his own skin? It's preposterous!"

"I agree. It does not sound like Harry," the earl said quietly, his voice heavy with resignation. "But I have had this confirmed by credible sources, Darcy. This is not something we can simply dismiss."

Darcy was left stunned. Further, the thought of his brother's honour being questioned like this was nearly unbearable. He looked up sharply. "Harry was no traitor. You knew him as well as I—he had principles. His loyalty to his men was unmatched. He would never abandon them."

The earl fell silent for a long moment, then spoke softly. "I am sorry, Darcy."

"Sorry?" Darcy's voice was sharp, his eyes flashing. "Sorry for what?"

The earl exhaled slowly, his expression grim. "For the storm you will face when you next return to London. It is already making its rounds. You will receive the cut direct. The Darcy name is tarnished—forever."

Darcy could not believe what he was hearing. His entire body shook with anger. He rose to his feet, pacing once more. "And do you think I care a jot about society and their bloody opinions? I have lost my only brother—a man of honour and courage—and now he is vilified in death by vultures who envied him. What does that say about them, Uncle? It says nothing of Harry's honour and everything about their jealousy!"

The earl raised his hands, trying to calm his nephew's fury. "Darcy, you must listen. You cannot let this consume you. You cannot fight the entire *ton*."

"Names, Uncle," Darcy demanded, his voice a low growl. "Give me their names. I will confront them myself."

"It is on everyone's lips, Darcy. Impossible to trace it back to a handful of sources. The accusations are everywhere." He paused, then added, "You could write to the colonel if you wish to hear the full tale. But I do not recommend it. The details are ugly."

Darcy continued to pace, his rage barely contained, when a knock interrupted the heated silence.

"What is it?" he barked, his voice harsher than he intended.

The door opened a crack, and Elizabeth peeked her head in, looking startled. "I did not think my knock was so offensive, Mr Darcy," she said with a teasing smile. But her eyes quickly flicked to the earl, and her expression turned more serious. "Forgive me, I did not realise you had company. I can return later."

Darcy immediately softened, the sight of her unwinding some of the tension coiled in his chest. "No, do come in," he said, stepping aside to welcome her. "Allow me to introduce my uncle, the Earl of Matlock. Uncle, this is Mrs Darcy."

The Earl stood, his eyes sharp as he took in Elizabeth's presence. His expression remained guarded, particularly after Darcy shot him a stern glare, but he bowed stiffly in greeting. "Mrs Darcy."

Elizabeth curtsied. "It is a pleasure, my lord."

The Earl raised an eyebrow, as if testing her mettle. "The pleasure must be all mine, I am sure. Tell me, madam, how are you adjusting to life at Pemberley?"

"It is a most beautiful place, and I find the people here to be kind and welcoming. I could not ask for better company."

"And," the Earl replied, his tone deceptively mild, "how do you find the management of such a large estate as Pemberley? It must be... quite different from what you are accustomed to," the Earl finished, smiling as though awaiting a misstep.

Elizabeth did not miss a beat. "Indeed, it is a great deal to manage, my lord," she said with a serene smile, folding her hands before her. "But I have had the excellent guidance of Mrs Reynolds and Mr Darcy to steer me through it. I find that one cannot help but rise to the occasion when supported by such capable hands."

The earl's eyes narrowed slightly, as though considering whether to press further. "And you have found no difficulties, then? Have you met any new acquaintances yet?"

Darcy tensed, sending his uncle another warning glare, but Elizabeth caught it with a wry smile.

"The household is in mourning, my lord," Elizabeth reminded him, "but I expect that with time and fair dealings, I might make one or two friends in Derbyshire."

Darcy could see the faint twitch in his uncle's brow, an indication that Elizabeth's composed response had not quite given him the opening he sought. The earl shifted slightly in his chair and, with a glint in his eye, ventured again, "And tell me, Mrs Darcy, what of London? How shall you fare there upon your return? Surely the circles you kept before were... somewhat different."

Elizabeth's smile did not falter. "Different, yes, but people are much the same wherever you go, are they not? The kindness of one's company speaks louder than their title, I have found."

The Earl blinked, clearly not expecting such a reply. "Quite so," he muttered, leaning back in his chair, the wind taken out of his sails.

Darcy hid a small smile. His uncle shifted uncomfortably, his test met and deflected with far more grace than it had been delivered. "Yes, well," the earl muttered, "it seems you have everything well in hand, Mrs Darcy."

Elizabeth dipped her head gracefully. "I certainly hope so, my lord."

As she curtsied and prepared to take her leave, Darcy could see the slight flush of frustration colouring his uncle's face. Elizabeth had answered every question with such effortless charm that the Earl had been left without a foothold.

"Excuse me, Uncle," Darcy said, inclining his head. "Mrs Darcy, was there something you wished?"

"I merely had a question about the household accounts," Elizabeth said, with a glance at Lord Matlock. "But it can certainly wait."

Darcy gave her a small smile. "Then I shall speak with you later."

She nodded, offering a parting glance that seemed to steady him before she slipped out the door.

As the door clicked shut behind her, Darcy turned back to his uncle, his thoughts still swimming with anger and frustration. But her presence had calmed him, as it so often did.

The earl watched her go, his face still slightly pinched with irritation, and Darcy couldn't help the small grin that tugged at his lips. "She is not what you expected, Uncle?" Darcy asked mildly, leaning back in his own chair.

His uncle let out a gruff chuckle, though his eyes narrowed at Darcy. "She is... something of a surprise," the earl admitted, shifting in his seat. "I will give her that. But I warn you, Darcy, the *ton* will eat her alive, and you with her."

"I look forward to seeing them try."

But the pleasure of congratulating his wife on comporting herself well before a sceptical audience must wait. Darcy paced back to the sideboard, returning his empty glass before turning round to his uncle once more. "What more, Uncle? What is to be done about these rumours?"

The earl sighed, his demeanour stiffening again. "What more *can* be done, Darcy? Captain Darcy is dead. You cannot undo his mistakes, nor can you save his reputation."

Darcy drew a long breath, forcing his mind to settle. "No," he said quietly, though the weight of his anger still simmered beneath his skin. "But I can try. And I will not let his name be ruined without a fight."

The earl rose from his seat, his expression resigned. "That is not why I came here, Darcy—to send you tilting after windmills. There is no more you can do. I merely felt it best you should hear it from me first, before others have their way with it."

Darcy gave a curt nod. "Thank you, Uncle."

E LIZABETH'S EYES NARROWED ON the Earl of Matlock's carriage in the distance as it rattled into view down the drive. She pushed her chair back, rising with a determined breath. Something was wrong. The earl's visit had been a surprise, but it was Darcy's sharp, frustrated shout when she had knocked on his study door... That was not the voice of a man at ease.

Perhaps he needed to talk. Perhaps he would prefer solitude. It was hard to tell with him, but she had learned enough in these few weeks to know that he would not voice his troubles unless pressed.

She made her way to the door, half-distracted by her thoughts, but before she even reached the hall, she froze. Darcy was already there, in the foyer. He yanked on his coat with a ferocity she had rarely seen from him, the hard set of his jaw betraying the storm swirling within him. He smashed his hat on his head, snatched up his walking stick, and moved toward the door, his strides long and brimming with frustration.

The footman barely managed to swing the door open before Darcy charged through it, the heavy wooden door creaking in protest. Elizabeth stood rooted in place, her heart thrumming. Whatever the earl had said to him had left a deep mark. She hesitated for a moment longer before making up her mind.

Slipping back upstairs to her room, she quickly pulled on her cloak and bonnet, tying the ribbons with practised ease. She hurried outside, stopping at the top of the steps to see where Darcy had gone. Halfway across the grounds, she spotted him, his tall figure storming toward the stables. His pace was quick, urgent, but then—without warning—he veered off, changing his direction entirely.

He was headed toward the lake.

That was as good as an invitation. He knew that was her favoured spot to think, and perhaps he had gone there for the same reason. Elizabeth quickened her pace as the lake came into view, her eyes fixed on Darcy's distant figure.

As she neared, his figure came into sharper focus, his pacing agitated, his hand raking through his hair in frustration. Suddenly, he halted, his figure contorting and fists clenching as he let out a sharp, wordless cry of anger that echoed across the water. Elizabeth froze in place, unsure whether to call out or remain silent, but before she could decide, he spun around, his gaze locking onto hers.

His body stiffened, and for a moment, he looked as though he might retreat from her presence entirely. Then, as if some unseen weight fell from his shoulders, he let out a long, shuddering sigh. His features softened, and he met her eyes with an expression that told her everything she needed to know.

"Harry is being accused of treason," he blurted out, his voice thick with outrage.

Elizabeth's breath caught, and her feet faltered for a moment before she hurried forward again. "What? What can you possibly mean by that? Who would even believe such a thing?"

Darcy shook his head, his eyes dropping to the ground as he paced once more, his fists clenching at his sides. "I do not know... I—" His voice faltered, and for the first time, Elizabeth noticed the tremor in his chest, the glimmer of a tear that he blinked away swiftly.

She swallowed, her heart aching at the sight of him like this, and though she slowed her steps, she continued toward him.

Without another word, Darcy reached for her, pulling her into his arms with a quiet desperation. His grip was firm, almost as if he feared she might vanish. Elizabeth slipped her arms around his neck, pressing her cheek to his chest, feeling the erratic rise and fall of his breath against her.

Neither of them spoke, and for once, words were unnecessary. She could feel the raw emotion, the vulnerability, the sheer agony of hearing the accusations against his brother—and all she could do was hold him tighter, offering her silent support as the heaving in his chest began to slow, and his arms grew tighter still.

E LIZABETH TURNED A PAGE, though her gaze barely brushed the words. From the corner of her eye, she glanced at Darcy. His book lay open, untouched. He had not turned a page in ages. The stillness in his posture, the way his brow furrowed slightly, spoke volumes. He wasn't reading. He wasn't even present.

Elizabeth lowered her own book, watching him more openly now. He seemed so far away, lost in the depths of his thoughts, and the blankness of his expression pulled at something deep within her. She knew the reason for his distress—the accusations against Harry still hung over him like a dark cloud. He had barely spoken after their conversation at the lake—not that there had been much conversation, even there—but there had been a shift in their silence. It was a sort of comfort in merely being near one another.

Finally, as if sensing her gaze, Darcy blinked and looked up from his book. His face was a mask of defeat, though he attempted a small, tired smile. "You do not care for your book, Mrs Darcy?"

She met his eyes, offering a gentle smile of her own. "I might ask you the same, sir."

He glanced down at the pages in front of him, then back up at her with a wry expression. "Caught, then. I suppose my mind has been elsewhere."

Elizabeth leaned forward slightly, her book forgotten. "Do you wish to speak of it?"

Darcy hesitated, his gaze flickering back to the fire. "I... It is difficult to know where to begin."

Elizabeth shifted closer. "Perhaps... you could tell me what your uncle said. You were too agitated to explain it earlier."

Darcy's jaw tightened, his eyes narrowing as the anger and disbelief from earlier began to surface once more. "He said he spoke with a colonel—Harry's commanding officer. Apparently, it was during the siege at Badajoz that these accusations arose. Harry... he was said to have ordered a retreat, to give ground to the enemy, against orders to the contrary. They call it treason."

Elizabeth's heart twisted at the pain in his voice. She took a deep breath, remembering that fight she had witnessed—the threats, the accusations. "Mr Darcy... when I overheard Mr Wickham speaking to Harry, it sounded as if your brother was trying to set right a wrong. Wickham was threatening him, saying that if Harry spoke out, he would be ruined. Could it be that...?"

Darcy's hand clenched around the book in his lap, his knuckles white. "I cannot believe it," he said, his voice low and fierce. "Harry was loyal. He was honourable. He would never—" He stopped, shaking his head as if trying to shake the very idea loose. "To accuse him of treason... it is unthinkable."

Elizabeth hesitated, choosing her words carefully. "But... could there be some truth in it? I do not mean to suggest he betrayed anyone, but perhaps, in the heat of battle, he made a decision that others have misunderstood."

Darcy's eyes flashed with anger as he looked at her. "No," he said firmly. "Harry was made Captain after that battle. He was recognised for his valour. How can they now claim he acted with dishonour?"

Elizabeth's gaze softened as she watched him, his shoulders tense, his entire body vibrating with barely contained fury. "It could be political, then," she murmured. "Someone could be using his death to settle an old score or to cast blame where it doesn't belong."

Darcy's breathing was heavy, his anger visibly mounting with every passing second. "I cannot stand it—the thought of people speaking of him like this. Harry... he—" His voice broke off, and for a moment, he stared down at the floor, his chest rising and falling in ragged breaths.

Without thinking, Elizabeth reached over and gently pulled the book from his hand. Darcy looked up in surprise, his brow furrowing as she took his hand in hers.

"There is nothing more we can do about it tonight," she said softly. "Perhaps... we can find some other way to spend our time. Something more enjoyable."

Darcy's brow smoothed slightly as he gazed at her, the tension in his face easing, though only a little. "More enjoyable?" he echoed, his voice carrying a note of curiosity.

For a fleeting moment, something shifted in his expression—something she couldn't quite place. Was it... desire? Or perhaps a flicker of uncertainty, even fear? Elizabeth's heart skipped, unsure whether to trust the way his eyes seemed to darken, as if his thoughts had leapt far ahead of her words.

Before she could examine that reaction too deeply, she grabbed his hand, rising from the sofa and pulling him up with her. "Come," she said as she led him toward the pianoforte. "I have a suggestion."

Darcy allowed himself to be guided, but his steps were hesitant, his brow clouded. "And what is it you have in mind, Mrs Darcy?"

Elizabeth gestured to the instrument with a playful smile. "We shall play a song together. Harry said once that your mother made both of you learn, so you *must* play some little."

Darcy blinked, then let out a small, reluctant laugh. "I have not played in at least five years."

"Good," Elizabeth replied, her tone light and teasing. "You will not sound any better than I do, then."

Darcy looked at her with a bemused expression, then glanced at the piano. "Harry was always the better player. He was the more agreeable student." He huffed softly. "And once I reached the age of ten, Father said I had more important things to learn, anyway. But I still played with Mother whenever I could."

Elizabeth's smile softened as she sifted through the sheet music. "Then you must prove her lessons were not wasted. Besides," she added with a mischievous glint in her eyes, "I have no intention of playing anything myself. You, Mr Darcy, will be the performer tonight."

Darcy shook his head, a smile tugging at the corners of his mouth. "You are determined, are you?"

"Absolutely," she said, pulling out a duet from the collection and setting it on the stand. "Now, sit. I shall play along if you pout convincingly enough, but only if you take the lead so your bad playing will obscure mine."

With a sigh of mock resignation, Darcy sat at the piano, adjusting his sleeves as though preparing for a grand performance. "I must warn you," he said, his fingers hovering above the keys, "I shall play terribly."

Elizabeth laughed, taking her place beside him. "Then I shall play terribly with you."

They began to play, but it was clear neither was focused on the music. Elizabeth's fingers stumbled over the keys, misjudging notes, her hand bumping into his again and again. The proximity of him beside her, his solid presence on the narrow bench, was making it impossible to concentrate. Every time his hand brushed hers, it was like a spark leaping between them, a fire that seemed to scorch her skin in a way that had nothing to do with the warmth of the hearth nearby.

"Perhaps," she quipped, grinning as she missed yet another note, "we should perform this duet blindfolded. I suspect it would make no difference."

Darcy chuckled. "I suspect it would only make things worse. I might take your fingers off entirely with my incompetence."

Elizabeth laughed, shaking her head, but the sound of his laughter wrapped around her, curling into her chest. He was so close. *Too* close. The heat of his leg against hers was sending a flutter through her stomach she had not expected, her pulse quickening with every brush of his hand.

At one point, their hands collided again, both reaching for the same key, and Elizabeth couldn't help but dissolve into laughter. "Are you trying to sabotage me, Mr Darcy? If so, you are doing an excellent job."

He smiled at her, but his gaze lingered a little too long, and Elizabeth felt the heat of it scorching the hair on her scalp. "Sabotage? Never. I would only do such a thing if I believed you had the upper hand." His voice dropped, and the shift in his tone made her pulse skip.

Elizabeth was still laughing, but there was a nervous flutter beneath it now. "I think I might have to accuse you of trying to throw me off, sir. You are clearly distracting me on purpose."

"Distracting you?" Darcy raised a brow, his hand hovering over hers on the keys, the warmth of it nearly burning her skin. "I wouldn't dream of it."

His voice was teasing, but there was something more beneath it, something that made the air between them feel thick as syrup and almost as sweet. Elizabeth's breath caught in her throat, and for a moment, she couldn't move. The fire crackled softly beside them, but it was the heat radiating from his body that made her feel light-headed, her pulse racing in her ears.

"Then," she said, forcing herself to speak lightly, "I'm afraid we are both hopeless. And I was so certain we would be the finest musicians in all of Derbyshire."

Darcy chuckled again, but this time his smile was softer, more intimate. "Well, I suppose we'll have to settle for being the worst duet in Derbyshire."

Elizabeth felt her heart race as his hand lingered beside hers on the keyboard, neither of them moving to resume playing. "Shall we try again?" she asked, though her voice sounded breathless to her own ears.

"Perhaps," Darcy murmured, his gaze slipping down to her hand resting on the keys. His fingers brushed against hers again, lingering this time, and Elizabeth's heart stumbled over itself.

"You are doing it again," she teased, though her voice was quieter now, softer.

"Doing what?" His eyes flicked up to hers, and for a brief moment, something hovered in their depths. A flash of desire, perhaps... or was it something else? Fear? Uncertainty? Elizabeth couldn't quite place it, but whatever it was, it made the space between them feel all the more charged.

"Distracting me."

For a moment, neither of them moved, the music forgotten, their hands hovering too close on the keyboard. Then, with a quick laugh that broke the tension, Elizabeth leaned back slightly, shaking her head. "I think we are hopeless."

"Hopeless, indeed." But his hand was still too close, and the nearness of him was still too intoxicating for her to focus on anything else.

"Perhaps we should play something less... complicated?" she suggested, but her voice wavered slightly, the words feeling like an attempt to cover up the heat building between them.

Darcy nodded, though he seemed just as distracted. "Perhaps." But neither of them moved to turn the page or choose another piece, their attention caught in something much more subtle, much more dangerous than music.

The silence between them stretched out, heavy with something unspoken. Elizabeth's skin prickled with awareness, every inch of her attuned to his presence beside her. She could feel the warmth radiating from him, more intense than the fire that crackled a few feet away. She glanced at him, only to find his eyes already on her, his gaze dark and searching, pulling at something deep inside her.

"Elizabeth..." Darcy's voice was low, almost hoarse, as if he were struggling to maintain control. He lifted his hand, hesitating for a moment before his fingers gently cupped her chin. The touch was soft but sure, sending a ripple of sensation down her spine.

She froze, her pulse fluttering wildly as their eyes locked. The moment hung between them, charged and fragile, like a taut string about to snap. His thumb brushed lightly along the edge of her jaw, and it felt as though the very ground beneath her shifted.

And then, without warning, he closed the distance, his lips finding hers in a kiss that was both tender and full of a quiet intensity. His touch was tentative at first, as though he feared to break something delicate. Elizabeth's senses flooded with the warmth of him, the pressure of his mouth on hers sending a rush of heat through her veins. She felt the keys beneath her fingers tremble as her hands rested against the piano, though all her focus was on him.

But just as quickly, he pulled away, his breath uneven, and dropped his hand from her face. They stared at each other, both stunned by the suddenness of it, the air between them almost brittle with everything that remained unsaid.

Darcy swallowed hard, his gaze shifting away from her to the piano, as though he could not trust himself to meet her eyes any longer. Elizabeth waited, expecting him to stammer out some sort of apology. Or, better yet, to throw caution to the wind and kiss her again. Instead, he drew in a sharp breath, then turned back to the sheet music with deliberate composure.

"Perhaps," he said, his voice tight but steady, "we should try something simpler. It seems we are not well-suited for more complicated pieces."

Elizabeth blinked, still reeling from the kiss, but nodded, her fingers trembling faintly as they hovered over the keys once more.

"Yes," she managed to murmur, "something simpler."

Darcy set the music on the stand, but even as they prepared to play again, the air between them simmered with an unspoken understanding. She was not sure what this new closeness meant, but there was no denying that something had deepened between them—something neither of them seemed ready to fully acknowledge, yet neither could ignore.

Chapter Twenty-One

ELIZABETH ADJUSTED HER CLOAK as she stepped down from the carriage, the chill air of the early winter breeze whipping the cloth about her legs. Mrs Reynolds followed close behind, advising Elizabeth on all the particulars of each family for this first outing as the mistress. Though she had encountered many at church, the prospect of truly getting to know them filled her with nervous anticipation.

"Mrs Darcy, these are good people," Mrs Reynolds said gently as they approached the first house. "I think you will find them most welcoming, but they are not without their struggles. The baskets will be well received."

Elizabeth nodded, holding her basket firmly. She had overseen their assembly herself, ensuring each family received provisions and small luxuries from Pemberley's stores. She hoped the gesture would make up for the missed harvest festival, a tradition here of some long standing. It was not the fault of these good people that the festival had not been held this year.

At the first cottage, a young couple greeted her with wide smiles and a toddler clinging to the mother's skirts. The house smelled of herbs and baking bread, and Elizabeth immediately felt at ease as the mother introduced herself as Mrs Hale. The little boy peeked shyly around his mother's legs before toddling forward, holding out a chubby hand. Elizabeth knelt to his level, smiling as he offered her a small wooden toy.

"This is little Peter," Mrs Hale said with a fond smile. "He's not yet three but already trying to help his father in the fields."

Elizabeth chuckled, handing the toy back to the boy. "A hard worker already, I see."

The family's gratitude for the gift basket was sweetly apparent, and as they shared a cup of tea, Elizabeth found herself exchanging easy conversation with the young mother. They spoke of the harvest, of how the estate's bounty helped the tenants, and how kind Mrs Reynolds had been in ensuring their needs were met.

At another cottage, an elderly woman named Mrs Blythe greeted them at the door. Her hands trembled as she welcomed Elizabeth and Mrs Reynolds inside, but her eyes were sharp with wit and experience. The interior was modest but immaculately clean, with simple, well-worn furniture that spoke of generations past.

"I thank you, Mrs Darcy, for the provisions," the older woman said. "I did not think I would see such kindness from the mistress of Pemberley herself."

Elizabeth smiled warmly. "It is my pleasure. I wanted to ensure everyone had something to see them through the winter."

Mrs Blythe eyed her with a shrewd glint. "You remind me of Mr Darcy's mother, Lady Anne. She used to visit, same as you're doing now. I see you've a good heart, like she did."

Elizabeth felt a warmth spread through her chest at the unexpected praise. It was a kind sentiment, one she wasn't sure she could live up to yet, but it was encouraging.

In another home, Elizabeth met Mrs Latham, who had five grown sons and one daughter still at home. The sons worked on various parts of the estate, and as Mrs Reynolds introduced them, Elizabeth noted how each family seemed to have their own unique role in the running of Pemberley's vast lands. Mrs Latham spoke proudly of her sons' contributions, though her face softened when she mentioned her daughter's prospects.

"A fine young lady like Miss Latham should have no trouble finding a good match," Elizabeth said kindly as the daughter stood by, her eyes downcast and cheeks flushed. "She's a great help to you here, I'm sure."

Mrs Latham nodded, but the younger girl gave no answer, only offering Elizabeth a shy smile as she helped her mother place the gift basket on the kitchen table.

The next few houses followed a similar pattern. Each family expressed first their welcome of the new Mrs Darcy, and then their grief over Harry's death in a way that felt almost ritualistic. But Elizabeth found comfort in the repetition. It made her feel, oddly, more connected to these people, even as she still struggled to comprehend the tragedy herself.

But it was at the last house that Elizabeth's world tilted ever so slightly.

The door opened to reveal a beautiful young woman, perhaps no older than Elizabeth herself, who greeted them with a shy, almost hesitant smile. Her hand rested gently on her abdomen, a protective gesture that highlighted the telltale sign of pregnancy, just barely visible beneath her modest gown. Elizabeth extended the basket, her expression warm and kind as always, but she could not ignore the flicker of anxiety in the girl's downcast eyes.

"Good afternoon, Mrs Henshaw," Elizabeth said softly, trying to put her at ease. "This is a small token of our appreciation for all that you do. I hope it will be of some use to your family."

The young woman glanced up briefly, her lips parting as if to speak, but she seemed to lose her courage and looked down again. Before the silence could stretch too far, her mother stepped forward, her hands outstretched to accept the basket. "Mrs Darcy, thank you for this kindness," she said, her voice steady but with a note of weariness. She glanced at her daughter, who stood silently at her side, staring down at her feet as if avoiding more than just the conversation. "We were all so saddened by Captain Darcy's passing. He... he was well loved."

The words hung in the air—strangely heavier, this time, than in other households. She offered a sympathetic nod, her gaze moving to the daughter again, noting how tightly the girl's hands were clasped in front of her. Elizabeth's throat clenched, but she kept her tone gentle as she replied, "I am sure he was very fond of this place and its people. It is difficult for us all to bear the loss."

The young woman's hand trembled slightly where it rested against her belly, and her mother's eyes flitted nervously between her daughter and Elizabeth, as if gauging how much more could be said.

The girl bit her lip, her eyes glistening as she tried to keep herself composed. Elizabeth felt a pang of sympathy. She knew the grief of loss, but this was different. The girl's reaction was raw, immediate.

"I am so sorry for upsetting you," Elizabeth said softly, reaching out to her. "Please, you needn't—"

But the young woman could no longer contain her tears. She choked out a sob and turned, rushing from the room with her hand clapped over her mouth. The sound of her faint crying echoed in the small house.

Elizabeth stood, stunned and distressed, watching the girl's retreating figure. "I am terribly sorry," she said to the mother, unsure of what had just transpired. "I did not mean to upset her."

The woman shook her head, more resigned than surprised. "It is no fault of yours, Mrs Darcy," she said, her tone almost matter-of-fact. "Clara's been this way since... well, since last summer."

Elizabeth exchanged a glance with Mrs Reynolds, but the housekeeper said nothing. They offered a few more words of comfort, but the atmosphere had shifted, and it was soon clear that the visit needed to end.

As they climbed back into the carriage, Elizabeth could not shake the unease that had settled in her chest. She turned to Mrs Reynolds, hoping for some clarity. "What... what happened to her? Why was she so upset?"

Mrs Reynolds hesitated, her normally composed expression faltering for a moment. "I ought to have warned you before we visited, Mrs Darcy," she began slowly, "but I thought the girl had been sent away by now."

Elizabeth frowned. "Sent away?"

"Clara Henshaw is unmarried, ma'am." Mrs Reynolds' voice dropped lower, and her eyes flicked up to meet Elizabeth's briefly. "She was found last summer, her gown torn, but she refused to name the man responsible. No one knows if she was attacked or if it was... something else. 'Tis a pity—she was always such a good girl, and so terribly fond of the young master."

"Captain Darcy?" Elizabeth asked.

"Aye." Mrs Reynolds clicked her tongue and shook her head. "She was often in his company at tenant gatherings, and..." Mrs Reynolds trailed off, her grimace deepening. "She took his death very hard."

Elizabeth sat in silence, her brow puckering in thought. Could Harry have been involved with this girl? The thought sent a shiver down her spine, but she quickly dismissed it. Harry had been in London most of the summer... hadn't he?

Except... she recalled something from when they first met at that party in July. He had told her he was being sent to Leicester for a week. Just a week, but perhaps... perhaps he had been in the country after all. That was the only time when no one she knew could vouch for his whereabouts.

Her thoughts grew darker. Could Harry have been the one? Had she misjudged him so completely? Oh, but that was preposterous! He had been on assignment, and surely his commander would have expected a swift return from his errand or whatever it was. To think of someone like Captain Darcy detouring to Derbyshire just to seduce a girl!

But he *could* have come further north to surprise his brother. Harry had even joked about doing just that, had he not? And if this... incident... happened before Harry made it to Pemberley, why, he might have turned round before anyone could place him in the county at that time.

Elizabeth hissed under her breath and shook her head, trying to put at bay such hideous thoughts. Her imagination was accusing and convicting a man who was not there to defend himself, whose very life and character would contradict the accusations decisively. The only smear on Harry's legacy was that bothersome accusation of some sort of treason, which... well, when put plainly, could be true but, in her estimation, was probably a product of battlefield confusion.

That, and the letter her husband had shown her. The one written by an outraged father over his compromised daughter.

Elizabeth swallowed and turned her gaze purposely out the window before Mrs Reynolds could see the darkness crossing her features. The remainder of the ride back to Pemberley passed in silence, Elizabeth's mind spinning with questions she had no idea how to answer.

D ARCY TOSSED THE LETTER onto his desk, rising abruptly to pace the length of his study. Richard's latest update was no better than the last—no progress, no answers. It was as though the truth about Harry's final battle had been swallowed up by the shadows of war, leaving nothing but suspicion and bitterness in its wake. The accusations, the rumours—it all churned in Darcy's chest, filling him with a restless energy that he could not dispel.

He leaned back in his chair, rubbing a hand over his face. His thoughts wandered to London, as they so often did now. Perhaps if he went, if he confronted those spreading these lies, he could silence them. But what would that accomplish? Harry was gone. No amount of defending him would bring him back. And London—London was already a quagmire of gossip. If he took Elizabeth there, it would only be worse. They could not attend social functions while in mourning, and he certainly did not wish to parade his wife in front of the very people who would revel in their misfortune. Perhaps... if he let things settle, the rumours would fade. That seemed a rational approach, though it filled him with no satisfaction.

He glanced at Richard's letter again. *Wickham.* The very name set Darcy's blood boiling. Richard had discovered that Wickham had been reassigned to Birmingham, ostensibly to deal with the Luddites. What a farce. Wickham, of all people, tasked with maintaining order?

And Birmingham was no distant outpost—just a day's ride from Pemberley. The idea of Wickham being so close unsettled Darcy more than he cared to admit. He considered doubling the watch on the property, perhaps taking extra precautions, but what good would that do? He would only seem paranoid, and Wickham would not dare come near Pemberley. Would he?

Darcy sighed, shoving his chair back from the desk with more force than intended. The letters scattered across the surface—too many unanswered questions, too many burdens. He could no longer concentrate. With a frustrated breath, he rose to his feet, glancing out the window. A walk. Perhaps fresh air would do what sitting in that stifling room could not.

As he moved toward the door, he reached for his coat, but something caught his attention—a flash of movement in the hallway. Elizabeth. He saw her just as she disappeared through the front door, her steps hurried, her skirts catching on the hem as she fled.

"Elizabeth!" he called after her, his voice echoing through the now-empty foyer, but she was already gone, moving too quickly to hear him.

Darcy hesitated for a moment, his hand on the doorframe. Where was she going in such haste? It almost looked as if something had ruffled her feathers, but the only thing at Pemberley capable of doing that was him. And while things between them seemed to have actually taken a step backwards since the night he kissed her at the piano—his own hesitancy, surely, was to blame—he had no reason to suppose he might be the cause of this. Shrugging into his coat, he followed her.

His gaze followed the path that led down to the lake, where he had often seen her walking in solitude. She was already far ahead, her form growing smaller as she hurried toward the water. Darcy watched her for a moment, feeling the distance between them more keenly than ever. She looked... distressed. And that bothered him in ways he could not ignore.

He sighed and pulled his collar tighter against the wind. His thoughts shifted, circling back to the same nagging question that had haunted him for weeks now. *Elizabeth*. What was he to do about her?

The more time they spent together, the more he found himself drawn to her—not just as a woman, but as his wife—his partner. He wanted her in ways he struggled to put into words, and the desire gnawed at him, refusing to be ignored. Yet, with every step closer, guilt threatened to swallow him whole. Harry's memory, still looming large between them, felt like a barrier he could not cross.

It was foolish, and he knew it. Richard had said as much—Harry was gone, and Darcy had his own life to live. But the guilt persisted, irrational as it was. And then there was Elizabeth herself. What did she feel? She had been so guarded, so measured in her interactions with him. Always polite, sensible of her duties as the mistress, and a bright spot in any room she entered, but there was a veneer over all their interactions. Was it even possible she felt something for him, as he did for her? Or had Harry's shadow stretched so long that it still stood between them?

As Darcy rounded a corner, the frozen lawns of Pemberley spread out before him. The gardens, once so vibrant, were now stark and white with frost. His breath fogged the air as he walked, but it was the sight in the distance that brought him to a halt. Elizabeth, as always, was sitting on her rock by the frigid lake. Even from afar, she looked so small, a figure dwarfed by the vastness of the landscape around her. But something struck him about the way she sat, the way her shoulders hunched just slightly, as if the cold were not the only thing pressing down on her.

Loneliness.

That was it! That was the missing piece. It had nothing to do with Harry—well, it was not *only* to do with Harry. She had lost far more than his brother, had she not? No, what weighed on her now wasn't grief over Harry—it was isolation. She was lonely.

She missed her family.

Darcy cursed himself under his breath. How had he not seen it sooner? Whenever he spoke with her, whenever they shared even the briefest of conversations, she brightened. She was a more social person than he—craving companionship in a way he could probably never comprehend. She came alive when she received letters from home, her face illuminated with a pleasure that was unmistakable. But when she was alone, when she thought no one was watching... there was a sadness in her, a deep, unspoken longing.

He swallowed hard, his eyes fixed on her distant figure. This, at least, was something he could fix. He might not be able to protect Harry's name, but he could do something for his wife. For Elizabeth.

With renewed purpose, Darcy turned on his heel and strode back toward the house. He might not have all the answers, but he had at least part of one of them.

E LIZABETH UNFOLDED JANE'S LETTER with a sigh, her fingers tracing the familiar handwriting as the rain pattered steadily against the windows. The crackling fire warmed the room, but her mind drifted far from the cozy library to the familiar comfort of Longbourn. She had hoped Darcy might be there—stormy afternoons often drew him to the fire with a book in hand—but today, the room was empty but for herself.

She read over Jane's words, smiling faintly as she imagined her sister's dearly beloved voice while writing.

P APA WANTS TO MEET *him, you know—this mysterious Mr Darcy who carried you away to "the far north of England," as he so dramatically puts it. Mr Bingley has assured him that your Mr Darcy is a man of good character, but you know that is not sufficient for Papa. I hope you might visit soon.*

ELIZABETH FOLDED THE LETTER with a soft sigh and slipped it back into her pocket.

Could she persuade her husband to visit Longbourn if they went to London? The thought filled her with both hope and apprehension. Her father's wit might amuse him, and Jane—oh, he would certainly approve of Jane. And it might be a chance for him to know Mr Bingley better, too.

Not that Mr Bingley could step into the hole left by his brother or even his cousin—Richard had been able to draw him out in ways that she fancied other gentlemen could not. But Mr Bingley was an open, cheerful sort who shared some measure of her husband's grief. Yes, he might be a very valuable friend, indeed.

But her mother... Lydia... Kitty... no, perhaps not yet. Perhaps not ever, unless Jane could give her some assurance that her own marriage to Mr Darcy, and Mr Bingley's interest in Jane had subdued Mama somewhat, and given her cause to rein in her younger daughters. And *that* was not likely. She reached for her book.

Only moments later, the door creaked open, and Darcy strode in, rain still dripping from his overcoat. He looked freshly in from the storm, his damp hair tousled, and there was an unusual gleam in his eye, a mysterious smile hovering on his lips. One hand remained tucked beneath his coat as if concealing some secret.

"Elizabeth," he said, his voice carrying a warmth she had not heard in some time. A rare grin spread across his face.

Elizabeth set her book aside and stood, her curiosity piqued by both his tone and appearance. She wandered over to him, brows lifted in mock surprise. "Fitzwilliam Darcy, what are you doing?" she asked, as her gaze swept over him. Rainwater trickled from his broad shoulders, the wild scent of the storm still clinging to him. She felt a strange pull, as though leaning closer might reveal more of that intoxicating scent—fresh air and untamed energy.

Oh, if he came to her like *that* more often, full of himself and smiling and fresh from the outdoors, she doubted very much that he would still think of her as a lady. She would have thrown over her dignity long ago, and would probably have more than one of his kisses to savour in her memories. Elizabeth forced herself to clear her throat and focus on his eyes rather than all the rest of him.

His grin widened as he pulled something from inside his coat. A small, wiggling form emerged—a terrier puppy, squirming and wriggling with boundless energy. Elizabeth gasped in delight, her hands flying up instinctively to catch the little creature as it tried eagerly to lick her face.

"Why in the world have you brought me a puppy?" she laughed, the sound bubbling up from her chest as she cradled the squirming ball of fur. The puppy's bright eyes sparkled, its tiny tongue licking furiously at her cheek.

Darcy stepped closer, resting a gentle hand on the puppy's back, feeling its excited little body wiggle beneath his palm. It was a small terrier, its coat a mix of soft brown and white, with bright, alert eyes that seemed to take in everything around it. The pup's ears twitched at every sound, its tiny paws tapping impatiently as if eager for adventure.

"I had begun to think you were lonely," Darcy said softly, his tone more serious than his grin implied. "I know you miss your family, and I am... perhaps... inadequate company." His gaze held hers, the warmth there unmistakable. "I hoped this little dog might cheer you up."

Elizabeth blinked, her smile faltering for a moment as his words struck her more deeply than she had expected. The puppy, unaware of the feelings her husband had just stirred in her, licked at her fingers, its tiny tail wagging furiously. "Where did you find him?" she asked, her voice quiet as she stroked the soft fur.

Darcy's smile widened, pleased by her curiosity. "One of my tenants raises terriers," he explained, watching the puppy with affection. "They are known to be bold little creatures, though small enough to accompany you anywhere—on your walks, even to London, should we travel there. And they are good company—energetic, brave. I thought..." He trailed off, then added, more gently, "I thought you might appreciate a companion, one who is always happy to see you."

She laughed. "Be careful, Mr Darcy. That statement sounds very much as if *you* are not always happy to see your wife, and I daresay, that is an impolitic confession."

His expression blanched. "I assure you, that is not at all..." His cheek flinched. "I *do* find pleasure in your company, madam. What I meant to say was that my... reception of your presence is too often tempered by my moods. That will not be the case here." His gaze lingered on hers with a strange heat for a moment, but then he cleared his throat and gestured to the puppy. "Look, he is already quite taken with you. Do you..." His brow furrowed. "Does he please you?"

Elizabeth's laugh was softer this time, more touched than amused, as she buried her face in the puppy's fur. She *had* been feeling a quiet loneliness, one she had hardly acknowledged, even to herself. Yet here he was, acknowledging it for her, seeing her more clearly than she realised.

"I know no one with such a hard heart they could not be pleased by such a winsome little creature," she replied. "But you may regret the gift when he soils the carpets, as puppies often do."

Darcy smiled and tugged at one soft ear. "I employ an excellent housekeeper for a reason, Mrs Darcy."

The puppy wriggled in her arms, its tiny paws pressing against her chest as it tried to reach her face for more kisses, and for the first time in a long while, she felt a warmth she hadn't expected—both from the lively little creature in her arms and from the man standing beside her.

"I do not know what to say," she murmured, the little dog's warm body wriggling in her arms. The absurdity and sweetness of the moment overwhelmed her. Unable to resist, she rose up on her toes and kissed Darcy lightly on the cheek. It was a brief, instinctive gesture, one that surprised her as much as it did him.

Darcy stilled, his eyes widening slightly at the touch of her lips. For a heartbeat, the air between them shifted, something unspoken passing between them. But before either could make sense of it, the puppy wriggled between them, nudging its head against Darcy's chest and breaking the spell.

Darcy blinked, his face briefly unreadable, then smiled faintly as the tension dissolved. "I see I've been replaced already," he teased, his hand brushing against hers as she held the puppy close.

"Not replaced, merely... supplemented," Elizabeth replied with a laugh, her gaze lingering on him for a moment longer before they both turned their attention back to the lively creature between them.

Chapter Twenty-Two

ARCY DISMOUNTED HIS HORSE with a grunt of effort, handing the reins to the waiting stable hand. The early morning ride had done little to ease the ball of anxiety that had built in his chest. His muscles ached from the cold, and his breath came in shallow pants, but none of it was enough to clear the fog that had settled over his thoughts. He was stuck—mired in frustration, unable to move forward, no matter how desperately he longed to.

He had lost count of how many nights he had stood outside Elizabeth's door, staring at the dark wood as if it held all the answers to his unspoken questions. Each night, something pulled him toward her, an invisible thread tugging at him to step across that threshold. Duty, desire, even the hope of her simple companionship.

And yet, every night, something equally strong held him back—guilt, hesitation, fear. What if he could never overcome this barrier in him? What if, despite all the growing feelings he harboured for his wife, he was incapable of bridging the gap between them?

His steps quickened as he crossed the threshold into the house, shrugging off his damp riding coat before retreating to his chambers. Once inside, he let out a long breath and began to unbutton his waistcoat, peeling away the cold, wet layers of his ride. He paused halfway through, glancing toward the window where the grey sky threatened more rain.

Perhaps he had been going about this all wrong.

In his mind, he had been picturing the sort of formal arrangement his parents had lived—civility outside the bedroom, each playing their roles but with little warmth or true affection obvious between them. He knew there had been some measure of love there—his father's grief after his mother's death had been the proof of that. But they never showed it to anyone.

It was what he knew, what he had always assumed was "correct." And yet... that life felt so distant from the one he truly wanted. What he wanted—what he longed for—was not just duty. It was love, honest and powerful feelings that would draw him and his wife together naturally, irresistibly. He wanted her to *want* him, to feel something real between them before he asked for anything physical.

And that was why he had been so ill at the thought of marrying her in the first place. He had thought, at the time, that he was giving up any modicum of choice he had in his partner—that all those things he wanted for his life were now dust and ashes. He expected to be saddled with an unholy burden, the sort of heedless strumpet he had imagined *must* be the case if all his other assumptions were true.

But instead, he had found *her*. How had Heaven blessed him so immeasurably? In regards to fortune and connections, she had none. Less than none, truly. She was a liability in every sense of the word. But what she had brought into his world more than compensated for any inconveniences in that regard.

Did she know that she was the reason he had not swallowed a pistol after Harry's death? All the guilt, all the shame that were his, and she was the one he had to be strong for. The one he wanted to live for, even when he did not understand her. Could she sense any of that?

Darcy pulled on a fresh shirt, trying to piece out what she did know and understand. She had warmed to him, in her way. Their conversations were easier with each passing day, their shared moments in the drawing room more frequent. The way her face had exploded with joy when he brought her the puppy—he had never seen her so delighted. She had named the little creature "Little Fitzy" just to tease him, and every time he saw her playfully chasing the dog, his heart swelled with a strange mixture of pride and affection. She did appreciate him—he was certain of that.

But did she desire him? Did she love him?

He just... could not know. And his pride had not yet permitted him to ask.

He fastened the last button of his waistcoat and ran a hand through his still-damp hair. Perhaps... perhaps he needed to change his approach. If what he wanted was more than just duty, he needed to show her that. A small smile tugged at his lips. Perhaps romancing her during the day, finding small ways to make her smile, would make their nights... warmer.

Darcy paced across the room, thinking. What could he do? He could take her on walks more often, perhaps to her favourite spot by the lake. Or bring her small gifts—not extravagant things, but thoughtful ones, things that showed he paid attention to her likes and needs. He could even join her in some of her activities—sitting with her when she read, playing a piece of music together again.

Yes, he thought, finishing his thoughts with a sense of resolution. He could start slowly, quietly, but intentionally. He did not want a life of formality and distance. He wanted love. And perhaps, if he could draw her closer to him in these small, tender moments, she would feel that same pull toward him.

With a deep breath, Darcy decided. Today, he would begin.

His resolve, freshly made, buoyed his spirits slightly. But as he stepped into the hallway, his eyes were drawn to something that spiked his blood like ice. Harry's room—its door open.

He stopped dead in his tracks, a wave of anger rolling over him. He had ordered that room to be left undisturbed. No one was to set foot inside without his explicit instruction. His fists clenched at his sides as he strode purposefully toward the door, his earlier intentions momentarily forgotten. When he entered, he found a young maid dusting the bookcase, her back to him as she worked.

For a brief moment, a rational part of him understood—this was her job, after all, the daily maintenance of the house's many rooms. But that rational voice was quickly drowned by the deeper, more visceral part of him that refused to accept the invasion. Harry's room was not just another room. It was sacred.

"Stop that at once!" Darcy snapped.

The maid jumped, nearly dropping her duster. She turned to him, her face pale with fright, and bobbed a quick curtsy. "I—I was only doing as instructed, sir. Mrs Reynolds said—"

"I do not care what Mrs Reynolds said," he interrupted, his tone clipped. "Leave this room immediately."

The maid fled without another word, her footsteps barely audible in her haste. Darcy's jaw tightened as he scanned the room, his eyes lingering on Harry's belongings. How dare they touch any of it? His mood darkened further. Had he not made it clear that this room was to be left untouched? It seemed he would have to set the matter right.

Striding through the house, Darcy's steps were heavy with purpose, his mind spinning with indignation. Harry's things—his books, his letters, the remnants of his life—were not for others to see, let alone disturb. The very idea filled Darcy with a storm of emotions he was barely able to contain. He would speak to Mrs Reynolds and have this nonsense stopped immediately!

Reaching the housekeeper's quarters near the kitchens, Darcy pushed open the door without waiting for an invitation. But instead of the solitary figure of Mrs Reynolds, his eyes were met with Elizabeth standing next to her, both women mid-conversation. Darcy's words crammed together in his throat, his frustration growing until they came out in a rush.

"Mrs Reynolds," he barked, his voice rough, "why are the maids cleaning Harry's room when I specifically ordered it to be left alone?"

The housekeeper's eyes flicked nervously to Elizabeth, who was staring back at him with an expression that was far from placid. She looked... irritated. Darcy's anger bristled, but before Mrs Reynolds could answer, Elizabeth spoke first.

"Mr Darcy," she said, her tone calm but with a hint of frustration lacing her words, "we discussed this more than a fortnight ago. The maids dust the room once a week, as they do with every room that is not currently occupied. I brought the matter to your attention before telling Mrs Reynolds to continue the practice."

Darcy swallowed hard. How dare she defy him with... And then, with a sudden flash of memory, he recalled the conversation. Yes, she *had* brought it up—while he had been still ruminating over a letter from Richard. He had given a distracted reply, barely paying her any heed. A wave of heat crept up his neck, a combination of frustration and embarrassment.

His jaw tightened, his gaze falling momentarily to the floor before snapping back to Mrs Reynolds. "Desist the practice at once. No one is to enter that room until I say otherwise."

Mrs Reynolds glanced uneasily between Darcy and Elizabeth, but she nodded. "As you wish, sir."

Without another word, Darcy turned and left, his steps hard and quick, the sting of his own lapse gnawing at him as he walked away.

ELIZABETH FOUND HIM IN his study, seated behind the large mahogany desk, but not truly working. Papers were scattered before him, ink drying on a forgotten letter, but his pen remained idle. His jaw was set, his brow furrowed, and his entire posture exuded frustration. She hesitated in the doorway for a moment before stepping forward, determined not to let this go.

"Mr Darcy," she said, her voice calm but firm. He did not look up. "I need to speak with you."

He sighed heavily, finally raising his eyes to meet hers. "I am busy, Elizabeth."

"That did not seem to be the case when I walked in," she replied, stepping closer. "And what you said to Mrs Reynolds earlier—it was uncalled for. You have never once, in all your life, raised your voice to the staff. Why would you shatter that trust now?"

Darcy's eyes flashed. "I do not wish for that room to be disturbed. That is the end of it."

Elizabeth's lips pressed into a hard line. "You are being unreasonable, sir. What was so great an infraction that you would wound Mrs Reynolds so deeply? She has only ever served you loyally. Are you hiding something in Harry's room?"

Darcy's hand clenched into a fist on the desk. "No!" he barked, standing abruptly, his chair scraping against the floor.

"Then what is it?" Elizabeth challenged, stepping forward. "What are you so desperate to protect? Do you think *Harry* had anything to hide?"

"No!" Darcy nearly shouted, his face twisting with emotion.

"Then why?" she demanded, her voice rising in exasperation. "Why are you being so obstinate?"

"Because my brother is dead, that's why!" The words exploded from him, raw and anguished. "My brother is dead, and it was *my* fault!"

Elizabeth's mouth dropped open, and for a moment, neither of them spoke. Then she thinned her lips, stepping closer still. "At last," she said quietly, "we have reached the crux of it."

Darcy's shoulders slumped, his face contorted in a mixture of sorrow and frustration, but she pressed on. "All this time, I wondered if it was simple grief that controlled you, but it is much more than that, is it not?"

He looked away, but she followed his line of sight, unwilling to let him retreat. "What did you do that day? What did you not do? Do you honestly believe a rational man could accuse you of being at fault?"

Darcy's voice was thick with emotion. "It does not matter. I was there! I should have been able to make it right. To save him. To do *something*. Instead, my brother died in my arms!"

"You could have done nothing," Elizabeth retorted, her voice trembling with anger. "*Nothing* would have changed what happened."

"You do not *know* that! You were not there!"

"No, I was not," she admitted, her voice cold. "But it is obvious now. Why you are so frigid, why you refuse to allow yourself any joy. You are punishing yourself, Fitzwilliam Darcy. And you are punishing me along with you."

Darcy's face flushed, but he stubbornly shook his head. "That is not true."

Elizabeth crossed her arms, staring out the window for a moment, trying to compose herself. "Is that why you really married me?" she asked in a quiet voice. "Not out of some noble sense of duty, fulfilling Harry's vow for him. But because you felt guilty? I was your penance?"

Darcy said nothing, his jaw tightening.

Elizabeth turned back to him, her eyes burning into his. "If that was your motivation, why stop at marrying me? Why not right all of Harry's other wrongs, too?"

Darcy stilled, his expression narrowing. "What do you mean by that?"

"If you are guilty of Harry's death, then why not answer the charges of treason against him yourself? Be the sacrificial lamb, face society and all their excoriation. Heavens, you could even don his uniform and stand at the block in his place! Would that not appease your guilt?"

"That's preposterous!" Darcy scoffed, his anger rising again.

"Is it really so preposterous?" she shot back. "There were accusations against him. Evidence. I heard it myself—he was in fear of being ruined but he *was* going to speak the truth, whatever it was. Is it really so shocking? He would not be the first good officer to make the wrong call. So, if it will appease your sense of wrongdoing, stand in his place and take the brunt of public opinion!"

Darcy's face flushed red with fury. "Harry was innocent! And besides, you are making a mockery of military law with your simplistic quid-pro-quo histrionics."

Elizabeth stalked forward, refusing to back down. "Very well, but what about the girl?" she demanded. "The one in the letter? Did you even try to find her?"

Darcy stiffened, his hand tightening on the back of his chair. "That would be like finding a needle in a haystack. There was no name—no way to trace her."

"Because you did not *try!*" she shouted, her voice breaking. "Harry had friends, people who knew his activities in Town. People who could have given some indication of the families he knew, the places he frequented. You at least owed her the dignity of trying!"

He bit down on his response, but she could see the battle waging behind his eyes. When he finally spoke, his voice was low, laced with heated wrath. "How do you even know there was any truth to that letter? It was not like Harry to dishonour a lady."

Elizabeth's eyes flashed. "You were willing enough to believe it when it suited you—when it gave you a reason to punish yourself by marrying me! But the moment you were off the market, you stopped looking. You made no more attempts."

Darcy's expression darkened. "Perhaps I should put myself *back* on the market," he snarled. "File for that annulment we both thought was unnecessary. But look at us! It is a sham of a marriage anyway. Two months wed, and you still do not even call me by my name. And I have yet to..." He gestured crudely with his hand, his face a contortion of aggravation. "Very well, then! Let us end it. Would *that* make you happy?"

Elizabeth paled, the words hitting her harder than she expected. He would really suggest that? Now, after all this time? But they had been starting to become closer! "No," she whispered, her voice barely audible. "It would not."

He glared at her, but she pressed on, her voice trembling. "And it would not be sufficient anyway. How do you know there is only one?" She held her head high, though her heart pounded. "There is a tenant girl."

He froze. "Which tenant girl?"

"Clara Henshaw. Last July, she was either seduced or attacked—she refuses to say which. All anyone can tell me about her is that she always fancied Harry with some unreasonable degree of fondness, and she took his death 'especially hard.'"

Darcy scoffed, rolling his eyes. "Now you are being outrageous. Harry dabbling with a farmer's daughter? Besides, he was in London all summer."

She shook her head. "No, he was not. The day after I met him, in fact, he was to journey to Leicester on an errand for his commander. He had just got through telling me that he came from Derbyshire and had a brother he would relish surprising, if he got the first half of his errand done swiftly enough. Do you not think it possible?"

His face hardened in disgust. "No, I do not. You are grasping at straws, madam. Harry detouring from Leicester to seduce a farm girl? It's ridiculous. One has to *try* to entertain such a fantasy, but perhaps it is not so difficult a thing for you."

She stiffened. "What is that supposed to mean?"

His features had twisted into a scowl, and he was raking his hands through his hair. "It means that I managed to marry the most ridiculous woman alive. A silly tradesman's niece who does not have the sense to stay out of things that do not concern her!"

Elizabeth's face flushed with white-hot anger. "Ridiculous? Silly? Is *that* what you think of me?" she spat. "Perhaps I should not be surprised. I had started to think of you as a generous-minded man. One who saw people for their qualities rather than their station, but I see that at the first opportunity, you fling my uncle's occupation in my face. How very petty of you, sir!

"Elizabeth—"

"No! You may make whatever excuses for your words you like, but they have been said and cannot be unsaid."

He extended a hand, as if he meant to reach forward to touch her arm, but his desk was between them. "Forgive me, I did not mean—"

Elizabeth drew back. "Forgive, I can, but forget? I shall not. You have been punishing yourself for Harry's death," she said, her voice shaking with emotion. "And now you are punishing me too. But I won't be part of it."

With that, she turned on her heel, fury burning in her chest as she stormed out of the study, the door slamming behind her.

Chapter Twenty-Three

D ARCY TOSSED RICHARD'S LETTER onto the desk with a sharp flick of his wrist, the crumple of paper echoing through the room. His cousin's words offered no new answers—only more of the same: apologies and uncertainty. No progress. No clarity.

He leaned back, rubbing his temples, as if he could massage the frustration from his thoughts. Everything—Harry, Elizabeth, London—felt like an impossible tangle he could not unravel. He had been trying, in vain, to push forward, to find a way to repair the growing distance between himself and his wife. But every effort felt inadequate. Useless. He pushed his way out of his desk to wander the room—his usual path from the fireplace to the window.

Darcy paused mid-step, staring out the window at the bleak landscape beyond. He had considered, again and again, what he should do, but each answer seemed to dissolve into nothing. London was out of the question—he had already resigned himself to that. Yet he was left here, trapped by his own indecision. He felt as though he were watching everything unfold from a distance, helpless to alter the course of events.

The accusations against Harry, the tension with Elizabeth—it all seemed to circle back to the same maddening question: what was his next move? He could not continue like this, merely waiting for time to ease the wounds. But every action, every decision, felt weighted by the fear of making things worse.

A sound from the hall broke his reverie, and Darcy looked up just in time to see Elizabeth pass the open door with her terrier bounding at her heels. His heart gave a little jump at the sight of her, dressed in a simple gown, her figure framed by the light from the corridor. She did not see him, or if she did, she made no sign of it. Her face was serene, as if her mind was far away.

Without thinking, Darcy turned toward the door. "Elizabeth," he called softly, stepping toward the door.

She paused, glancing over her shoulder, and "Little Fitzy" careened into her legs at her abrupt halt. For a brief second, their eyes met. There was something in her gaze—was it curiosity? Or perhaps a lingering hurt from their last argument? Darcy could not tell. He swallowed. "I..." He took a breath. "Tell Cook that I prefer a lighter dinner this evening."

Elizabeth studied him for a moment, the lower lid of one of her eyes twitching before she nodded politely and continued down the hall.

He watched her go, an odd tightness settling in his chest. He wanted to speak to her, to say something—anything—but the words were so garbled in his head, he had no hope of stringing them together. How could he bridge this growing chasm between them when his own emotions were still so tangled?

He sighed heavily, leaning against the doorframe. He was a fool. A coward. Night after night, he stood at the threshold of her room, torn between desire and guilt, unsure of what to do. Each time, he turned away, leaving the door closed and his heart more confused than ever.

A sharp rap on the doorframe pulled him from his thoughts. One of the servants stood there with a fresh stack of correspondence. Darcy groaned silently and gestured for the servant to set the tray on his desk and leave him. He was not in the mood for more letters he could not answer.

His gaze drifted back down the hall, towards where Elizabeth had disappeared. His mind filled with thoughts of her—her laughter, her wit, the way her eyes sparkled with mischief when she teased him. His fists clenched at his sides, filled with an ache he could not put into words.

How had it come to this? How had he, a man so in control of his world, allowed himself to become so lost in his marriage? And here, he had almost permitted himself to believe she was a gift to him! A token of Heaven's mercies after such a cruel blow—some sign that his heart's cry had been answered and he had been granted more than he deserved.

Darcy's breath hitched as he turned back to his desk. Richard's letter lay open, reminding him of his cousin's words—*no dishonour to Harry's memory if you fall in love with your wife.*

Oh, that ship had sailed. Long ago—probably the night he found her shivering and frozen in the garden after their first argument. He had fallen in love with Elizabeth Darcy from the earliest days of their marriage. He just could not find a way to tell her that.

Each time he tried, each small gesture of affection, Elizabeth seemed to step farther away. Or was it him, retreating before he could be hurt?

His fingers tightened on the edge of the desk, knuckles white. Perhaps it was time to change his approach. If he wanted something real—love, desire, companionship—he would need to earn it, not simply expect it to grow from duty.

But how? Darcy's head swirled with possibilities, with doubts, with a sense of helplessness he had not felt in years.

E LIZABETH CLOSED HER DOOR with a soft click, pressing her back against the wood. That argument with her husband still haunted her, playing over in her mind like a nightmare she could not wake from. His accusations, her own sharp words—they had both been so foolish. How had it come to this?

She sighed, moving away from the door and crossing to the window. The view of the snow-dusted landscape did little to soothe the restlessness within her. She longed for the comfort of a letter from Jane or some sign that the battle lines drawn between her and her husband might break. But no letter had arrived, and Darcy had remained distant ever since that day in the study.

She had seen him, of course—passing her in the halls, a nod at dinner, the occasional stiff pleasantry when they shared a room. But there had been no warmth, no shared smiles or casual conversations. Nothing to bridge the widening gap between them.

But there was still that puppy—little Fitzy—who had become her constant companion over the past week. He, at least, was a reminder that her husband had once tried to make her happy. But now? Now, she feared Darcy might regret even that small kindness.

Fitzy scampered across the room, chasing his tail before collapsing at her feet with a soft whimper. Elizabeth reached down and scratched behind his ears, her heart aching with the sense that something precious was slipping through her fingers.

How could she mend things between them when she barely understood what had gone so wrong? Darcy's guilt over Harry, his anger, his guarded heart—it all seemed so unreachable. And the argument had only built more walls between them.

Pushing the lace curtain aside, she caught a glimpse of her husband striding across the lawn, his dark coat standing out against the frost-covered ground. He was heading toward the stables, likely for another of his long, solitary rides. Should she go after him, say something—anything—that might break this silence between them? But no. Her pride stung from their last confrontation, and a small voice in the back of her mind warned her that he might not want to see her at all.

Turning away from the window, Elizabeth tried to bury herself in the letters on her desk. There was so much to do, tenants to respond to, household matters to arrange. But her gaze wandered, unfocused, and all she could think of was how deeply she missed him.

It was a ridiculous thought, she chided herself. They were in the same house, in each other's company nearly every day, and yet... she felt as though they were worlds apart.

D ARCY STOOD BY THE window in his study, arms crossed tightly over his chest as he stared out at the wintry landscape. The snow had started falling again, light flakes swirling in the wind and settling on the grounds below. Elizabeth's favourite spot by the lake was barely visible, shrouded by the mist rising from the water's edge. He wondered if she would venture out again today, despite the cold.

He turned away from the window, restless. The silence of the house pressed in on him, a silence he had once prized but now found unbearable. His gaze landed on the stack of papers at the corner of his desk—letters from tenants, estate matters, documents he needed to review—and he sighed, knowing he would accomplish little today. His thoughts were far too tangled for business.

By now, he had torn and hacked at his conscience over the argument with Elizabeth enough, not just about the words they had spoken but about even more basic truths that lay beneath. She had come out and accused him of punishing himself, of punishing her, and he saw it in his own heart. He wrapped himself in duty, in guilt, and let those protect him from the agony of Harry's loss.But in doing so, he had distanced himself from the one person who might have helped him heal.

And now, what was left between them? A fractured bond, an ever-growing chasm he had no idea how to cross. He wanted to speak to her, to apologise, to make things right. But every time he saw her, something in him locked up. His pride, his fear—he could not tell. The mere sight of her stirred up a mix of emotions he struggled to navigate.

His eyes drifted to the doorway, half-expecting her to appear. He had grown so accustomed to her presence, to the soft rhythm of her steps down the hall, the occasional glance she would send his way when they passed each other. And yet, in all those fleeting moments, they had not truly *seen* one another in days.

The door opened softly, and for a fleeting moment, his heart leapt, hoping it might be her. But it was only a servant, bringing another letter. Darcy waved the man away without a word, sinking down into the leather chair by his desk.

The letter lay unopened before him, but he knew it was of no consequence. His mind was elsewhere—back on that conversation that had shattered their fragile peace, on the ways he had failed her, and on the stubbornness that kept him from making amends. He had told himself he was protecting her from his own turmoil, from the darkness of his grief, but the truth was... he had been hiding.

Hiding from the vulnerability that came with loving someone, hiding from the risk of losing again.

He ran a hand through his hair, exhaling sharply. He could not go on like this, pacing the halls, suffocating under the weight of his own silence. Elizabeth deserved better—better than the half-hearted attempts at conversation, better than the cold distance he kept between them.

But how could he explain any of this to her? How could he tell her that every time he looked at her, he felt the ghost of Harry standing between them, a barrier he could not surmount?

His eyes closed, and in the quiet of the room, he let himself admit it: he was in love with her. Deeply, painfully in love with her. But love, he had learned, was not enough to overcome everything.

E LIZABETH LAY IN HER bed, staring up at the canopy, her eyes wide open, unblinking, while the wind outside howled against the panes. The covers, once a comfort, now felt suffocating, as if they were holding her in place, trapping her within her own thoughts. It had been days since their argument, and every passing moment felt like a stretch of silence too vast to cross.

She could hear him again. Pacing. The rhythm had become so familiar over the past nights. Back and forth, forth and back, as if his steps could wear a chasm in the floor that neither of them could breach.

A sigh slipped from her lips as she turned onto her side, clutching the pillow tightly. Every part of her ached to go to him, to reach across the distance that now seemed to define their every interaction. It had been a foolish argument, and yet... had it really been about Harry's room? Or had they both used it as an excuse for the deeper frustrations they each carried? She missed him—truly missed him. More than she had realised was even possible in a marriage built on duty rather than affection.

The clock ticked loudly in the corner of the room, its hands inching closer to midnight, but sleep was impossible. Every creak of the house, every gust of wind outside, every footstep from his pacing brought her closer to a decision she had been too hesitant to make.

Enough.

Before she could reconsider, she threw off the covers, her feet hitting the cold floor. Wrapping her robe tightly around herself, she crossed the room with a swift determination she had not felt in days. The chill in the air bit at her exposed skin, but it was nothing compared to the coldness that had grown between them.

Crossing the room, Elizabeth hesitated for only a moment before stepping toward the adjoining door between their chambers. The sound of his footsteps, heavy and restless, filled the silence.

Her hand hovered over the door handle, her heart racing. The footsteps inside suddenly paused, as though he had sensed her nearness. For a fleeting second, she considered turning back—perhaps it was a mistake—but no, she could not leave him like this.

Taking a deep breath, Elizabeth gently knocked, her knuckles grazing the wood.

Her knuckles rapped against the door, once, softly, almost hesitantly. There was no answer. She knocked again, a little more firmly, then held her breath to hear better as the footsteps inside stilled.

"William?" she called softly, her voice barely above a whisper. She had never called him that before, but what else could she call him now?

For a long moment, there was nothing but silence. Then, in a rush of movement, the door swung open.

There he stood, his chest rising and falling rapidly, his nightshirt clinging to his damp skin. His hair was tousled, the evidence of his pacing clear in the tension of his muscles, in the way his shoulders slumped as if he had been carrying the weight of the world. But it was his face that made her heart squeeze—the anguish in his eyes, the desperation in the way he looked at her. He seemed... broken.

Elizabeth froze, her heart pounding at the sight of him. He looked like a man teetering on the edge of something deep and dark, and she wanted nothing more than to reach out and pull him back.

For a moment, neither of them moved. She was tempted—desperately tempted—to fling herself into his arms, to wrap herself around him and offer the physical and emotional comfort she knew he needed. But even as she took a step forward, she stopped.

That was not what he needed. Not yet.

Instead, she studied him—his eyes, full of pain, full of heartbreak. And then, without saying a word, she reached out and took his hand.

"Come with me," she whispered.

Darcy blinked, his brow furrowing slightly in confusion, but he did not resist. He let her take his hand, his fingers curling around hers as if it were the only solid thing he could grasp.

Chapter Twenty-Four

WHEN HER HAND SLIPPED into his, Darcy's body hummed like a piano string. For an instant, as her fingers curled around his own, he shuddered with a sudden, desperate hope. Was she finally... inviting him to her? They had barely spoken since that argument, the words they had hurled at each other almost physical things between them, yet here she was, standing before him in her nightdress, her face pale but determined.

Surely, she was leading him to her bed. Why else would she have come? He could see it in her eyes—a glimmer of understanding, or perhaps acceptance. Could this be the moment he had not dared to ask for? His need for her had become an insistent drumbeat, a pulse he could not quiet, no matter how hard he tried to push it away. Each night, he lay in bed, thinking of her just a few feet away, the barrier of their adjoining door feeling like miles. The tension between them had mounted so unbearably, it was suffocating.

She tugged on his hand gently, leading him from the threshold of his room. Darcy followed willingly, almost panting with the agony of his longing. The thought of being welcomed into her warmth, of finally being free to express all he had held back, twisted a knot of aching desire in his chest. It did not matter that their last words had been harsh, that their relationship was still a confusing muddle of unspoken fears and unsorted feelings. Right now, none of that mattered.

He would take whatever she was willing to give.

But when they entered her room, she did not pause. Elizabeth kept moving, pulling him through her chamber and out into the hallway again, her pace quickening. Darcy blinked, his breath faltering. Confusion began to creep in.

What... what was she doing?

His mind scrambled to keep up with her sudden change in direction. If not to her bed, then...?

She said nothing, her grip firm but gentle as she guided him down the hall, their footsteps muffled on the plush carpeting. His eyes darted between her face, set with determination, and the corridor stretching before them, lit only by the occasional candle. Darcy's stomach twisted with uncertainty. Where could she be taking him at this hour?

They passed by several rooms, and then it hit him. His heart clenched painfully when she led him directly to the threshold of *that* door.

Harry's room.

Darcy froze, his feet stumbling to a halt, but Elizabeth pressed forward, tugging him along until they crossed the threshold. He followed, albeit reluctantly, his steps slow, his gaze flickering back to the hallway. It felt wrong—this room was meant to be untouched, his silent monument to the memory of his brother. The air itself seemed to still in here, thick with ghosts of the past. Why would she drag him to *this* place?

His heart nearly stopped when she marched him into the middle of the room, halting in front of Harry's old trunk. The very sight of it made his chest ache, as if the air was being slowly pressed out of his lungs.

"Elizabeth..." His voice was low, hoarse. He could not look at her; his eyes were fixed on the trunk, on the dust-laden reminders of the man he had lost. "What are we doing here?"

She did not let go of his hand, but the firm grip of her fingers was now unmistakably deliberate. "You need to let go," she said softly but firmly, turning to face him fully. Her words were like a key unlocking something tightly wound within him. "Let go of Harry, William."

His head snapped up at the sound of his name on her lips. She had never used it before. She had always called him 'Mr Darcy,' or even 'sir'—had kept a distance in her formality that mirrored the distance between them in every other respect. But here, in the middle of the room where his brother's presence lingered like a spectre, she called him by his given name. And not only his given name, but the gentle moniker his mother used to use.

"I cannot..." he began, but his voice faltered. He could feel the cracks beginning to form, the dam he had so carefully constructed around his grief trembling at the edges. "Elizabeth, I..."

"You *can*," she interrupted gently, her eyes searching his. "You *must*. This... this pain you carry, it is destroying you. You cannot go on like this."

"I do not want to talk about it," Darcy said sharply, pulling his hand free of hers. He turned away, running a hand through his hair, trying to regain control of the riot of feelings inside him. "I cannot."

"William, your brother is gone, and you are holding on to his memory like a chain around your neck. You need to let him go. Let go of the mistakes, the guilt. You did not kill him."

The words stung, sharper than any blow he could have imagined. He recoiled as if struck, his chest tightening painfully. His throat burned with the need to shout, to rage at the unfairness of it all, but when he opened his mouth, nothing came out.

"Let yourself grieve him," Elizabeth said, stepping closer. "Truly grieve him, and forgive yourself. You do not have to bear this alone."

Darcy turned away from her, his hands trembling at his sides. His gaze fell to the trunk again, to the leather-bound memories of his brother's life. The ache in his heart was unbearable. How could he let go? How could he release the guilt that had defined him for so long? He had been *there* when it happened. He should have been able to save him.

"I *should* have done something," he rasped, his voice barely audible. His hands clenched into fists. "I should have been able to stop it, to make it right. But I did not... I *could not!*"

"You could not have saved him, Fitzwilliam. Sometimes... sometimes there is nothing we can do."

Darcy shook his head, swallowing hard against the lump forming in his throat. "You were not there, Elizabeth. You... you do not know what it was like!"

"No, I was not there," she said softly. "But I know you. And I know that if there were anything you could have done, anything at all, you would have done it. You loved him. But you cannot change what has happened, no matter how much you wish you could."

"I *failed* him," Darcy choked out, his chest heaving as his hand swept over his eyes. "He was my brother, my younger brother! I was supposed to look out for him, and I could not save him!"

Tears welled in his eyes, blurring his vision. He blinked rapidly, trying to fight them back, but it was useless. The floodgates had opened, and the sorrow he had kept buried for so long came rushing to the surface.

Elizabeth moved closer, her hands gentle as she reached out to him. "You have not failed him," she whispered, her voice a soothing balm to the rawness of his grief. "You loved him. That is not failure."

Darcy's shoulders trembled as the first tear slipped down his cheek. He tried to hold it back, tried to push it all down again, but it was too late. The grief he had been carrying for so long broke free, and before he knew it, the tears were falling in earnest.

He let out a shuddering breath, his chest wracked with sobs. His knees buckled, and he sank to the floor, his hands gripping the edge of Harry's trunk as if it were the only thing anchoring him to the world.

Elizabeth knelt beside him, wrapping her arms around his trembling shoulders. "William," she whispered. "It is all right. Let it out. Let it go."

Darcy leaned into her embrace, his body shaking with the force of his sobs. He had never wept like this, not since the day Harry died in his arms. He had kept it all inside, the grief, the guilt, the anger, until it had festered and consumed him.

Now, in Elizabeth's arms, it all came pouring out.

"I am so sorry," he gasped between sobs, his voice strangling in his throat. "I am so, so sorry…"

Elizabeth held him tighter, her hand stroking his hair as she whispered soothing words in his ear. "It is not your fault, William. You did everything you could. You loved him, and that is what matters."

For what felt like hours, Darcy wept. The weight of his grief, the burden of guilt, all of it came tumbling out in waves, and Elizabeth held him through it all.

When the storm of his tears finally began to subside, Darcy pulled back slightly, his breath coming in ragged gasps. His face was wet with tears, his body exhausted from the effort of it all.

Elizabeth's eyes were full of compassion as she looked at him, her hand still resting on his shoulder. "You are allowed to grieve, William," she said softly. "But you are not allowed to carry this burden alone. Not anymore."

Darcy nodded, his throat too tight to speak. He had never known such tenderness, such understanding. He had always believed he had to bear his pain in silence, that it was his duty to shoulder the responsibility alone.

But now, in Elizabeth's arms, he did not have to.

"Thank you," he whispered.

Elizabeth smiled softly, her fingers brushing a stray lock of hair from his forehead. "You are not alone," she repeated, her voice a gentle promise.

Darcy closed his eyes, letting her words wash over him. For the first time in what felt like an eternity, he felt something loosen in his chest—a release, a small breath of relief from the suffocating weight of guilt and sorrow that had hung over him for so long.

He drew a deep, shuddering breath and opened his eyes, looking into hers, and for a moment, they simply stayed like that—silent, connected, and understanding more in that stillness than any words could express.

"Elizabeth..." he whispered her name softly, as though tasting it for the first time. There was so much he wanted to say, but the words wouldn't come. Instead, he tightened his grip on her hand, drawing strength from the steady, unwavering presence she offered.

Slowly, she smiled at him, a soft, knowing smile, and that simple gesture was enough.

I T WAS LIKE HE could breathe again. Darcy had a new lightness to him as he led her back to his room. After the tears and the rawness of his emotions, part of her feared he might retreat again—back behind the walls he so often hid behind. When his hand lingered at the small of her back, guiding her through the door and gently pulling her into his room, it was that he was no more ready to part from her than she was from him.

He closed the door softly, the latch clicking shut as if sealing them off from the rest of the world. Without a word, he crossed to the side table, pouring two glasses of brandy, the amber liquid catching the glow of the firelight. Elizabeth stood quietly by the hearth, watching him as he poured. There was something reassuring in the way his hands moved—steady and relaxed, despite everything they had been through.

When he turned, he caught her eye, offering the glass with a small, tired smile. "For you," he said, his voice low and rough. He handed it to her, then tugged a warm blanket from the bed and sat on the large sofa in front of the fire.

Elizabeth seated herself beside him, curling her legs underneath her and leaning against his shoulder as she took her first sip of the brandy. It was stronger than anything she was used to, and she coughed lightly, her eyes widening at the burn it left in her throat.

Darcy glanced over at her with concern. "Too strong? I can send for something else if you prefer."

A grin tugged at her lips despite the warmth spreading down her chest. "No, no." She raised the glass to him, her eyes sparkling with a playful glint. "I will survive." Another cough escaped, but she swallowed it down, determined. "See? I am quite well." To prove it, she took another sip, nestling closer to him under the blanket.

He chuckled softly, pulling her nearer, his arm wrapping securely around her shoulders so she could pillow her head against him. And in a gesture of pure sweetness, he tugged the blanket high up on her shoulders, tucking it snugly around them both. Elizabeth relaxed into the warmth of his body, feeling the steady rise and fall of his chest beneath her cheek.

The brandy left a comforting heat in her belly, but it was nothing compared to the quiet contentment of being in his arms. For a long time, neither of them spoke. They did not need to. After the emotional toll of the evening, words seemed like too much effort. It was enough just to sit there, letting the fire warm them as they shared the same breath.

Darcy's fingers had stretched to cup her neck and played absentmindedly with a strand of her hair. Elizabeth closed her eyes at the sensation, tilting her head slightly to give him better access. The simple touch sent a shiver down her spine, and she couldn't help the sigh of pleasure that escaped her lips. He had never touched her so tenderly before—not like this. It was as though, for the first time, he allowed himself the indulgence of just being close to her.

She shifted slightly, her toes brushing against his calf beneath the blanket. She paused, then wiggled them mischievously against his leg. His immediate flinch told her all she needed to know.

"Good Heavens, Elizabeth, your feet are freezing!" Darcy exclaimed.

She laughed. "Have you gone soft?" she teased, looking up at him with a smirk. "Surely a little cold should not bother you like that."

"A *little* cold? These are blocks of ice!" He raised an eyebrow, feigning indignation. "There is a vast difference, madam, between a little cold and solid glaciers being pressed against one's skin."

Elizabeth grinned wickedly and leaned closer, her breath warm against his neck. "Perhaps," she murmured, her voice dropping to a sultry whisper, "I shall have to find a way to warm you up."

Darcy's breath faltered, his chest rising beneath her hand as her words seemed to settle between them. His dark eyes glittered in the firelight, filled with a curiosity—and something more. "What did you have in mind?" he asked softly, his voice rough with the unspoken emotions he'd been holding back.

Elizabeth did not answer immediately. Instead, she reached up, her hand sliding to the back of his neck. His skin was warm beneath her fingers, his pulse quickening slightly at her touch. Slowly, deliberately, she leaned up, her lips just inches from his, and whispered, "This."

Before he could react, she kissed him.

She felt his surprise, the briefest hesitation as though he was unsure if he should let himself fall into it. But Elizabeth did not hold back. She poured everything she felt into that kiss—the longing, the weeks of frustration, the growing warmth between them. Her arms wound around his neck, pulling him closer as if she could close the space between them forever.

Darcy groaned softly against her lips, and suddenly, the dam holding back his restraint broke. His arms tightened around her, his hands tangling in her hair as he deepened the kiss, returning her passion with a fervour she did not know he was capable of. Was this her reserved, restrained husband, who never had a hair out of place and probably thought "passion" was a word reserved for anger? He kissed her as though she were the very air he needed to breathe, his lips moving over hers with a hunger that sent shivers racing down her spine.

When they finally broke apart, both of them were panting, their foreheads resting against each other as they tried to catch their breath. Elizabeth's heart was pounding—no, racing in a way she had never experienced before. His hands were still in her hair, his fingers gently tracing the line of her jaw.

"I love you," she whispered against his lips, her voice trembling with the weight of the confession. "Foolishly. Irredeemably. Whether you love me or not."

Darcy's response was immediate, his voice rough with emotion. "I love you too," he breathed, his forehead pressing harder against hers. "You are my life's blood, Elizabeth." He kissed her again, more gently this time, but the intensity of his emotions was unmistakable.

Without another word, he stood, lifting her effortlessly into his arms. Elizabeth gasped, her arms instinctively wrapping around his neck as he carried her across the room toward the bed. His eyes never left hers, the depth of his feelings shining through every glance, every touch. Gently, he laid her down on the bed, his body hovering over hers as he stared down at her, his breathing ragged.

"William," she whispered, her fingers tracing the lines of his face. His name, spoken like that, felt like a promise.

He leaned down, pressing his lips to hers again—slowly, reverently, as though this moment was something sacred. And for all she cared, it was.

Chapter Twenty-Five

THE MORNING WAS HEAVY with the sound of rain against the windows, a steady, rhythmic backdrop to the fire crackling in the hearth. Darcy sat on the sofa in the library, a book in his hand, though his eyes rarely lingered on the pages. Elizabeth was nestled beside him, her head nearly resting on his chest as she leafed through her own book, her little dog curled up contentedly on her lap.

The stormy day... and the fact that there were better allurements indoors... had kept Darcy from venturing forth out of doors for his morning ride. Neither he nor Elizabeth had wanted to attend to business or letters—their usual routines—choosing instead the quiet companionship of one another. Darcy's arm rested comfortably around Elizabeth's shoulders, his thumb idly tracing the fabric of her sleeve.

They had shared few words this morning, content in the peace that came from being near one another. The fire warmed the room, but it was Elizabeth's presence that made Darcy feel, for the first time in what seemed like forever, that there might be a way forward—a future beyond grief, beyond guilt.

A sudden knock on the door shattered the stillness. Darcy straightened, the book in his hand falling shut.

"Mr Darcy, I beg your pardon, sir," the footman entered, his expression careful. "Lady Catherine de Bourgh has arrived and requests an audience with you in the drawing room."

Darcy's jaw clenched. She had ventured all the way from Kent to Derbyshire at *this* time of year?

There could be no ambiguity about why. He knew what was coming before the words were even fully spoken. Lady Catherine's visits were never idle, and given the swirling rumours in London, he had no doubt what had brought her to Pemberley. A storm of a different sort, one with far more bite than the rain outside.

He turned to Elizabeth, his voice softer. "Wait here. This will not take long."

Elizabeth looked up at him, concern flickering in her eyes. She shifted on the sofa as if she might argue, but she only nodded. "Of course."

Darcy kissed her forehead, lingering just a moment longer than usual, then rose from the sofa. His mind already steeling itself for the confrontation to come, he strode to the drawing room, where Lady Catherine would surely be sharpening her claws.

Upon entering the drawing room, he found his aunt pacing by the window, her bonnet still tied, a grim expression on her face. Beside her, Anne de Bourgh sat, her small, frail frame perched on the edge of a chair, her hands folded demurely in her lap. She barely glanced at Darcy as he entered, though Lady Catherine whirled at once, her eyes narrowing as she took him in.

"Fitzwilliam," she barked, her voice sharp and commanding as always. "What is the meaning of this? I have heard the most dreadful rumours—rumours that you have entangled yourself with some... ruined strumpet and, worse, married her!"

Darcy drew a long breath, already feeling the cold waves of his aunt's fury wash over him. He crossed the room, placing himself firmly between her and Anne, as if to shield his cousin from the tirade. "I have not 'entangled' myself with anyone, Aunt Catherine. Elizabeth Darcy is my wife, and you will speak of her with the respect due to her station."

Lady Catherine's eyes bulged, her nostrils flaring. "Respect? Respect for a woman of such scandalous reputation? I will not tolerate such insolence, Fitzwilliam! Have you lost all sense of propriety? The whole of London is in an uproar over this disastrous marriage!"

Darcy crossed his arms, his posture stiffening. "It is no concern of theirs—or yours—whom I marry. Elizabeth is my wife, and I swore an oath to her."

Lady Catherine's mouth twisted in disgust. "An oath? What does an oath mean if sworn to a deceitful chit? It is meaningless, and you are a fool if you think otherwise. Your duty is to your family, to your name! You have failed miserably in your responsibilities. First, allowing your brother to wander into danger, and now, letting this scandal stain the Darcy legacy! Harry's disgrace is already enough, with those vicious rumours about treason hanging over his name. And you... you are adding to the ruin by wedding that girl!"

At the mention of the blame being cast upon Harry, a deep ache stirred within his heart. But he forced himself to remain calm, though his hands clenched into fists at his

THE MEASURE OF HONOR

sides. "I loved my brother. I tried to protect him as best I could, but I will not allow his mistakes to define me—or to define Elizabeth. Whatever rumours you have heard about her are lies. She is a woman of integrity, and I will not entertain any more of your slander against her."

"Slander?" Lady Catherine sneered, stepping closer, her eyes flashing. "Do not be so naïve, Fitzwilliam. That Bennet girl has deceived you! She is no more worthy of the Darcy name than a common street wench. My parson, Mr Collins, is a relative of the Bennet family, and he has written to me all about her ruin. You are a disgrace to this family, Fitzwilliam. You were supposed to marry Anne, to keep the bloodlines pure. Instead, you have bound yourself to a woman whose reputation is in tatters!"

Darcy's jaw clenched tighter, his voice growing colder with each word. "No, Aunt Catherine. You are the one who has been deceived—deceived in my character if you think I would ever abandon my wife. The woman I love. My loyalty is to her now, not to the whims of society or the dictates of a bitter old woman."

"Love!" Lady Catherine spat, her face contorting with fury. "What does love have to do with anything? You are a worthless milksop if you think sentiment is more important than duty! Your duty is to your *family*, to Pemberley, to the Darcys who came before you!"

"Enough!" Darcy's voice cracked like a whip in the room, silencing his aunt's tirade. His chest heaved with the effort of controlling his anger. "I will not allow you to speak of my wife this way. Elizabeth is a Darcy now, and nothing you or anyone else says will change that."

Lady Catherine recoiled, stunned into momentary silence by the force of his words. For a moment, she looked almost bewildered, as if she had never expected him to defy her so openly.

"You will regret this," she hissed after a long pause. "You have cast aside your duty, your family, your very name. You have chosen ruin, and you will suffer for it."

Darcy remained unmoved. "I have chosen my wife. And that is enough."

There was a charged silence as Lady Catherine glared at him, her breath coming fast and hard. Before she could speak again, Darcy turned to Anne, his voice softening. "Anne, it has been a long journey for you both. Would you care for some refreshment? You are always welcome here. If you wish to stay, I shall have rooms prepared immediately, and I know Mrs Darcy would be pleased to make your acquaintance."

Anne's eyes flickered with a faint glimmer of hope, her lips parting slightly as if to accept the offer. But before she could speak, Lady Catherine cut in sharply.

"I take no notice of your false pleasantries, Fitzwilliam," she snapped, her voice rising. "We will not stay—certainly not under *your* roof!"

Darcy met her gaze with calm, though his concern for his cousin did not waver. "Surely, Aunt, Anne's health must come first. You have always spoken of it as your utmost priority. Would you not allow her a rest in a comfortable room before returning on such a journey?"

Lady Catherine's eyes narrowed into cold slits. "If you had so much concern for Anne's well-being, you would have done your duty and married her! That would have spared us all this disgrace."

Darcy's voice remained steady, though his eyes hardened. "That is something I cannot do."

Lady Catherine snorted in contempt, turning on her heel with a flourish. "Come, Anne. We shall not waste another moment here."

Anne hesitated for the briefest of moments, casting one last, lingering look at Darcy, as if silently wishing for something that could not be. Then, with a resigned sigh, she turned to follow her mother, her step lighter than Lady Catherine's but no less final.

Darcy watched as they left, the air still heavy with his aunt's accusations. He remained in the drawing room for several long moments, steadying himself, but the sting of the confrontation lingered. He had known it would come, yet it had cut deeper than expected.

He had made his choice. And not for a day in his life would he regret it.

DARCY ENTERED THE LIBRARY, his expression guarded, though the firelight caught the tension lingering in the line of his shoulders. Elizabeth looked up from her book, instantly seeing the thrumming of his pulse at his throat.

"Well?" she asked, setting the book down and sitting up straighter. "Did you speak with your aunt?"

Darcy let out a slow breath, crossing the room to stand before her. "I did. As expected, it went about as well as a negotiation with a storm cloud."

Elizabeth raised an eyebrow, a teasing smile tugging at her lips. "And did the storm cloud and her daughter decide to stay?"

Darcy shook his head, sighing as he glanced toward the door. "No, it is already too late for that. I have offended my aunt sufficiently for one day. You will have to take your turn some other time."

Elizabeth chuckled and patted the space beside her on the sofa. "A shame," she mused. "I did so hope to make her acquaintance."

"No, you did not. Insincerity does not become you, Elizabeth."

She shrugged with a grin. "Perhaps not, but after meeting your uncle, the earl, I had dearly hoped to make a better impression on your next relation."

Darcy gave her a rueful look but sank into the offered seat, his hand rubbing absently at her thigh. "I would not take it to heart. Lady Catherine is... as one might expect."

"Oh, I already know something of your aunt," Elizabeth said with a glint in her eye.

Darcy turned toward her with some curiosity. "Do you?"

She nodded, tucking her legs beneath her on the sofa. "Indeed, through my father's cousin, Mr Collins. He is to inherit my father's estate."

"Ah, yes. She mentioned that. I had never heard of his connection to the Bennets before now."

Elizabeth wrinkled her nose playfully. "An oversight you may surely not regret. He is... well, let us just say he is a man of such obsequiousness that he makes flattery seem like a chore."

Darcy grunted. "That does not surprise me. Precisely the sort of man my aunt would approve of."

Elizabeth laughed softly, her fingers trailing through his hair. "No, I suppose it would not. So, let me guess. You are hereby ordered to divorce me forthwith and do your duty by your cousin, is that correct?"

"That is a fair summation. What do you think, ought I to cave?" He let his fingers trail down the length of her calf until they tickled the arch of her foot, leaning forward as he did so to nibble kisses down her neck.

"Oh, indeed," she sighed, curving her neck so he could reach her better. "I am sure Miss de Bourgh would give you far less trouble than I am apt to."

"I am afraid..." He wrapped an arm under the small of her back and pulled her up until her shoulders fell back and the shoulder of her gown slipped some little. "... I do not care for ladies who give me no trouble at all. In fact, I..." He tugged at her ear lobe with his lips. "... I rather abhor them."

Elizabeth lay her head back, but his ministrations tickled, and she could hardly keep from spasming with each new brush of his lips. "Then you certainly married the right woman, no matter what Lady Catherine says," she managed breathlessly. "I shall make it my mission to give you trouble, as well and as often as I may."

He smiled and pressed a softer kiss to her collarbone before easing her upright again. "I would hope for no less. We cannot have my family thinking my wife disappointed my expectations."

Elizabeth laughed and trailed a finger along the edge of his ear, then traced it down his jawbone. "Certainly not." Then, in a quieter voice, she added, "But it is more than that, isn't it? More than their disapproval of me?"

Darcy shifted under her touch, his jaw tightening once again. "Perhaps," he muttered, his voice low. "I suppose I am still a little unsettled. It has more to do with the rumours she claims to have heard about Harry than any of her opinions on our marriage."

Elizabeth grew still beside him, her hand resting on his shoulder. "What sort of rumours?" she asked, though she could already guess.

Darcy's brow furrowed, and his eyes darkened. "The accusations of treason. Of dishonour. It is nothing new—in fact, I ought to have expected her to have heard them by now, but every time they are repeated, it feels like they cut deeper."

Elizabeth frowned in thought, tracing her fingers absently along his arm. "Do you think anything can be done?"

Darcy's eyes narrowed. "Like what?"

She shrugged slightly, her expression contemplative. "Perhaps we could look through Harry's things again. I know you did once already, but you were not looking for that, specifically. If there is something that might help..."

Darcy exhaled through his nose, his fingers running through his hair in frustration. "I do not think I have the strength for that just now," he admitted. "And what would we even hope to find?"

Elizabeth's brow furrowed. "Well, you remember what I heard Harry say to Wickham the night they fought. He claimed he had evidence. Proof of something. Maybe he wasn't bluffing."

Darcy's expression changed, a flicker of realisation crossing his face. "That is true... But if there was something, perhaps Wickham found it when he ransacked Harry's flat. If not, it may still be here." He paused, thinking aloud. "I saw nothing unusual among the things I recovered, though."

"Could there have been another place Harry secreted something away? Did he go anywhere else? Stay anywhere?"

Darcy frowned. "Not to my knowledge. Only here. He was here only one day before his death, and we had no time to speak of almost anything important. But as far as I know, there was nowhere else."

Elizabeth untucked her feet and sat up straighter, pulling on Darcy's hand. "What about Harry's room here at Pemberley?" she suggested. "Is it possible he left something behind?"

Darcy's eyes widened slightly, a spark of hope flickering in the depths of his gaze. "I... I have no way of knowing. I never went through his room. I never permitted anyone else to do so either."

Elizabeth stood, tugging him gently to his feet. "Then it is time we look," she said with quiet conviction. "If you have the courage to search, I will be right there with you."

Darcy hesitated for a heartbeat, his gaze searching hers. Then, with a determined nod, he allowed her to lead him forward.

D ARCY KNELT BESIDE THE trunk, its leather bindings creaking as he lifted the lid. The contents were familiar, too familiar, a reminder of all that had been lost. His hand brushed over the neat stacks of papers, letters, and maps—Harry's personal things, returned from London after his death. Darcy had combed through them once before, but with Elizabeth beside him, he felt a strange sense of purpose. Perhaps now, with her fresh eyes, something new might emerge. But it was hard to see how.

With a heavy sigh, he began pulling out the papers, one by one, laying them on the floor. "There is nothing here," he muttered after several minutes of sorting. "Nothing of importance."

Elizabeth, sitting cross-legged on the floor beside him, remained silent. She was methodical in her handling of the papers, her sharp gaze missing nothing as she examined each item. She set aside the maps first—military sketches, lines and arrows indicating troop movements, all of which Darcy recognised as outdated and perfectly ordinary. Still, Elizabeth gathered them carefully, tucking them into a neat pile at her side.

Darcy shook his head. "These are just routine dispatches. Records. Correspondence between Harry and his commanding officers, and some with other men from the regiment. Nothing of consequence. Nothing about..." He trailed off, unwilling to voice the ugly word that hovered at the back of his mind: *treason*.

Elizabeth glanced up. "Perhaps not. But Harry saved them for a reason."

Darcy sighed, pulling out a small stack of personal letters, many of which he had already read. The edges of the paper were worn, the ink faded in some places. Letters from old friends, discussions of family matters, and pleasantries exchanged during quieter moments of the war. Again, nothing that seemed to hint at what he had been hoping to find.

Time stretched as they worked, the soft rustle of paper the only sound in the room. Darcy's fingers moved through the rest of the contents quickly, his frustration mounting. "It's useless," he said, his voice tight with exasperation. "I've seen all of this before, and there is nothing here that would—"

"Wait," Elizabeth interrupted gently, standing up suddenly. Darcy paused and looked up at her, watching as she turned to scan the room.

Elizabeth's little dog, "Little Fitzy," was scampering near the bed, paws scraping the floor in an eager attempt to dig at something beneath. "Fitzy!" Elizabeth scolded softly, stepping forward. "Mind your manners and come back here."

Darcy's brow furrowed, a faint curiosity stirring in his chest as he rose and crossed the room. "What is he after?" he asked, shooing the little terrier out of the way.

Dropping to one knee, Darcy peered under the bed. It took a moment for his eyes to adjust to the shadows, but then he saw it—a flat box, half-hidden beneath the bed frame. It was pushed up against the wall, as if deliberately placed there, out of sight.

"Strange," he murmured, reaching under to drag the box into the light. "I do not recall this."

Elizabeth stood beside him, her eyes wide with intrigue. "What is it?" she asked, bending closer.

Darcy shifted the box aside and pulled off the lid. The terrier was still snuffling around, and as Darcy glanced back, he realised what had caught the little dog's attention. With a grimace, he reached in and pulled out an old tin of army rations—long ago "turned", judging by the smell that wafted faintly from the rusted edges.

"This," Darcy said, holding it up with distaste, "is what the dog must have been smelling. It has gone completely rancid."

Elizabeth wrinkled her nose, stepping back as he offered the tin toward her. "Good Heavens," she said with a laugh, waving it away. "That's enough of that! I will have a maid dispose of it at once."

But Darcy was already distracted, his focus returning to the rest of the box's contents. With one hand, he passed the tin to Elizabeth, but with the other, he was searching what remained inside.

"Some of Harry's old boots and one of his uniform coats," he said, though his voice softened as he gently pulled out a pair of worn leather boots. They had been buffed to a spit shine, but the soles had worn down from many miles.

For a moment, Darcy did not move. His hand lingered on the soft leather, and a knot tightened in his throat. His brother must have worn these when he was in Spain. Darcy could almost see Harry standing before him, grinning, his boots muddy from the field, his hair tousled from the wind. The memory was too real, too vivid.

Elizabeth's hand came to rest gently on his shoulder, pulling him back to the present with a snap and a sigh. He stood back to allow her to see inside. She bent beside him and reached into the box, pulling out Harry's dress uniform jacket. Darcy had been wondering what had become of that—he had found two other uniform coats, one for summer and one for winter, but not Harry's dress jacket. She laid it flat on the bed, her fingers brushing over the fabric.

"Look at this," she said softly, her tone contemplative. "There is a stain here."

Darcy looked up from the boots, his eyes narrowing as he leaned over her shoulder. Elizabeth was right—a small, dark stain marred the lapel of the jacket. Blood. Harry's?

"This must have been from the night at the ball," she mused, her voice hushed. "When Harry gave me his coat. After Mr Wickham..." She trailed off, touching the spot where the blood had dried into the fabric.

A surge of anger swept through Darcy. He had seen the scar on Elizabeth's breast last night... and again this morning—the faint ridge that still marked her skin, a reminder of Wickham's cruelty to an innocent woman. He clenched his jaw, his hands tightening into fists.

How had he kept his rage in check last night? The sight of her, vulnerable in a way she had never shown him before, had stirred a protective fury in him that nearly overpowered his reason. But now, looking at the bloodstain on Harry's jacket, that rage returned with renewed force.

"He did this to you," Darcy said, his voice tight with suppressed emotion.

Elizabeth turned her head toward him, her eyes softening with understanding. "He did," she admitted quietly. "But Harry tried to stop him. That night... it was Harry who saved me."

Darcy's hand reached out, his fingers brushing the edge of the lapel, where the blood had soaked into the fabric. He flipped the coat open all the way to see how far the blood stretched—how far his Elizabeth had truly been wounded. As he did so, his gaze caught something—a corner of paper, tucked inside an inner pocket of the coat. Frowning, he gently tugged at it, pulling the paper free.

"What is that?" Elizabeth asked.

Darcy's heart pounded as he unfolded the paper, revealing not one but a handful of letters. The handwriting was unmistakably Harry's, and the papers were worn, as though they had been folded and refolded together many times. His eyes flickered up to Elizabeth, who was watching him with bated breath.

He glanced back down at the letter. "This might be what Harry was talking about."

Chapter Twenty-Six

ELIZABETH SAT QUIETLY IN the morning room, the fire crackling in the hearth, casting a gentle glow over the room. She glanced toward the door just as Mrs Reynolds entered, leading Clara Henshaw and her mother into the room. Elizabeth could sense the nervous energy radiating from them as they entered—Clara's mother avoiding her gaze, and Clara herself wringing her hands, her knuckles white against the dark fabric of her dress. They clearly expected a reprimand, perhaps even worse.

"Thank you, Mrs Reynolds," Elizabeth said, dismissing the housekeeper with a kind smile. The older woman curtsied and left the room.

"Good morning, Mrs Henshaw, Clara. Please," Elizabeth gestured to the chairs before her, "make yourselves comfortable."

Clara and her mother exchanged a look, their hesitation painfully clear. With visible reluctance, they sank into the chairs, Clara keeping her gaze firmly fixed on her lap, while her mother glanced nervously around the room.

Elizabeth moved toward the tea tray, deciding to break the stiffness with a simple gesture. "I thought we might have tea. I'll serve."

Their bewildered looks did not go unnoticed by Elizabeth as she poured, but she remained calm, offering them both a delicate china cup. They both accepted, though Mrs Henshaw's hand trembled as she reached for the cup.

"There is no point in beating around the bush," Elizabeth said gently but directly, watching as both women tensed immediately, their bodies stiffening as though bracing for a storm. "I understand Miss Clara is..." She cleared her throat and smiled.

Clara's face drained of colour, and her eyes darted to her mother before returning to the floor. "Yes, ma'am."

"You've nothing to fear from me, either of you. I have hardly asked you here to cause you more discomfort or pain. Quite the opposite." Elizabeth sipped lightly from her cup before lowering it. "I should like very much to help, but there is something I must know. How far along are you, Miss Clara?"

The girl swallowed. "Four months gone," she whispered after a moment, her voice barely audible.

Elizabeth nodded, calculating quickly. July, as she had suspected. Her mind turned over the possibilities, the suspicion of what she had feared most sitting heavy in her heart. She met Clara's nervous gaze and offered a small, reassuring smile. "I see. I cannot imagine how difficult this has been for you both."

Mrs Henshaw stammered a reply, "We—we are grateful for your kindness, ma'am. 'Tis... most unexpected."

"I wish to help," Elizabeth continued. "I have four sisters of my own, and I cannot think what it would be like for any of them to be in need of help and find themselves shunned." Elizabeth's words seemed to reach them, as both Clara and her mother visibly relaxed, the rigid tension in their postures easing.

Elizabeth folded her hands in her lap, glancing briefly between the two women before laying her cards on the table. "There have been rumours, you see, about my brother-in-law, Captain Darcy." She watched their reactions closely. "I am trying to protect his name, as well as your own."

At the mention of Harry, Clara's eyes widened, and she immediately shook her head, her voice breaking through with sudden emotion. "No, ma'am, never. Captain Darcy was never anything but kind to me. He would not... He would never..."

Elizabeth's expression remained kind, but she pressed gently. "I am not asking if he forced himself upon you, Clara. I am asking if he may have... seduced you. It would reflect poorly on him, even if you were willing."

"Capt..." She gulped. "Darcy, he..." At this, Clara began to crumble, her face crumpling in tears as she collapsed against her mother's shoulder, sobbing. Mrs Henshaw's eyes shimmered with unshed tears as she brushed away her daughter's grief, urging her gently, "Go on, Clara. Tell Mrs Darcy the truth."

For a few moments, the room was filled with Clara's quiet, gasping sobs. Elizabeth rose and moved to comfort her, but Mrs Henshaw lifted a hand, her arm wrapped protectively around her daughter's shoulders. Clara took a deep, shuddering breath, composing herself just enough to speak.

"It wasn't... it wasn't Captain Darcy," she said in a shaky voice. "I haven't seen him in over two years."

Elizabeth's brow furrowed. "Then... who was it?"

Clara hesitated, her face twisting with shame, but after a moment, the words tumbled out. "It was his friend. Lieutenant Wickham."

Elizabeth's stomach clenched as the pieces began to fall into place. *Wickham.* Of course.

Clara swallowed hard and continued. "He was riding up the lane one day. He was in uniform, and from a distance, I thought it was Captain Darcy, come back to the manor. I ran to him, waving to greet him. He was always so kind to me—like a brother—but when I got close, I saw it was Mr Wickham."

Elizabeth remained silent, her gaze steady as Clara spoke, her heart breaking for the girl.

Clara's voice grew shakier as she went on. "He called me over, said that Harry had just been speaking of me and that he had a letter from him. He promised to find it in his bag if I came closer, so I did."

Elizabeth's eyes narrowed. "And that sounded... credible to you?"

Clara looked miserable. "No, ma'am, but... why would he say it if it wasn't true? I wanted to find out if..." Clara broke off, covering her face as fresh tears streamed down her cheeks. "He... He grabbed me, ma'am. I couldn't get away."

Elizabeth felt a surge of anger twist inside her chest, but she kept her voice gentle as she knelt beside the weeping girl. "It's all right, Clara. You've done nothing wrong. I will help you."

The room fell into silence, broken only by Clara's quiet sobs. Elizabeth rose and smoothed the girl's hair with gentle fingers, offering whatever comfort she could.

"There is a place, in another town," Elizabeth said after a moment, "where girls in circumstances like yours can go for a time. I will pay for your expenses if you choose that path." She hesitated, watching Clara closely. "Or, I could provide you with a dowry and help you find a husband who will treat you and your child with dignity and kindness."

Clara's sobs softened, and she blinked through her tears, wide-eyed at the offer. "You... you would do that for me?"

Elizabeth nodded. "Think on it tonight, and come tomorrow to tell me what you wish to do. I only ask that if you find yourself in need, you come to me. You must promise."

Clara's mother gripped her daughter's hand tightly and nodded through her tears. "We promise, ma'am. Thank you... thank you."

As they gathered themselves to leave, Elizabeth saw them to the door, offering one last reassuring smile. Once the door closed behind them, she let out a long, slow breath, her body still trembling. She didn't turn right away but instead waited, knowing he would come.

From the back of the room, Darcy emerged from the hidden door that led into his study. His footsteps were quiet, his face drawn but attentive, and as he came to stand beside her, their eyes met—his dark with concern.

"She named Wickham," Elizabeth said. "And it was not... voluntary."

Darcy nodded, his jaw tightening. "I feared as much," he murmured. "I wanted to be sure, just in case Clara could not name the man or could only describe his face. You handled it well, Elizabeth."

She gave a small smile, grateful for his presence, his support. He hadn't needed to speak, but his quiet vigilance had meant everything.

"That brings up two questions." He paused, staring at the floor as his mind worked. "First, if Wickham was here in July, what was he doing? Was he trying to approach Pemberley?"

"And second," Elizabeth added, meeting his gaze with her own troubled thoughts, "this might mean that Harry did not father the child in that letter you found. Could it be that Wickham has been deceiving everyone, trying to frame Harry to ruin him?"

Darcy's jaw clenched, his fists tightening at his sides. "It would explain much... including why Wickham was so determined to ruin you. All of it—everything he did to you, to those other girls—was meant to weaken Harry's credibility."

Elizabeth nodded. "Can we find the other girl? And what can we do about the rest?"

He pulled her into his embrace, kissing the top of her head and letting his chest sink in a sigh that dropped her heart rate. "We can try. I've written to Richard, and as soon as you've had your second meeting with the Henshaws, we are bound for London. I mean to put this right."

T HE STORM OUTSIDE DARCY'S London townhouse had been raging since the early
      morning, but the drumming of rain against the windows was a dull background to
the storm in Darcy's mind. He had travelled four days from Derbyshire to London with
Elizabeth, but after days of being strung taut as a bowstring, his toes tapping anxiously
on the floor of the carriage with every mile, there had been little rest since their arrival. He
had written to Colonel Fitzwilliam before leaving Pemberley, and after several agonising
days of waiting, Richard had finally arrived in Town.

Darcy's study, usually a refuge of order and calm, was cluttered with letters, maps, and
scattered correspondence. His focus was drawn to one thing alone: Harry's legacy, his
reputation, and the truth that lay hidden somewhere between those papers. Now, at last,
Richard was here, and Darcy hoped his cousin's military insight would shed light on what
Harry had been facing before his death.

The door to the study creaked open, and Richard strode in, his military boots muffled
on the thick carpet. His coat was damp from the rain, and his dark hair was slicked back,
water droplets clinging to his brow. "Darcy," Richard greeted as he stepped into the room,
then shut the door behind himself, sealing them both in.

"Richard," Darcy replied, nodding. He gestured toward the desk piled with papers.
"You got my letter. Did you find anything?"

Richard tugged off his wet gloves and sighed, rubbing his temples. "I have, and what
I've uncovered... well, we have much to discuss. But first, I need to know—what exactly
did you find among Harry's things?"

Darcy's jaw tightened as he turned toward the desk. He picked up the worn letter that
he and Elizabeth had discovered hidden in Harry's uniform coat, its edges still creased
from where it had been folded and tucked away. "This," he said quietly, handing it to
Richard. "I wasn't certain of its significance at first, but after your last letter, it seems
clearer."

Richard took the letter, his brow furrowing as he began to read. The minutes stretched in silence, the only sound the crackling fire in the hearth and the rhythmic tapping of rain against the window. Darcy watched his cousin's face carefully, noting the deepening furrow in his brow as Richard's eyes flicked over each line.

When he finished, Richard set the letter down with a long exhale. He leaned back in his chair, the creaking of the wood barely masking the gravity of his thoughts. "This explains a great deal," he murmured.

Darcy's pulse quickened. "Explain it to me, then. I need to know the full truth of what Harry was caught up in."

Richard steepled his fingers and considered for a moment. "This letter... it's more than just a record of some minor mistake. It's a damning piece of evidence about a cover-up during the siege at Badajoz. Friendly fire, Darcy—Harry witnessed it. He tried to stop it, tried to order a cease-fire to avoid more casualties, but his orders were countermanded by a superior officer. And when the battle ended with heavy losses, and the truth became apparent, they promoted him, likely to keep him from reporting the truth."

Darcy clenched his fists, his knuckles turning white. "Promoted to keep him silent. That makes sense now, but I still do not understand... why treason? Why is my brother's name being dragged through the mud like this?"

Richard leaned forward, his voice lowering as if to shield the words from the storm outside. "After the battle, rumours began to circulate—rumours that Harry had deliberately allowed the French to breach the walls, that he had collaborated with them. It was all lies, of course, but lies spread quickly, especially when the men involved in the cover-up had much to lose if the truth came out. And..." He thinned his lips and lowered his voice. "Harry was no longer here to defend himself. Throwing him to the wolves—why, I suppose it was a way to make sure nobody else was ever able to bring truth forward, either. You know Harry was not the only one who could have reported this. He was just their scape goat because he was the first to raise the alarm."

Darcy swore under his breath, pacing in front of the fireplace. "And Wickham? Where does he fit into this?"

Richard's expression darkened. "That's where things take a more personal turn. Wickham was with Harry during the siege—some reports place him within an arm's length of Harry, though I've not been able to discover whether Wickham tried to stop the mistake or just carried forward with the attack—I am supposing the latter, because it explains the rest better."

Darcy narrowed his eyes. "How? What 'rest'?"

"My contacts confirmed that Wickham was involved in spreading the rumours. He clearly stood to gain from discrediting Harry—perhaps even blackmailing him. If Harry tried to expose the truth, Wickham would have used those rumours to destroy him."

Darcy froze mid-stride, his heart thudding with fury. "Wickham." The name hissed from his lips like venom. "That blackguard has haunted my family for years. He was looking for these papers when he tore apart Harry's flat. When he didn't find them, he ran. And now, he's been reassigned to Birmingham."

"A convenient assignment, just a day's ride from Pemberley. But he cannot hide forever. Not now that we have this."

Darcy stopped pacing and turned to face his cousin. "I want his head for this, Richard. Harry died with the accusation of treason hanging over him. He died knowing he would be betrayed, slaughtered on the altar of public opinion and 'military justice' if he told the truth. I will not rest until Wickham and whoever else is responsible are brought to justice."

"You always were the protective older brother, Darcy. But you'll need more than vengeance if you're going to clear Harry's name. We have this letter, but it's not enough to expose the entire cover-up. We'll need corroboration from others who were at the siege—officers who can confirm what really happened."

"Then we find them. Every last man who was there. I don't care what it takes. We will clear Harry's name."

Richard stood, placing a steadying hand on Darcy's shoulder. "We will, cousin. But we must move carefully. Whoever these men are who are protecting their careers, their reputations, they will not go down easily. You could be going against some rather formidable names. They *promoted* him, Darcy—promoted him to keep him quiet. Do you think this will stop with some field commander? No, I tell you, it goes much higher up the chain. Why Wickham is so vested in this, I've no idea, but he is slippery. He'll run if he thinks we're onto him, and he'll talk if he suspects we're looking about for answers."

Darcy straightened, resolve hardening in his chest. "Then we'll strike before he has the chance. Find someone trustworthy, someone you can bring this evidence to who has the authority to set the matter straight."

Richard gave a curt nod, his eyes narrowing with determination. "I've already reached out to a few men from the War Office—men we can trust. They're beginning to gather information on that battalion's movements, and I've asked for a complete list of men from that regiment. If we move quickly, we can expose this whole mess before it festers any longer."

Darcy allowed himself a small sigh of relief. It wasn't over—not by a long shot—but they finally had a way forward. They had a plan. And for the first time in weeks, Darcy felt the faintest flicker of hope.

E LIZABETH STEPPED INTO THE grand entrance hall of Matlock House, her hand resting lightly on Darcy's arm. The interior was as grand as one might expect of an earl's residence—ornate plasterwork and towering portraits of stern-looking ancestors lining the walls. Yet, despite its grandeur, an undeniable chill settled in Elizabeth's stomach. This meeting held more weight than any previous introduction, and she was painfully aware of the judgment hanging in the air.

Darcy stood tall beside her, his features perfectly composed, though occasionally his jaw shifted, and his gaze flicked to her as they waited. The moment they had entered Matlock House, his grip on her arm had tightened ever so slightly. It was a signal, not of fear, but of quiet determination. He would stand by her—he had made that clear. And for that, Elizabeth felt a swelling of gratitude and love for the man who had defied society, his family, and even himself to claim her as his wife.

Lady Matlock entered the hall with a measured step, her gown sweeping behind her in a rustle of silks. Her features were striking, her expression one of guarded politeness, though Elizabeth did not miss the flicker of reluctance in her eyes. The older woman's gaze shifted briefly to Darcy, perhaps searching for a clue as to why he had chosen this particular path. But it wasn't Darcy who had to prove himself—it was Elizabeth, the family spectacle, who must now prove she belonged.

"Mrs Darcy," Lady Matlock greeted her at last, her voice cool but not without civility. She extended her hand with the practised grace of someone who had long been accustomed to receiving guests of all ranks. "How kind of you to come. Such a... surprise."

"Lady Matlock," Elizabeth responded, taking the offered hand as she dipped a curtsey. "It is a pleasure to meet you." She was proud of how stately her voice sounded, though inwardly, her nerves danced. This was no ordinary meeting of polite society. This was her husband's family—the people whose acceptance or rejection would ripple through their social sphere.

Lady Matlock inclined her head. "The pleasure is ours," she said, though there was no mistaking the slight emphasis on the word 'ours' as though she spoke on behalf of her husband's more pragmatic considerations rather than any personal warmth.

As if on cue, Lord Matlock appeared, his demeanour slightly more welcoming but tinged with the pragmatism that Elizabeth expected. He smiled, though it was the kind of smile one reserved for an important business association rather than family.

"Darcy," the earl greeted his nephew with a firm handshake before turning to Elizabeth. "Mrs Darcy, welcome to Matlock House."

His words were polite enough, but Elizabeth could see it—the calculation in his eyes. She understood it. Darcy had forced his hand, after all, by just appearing here unannounced. To openly snub Elizabeth now, given her position as Darcy's wife, would be to risk severing their financial and social ties, a prospect the earl would be reluctant to entertain.

She felt a surge of pride in her husband at that moment. Darcy had brought her here, not as a mere gesture, but as a statement of defiance against those who sought to undermine her reputation and the Darcy family name. He was staking his loyalty to her in the heart of the very family who had questioned his decision. He had made his choice clear.

"Thank you, my lord," she said with a smile. "I am deeply honoured to meet you again."

Lord Matlock gave a nod, turning back to Darcy. "Your timing is... unexpected, but we are, of course, always happy to receive you."

"I thought it time," Darcy said evenly, his hand reaching for Elizabeth's, "that you meet my wife properly."

The subtle tension between the words was not lost on anyone. Lady Matlock's eyes lingered on Elizabeth as if weighing every inch of her, not with malice, but with the practical judgment of a woman who had spent her life assessing the worth of those who entered her circle. But Elizabeth refused to shrink under her gaze. She met the older woman's eyes with quiet confidence.

"Indeed," Lady Matlock said, at last, her voice softer now, though still reserved. "I hope you find Matlock House agreeable, Mrs Darcy. Perhaps you would join me for tea while we become better acquainted?"

The conversation was formal, stilted, but not entirely unkind. Elizabeth could sense the delicate dance they were all engaged in. No one wished to openly acknowledge the scandal that had surrounded her name in London, nor the fact that her presence here was a deliberate challenge to the unspoken rules of their world. And yet, by standing here, by being welcomed—however reluctantly—Elizabeth had crossed a threshold.

Darcy's loyalty had carried her across it.

They were ushered into the drawing room, where Lady Matlock offered Elizabeth a seat beside her. The gesture, however minor, was not lost on Elizabeth. It was a small step, but a step nonetheless.

As she sipped her tea, Elizabeth glanced across the room to where her husband and Lord Matlock were quietly retreating to the study. He looked once over his shoulder, just before the door closed behind him, and she caught just the edge of his smile. That was all the reassurance she wanted.

Lady Matlock set her cup down with a soft clink, drawing Elizabeth's attention. "Your husband appears to hold you in great esteem," she remarked, her tone no longer sharp, but softened, as though some invisible barrier had been quietly lowered.

Elizabeth returned the older woman's gaze, a faint smile on her lips. "As I do him, my lady."

D ARCY STOOD BY THE window in Lord Matlock's study, his hands clasped behind his back. The faint hum of the city filtered through the glass, a distant reminder of the world outside this room, but his mind was entirely focused on the man sitting across from him. Lord Matlock remained in his chair, his posture stiff, though not entirely hostile. A fire crackled in the hearth, its warmth doing little to thaw the coolness that had settled between them since Elizabeth had entered Matlock House.

"You've brought her here," the Earl began, his tone low and measured. "You must know what that means."

"I do," Darcy replied, turning from the window to face his uncle. "It means I expect her to be welcomed. She is my wife, and I will not have her slighted. By anyone."

The Earl's lips tightened, and for a moment, silence fell between them, save for the crackling fire. "It is not that simple. The girl's reputation precedes her, and you've put yourself—and your family—in a difficult position. Do you truly think this will be forgiven so easily? That society will simply look the other way?"

Darcy crossed the room with slow, deliberate steps, stopping just short of his uncle's desk. "Society can think what it likes. I care little for its whispers, and if any man has the audacity to question my wife's honour, he will answer to me directly."

"You always were stubborn," Lord Matlock muttered. "But it is not just about you. The Darcy name means something. You've always known that. It carries weight, responsibility. Your actions affect more than just your own household."

Darcy's jaw clenched, and for a moment, he said nothing. Then, with a steady voice, he replied, "Do you think I take that lightly? The Darcy name means everything to me, but it will not be sustained by cowering in the face of false judgment. Elizabeth is my wife—she deserves respect, not condemnation. And I will not allow anyone to treat her otherwise."

Lord Matlock studied him, his eyes narrowing slightly as he leaned back in his chair. "Respect? Do you think respect is all that is needed to silence the rumours? There are things being whispered about her... about Harry. You will need more than respect to counter those."

Darcy's gaze darkened at the mention of his brother. "Yes, I am aware of the rumours," he said, his voice cold. "And I mean to put an end to them. But I need your support, Uncle. You have always been respected—if you stand with me, with Elizabeth, it will go a long way toward quelling the gossip."

The earl exhaled sharply and stood, moving toward the decanter on the sideboard. "And what of Harry? These accusations that have come to light..."

Darcy stepped closer. "I know the truth. I have the evidence to clear Harry's name, and I intend to do so. Harry was no traitor, Uncle. He tried to stop his commander from firing on their own troops."

Matlock's brow puckered. "What?"

"I showed everything to Richard—Harry's maps, his letters, and the statement he wrote out, probably intending to publish if he were ever pressed to do so. Richard believes a squadron was in the wrong place at the wrong time. It was dusk, with smoke in the air, so it was difficult to see them properly, and the riflemen behind the wall were ordered to fire on them. Harry saw what was happening and ordered a cease-fire but was overruled, resulting in... egad, there is no way of knowing how many unnecessary fatalities."

"Is this... verifiable?"

"I have a copy of the initial report. Harry must have spirited it away before it was destroyed, but it bears the colonel's signature."

"Good Heavens." The earl's face fell, and he bent to rummage in his desk drawer for a cigar to puff away his thoughts. He never even bothered offering one to Darcy—not that he would have accepted. He was too angry, too bent on his purpose to puff away on tobacco as if this were a leisurely afternoon of drinks at the club.

"And this... this report," his uncle mumbled as he cut the end of his cigar. "What do you mean to do with it? Make it public knowledge?"

"As public as public can possibly be. But first, I need the names of all those responsible for slandering Harry, so I know whom I may trust. Do you recall Wickham, son of my father's steward?"

Matlock frowned. "Disreputable cad. Never understood why your father tolerated him."

Darcy's voice lowered, thick with frustration. "Neither did I, and Harry's trust in him was his undoing. Wickham may not have ordered the attack, but he is the one who let the accusations fester. He knew—he *had* to know Harry's attempts to stop the attack, and he still stood by while the rumours of treason spread. I daresay he was the one who pointed the finger at Harry when the general demanded answers about the high death toll."

The Earl paused, the smoking cigar halfway to his lips, his brow furrowing as the implications sank in. "Wickham?" he repeated, slowly. "I never liked the blighter, but you believe him capable of betraying his own friend?"

"More than capable. What he did to Mrs Darcy—he was threatening Harry with the very gossip you have been hearing for the past several weeks. It was at a party, outside on the portico. She saw it, tried to put a stop to the fight, and Wickham cut her gown open and threw her at Harry, just for the pleasure of ruining both of them. I daresay you were told quite a different version of events."

A puff of smoke briefly concealed the earl's clouded face. "Aye." He stabbed out his cigar and leaned forward on his desk. "All the talk has her ravished and likely pregnant. I never could have guessed…"

"Now, do you see, Uncle? I want my brother and my wife dignified with the truth."

The earl sucked in a breath, releasing it slowly as his chest fell. "Very well. Wickham, then. What do you mean to do?"

"He's in Birmingham on some sham assignment. I shall have to confront him later, but he's only part of it. There are men with far more to lose than Wickham—higher ranks that orchestrated this, used Harry as a scapegoat to cover their own blunders. Wickham merely seized the opportunity, throwing Harry to the wolves while he protected his own skin."

Lord Matlock set his glass down, his gaze sharpening. "And you mean to bring this all into the open, do you? How do you plan to preserve even a scrap of your family dignity when you shed light on everything?"

Darcy swallowed. "Carefully, uncle."

Lord Matlock stared at him for a long moment, then downed his brandy in one swift gulp. "You're playing a dangerous game, Darcy. But if you're determined to see it through, you shall have my support. I only hope you know what you're doing."

Darcy nodded, his expression grim. "I appreciate that. So do I."

The earl set his empty glass aside and turned toward the window, his voice softening slightly. "And your wife… Mrs Darcy. I hope, for your sake, that she's as strong as you believe her to be."

Darcy's lips twitched into a faint smile. "Stronger, Uncle. Much stronger."

Chapter Twenty-Seven

DARCY STRODE THROUGH THE entrance of the gentlemen's club, his coat dripping slightly from the persistent drizzle outside. The familiar scent of tobacco and polished wood greeted him as he handed his hat to the waiting valet. A few heads turned in his direction—recognising him, no doubt—but Darcy paid them no mind. His thoughts were focused, his purpose clear.

The room was warm and crowded, filled with men discussing politics, estates, and the latest scandal to surface in London. It was a place Darcy had frequented often enough, though rarely for pleasure. Today, however, he had come with a specific goal: answers. Answers that, he hoped, would lead him closer to the truth about Harry—and perhaps even Wickham's involvement in the cruel game that had been played against his brother.

He made his way toward a corner table, where a few men sat in low conversation. Among them was Sergeant Michael Langley, the man Richard had written to—a soldier who had served alongside both Harry and Wickham during their campaign. Langley looked up as Darcy approached, his expression shifting from polite recognition to cautious curiosity.

"Mr Darcy, I presume?" Langley greeted, rising slightly in his chair as Darcy approached. "I wasn't sure I'd be seeing you today."

"I came as soon as Colonel Fitzwilliam told me where to find you. Thank you for agreeing to meet," Darcy replied, putting out his hand.

Langley shook Darcy's hand and gestured to the empty chair beside him, but Darcy hesitated, his eyes flicking toward the other men at the table. "Would you mind if we spoke somewhere more private? The matter concerns my brother, Captain Darcy, and it is not for public ears."

Langley's brows lifted in understanding. He glanced at his companions, then nodded. "Of course, Mr Darcy."

Darcy led the way toward a quieter alcove near the back of the room, the sound of murmured conversation fading behind them. Once they were seated in relative privacy, Darcy leaned in slightly. "I'm looking for some information—about Captain Darcy's actions at the Siege of Badajoz and the rumours that have sprung up after the battle."

Langley's face softened at the mention of Harry's name. "Your brother was well-regarded, Darcy. A good man. A bloody shame what happened."

Darcy swallowed, forcing back the familiar sting of grief. "Yes, it was. But I've come across something... unsettling. I need to know what you've heard, Langley. There are whispers... treason—surely, you've heard them, but I cannot credit any of it. And I have reason to believe Lieutenant Wickham may have had a hand in this."

Langley leaned back, exhaling slowly as he regarded Darcy with an appraising look. "I figured this would come up sooner or later. Wickham's name's been floating around, but it's not just him. The accusations started long before that, during the siege. Men have been talking, though not many with enough guts to say it aloud."

"So, it's true then? Not the treason, but that Wickham's been stoking these fires?"

Langley gave a grim nod. "Wickham's no innocent, but he wasn't the one who started it. Word is, Captain Darcy saw something he 'shouldn't have' during the siege—something that could've got the wrong men in a lot of trouble. They promoted him to shut him up, even though he protested and said he was going public with the truth. But Wickham... he was the one who first pinned Captain Darcy for calling the cease-fire, saying it was treason so he could cover for the colonel who was at fault. Wickham was in a rage when Darcy got promoted, but he didn't, and he said he'd see him ruined."

Darcy's jaw clenched, anger rising. "And what about the others? Who else is involved?"

Langley glanced around the room, his voice dropping lower. "High-ranking men. This goes deeper than just Wickham, Darcy. If you're going to take this on, you'll need more than a few suspicions and the word of a few sergeants to clear the captain's name."

"I know. But Wickham's the one who has been trying to ruin my brother, even from beyond the grave. I start with him. Were you in London at the same time as he was this summer? I'm curious about... social functions. Company he kept. Anything."

Langley nodded slowly. "I did hear something recently... at a gathering, about a month back. Someone mentioned Wickham in connection with Darcy. They said he'd been seen fighting with the captain—shouting in public during those last few months. More than that, though, I'm not certain."

Darcy leaned in. "What about women?"

Langley blinked. "There was always a woman," Langley said slowly, glancing around as if to ensure no one else was listening. "You know Wickham. Lots of them, in fact."

"And can the same be said for my brother?"

The sergeant pursed his lips, then shook his head. "He went to more respectable parties—the Darcy name, you know. I'm sure he was in the company of ladies—real ladies—but I never heard any gossip tying him to any particular ones until... well, that is..." He cleared his throat and gestured to Darcy. "Colonel Fitzwilliam said something in his letter about the former Miss Bennet."

He smiled faintly. "Mrs Darcy now. My brother was trying to salvage her honour after Wickham blasted it."

The sergeant lifted his shoulders. "As you please, sir."

"What I want to know—" Darcy said, drawing his chair closer— "is names. Can you tell me who Wickham kept company with the most? Male as well as female... perhaps particularly female."

"Ah, I got you now, sir." Langley rubbed his chin in thought. "There was a young lady who was seen in Wickham's company more than once. Not his usual sort of strumpet, but a classy one. It could have been nothing, just rumours, but... well, you know Wickham. He doesn't leave a good reputation in his wake."

"Do you recall who mentioned this?" Darcy pressed. "Or can you find out?"

Langley frowned. "I can keep my ear to the ground, sir. So to speak."

"Excellent." Darcy put his hand in his pocket and withdrew a coin to toss it on the table. "Buy your friends a round on me, and I appreciate anything you can pass on, Langley."

The sergeant tipped a casual salute as Darcy rose. "Will do, sir, and thank you."

T HE DRAWING ROOM AT Darcy House had always seemed too grand to Elizabeth at first—on her wedding day, she had barely had time to even glance around it in the flurry of introductions and formalities.

Now, however, as she waited for William to return, with Fitzy curled up at her feet, she found herself appreciating its quiet elegance. The afternoon light filtered through the tall windows, casting a golden glow over the polished wood and soft drapery, and for the first time, she truly felt like its mistress. She had learned her way through the house, come to know Mrs Hodges, the capable housekeeper, and now moved through the space with a sense of belonging.

A glance at the clock told her it was late—William should have returned by now. Fitzy lifted his head as if sensing her impatience, his small body alert to the change in her mood. She reached down to stroke his soft fur, the action soothing her own restless thoughts. William had been out all day, chasing leads, trying to uncover more about Harry's past and the tangled web Wickham had spun. It would take weeks, if they were lucky, to learn all there was to know.

But she knew him too well now. He would come home frustrated if he had not found the answers he sought on the very first day.

The sound of the front door opening below made her sit up straighter. She could hear the hurried steps of the footmen, the soft murmur of voices. And then, William's unmistakable heavy tread as he made his way toward her. Elizabeth rose to meet him, standing by the fire as the drawing room door opened.

He stepped inside, dripping wet from the rain outside, his face drawn tight with frustration. His dark hair clung to his forehead, and his coat was soaked through, the damp fabric clinging to his broad frame.

"William," she chided, moving toward him. "You are drenched."

He shook his head, brushing aside her concern. "It is nothing," he said, his eyes narrowing with frustration. "I have not learned enough yet. Every lead seems to go nowhere, and I am running in circles."

Elizabeth stepped closer, allowing the footman behind him to take his wet things. Her gaze never left her husband as he shrugged out of his coat with a rough gesture, his irritation rising with every jerk and tug. She reached for his arm, her touch light but insistent. "You have only just begun, William," she said softly, offering a reassuring smile, though she could see the tension etched into his face. "It will take time. You will find what you are looking for, but not like this—not when you are exhausted."

He let out a low breath, glancing toward the drawing room, with its inviting fire and comfortable sofa, as if it might hold some answer to his frustration. "I cannot rest while these questions remain unanswered," he replied, shaking his head once more, as though determined to push through his weariness. "I am not used to waiting idly, nor relying on others for help. I must have names—learn where this began so I do not run into a brick wall in attempting to expose the truth."

"And you will," she said, stepping in front of him to block his path. She placed her hands on his chest, feeling the steady rise and fall of his breath beneath the damp fabric of his shirt. "But not tonight. Tonight, you need to let it go, if only for a few hours."

He opened his mouth to protest again, but she cut him off, her gaze unwavering as she tilted her head slightly. "Come with me," she insisted, her fingers brushing lightly against his damp shirt. "I will not let you drive yourself into the ground over this."

He hesitated, his jaw tightening as he glanced away, struggling with his own sense of duty and pride. "Elizabeth, I—"

She raised an eyebrow, the corner of her lips lifting in a teasing smile. "Do you think I am asking, husband?"

That caught him off guard, and he blinked down at her, the faintest hint of amusement flickering in his eyes. "You are quite determined, I see," he said, his tone softening, though the conflict in his gaze remained. "Very well. But I do not need—"

"You need rest," she interrupted firmly, taking his hand in hers and leading him toward the door. "And for once, I will make certain you have it."

He muttered something about not needing help, insisting that his valet could attend to him, but she ignored him, pulling him along with a quiet smile until they reached his chambers. Fitzy trotted behind them, but Elizabeth closed the door firmly in his face.

"Well! I shall take care not to offend you, Mrs Darcy, if that is how you treat your most loyal friend."

She grinned. "I am merely demonstrating my preference for one 'Fitzy' over the other. Come here." She began working on the buttons of his waistcoat, ignoring his weak protests.

"I can manage—"

"No, you cannot," she laughed, stripping the waistcoat from his shoulders and tossing it aside. "You have been out all day in the rain, and now you are going to let me help."

He watched her, his frustration softening into something else as she moved on to his cravat, loosening it with deft fingers. His hair, damp and tousled, fell over his forehead, and she pushed it back gently. "I employ a valet for this," he reminded her, his voice quieter now.

She placed a finger over his lips. "Your valet is an excellent fellow," she murmured. "But he cannot do what I have in mind."

He let out a breath, his protests fading as she unbuttoned his shirt, her touch lingering over his chest. His boots followed, then the fall of his breeches, and before long, he stood in his unbuttoned undershirt, watching her with a half-smile that looked almost wolfish.

"Is this what you wanted, Mrs Darcy?" he murmured huskily.

Elizabeth moved closer, sliding her arms around his neck as she whispered, "You are home now, and quite my own for the moment. That is all I wanted."

He sighed, the weight of the day slipping away as he finally let himself smile. "You always know how to bring me back to myself," he said softly, his hands resting at her waist.

She rose onto her toes, her lips grazing his. "Because I love you," she whispered, pulling him closer.

And that was the last thing either of them said for a long while.

DARCY PUSHED THE PAPERS across his desk in frustration, the scattered documents refusing to yield any answers. His fingers drummed on the table as he stared at the cryptic notes Langley had sent him earlier. Names, half-sentences, military jargon—none of it fitting together in any coherent way. He exhaled sharply, rubbing a hand across his temples, as if by sheer will he could force the tangled mess to make sense.

The fire crackled behind him, but its warmth only served to remind him how little comfort there was in his current predicament. With every new piece of information, the truth seemed further out of reach. Darcy clenched his jaw, leaning back in his chair. What was he missing?

The sound of footsteps in the hall caught his attention, and a moment later, the door to his study swung open. Darcy looked up, surprised to see Richard standing there, silhouetted against the doorway.

"Richard?" Darcy rose to his feet. "I did not expect you."

"I thought it best to come in person," Richard replied, stepping inside and closing the door behind him. There was a grim look on his face—one that told Darcy the news was not going to be easy. "I have names."

"Names?"

Richard nodded, crossing the room to stand beside the desk. "I've spoken to a few more men—trusted sources. They were reluctant to talk at first, but once I mentioned the fact that we had proof, eyewitnesses... well, it opened a few doors. I have the names of the officers involved."

Darcy gestured to the chair beside him. "Sit, tell me everything."

Richard sat down, setting his hat on the arm of the chair and pulling out a folded piece of paper from his coat. "The officer who ordered the charge was Colonel Frederick Halton," he began, his tone low.

"Halton!" Darcy sucked in a breath. "But he was the very man who confirmed Harry's treason to your father!"

"The same."

Darcy blinked, staring off into the distance. "I spoke with him in person when Harry died. The blackguard! Offered me his condolences and acted as if he had just lost his right-hand man!"

"He probably did. I've no doubt Harry was his best officer before he happened to catch the colonel in a career-ending error. It was a mistake, and Harry knew it from the start.

He reported the error to Major James Bellamy, but Bellamy covered it up—claimed it was a 'miscommunication,' though we both know that's not true."

"I am not so sure that I do not find him even more culpable than the colonel. Halton's signature actually appears on Harry's initial report—he was probably facing a court-martial when that report came out, but he did sign it. Bellamy must have decided to cover for him. Or for himself."

"That's my opinion as well," Richard agreed. "Now, the one who orchestrated the promotion to silence Harry was General Townsend, trying to save face so he did not have to justify the matter to Wellington. He's the one we need to avoid at all costs."

Darcy's brow furrowed as he took in the names. "And Wickham?"

"He was involved, yes," Richard confirmed. "He was feeding these officers the information they needed to keep Harry in check, playing it for a promotion for himself, no doubt. And when Harry refused to stay quiet, Wickham took it a step further—started spreading the rumours of treason—as well as that nice little touch about ruining women—knowing full well what it would do to your brother's reputation."

Darcy stood, pacing the length of the room as he absorbed Richard's words. "So now we know who they are. Halton, Bellamy, and Townsend." He stopped in front of the fire, staring into the flames. "They wanted to bury Harry's truth with him."

"Exactly," Richard replied. "And if you want to bring Harry's evidence forward, you'll need to make sure it gets into the right hands. These men have influence, Darcy—enough to turn the tables if they catch wind of the fact that you still have Harry's statements."

Darcy nodded. "I will be careful."

Richard leaned forward in his chair, his expression thoughtful. "There's one more thing, though. You mentioned before that you were looking into that letter—the one about a girl Harry might have... wronged."

Darcy's jaw tightened. "Yes. But I no longer believe Harry was responsible. I suppose it is *possible*... but it just does not sound like something Harry would do."

"Agreed. So?"

"We already know Wickham was trying to do anything he could to ruin Harry's name. He has a history of seducing and abandoning women, and I believe he has done the same here, even to the point of letting the girl believe he *was* Harry. The problem is, we have no idea who or where she is. The letter gave no name, no real clues."

Richard frowned. "But why does it matter now? If Wickham was behind it, and the girl is long gone, why are you still searching? There is no way of tracking her down after all this time."

Darcy's shoulders tensed, his back still to his cousin as he stared into the fire. His voice was softer when he spoke again. "I married Elizabeth intending to right my brother's mistakes. At least, that is what I believed at the time. But now... now I see that *she* was no mistake at all. Even so, I made a promise to her—to set things right, wherever I could. If there is another woman out there who was wronged by this situation... I cannot turn my back on that. Elizabeth would never forgive me if I did nothing, nor could I forgive myself."

Richard was silent for a long moment, watching his cousin with quiet understanding. "You are a better man than most, Darcy," he said finally. "But you cannot fix everything. You may never find this girl."

"I know. But I promised my wife that I would try."

There was a long silence between them, the crackling of the fire the only sound in the room. Finally, Richard stood, clapping a hand on Darcy's shoulder. "We will find the truth. And we will make sure Harry's name is cleared. But take care of yourself, cousin. You cannot fight this battle alone."

Darcy turned to his cousin with a grin. "I'm not."

Chapter Twenty-Eight

"**B**LAST THESE BUTTONS," DARCY muttered under his breath, fumbling with his coat as he tugged it into place. The morning promised to be crisp, to be sure, but it was his fraying patience that had him snapping at his coat.

Richard raised an eyebrow, his lips twitching with amusement. "Having trouble already, cousin? We have not even left the house."

Darcy shot him a look. "It is the coat, not me," he replied, jerking the lapels into position with one last tug.

"You could have had your valet help you, if you had half a moment of patience."

Darcy scowled. "Are you ready?"

Richard reached for his gloves, pulling them on with a nonchalant shrug. "I have been waiting on you for the better part of an hour."

"You were drinking my brandy," Darcy muttered, though the corner of his mouth twitched slightly. He slipped on his gloves, the leather creaking softly as he flexed his knuckles. "But yes, I'm ready."

Their eyes met briefly, a look that carried more weight than words could manage. Richard's usual ease was still present, but his posture was too rigid, his movements measured. Darcy could sense the same unspoken strain in himself. Neither would voice it, but the silence between them was thick with purpose and something that bordered on unease.

"This is the last time," Darcy said quietly, his voice rougher than he intended. "We take Harry's report, we hand it over directly, and we make bloody sure they listen."

Richard nodded, pulling open the door. "Right. Let's get it done."

They stepped into the morning chill, the cobbled streets of London slick from the rain that had fallen overnight. Horses clattered by, and the hum of the city began to rise with the dawn, but Darcy's mind was elsewhere. Whitehall was only a short ride away, but the weight of what they were about to do felt larger, graver than the distance suggested.

"I do hope you've prepared yourself for the sheer joy of bureaucratic stonewalling," Richard said as they mounted the carriage.

Darcy snorted. "I have dealt with men in Whitehall before, Richard."

"Ah, but not like this," Richard said with a grin. "They'll make a sport of slowing us down, you know. It is practically a game to them."

"I will break their game if I have to."

Richard chuckled, though there was little humour in it. "I almost want to see that."

They climbed into the carriage, the door closing with a soft thud behind them. The horses lurched forward, and the familiar jostle of the cobblestones beneath the wheels seemed to mirror the noise roiling in Darcy's mind. Harry's report sat tucked inside his coat, and though it was only a few pages, it felt like the heaviest burden he'd ever carried.

Richard stretched his legs out in front of him, his gaze wandering to the window. "You are quiet, cousin."

Darcy pressed his lips together, glancing at the leather pouch at his side. "I am thinking."

Richard turned toward him, studying him with a rare seriousness. "Wondering if it will be enough?"

Darcy sighed, his fingers brushing the edge of the pouch. "I have to believe it is. For Harry's sake."

They fell into silence again, the city passing by in a blur of grey and damp stone.

They arrived at Whitehall shortly after noon, the building alive with the constant shuffle of officers, secretaries, and couriers weaving in and out of rooms. Darcy barely registered the movement around him. Together, he and Richard approached the outer office of General Sir Edward Hamilton.

A young secretary sat behind a polished desk, eyes darting over ledgers and correspondence. As Darcy and Richard stepped forward, the man barely glanced up.

"We need to see the general," Darcy said firmly.

The secretary's pen stilled, and he looked up, his expression impassive. "I am afraid that is impossible without an appointment. The general's schedule is full for the day."

He turned his attention back to his papers, dismissing them as if they were a minor inconvenience.

Richard cleared his throat, stepping forward with a practised smile. "Perhaps you did not catch my name. I am Colonel Fitzwilliam, and this"—he gestured toward Darcy—"is Mr Darcy of Pemberley. We are here on urgent family business that cannot wait."

The secretary frowned, glancing between them. "Colonel Fitzwilliam, you say?" His tone had softened slightly, but he still looked hesitant.

Richard leaned in just enough to make the secretary straighten in his chair. "Indeed. The Earl of Matlock is my father. I suggest you mention my name to the general. I believe he will make time for us."

The young man hesitated for a moment, then rose from his desk with a sharp nod. "Wait here," he said, disappearing through a side door.

Darcy exchanged a look with Richard, who simply raised an eyebrow as if to say, *patience.*

Minutes later, the secretary returned, his posture noticeably more respectful. "The general will see you now, Colonel Fitzwilliam, Mr Darcy. Follow me, please."

As they entered the office, General Sir Edward Hamilton rose from his desk. His eyes flicked between Darcy and Richard, curiosity sparking in his expression. "Mr Darcy, Colonel Fitzwilliam," he greeted, gesturing to the chairs across from him. "To what do I owe this unexpected visit?"

Richard spoke first. "We've come to deliver a report, Sir Edward. A report that was written by Captain Harold Darcy before his death, concerning troubling events during the Siege of Badajoz."

Sir Edward's brow furrowed slightly as he accepted the packet of papers Darcy held out. He flipped through them, his face unreadable. "And why bring this to me directly?"

"Because," Darcy answered, leaning forward slightly, "we believe it was deliberately covered up. The details of what happened during the siege were hidden, and my brother was promoted as a way to silence him. We are here to ensure that his voice is finally heard."

Sir Edward's eyes narrowed as he glanced back down at the papers, his fingers brushing over the official seals and signatures that adorned the documents. "These are serious accusations."

"They are the truth," Richard replied firmly. "And we trust that you will ensure they are investigated properly."

Sir Edward sat back in his chair, studying both men carefully. After a long pause, he nodded. "Why should I believe any of this is true?"

"We only ask you to investigate it, sir," Richard urged. "We trust the facts will speak for themselves."

Sir Edward frowned at them, then turned his attention to the papers in his hand. With a sceptical arch of his brow, he unfolded them, and his eyes flicked over the first page. His brow furrowed, and his lips began to move as he kept reading.

"Firing on their own troops?" he muttered, straightening in his chair and continuing to the next page.

"There is more, sir," Darcy added. "Captain Darcy tried to put a stop to the mistake and was villainised by the very officers who ought to have been corrected by him. I would like very much for the truth to be known."

Sir Edward arched a brow. "I am sure you would, Mr Darcy. And I would like very much for the war to be ended today. But you would ask me to acknowledge a report that could damage public sentiment—the nation's confidence in the war effort. Even the reputation of Wellington himself!"

"We understand that," Darcy said. "But my brother was not the only witness. Others can testify to this, and I will find them if I must. The truth will come out, whether you take the credit for uncovering it, or a mutiny stirs among the ranks."

Sir Edward's features darkened. "Are you threatening me, Darcy?"

"My brother died with the weight of this on his shoulders, and I will not allow his memory to be tarnished by lies."

Sir Edward sighed, then gave a curt nod, slipping the papers into his desk. "I will do what I can. But be prepared for disappointment. If even half of this is true, it will be... a delicate matter."

Darcy exchanged a glance with Richard. "We expect nothing less."

D ARCY STEPPED OUT OF the carriage with long, purposeful strides, barely sparing Richard a glance as he disembarked. Richard followed him with a bark of laughter.

"In quite the hurry, are we? You know, cousin, it's quite something to witness this transformation in you. One might even say you've become completely besotted."

Darcy shot him a glance, though a smile tugged at the corner of his lips. "Besotted, am I?"

"Absolutely. I might as well be invisible the moment you catch sight of your wife."

"There you prove how preposterous you are. She is not even outside for me to see."

Richard shook his head as he followed Darcy into the hall. "That must be why you are in such a hurry to go find her."

"She will be eager to hear how the report was received," Darcy replied as he marched toward the stairs. But he concealed a grin that he hoped his cousin could not see.

Richard was right, of course. There was nothing quite like returning to Elizabeth—no matter the business or concerns he carried, being in her presence soothed him in ways he still found difficult to explain. One of the many joys that had been his comfort in the wake of Harry's loss.

"Do me a favour," Richard added, clapping a hand on Darcy's shoulder as he began to take his leave. "Try not to forget the rest of us exist in the meantime, will you?"

"I make no promises," Darcy called back, already hurrying up the stairs. Inside, he removed his coat and asked the housekeeper where Mrs Darcy was.

"Upstairs, in her sitting room, sir," the housekeeper replied, smiling as she took his gloves. "She has been writing her letters this afternoon."

Darcy nodded his thanks and immediately made for the staircase. His steps were light, his heart quickening as he imagined her there—perhaps by the window, her head bent in concentration over her correspondence, that soft smile he loved gracing her lips. A familiar warmth spread through him at the thought.

As he reached the door to her sitting room, an idea took hold of him—mischievous and delicious, and entirely unlike him. He would sneak in behind her, press a kiss to her cheek, and feel that delighted startle of surprise she always gave him. He opened the door quietly, taking care with each step, but before he could close the distance, the small bundle of fur that was her terrier puppy leapt off her lap and bounded toward him, barking in a frenzy of excitement and taking a blind leap, forcing Darcy to catch him.

Oh, blast. He laughed, though the element of surprise was now completely ruined. Elizabeth turned in her chair, her eyes sparkling with laughter as the puppy leapt to lick his nose, his chin, his ears, and anything else within reach.

"Ah, you thought you were giving me a sweet companion, but it seems you've got me a watchdog instead."

"A rather poor one at that," Darcy replied, trying to control the squirming puppy. "He's hardly threatening."

The dog wriggled in his arms, tail wagging so furiously that Darcy couldn't help but laugh. He crossed the room, still holding the dog, and leaned down to kiss Elizabeth. She met his lips with a smile, her fingers brushing his cheek before she took his free hand in hers.

"How did your errand go?" she whispered against his lips, studying his face.

"It went as well as could be expected. We will hear soon enough if it is believed."

Elizabeth offered him a sympathetic smile, but her eyes brightened a moment later as though a thought had just come to her.

"Well, *I* have some good news to share, at least," she said, her voice lighter. "Before we left Pemberley, I wrote to my father about one of his tenants' sons."

Darcy frowned. "Why?"

"Well, John Michaels is a young, strong lad who would like very much to take over his father's farm, but his mother has been ill, and it was looking as though they would have to give it up altogether over the winter. He's a good lad... and a single one."

Darcy raised a brow, intrigued. "You've proposed a match? With Clara Henshaw would be my guess."

Elizabeth smiled and nodded. "Indeed. And I just received Papa's reply. John and his family are in favour of the match, and I believe it has charms for both Clara and John. I feel confident they will treat each other well."

"And how much are we paying to make this match take place?"

Elizabeth put on a mock pout. "Now, Mr Darcy, that is not fair. You said I might have full discretion in the matter, and now you wish me to answer your questions?"

"I only wonder if I ought to have my banker look over the accounts. Is Pemberley still secure for at least another year?"

She arched her back primly. "Pemberley is quite safe, and I've no doubt this little notion of mine will benefit both families. There, are you satisfied?"

"Perfectly so, if you are," Darcy said, pleased. "You have done a good thing, Elizabeth. A kind thing for that girl. I think my own mother would not have done more."

Her features softened at his words. "So, you approve of my idea, do you?"

"Very much." Darcy's expression shifted into something more playful. He tightened his grip on her hand. "I, too, have an idea to propose," he said, his voice lowering in a way that made Elizabeth narrow her eyes in playful suspicion.

"Oh?" she asked, her tone teasing as she met his gaze. "And what exactly is your idea?"

Before she could react, Darcy swept her up into his arms with such suddenness that she yelped in surprise, her hands flying to grasp at his neck for balance.

"William!" she gasped, though laughter bubbled up from her lips. "You seem to be forever carrying me places these days. Are you not tired of it yet?"

He paused for just a moment, his expression turning serious. "I have relished every opportunity to carry you, Elizabeth. From the very first day you came to my life—I have always loved having you in my arms, even before I could admit that to myself."

Her laughter faded, and she gazed up at him in some wonder. Before she could find an answer, he closed the remaining distance between them, pressing his lips to hers in a kiss that spoke more than words could. She smiled against his lips, her hands tightening at his neck.

Without another word, Darcy kicked open the door leading from her sitting room to her bedroom, the soft creak of the hinges and Elizabeth's laughter the only sounds as they disappeared into the room together.

A WEEK HAD PASSED with no word of success or failure. Each day of silence seemed to darken her husband's mood. Not that William had been anything less than warm with her, but she was not blind to the cloud of doubt that hovered over him—the tightness in his jaw when each new morning passed without the new Mrs Darcy receiving even one caller in her drawing room, and no Christmas party invitations arrived for either of them.

Elizabeth sat across from her husband, her spoon paused over her bowl of porridge, watching the icy sunlight filter softly through the curtains. It was a rare, quiet morning—one of the few where neither seemed pressed with immediate tasks. Fitzy lay curled at her feet, snoring softly, while Darcy, lost in thought, absently swirled his tea.

Just as she was about to speak, the butler entered with the morning paper, folding it neatly and placing it beside Darcy's plate. He glanced at it and waved it away with a sigh.

"Not today. I've no desire to read the latest scandals," he muttered, lifting his cup. "It is probably full of gossip about things I care nothing for."

Elizabeth, however, reached for the paper. "Oh, come, William," she said with a playful smile, "As if we are so very exciting ourselves today. One can never tell what morsels of news the world might offer." She unfolded it, skimming the front page. Her eyes widened as the headline caught her attention.

"William," she said softly, "you may want to reconsider."

Darcy frowned, setting his cup down. "What is it?"

Wordlessly, she turned the paper around for him to see. The headline blared back at him: *INVESTIGATION INTO MILITARY SCANDAL: REVELATIONS SHAKE THE ARMY.*

His expression shifted from mild disinterest to sharp attention as he scanned the article. "Can it be?" he murmured in awe. "Did they actually read Harry's statement?"

"With such esteemed personages as Colonel Fitzwilliam and Fitzwilliam Darcy standing in their office, how could they not?" Elizabeth teased.

He glanced up. "General Sir Edward Hamilton owes the second son of an earl and a private gentleman like me nothing at all. He saw us on a whim. That was a bit of luck—or pity, perhaps. We certainly did not possess the clout Richard seemed to pretend we had, but it worked."

She watched his eyes drop to the paper again—watched how they darted across the page with increasing speed, the further he read.

"The names," he muttered, "they've listed all of them." His voice caught slightly. "As well as that of a Lieutenant Daniels and a Captain Hunt, who both corroborated Harry's account. I didn't expect to see this so soon." He stared at the paper in disbelief.

Before he could say more, the door to the breakfast room opened again, and Richard strode in, looking far too pleased with himself. His grin, usually mischievous, seemed almost triumphant today.

"You're late, Richard," Darcy said, still peering at the paper. "I have already seen the news."

Richard waved the broadsheet off with a laugh. "Oh, I know, cousin. But that's not why I'm here." With a flourish, he pulled another paper from his coat, this one far less respectable, its edges worn and cheap ink smudging his fingers. "I bring you something even more scandalous—compliments of my mother, Mrs Darcy."

Darcy narrowed his eyes as Richard handed him the paper. "What on earth is this?" he asked, glancing at the title: *Lady Marlina's Mirror*.

Elizabeth stifled a giggle. "That sounds delightfully terrible."

Richard grinned, his eyes dancing with mirth. "It is a gossip column my mother insists on reading. And today, it contains a rather interesting tidbit about a certain major whose name is currently all over London."

Darcy raised a brow. "Go on."

Richard flipped to the page in question and read aloud: *"A certain major, whose name is now in the public eye for rather a different scandal, has been the subject of whispered rumours for months. Word has it, his daughter has been sent away after finding herself in some... delicate condition. Naturally, those in the know are aware of who this major is. One cannot help but wonder—was there more behind the promotion that catapulted a different officer's fortunes than we've been told?"*

Richard glanced up, the corners of his mouth still curled in amusement. "This major... must be Bellamy. And they're talking about Harry's sham of a promotion."

Darcy blinked, still processing the implication. "Bellamy's daughter?"

Richard leaned forward, his tone more serious. "Think about it. If it really was Wickham who ruined the lady from that letter, and not Harry... Wickham may have chosen her specifically and used Harry's name to further sour things between Bellamy and your brother. It makes perfect sense. Bellamy would already despise Harry for whatever involvement he thought he had in the scandal surrounding the military incident, and this—this would drive him over the edge. Wickham wanted to lock up that promotion and lock out Harry."

Darcy stared at him, astonishment blooming in his eyes. "You're suggesting he deliberately used Bellamy's daughter to damage Harry politically?"

Richard nodded. "Exactly. Wickham could have easily spun a lie—you know how skilled he is at that—and if Bellamy's daughter was misled... it would explain a great deal."

Darcy sat back, stunned. "Is there any way to confirm this? To find her?"

Richard shrugged. "It's difficult. If she *has* been sent away, the family would have done everything they could to keep it quiet. But servants talk, and if we grease the right palms, we might uncover something."

Darcy stood abruptly and strode down the hall, toward his study. Elizabeth and Richard exchanged a glance, and the colonel shrugged. What was William about? She set aside her napkin and rose to follow him, with the colonel right behind her.

In Darcy's study, they found him unlocking a drawer in the bottom of his desk. Before he pulled it open, his gaze moved to Elizabeth, and she was certain he was holding his breath. Then he withdrew a small, intricately carved box and rummaged through its contents. Elizabeth drew close, peering over his shoulder.

There were four portrait miniatures in there, and her husband's hand stilled over the lid—his fingers trembling faintly. One, she recognised as his mother. Another was obviously himself—younger, probably when he had just reached his majority. And then there were the other two.

William swallowed audibly as he withdrew the other two portrait miniatures. One, he held up to the light—a likeness of his brother, Harry, his expression captured forever in the easy smile she remembered so well. The other, he handed to Richard.

"Here," he said, his voice tight with emotion. "This is Wickham's portrait. My father had it commissioned, though Heaven only knows why. Take both of these. If you find Bellamy's daughter, show her these portraits. Ask her to identify the man."

Richard took the miniatures, nodding grimly. "I'll get to work."

Chapter Twenty-Nine

WORD CAME RATHER MORE swiftly than Darcy had anticipated.

The sun was beginning its slow descent over the London streets when Darcy entered the drawing room, an express letter from Richard in hand. Elizabeth sat near the window, her needlework resting in her lap as she glanced up, immediately curious.

"An express from Richard," Darcy said, crossing the room and handing her the envelope. He pulled up a chair beside her, unfolding the letter as she peered over his shoulder.

She leaned forward intently, breaking open the seal with fingers that trembled in excitement. "Does he send good news?"

Darcy scanned the page quickly, a smile tugging at his lips. "It seems so," he murmured before beginning to read aloud.

"My dear cousin,

I bring tidings of a matter that has weighed on us both for some time. After considerable effort, I was able to find Major Bellamy's daughter. She was married off in haste to a Lieutenant of the Regulars—now Captain, as he has recently been promoted—just before they were both shipped off to Newcastle. Very convenient, indeed. Her father, I assume, wasted no time in arranging the match to preserve her reputation.

I was able to meet with her discreetly, and I showed her the miniatures as we discussed the matter. She did not recognise Harry's likeness at all. However, upon seeing Wickham's portrait, the poor girl flew into a wrath such as I have never witnessed in any lady... or, no lady since Lady Catherine learned of your marriage, at least. I've no doubt you can imagine the reason for her distress."

Darcy paused, shaking his head slightly as Elizabeth's lips tightened with disbelief. "So, it *is* true," she mused. "She has every right to be indignant."

He cleared his throat and kept reading.

"I had been prepared to pledge help to the girl on your behalf, but it appears her father has already pulled the necessary strings. They seem to be as settled as they can be under the circumstances, and there is little more to be done. Her new husband has been rewarded well enough for his part in all this."

Darcy's eyes flicked up from the letter, meeting Elizabeth's knowing gaze. "It seems Major Bellamy was quite adept at managing the situation. No surprise there."

Elizabeth nodded slowly, her brow furrowed. "Poor girl. To think she was deceived so cruelly."

"I am now on my way back to Chatham to rejoin my regiment, but I intend to detour through Derbyshire and break my journey at Pemberley for a few days. I hope you and Mrs Darcy will also be there by the time I arrive. But if I should miss you, fear not. I am quite adept at making myself at home with your brandy and your house. I will return Harry's miniature when I see you. As for the other... Well, I regret to inform you that it has been flung into the sea by a very angry young captain's wife. And I say, good riddance to it."

Darcy chuckled as he finished the letter, setting it aside. "I cannot say I disagree with her decision."

Elizabeth's lips twitched into a smile. "Wickham deserves nothing less. Perhaps it is best if his image remains at the bottom of the sea."

"Indeed." Darcy leaned back, the tension in his shoulders easing as he reflected on Richard's news. It was a small victory, but a victory nonetheless. Harry's name, at least in this case, had been cleared, and the girl was safe—married and taken care of.

Elizabeth reached over, taking his hand and squeezing it gently. "You have done all you can, William. Harry would be proud."

"I hope he would be. And now, Mrs Darcy, it seems we had best prepare for our return to Pemberley at once, before Richard takes it upon himself to empty my cellars completely."

Elizabeth's laughter... well, it was all he wanted in the world.

I T HAD BEEN TWO weeks since Darcy and Elizabeth returned to Pemberley from London. The change from the whirlwind of the city to the quiet grandeur of their Derbyshire estate was both welcome and strange. Though Pemberley had long been home to Darcy, it felt somehow transformed now that Elizabeth was truly settled into her role as mistress of the house. She had flourished in her duties, a natural grace in her interactions with the staff and tenants.

And after the news broke in London... why, the Darcy name was suddenly popular. Harry had gone from a blackguard to a posthumous hero overnight, and as for Elizabeth—why, perhaps it was the novelty of the mystery, perhaps attention spans truly were that short, but there were few left who would think to shun Mrs Darcy. Letters and invitations had begun to pour in, and the morning post had been full of social obligations from neighbouring families.

Elizabeth sat at the writing desk in the drawing room, the soft light of the morning streaming through the windows, illuminating the many papers before her. Darcy, seated nearby on the sofa, was reading one of the reports he had brought from London, his brow furrowed in concentration. But every now and then, he glanced up, a soft smile warming his face as he watched his wife, who, though occupied, would occasionally reach down to pat the eager little terrier at her feet.

"Mrs Darcy," he mused aloud, his voice warm with affection, "it appears you are quite in demand. Social engagements left and right."

Elizabeth laughed softly, holding up an embossed invitation to a dinner party in a nearby estate. "Indeed. We have been invited to more events in the past week than I care to attend in a lifetime." She placed the card back down, shaking her head with a smile. "Though I suppose it would be impolite to refuse all of them."

"Not all," Darcy agreed, leaning back in his chair. "But perhaps we can be selective. I have no desire to spend endless hours trapped in stifling parlours."

Elizabeth glanced at him, a playful twinkle in her eye. "Afraid you'll have to endure a ball or two, my love. I am sure you will survive, although I daresay you might require medical attention to accomplish the feat."

Darcy sighed dramatically. "If I must, I shall. Though I confess, I would much prefer our quiet evenings here."

Before Elizabeth could respond, the dog, little Fitzy, leapt onto her lap, wagging his tail furiously. She laughed, scratching behind his ears as he tried to lick her face. "Down, you scamp! Let me finish, and I will pet you."

"He's quite the lively creature, isn't he?" Darcy remarked with a grin, watching the small terrier bounce with energy.

Elizabeth nodded, setting the dog back down on the floor, where he proceeded to run in circles around the table. "He certainly keeps things interesting, but he may soon find himself replaced in that regard."

Darcy's brow furrowed in mock concern, his voice playful as he leaned closer. "Another companion? Who might that be?" His tone lowered conspiratorially. "Tell me you did not acquire a cat. I am afraid I would have to draw the line there."

She pursed her lips. "It is not a cat. Something rather more demanding of my attention, I am afraid."

"You should know, Mrs Darcy, I am very much the jealous type."

"Indeed! Why, then, I suppose you might be *very* interested to know who might be keeping me company."

"Madam, you have my *rapt* attention, I assure you. Who would be so impudent as to steal my lovely bride's attention from her dog? Or from me, for that matter?"

She grinned and glanced over at him. "Do you remember that time you had to help me up the stairs because my courses took me by surprise? You were all gentlemanly awkwardness in the face of my distress."

Darcy's face flushed immediately, his composure faltering. He stammered slightly, "I— I try not to dwell on such things."

Elizabeth waved a hand dismissively. "Yes, well, I have been doing a good job of 'forgetting' that embarrassing incident, too. In fact, I had forgot it *so* well that I failed to notice something rather important until recently."

Darcy's expression softened, his teasing gone as he looked at her. "What do you mean?"

Elizabeth met his eyes, her smile brightening as she leaned back in her chair. "That was the last time I had my courses at all."

The words hung in the air for a moment as Darcy processed them, his face transforming from confusion to shock, then to joy. "Elizabeth!" he whispered, the happiness swelling in his chest. Without another word, he stood abruptly, scooping her out of her chair and twirling her around the room, her laughter ringing out in delight.

"I—" he faltered, his voice breaking with emotion. "I had married you expecting to raise Harry's child, and now—this—this is more than I could have ever hoped for!"

She wrapped her arms around his neck, her face glowing with happiness as he set her gently back on her feet. "More than *we* could have ever hoped for."

Darcy held her close for a long moment, his hand resting against her back as the little terrier barked and danced around their feet, wagging its tail furiously.

As if on cue, there was a sharp knock at the door. Fitzy immediately turned toward the sound, barking as he ran to the door. Elizabeth rolled her eyes fondly. "See? Ever the vigilant guard."

Darcy smirked and stood, waving a hand dismissively. "A fine watchdog, indeed. I will see who it is and send them away post-haste. I have not yet finished my moment of euphoria."

The door opened, and one of the footmen stepped in, his face slightly pale. "Mr Darcy," he began hesitantly. "There is... a gentleman here. A man, rather."

Darcy set Elizabeth back on her feet and turned back. "What is this about a man, Wilson?"

The footman cleared his throat. "It is Mr Wickham, sir."

Darcy froze in place, the name landing like a heavy stone between them. Elizabeth looked up, her expression turning serious, and she immediately called her dog and crouched to pick him up. Darcy's face darkened as he turned back to the footman. "Wickham? Here?"

"Yes, sir. He insists it is urgent. Shall I have him sent away, sir?"

Darcy's hand gripped the edge of the table, his knuckles white with the pressure. The sheer gall of the man, to show up at Pemberley unannounced—and after everything!

"Stay here," he muttered to Elizabeth, his voice low with anger.

"William," Elizabeth began, her tone firm, but he silenced her with a look.

"I do not want you anywhere near him."

"And *I* do not *you* anywhere near him! Why grant him an audience at all?"

Darcy balled his fists. Indeed, why *should* he see Wickham? The man ought to have been arrested by now—dragged before a court-martial like the others. The fact that he was here must have meant that he had run, was a fugitive of some sort. And that meant he wanted money.

"Do you know," Darcy growled, "I've not the least idea. But I will take deep... *personal* satisfaction in refusing whatever he came here to ask."

Elizabeth met his gaze, her lips thinning in protest, but she understood the look in his eyes. She gave a small nod. "Be careful."

Darcy turned and followed the footman toward the entrance hall, his heart pounding with outraged disbelief. Wickham, of all people, had no business being anywhere near his home!

And yet, the moment he stepped into the hall, there stood George Wickham—his clothes wet from the rain outside, his hair dishevelled, but his smirk ever-present. He looked up as Darcy approached, his eyes gleaming with something between desperation and arrogance.

"Darcy," Wickham greeted casually, though there was a tremor beneath his usual bravado. "I was hoping you might hear me out."

Darcy did not move. His gaze was cold, cutting through Wickham like a blade. "Lost your uniform, I see."

Wickham's features froze, then broke into his old smile as he shook his head and wagged a finger. "Still the same Fitzwilliam Darcy, I see. My uniform, as you well know, is something more akin to a target at the moment. But you know that already, don't you?"

Darcy crossed his arms. "Why are you here, Wickham? What possible business could you have with me?"

Wickham spread his hands in a gesture of feigned innocence. "Business, yes, exactly. I am in need of a little... assistance."

Darcy's eyes narrowed. "Assistance? You're fleeing army justice because you betrayed my brother—betrayed good men who were killed needlessly, and broke the trust of more than one lady. After everything you've done, you think I would help you?"

Wickham had the audacity to smile again. "We've had our differences, I grant you that, but surely we can come to an arrangement. Harry, now, he was the hot head, but you've always been the rational one, Darcy."

Darcy took a step forward. "I am not interested in anything you have to say. Wilson! Have word sent to the commander of the militia regiment in Derby. We have a wanted fugitive, and he needs to be collected."

Wickham's expression shifted, desperation creeping into his voice. "Wait, hear me out. You've heard about the investigation, I'm sure. Egad, I would not be surprised if you were the one who started it!"

Darcy just stared at him, his jaw ticking involuntarily, but not another muscle moved.

Wickham eased closer. "The accusations against me—they're false, all of it. Harry saw it wrong. I just need a small favour from you to clear my name."

Darcy's eyes blazed with fury. "You have the gall to come to me, after all the lies you spread about Harry? After betraying him and now trying to save yourself from the consequences?"

Wickham's smile faltered. "Lies, Darcy? Harry was a good man, but even good men make mistakes. You know that better than anyone. I heard he died right before your eyes. You mean to tell me you made no mistakes? That you would not have that day back to do all over again if you could?"

Darcy turned away. "Carter, call for four strong lads to come bind this man. He is wanted by the army for his court-martial."

"Darcy, you have got it all wrong! I just need you to... create something for me. A document, a statement from Harry, exonerating me. He would have done it if he had known about all this. You could say he left it with you, and you just discovered it!"

Darcy's temper flared, his fist itching to strike Wickham where he stood. "You expect me to fabricate evidence? You are lower than I thought!"

Before Wickham could respond, Elizabeth appeared in the doorway of the drawing room. Wickham's gaze shifted, and his expression turned smug. "Mrs Darcy," he drawled. "What a pleasant surprise."

Darcy stepped protectively in front of his wife. "Do *not* speak to her!"

Wickham chuckled darkly, his gaze shifting between them. "Oh, I remember her. Thought she looked familiar. You were that... that tradesman's daughter, were you not? Harry's... woman. I see you found the wealthier brother to attach yourself to, in the end." He raked his eyes over Elizabeth's figure in a way that made Darcy's blood boil. "I liked your *other* gown better."

Before he could say another word, Darcy's fist connected with Wickham's jaw. The force of the blow sent him staggering backwards, clutching his face in shock. "How *dare* you!" Darcy growled, standing over him. "How dare you insult my wife in my home!"

Wickham scrambled to his feet, blood trickling from his mouth, his bravado crumbling. "Wait—wait, Darcy. Please, just listen—"

"Enough." Darcy turned to the footmen who had been watching in stunned silence. "Take him to the stables. Inform the colonel of the regiment that Wickham is here, awaiting transport to London for his court-martial."

The footmen moved swiftly, seizing Wickham by the arms. He struggled weakly, but he was no match for their strength. As they dragged him toward the door, he looked over his shoulder at Darcy, his eyes filled with desperation. "Please, Darcy! You don't understand—"

"I understand more than you know," Darcy said coldly, watching as Wickham was hauled away.

As the door slammed shut, leaving Wickham in the hands of the footmen, Darcy turned to Elizabeth, his expression slowly softening as he reached for her hand. She stepped forward, her eyes searching his before she gently placed her hand in his. Without a word, she moved into his embrace, her head finding its place against his chest, where she could feel the rapid beat of his heart.

"It is done," she whispered, her voice low and soothing, as if trying to absorb the tension that still lingered in him. Her fingers gently traced the line of his sleeve. "You need not carry this burden any longer."

Darcy exhaled a long, slow breath, his arms tightening around her as though she were the only thing anchoring him to the moment. He pressed a kiss to the top of her head, his lips lingering against her hair as a tremor of relief passed through him.

"Harry's honor is avenged," he murmured, though the words felt more like a promise than a declaration. His hand slid up to cradle the back of her neck as he held her a little closer, needing the reassurance of her presence. "Finally."

Epilogue

One Year Later

ELIZABETH STOOD BY THE hearth at Longbourn, smothering a proud smile as she watched her family dote on her son. Little Harry Darcy, now six months old, was passed from one eager pair of arms to another, his chubby hands grabbing at everything within reach as he gurgled in delight. Jane, glowing with happiness, sat beside her husband, Mr Bingley, both of them laughing as Harry tugged at one of Mr Bennet's waistcoat buttons.

The room was warm, filled with the laughter of her sisters, the steady hum of conversation, and the rich scent of evergreens woven into garlands along the mantel. Sprigs of holly and ivy adorned the walls, their glossy leaves catching the candlelight. The Gardiners had arrived from London that morning, and her uncle was currently deep in discussion with Mr Bingley about some investment matter, while her aunt sat close to her father, watching the baby with soft adoration.

Elizabeth's gaze drifted to her husband. Darcy sat in a corner, valiantly attempting to keep up with her mother's rapid stream of conversation. He nodded politely, though it was clear from the faint crease in his brow that he was struggling to follow her ever-changing topics. Yet, to his credit, he remained attentive, doing his best to engage with her as she prattled on about Jane and Bingley's wedding last spring at the Meryton church, the latest rumours about the neighbourhood, and her newest delight over Lydia's flirtations.

How William had changed since their marriage! Elizabeth marvelled at the man sitting across the room, scarcely able to reconcile this attentive, quietly amused figure with the reserved gentleman she had first come to know. In those early days, he had been a mystery to her—so composed, so distant—almost as though he stood apart from the world, watching it but never partaking in it. But now, here he was, leaning into the conversation with her mother, of all people, enduring her endless prattle about the neighbourhood's intrigues with a patience and grace she had never expected of him. The transformation was not loud or obvious, but it had shaped every corner of their life together, and for that, she felt a warmth bloom in her chest—gratitude, affection, and something deeper still.

She reached for the delicate box on the table beside her, her fingers brushing over the embossed emblem. "Mama," she called, interrupting their conversation. "I have something for you."

Her mother's attention shifted immediately, her eyes alight with curiosity as Elizabeth crossed the room to hand her the gift.

"Oh, what is this, Lizzy?" her mother exclaimed, her fingers already working to open the small box.

Elizabeth smiled. "It is from Mr Darcy's aunt, Mama. A gift for you, from the Countess of Matlock."

Her mother's mouth opened and closed in surprise, her eyes widening as she lifted the fine lace handkerchief from the box. "The countess? Oh my... Oh, Lizzy! This is... this is most elegant." She looked up at her daughter, her expression softening in rare gratitude. "Well, I never thought I should receive such a thing."

Elizabeth chuckled softly. "It seems you have impressed her, Mama."

Mrs Bennet blinked in disbelief, clutching the handkerchief to her chest. "I dare say I have, indeed."

Elizabeth caught Darcy's eye as he glanced her way, a small, knowing smile tugging at the corner of his mouth. She returned it, the brief exchange saying more than words could—an understanding, a quiet acknowledgment of how far they had come.

Meanwhile, Colonel Fitzwilliam, who had arrived not half an hour ago, had found refuge at the opposite end of the room. The younger Bennet sisters had taken quite a fancy to him, and though he bore their attentions with his usual good-natured humor, Elizabeth noticed he had subtly migrated toward a quieter corner, where he was now sitting in peaceful conversation with Charlotte Lucas. Elizabeth hid a smile. It seemed that Charlotte was just as pleased by her companion for the moment as he appeared to be with her.

As the evening wound down, and little Harry was finally returned to Elizabeth's arms, Darcy excused them both. With the Gardiners staying at Longbourn, the house was rather crowded, so the party from Pemberley were all to stay at Netherfield. "We shall take our leave now, Mrs Bennet. I fear we must make our way before the roads become any worse."

Her mother dabbed at her eyes with that new lace handkerchief, her voice breaking as she clung to Elizabeth's arm. "You will come back early, won't you, Lizzy? I cannot bear to wait too long. And do bring little Harry. Your aunt Philips has been telling everyone how handsome he is—we mustn't disappoint them!"

Elizabeth exchanged a glance with Darcy, but before she could reply, her husband stepped forward, his expression softened with understanding. "We will come as early as we are able, Mrs Bennet," Darcy said gently. "I shall see to it personally."

Her mother beamed, clinging to his hand for a moment as though he had offered her the world. "Oh, Mr Darcy! So kind, so thoughtful. What a blessing you have been to this family."

As they finally made their way to the carriage, she leaned in slightly, whispering, "Thank you for that."

He glanced down at her with a smile as he took Harry from her arms and helped her into the carriage. "It was nothing, my love."

"No." She cupped his cheek with her gloved hand. "It was everything."

ONCE INSIDE THE WARMTH of Bingley's home, Darcy helped Elizabeth out of her cloak, the house quiet as they retired to their private chambers. The day had been long, and he felt the ache of it in his limbs, but the sight of Elizabeth, seated on the edge of the bed, her face illuminated by the soft glow of the fire, filled him with a sense of peace.

Harry lay fast asleep in his cradle nearby, his tiny breaths almost audible in the silence of the room. Darcy moved to the fire, pouring himself a small glass of brandy. He swirled it absently, watching the flames flicker, his thoughts drifting back to the chaotic evening they had just left behind. Mrs Bennet was... He gulped down a rather large swallow of brandy. All he could think was that Heaven had been merciful to him, for Elizabeth seemed to have inherited only her mother's finer qualities.

Elizabeth's voice broke through his reverie. "You endured it all very well," she teased, her eyes bright with amusement as she stretched out her hand toward him.

Darcy raised an eyebrow, setting the glass aside before crossing the room to her. She was more interesting, anyway. He took her hand, allowing her to pull him closer. "Did I? I suppose I ought to thank your family for their... enthusiasm."

Elizabeth laughed. "You had no idea what you were getting yourself involved with when you married me, did you?"

Darcy pretended to consider her words, his brow furrowing in mock seriousness. "Indeed, I did not," he agreed, his voice rich with humour. "But I have never been one to shy away from a challenge."

She grinned, her fingers tracing idle patterns over his chest. "Oh, a challenge, am I? So, tell me then," she said, her voice soft yet teasing, "why did you do it? Why did you decide to marry a perfect stranger, thinking it would somehow vindicate your brother's honour?"

For a moment, Darcy said nothing, his eyes tracing the curve of her lips, the softness in her gaze. He had never been good at answering this particular question—why he had married her. In truth, he had married her because... because it had been the only thing he *could* do. But when had it ceased to be about Harry and more because he could not bear the thought of anyone else caring for her, anyone else having the right to call her theirs? He could not fix the spot or the hour, but it seemed to have always been there.

Darcy's expression shifted slightly, the playful gleam in his eyes giving way to something deeper. He reached down, lifting her effortlessly into his arms, and she let out a small, surprised yelp. He smiled at her reaction, the warmth of her body against his filling him with an almost overwhelming sense of contentment.

"The *honour*, Mrs Darcy," he said, his voice dropping to a low, intimate murmur as he gazed into her eyes, "was *mine*."

"Oh, that will not do at all! That is a clever play on words, sir, but you are evading the question."

His smile softened, and he set her gently on the bed, kneeling beside her, his hand coming up to brush a lock of hair from her face. His thumb lingered on her cheek, his touch tender as he looked at her with a seriousness that made her eyes widen. "I imagine there were moments when you thought I had lost my mind."

Elizabeth smiled, shaking her head slightly. "Oh, many times. But then, I believe we both walked into this marriage not fully knowing what to expect. You might have shocked me, William, but I like to think I surprised you as well."

Darcy chuckled, his thumb tracing small circles over her hip. "Surprised me? Elizabeth, you turned my life upside down." He leaned in a little closer, his eyes fixed on hers. "But I confess, I would not have it any other way."

She laughed, leaning forward to press a kiss to his forehead. "Perhaps I did you a favour, then. And now look at us... a year later, with our little Harry asleep in his cradle, my mother fawning over you like you are the most perfect man in the world. Little does she know!"

Darcy groaned softly, leaning his forehead against her shoulder. "Your mother... she will be the end of me, I swear it."

Elizabeth laughed, gently running her fingers through his hair. "And yet you were so kind to her tonight, William. I could hardly believe it. What has become of the stern, proper man I married?"

He lifted his head, arching an eyebrow at her teasing tone. "I suspect that man still lurks somewhere beneath the surface. But... perhaps I have learned a thing or two about life beyond duty."

She nodded thoughtfully, resting her head against his as she softly replied, "It seems we both have."

Darcy reached up to cup her cheek, his fingers lingering at the base of her neck. "Do you know what I never expected, Elizabeth?" he asked quietly.

Her brow furrowed slightly. "What is that?"

"That you would become so much a part of me. That I would come to need you in ways I never thought possible." His hand lingered on her cheek, the feel of her skin against his thumb grounding him in this moment—this life he had almost never known. "There was a time," he began quietly, his voice rougher than he intended, "when I thought Harry had left me with a mess. Something to set right. That I had to—" He paused, searching her face as the words caught in his throat.

Elizabeth's eyes softened, her hand finding his and squeezing gently, as if urging him on, waiting.

Darcy exhaled slowly, his hand moving from her face to cradle her hand in his. His gaze held hers, steady, certain, filled with all the love he had struggled to express until now. "But now I see," he said, his voice quiet, full of emotion, "you were Harry's last gift to me."

From Alix

T HANK YOU FOR INDULGING with me and spending a little time with Darcy and Elizabeth.

I hope you've had a delightful escape to Pemberley. I'd love it if you would share this family with your friends so they can experience a love to last for the ages. As with all my books, I have enabled lending to make it easier to share. If you leave a review for ***The Measure of a Man*** on Amazon, Goodreads, Book Bub or your own blog, I would love to read it! Email me the link at **Author@AlixJames.com.**

Would you like to read more of Darcy and Elizabeth's romance? I have a delicious bit of Darcy and Elizabeth swoonery for you to try next! Dive into ***All Bets are Off*** and see who wins whose heart first!

And if you're hungry for more, including a free ebook of satisfying short tales, stay up to date on upcoming releases and sales by joining my newsletter: https://dashboard.mailerlite.com/forms/249660/73866370936211000/share

Preview All Bets Are Off

Chapter One

"SHE IS TOLERABLE, I suppose, but not handsome enough to tempt me."

Elizabeth nearly choked on her punch.

Tolerable? *Tolerable?*

Her grip tightened around the glass, and for a brief, delicious moment, she imagined spilling the punch all over Mr. Darcy's perfectly tailored coat. She wasn't close enough to pull off the move, but oh, the satisfaction it would bring. He stood across the room, his voice low but clear enough to ring in her ears.

The ballroom seemed to still, the glaring humiliation of his words hanging in the air, stinging as sharply as if he'd directed them right at her. Elizabeth glanced toward Jane, who was entirely absorbed in conversation with Kitty, perfectly unaware of the insult that had just battered her sister's pride.

Elizabeth's toes curled inside her slippers. She shifted her feet, trying to shake off the burning humiliation crawling up her spine. Not handsome enough? Well, if she had any doubts about the man's character, they had just been soundly confirmed.

"Did you hear that?" Charlotte Lucas's voice came from beside her, laden with the hint of restrained laughter.

"Every mortifying word," Elizabeth muttered, setting her glass down on the nearest table with a bit more force than necessary. "I suppose I should be grateful he doesn't think me a complete horror."

Charlotte bit her lip, a sparkle of amusement in her eyes. "I never thought a man's bad manners could be so entertaining."

"Entertaining?" Elizabeth shot her a sharp look. "It is outrageous, and I have half a mind to—"

"To what? March up to him and correct his perception of your charms?" Charlotte tilted her head, an eyebrow lifting. "He might take that as a sign of interest, you know."

Interest! Elizabeth would have laughed, but it... well, it wasn't funny. At all. She turned back toward Mr. Darcy, who stood brooding like a dark cloud over the festivities. As if anyone could inspire interest in that man!

"No. A gentleman so full of himself is hardly worth the trouble," she said, with a haughty lift of her chin. "I'm more likely to ignore him."

Charlotte didn't look convinced. "Well, if you're ignoring him, you're doing a poor job of it. You haven't looked away since he insulted you."

Elizabeth blinked. She hadn't realized her eyes were still pinned to Mr. Darcy as though her gaze alone might convey all the contempt she felt. She pulled herself back, smoothing her skirts with a quick brush of her hands. "I don't know why I care. It's not as if I've any reason to impress him."

"Exactly," Charlotte said lightly, "and you've never been one to let some stranger's opinion wound your pride."

"I don't believe it's about my pride," Elizabeth protested, but her words felt weak, even to herself. "It's a matter of decency."

Charlotte let out a quiet laugh, shaking her head. "Well, if you say so."

Elizabeth crossed her arms, but Charlotte's amusement had already worked under her skin. Why did she care? A stranger's insult—particularly one from a man as dull and disagreeable as Mr. Darcy—shouldn't have any power over her. Yet here she was, turning three shades of crimson over his words as though they actually held weight.

As if sensing her thoughts, Charlotte stepped a little closer, her voice dropping into a teasing whisper. "In fact, I'd wager that if Mr. Darcy were forced to spend any real time with you, he'd fall quite desperately in love."

Elizabeth let out a bark of laughter. "I think not! The man barely looks capable of emotion, let alone love."

"Oh, I don't know about that. Perhaps if he were shown the proper attention—"

Elizabeth shook her head, cutting her off. "I have no intention of wasting any attention on him. Nor do I care to tempt him, as you so amusingly suggest."

"But that's exactly what makes it interesting!" Charlotte's eyes gleamed now, sensing a game. "I'll bet you, Elizabeth."

"No! No more betting. The last four times I have wagered against you, I have lost—lost more than my pride, too."

"You certainly did." Charlotte stretched forth her arm, rolling her wrist about. "By the by, how do you like my new gloves? And the ribbon on my gown—now, I daresay that green is not usually my color, but I could not let it go to waste, could I?"

Elizabeth grimaced. "I was sure Mama would recognize those and announce it for all the world to hear, but it seems the presence of two wealthy, single gentlemen tonight was quite enough to distract her from the topic of my 'missing' gloves."

"Oh, come, Lizzy, it is not as if anyone is surprised. I always win my forfeits."

"Which is why I am not betting against you. You flirt with Mr. Darcy as much as you please. I have no intention of suffering further humiliation at his hands... or yours."

"What are we talking about?" Jane appeared from behind Charlotte—features flushed and slightly out of breath. "Is Charlotte putting you up to something again, Lizzy?"

"No, because I do not intend to do it. Tell her, Charlotte. Surely, she could use a laugh."

Jane blinked innocently. "Tell me what?"

"Mr. Bingley's friend insulted Lizzy. But honestly, Lizzy, it sounded to me like the sort of thing a man says when he means precisely the opposite and is terrified to admit the truth."

"There, do you see, Jane?" Elizabeth gestured toward her friend. "She is at it again. If I am not careful, Charlotte will own my best ball gown, my new bonnet, and half my pin money,"

Jane laughed. "Let me guess, Charlotte. You put Lizzy up to provoking a dance invitation from Mr. Darcy to force him to publicly favor her after being heard insulting her? Lizzy, how could you pass that up?"

"Oh, not just a dance," Charlotte corrected. "Lizzy, if you set your mind to it, you could make 'Mr. Darcy of Pemberley with ten thousand a year' fall in love with you. I have every confidence in it."

"Now you're just being preposterous."

Charlotte gave a soft shrug. "Is it preposterous? Or are you afraid it might actually work?"

The challenge sat between them, hanging in the air. Impossible! There was no way a man as proud and insufferable as Mr. Darcy could ever be tempted by her. And why would she want him to be?

"You're serious?" Elizabeth asked, eyes narrowing.

"Absolutely. I stand by my wager."

The absurdly of it was almost too much to consider. "And if I don't succeed?"

"The usual terms," Charlotte said, a glint in her eye. "But I think we both know you're far too clever to fail."

Elizabeth raised an eyebrow. "And if by some miracle I do succeed? What then?"

"Then you own the forfeit." Charlotte's tone was light, but there was a knowing look in her eyes, the kind that made Elizabeth suspicious.

Elizabeth smiled, her head shaking in disbelief. "I think I would much rather let Mr. Darcy keep his indifference."

But even as she spoke, the idea of forcing Darcy—Mr. Darcy—to fall for her, only to have the pleasure of rejecting him, sparked something wicked in her.

"Lizzy, do not let her bait you again," Jane cautioned. "You know she sees you as a soft mark by now."

"Indeed, and yet I let her swindle me time and again, because she is simply too persuasive—and persistent—for me to refuse indefinitely."

Charlotte laughed. "What else have I to amuse myself at these Assemblies? I scarcely ever have a dance, but I do usually find other diversions. What say you, Lizzy? Do you feel confident enough to venture it? Or has Mr. Darcy's insult shattered that courage you are so proud of?"

That did it. Somehow, Charlotte always found just the right leverage to work upon her. She straightened. "Very well, Charlotte. If you are so confident in this ridiculous wager, I'll play along."

"And your forfeit?" Charlotte asked.

Elizabeth's stomach roiled with denial. She already knew what Charlotte would demand—the thing she had been trying to force for years. The very thought made her bristle. No. It couldn't come to that.

Charlotte merely smiled, leaning in closer. "You know what you'll have to do."

Elizabeth tried to swallow the lump forming in her throat, but Charlotte's knowing look only made her heart beat faster.

"No," she decided. "Because I do not intend to lose."

"I HAVE NOT SEEN a more spectacular example of buffoonery since Eliza Townsend exposed herself with George Whitmore at Lady Framton's ball," Caroline Bingley declared, sinking into her chair with a sigh of exaggerated suffering.

Darcy kept his focus on the fire, willing himself not to engage. The conversation was predictable: provincial gatherings were beneath her; the company lacked refinement. It was a routine he knew too well.

"Really, Charles, I don't know how you can find any pleasure at all in such company," Caroline continued, swirling her wine. "The conversation was insipid, and as for the dancing—"

"Indeed, the dancing," Bingley interrupted. "I thought it was rather enjoyable. And as for the company, you do them too little credit, Caroline. Why, everyone was lively, their manners pleasing. Perhaps a bit more... vigorous than a London ball, but I have never passed a more delightful evening in my life!"

"Charles, you cannot be serious. Why, there were children there—girls not more than fourteen, dancing and flirting shamelessly!"

"Caroline, this is not London. I saw nothing inappropriate—why, every family in the neighborhood was there, and it is rather common in the country for the children to attend such events."

"Well!" Caroline sniffed. "I thought the entire affair rather tawdry."

"Tawdry! You are far too harsh on people you met only this evening. I, for one, have never met so many charming people anywhere. Even in London. Darcy, you do not agree with my sister, do you?"

Darcy's mouth twisted in discomfort. He might as well come out with it. "I thought there was little breeding and no beauty whatsoever."

Caroline Bingley hid a smile behind her wineglass, but Bingley cried out in dismay. "Surely you exaggerate! You gave yourself little enough trouble to seek enjoyment. Surely you could have joined us on the floor and had a more pleasant evening?"

Darcy turned to meet his friend's gaze, his arms folding across his chest. "I did not see the need."

"No need?" Bingley frowned. "Was it the music, or was the company not to your liking?"

Darcy allowed a pause. The music had been tolerable enough, though the room... not so much. "The company was adequate, but you know how these things go. Too much attention paid to the wrong dance partner, and suddenly, there are expectations."

"Expectations?" Bingley blinked, incredulous. "From a dance?"

"Yes, a dance. You have seen it happen. A man dances twice with the wrong woman, and by the next day, half the town believes there is an attachment."

Bingley stared at him as though Darcy had suggested something utterly nonsensical. "Darcy, you're being melodramatic. It was an assembly, not a proposal."

Darcy held his ground. "You underestimate the power of idle chatter. It only takes a little encouragement for desperate ladies to start assuming more than they should."

Caroline let out a delicate laugh. "Oh yes, they must all feel dreadfully forsaken that Mr. Darcy did not condescend to dance. How thoughtful of you to spare the ladies their broken hearts."

He ignored her, his focus still on Bingley. There was no use in trying to clarify himself to someone like Caroline, but Bingley... perhaps Bingley could still be reasoned with.

"You may find it absurd," Darcy continued, "but when you've spent as long as I have, fending off fortune hunters and overly ambitious mothers, you begin to tread carefully."

"Fortune hunters? In Meryton?" Bingley was laughing now, his eyes bright with disbelief. "Darcy, I've danced with a dozen ladies tonight, and I've no reason to believe any of them expect to marry me tomorrow."

Darcy's expression remained unchanged. "You may be fortunate in that regard, but that has not been my experience."

Bingley leaned back in his chair, crossing his arms. "You truly believe that behaving like a gentleman—a gentleman, Darcy, not a cad—necessarily leads straight to matrimony?"

"All too often, when one has wealth and no inclination to marry," Darcy replied curtly. "A few dances here, a bit of polite conversation there, and suddenly a man is trapped in expectations he never intended."

Bingley grinned, clearly unconvinced. "You make it sound like common courtesy is a trap. Surely, a man can be pleasant without every woman assuming he's about to propose."

Darcy shook his head slightly. It wasn't that simple, and Bingley knew it. "You've been spared the worst of it, but not every man can enjoy such freedom."

Bingley sat up straighter, his eyes narrowing with an almost mischievous gleam. "I think you're making excuses."

Darcy raised an eyebrow. "Excuses?"

"Yes. I believe you're avoiding courtesy simply because it's easier to stand aloof and judge the room than actually engage with people."

Darcy fixed him with a sharp look. "That is absurd."

"Is it?" Bingley's grin widened. "I'll wager you can't be a perfect gentleman without giving anyone the wrong idea. All I'm saying is that you're overcomplicating things."

Darcy frowned, his patience wearing thin. "I'm not entertaining this."

But Bingley leaned forward, too amused to let the moment pass. "No, listen. Sir William Lucas tells me it is quite the thing here in Meryton to wager—why, even the ladies have their own amusements. Perfectly respectable and expected, and I think it a harmless amusement."

"I do not." Darcy crossed his arms.

"Yes, well, I am now a part of this town, and I shall do as they do. I will wager you, Darcy, and I challenge you on your honor to consider accepting. You claim that behaving as a gentleman leads to unwanted expectations. I'm saying it's entirely possible to be polite—dance, talk, the whole lot—without sending anyone rushing to the altar."

Darcy exhaled slowly. Bingley's optimism was charming but misguided. "It is not as simple as that."

"Then prove it," Bingley dared, his smile still in place. "Let us see if your theory holds up. For the rest of our stay in Hertfordshire, you act as a perfect gentleman—dance, converse with every lady in your path, and show the courtesy you claim leads to disaster."

Darcy gave him a long, level look. This was foolishness. A game. "And if I refuse?"

"Then I suppose I'll never know whether you're right," Bingley said, still grinning. "But I'll wager you are overthinking the whole thing."

"I do not need to prove that I am right. I know I am. That is enough."

"Yes, but how are you going to prove it to me? You see, I know you, Darcy. You can hardly stand for anyone not to think you are in the right."

He kept his face impassive. "It matters little to me whether you believe me to be right or wrong. I have no intention of putting myself out merely because you desire to engage in some local amusement by trying to provoke me into acting out of character."

"So, you admit that you are unsociable? That you are downright unapproachable and prideful, above your company?"

Darcy narrowed his eyes. "I am no such thing. I simply do not lower myself to indulge in ribaldry."

"Poppycock. That Assembly was everything respectable. You, however, were little better than a wall hanging adorning the edge of the room. Can you deny it?"

"I have no wish to deny it."

"Then you may as well admit it, Darcy. You are unpleasant in company because you find it expedient. You will not give yourself the trouble of being merry and engaging because you prefer to be miserable and alone."

Darcy sighed. "I am perfectly willing to return to London if you find my company tiresome."

"No, no, don't you dare!" Bingley laughed. "You cannot show up as my guest, looking like a black cloud, and then leave town the next day. Think of the questions I shall have to answer! I repeat my challenge, Darcy. If you refuse, I shall form my own opinions on your manner."

He pursed his lips. "And if I accept your wager?"

Bingley leaned back, his grin widening. "Then we'll see just how easily you can behave like a gentleman without being 'trapped in expectations.' I daresay you will surprise even yourself."

Darcy considered this for a moment. It was ridiculous. But the idea of proving Bingley wrong—of showing him the truth of how these situations unfolded—was almost tempting. "And if you're right?"

"If I'm right," Bingley said, shrugging lightly, "you owe me nothing. I will have the satisfaction of knowing my dearest friend in the world does not send my neighbors running for the woods in fear of his displeasure."

"And if you are wrong? If I show myself to be everything you deem 'amiable' and half the mothers of Meryton do not begin buying wedding clothes for their daughters?"

Bingley laughed. "Darcy, if I am wrong, it will not be because of raised expectations among the town, but because you failed to be properly 'amiable.'"

Darcy sucked in a sigh and shifted in his seat. "Try me."

"Very well. If you win... well, then I'll finally take your advice about the business."

Darcy's expression darkened. "The business?"

"You know exactly what I mean," Bingley said, more serious now. "You've been telling me to sell my father's business for years. And I've resisted every time. But if I'm right and you lose the wager, I'll sell it and reinvest as you've been advising."

Darcy studied him in silence. There was no joking in Bingley's tone now. They'd had this conversation before, many times. And though it was in Bingley's best interest to let the business go, the younger man had never been able to sever the sentimental tie. But here was a chance to prove a point—and perhaps to do some real good.

He stared at Bingley, who was still watching him with that maddening grin. Darcy exhaled slowly, the flicker of a smile tugging at the corner of his mouth. "You are incorrigible, Bingley."

"And you're a cynic, but we've always known that."

Darcy shook his head, already regretting the decision, but there was something about the challenge he couldn't resist. "Very well. I accept your wager."

G RAB YOUR COPY OF ***All Bets are Off*** now!

Also By Alix James

The First Impressions Collection:

All Bets Are Off

The Measure of a Man Collection:

The Measure of Love

The Measure of Trust

The Measure of Honor

The Measure of a Man Box Set (Coming December 2024)

The Mr. Darcy Collection:

Mr. Darcy Steals a Kiss
Mr. Darcy and the Governess
Mr. Darcy and the Girl Next Door

Mr. Darcy: Swoonworthy Collection

The Heart to Heart Collection

These Dreams
Nefarious
Tempted

Darcy and Elizabeth: Heart to Heart Box Set

The Sweet Escapes Collection

The Rogue's Widow
The Courtship of Edward Gardiner
London Holiday
Rumours and Recklessness

Darcy and Elizabeth: Sweet Escapes Box Set

The Sweet Sentiments Collection:

When the Sun Sleeps
Queen of Winter
A Fine Mind

Elizabeth Bennet: Sweet Sentiments Box Set

The Frolic and Romance Collection:

A Proper Introduction
A Good Memory is Unpardonable
Along for the Ride

Elizabeth Bennet: Frolic & Romance Box Set

The Short and Sassy Collection:

Unintended
Spirited Away
Indisposed
Love and Other Machines

Elizabeth Bennet: Short and Sassy Compilation

Christmas With Darcy and Elizabeth

How to Get Caught Under the Mistletoe: A Lady's Guide
The Scotsman's Ghost: Or How to Wreck a Yule Party

North and South Variations

Nowhere but North
Northern Rain
No Such Thing as Luck

John and Margaret: Coming Home Collection

Anthologies

Rational Creatures
Falling for Mr Thornton

Spanish Translations

Rumores e Imprudencias
Vacaciones en Londres
Nefasto
Un Compromiso Accidental
Reina del Invierno

Una Mente Noble

Cuando el Sol se Duerm

A lo largo del Camino

Reina del Invierno

Una Mente Noble

El señor Darcy se roba un beso

Italian Translations

Una Vacanza a Londra

About Alix James

Short and satisfying romance for busy readers.

Alix James is an alternate pen name for best-selling Regency author Nicole Clarkston.

Always on the go as a wife, mom, and small business owner, she rarely has time to read a whole novel. She loves coffee with the sunrise and being outdoors. When she does get free time, she likes to read, camp, dream up romantic adventures, and tries to avoid housework.

Each Alix James story is a clean Regency Variation of Darcy and Elizabeth's romance. Visit her website and sign up for her newsletter at AlixJames.com

www.ingramcontent.com/pod-product-compliance
Lightning Source LLC
Chambersburg PA
CBHW030421180626
46812CB00005B/2108